The Protector

Bridget Essex

The Protector

Other Books by Bridget Essex

A Knight to Remember
Date Knight
A Dark and Stormy Knight
Just One Knight
Forever and a Knight
Cry Wolf
Love Spell: Tales of Love and Desire
Beauty and the Wolf
Under Her Spell
The Longing
Raised by Wolves
Meeting Eternity (The Sullivan Vampires, Vol. 1)
Trusting Eternity (The Sullivan Vampires, Vol. 2)
Wolf Pack
The Guardian Angel
Holiday Wolf Pack
Don't Say Goodbye
Wolf Town
Dark Angel
Big, Bad Wolf
The Vampire Next Door (with Natalie Vivien)

Erotica

Wild
Come Home, I Need You

The Protector

About the Author

My name is Bridget Essex, and I write love stories. Many are about werewolves, vampires and lady knights; but always, they're about two strong, courageous women who fall deeply in love with one another, living love stories that transcend time. I'm married to the love of my life, author Natalie Vivien.

I'm best known for my Knight Legends series, stories about women knights, real world hi-jinks and love stories that are out of this world. My Sullivan Vampire novellas are a popular series lauded as "TWILIGHT for women who love women," and I have several other series and stand-alone novellas, and I'm always putting out something new.

Together with my beautiful wife, we live in a little fairy tale cottage in Pittsburgh, and take care of several furry children who we love with all our hearts. ♥

Find out more about my work at
www.LesbianRomance.org and
http://BridgetEssex.Wordpress.com

The Protector
Copyright © 2016 Bridget Essex - All Rights Reserved
Published by Rose and Star Press
First edition, April 2016

This is a work of fiction. Names, characters, places and incidents either are products of the author's imagination or are used fictitiously. Any resemblance to actual events or locales or persons, living or dead, is entirely coincidental.

This book, or parts thereof, may not be reproduced without written permission.

ISBN-13: 978-1977994349
ISBN-10: 1977994342

The Protector

The Protector

DEDICATION

For the love of my life.

And for Ruby and Marian, two of the best friends I could ever have wished on a star for. Thank you so much for believing in me. This wolf's for you!

The Protector

Chapter 1: Close Call

On the day of my accident, my father hired the bodyguard.

I was on my way downtown to rehearsal. I was first violin in the Buffalo Philharmonic Orchestra, and my fiddle was in the backseat, my sheet music haphazardly stuffed into my backpack, because I was a little late. I still remember what I was listening to on the radio, some shock jock DJ talking about a supposed monster sighting in the bay. I was turning up the radio when I felt my car...shudder.

I felt that car quaking all around me as the sleek black SUV hit my smart car's rear. I'd glanced in my rear-view mirror at the driver with the meaty, black-gloved hands on the steering wheel, the black sunglasses blocking out any emotion in his eyes, his thin lips set in a tight frown as he laid into the gas pedal and the SUV slammed into me again, so hard that if I hadn't been watching the vehicle ram into me, I never would have thought such a big, bulky vehicle could move so quickly.

I don't remember much after that except spinning and spinning, my head whipped against the window so hard that I saw stars and then...darkness. There was this metallic *crunch* that I'll probably be hearing in my nightmares for the rest of my life.

When I woke up in the hospital, my father was hovering over me. Alexander Grayson, a staggeringly tall and usually intimidating (well, to anyone but me) man, *doesn't* hover. But he did that day, his handsome face contorted into a grimace of pain as he stared down at me, brown eyes wide and tear-filled. He was wearing his usual designer suit because he'd probably come right from the office, and his shoulder-length salt-and-pepper hair was swept back into a loose ponytail. I teased him about that ponytail all the time, which I think only made him wear it more, just to provoke me. His gaze glittered as he took a quavering breath, and then I exhaled a sigh, blinking, my eyes adjusting to the light, and the boring white-tiled hospital ceiling came into focus.

"Hi, Dad," I croaked. I immediately wished I hadn't spoken: my sides squeezed, and my lungs ached as if I'd swallowed a handful of glass shards. My whole body hurt like a *sonofabitch*.

"Elizabeth?" My dad seemed to crumple, kneeling down beside me, and then he was *really* crying, bright, shining tears that snaked their way along the smooth skin of his face, getting caught in his trim mustache and tiny beard that—he insisted, much to my chagrin—made him look "devastatingly dashing."

"God, I thought this was it, sweetheart. I thought you were going to…going to…" He trailed off, gripping my hand so tightly that I wondered if he'd bruise my fingers. His eyes were fierce, flashing with a light I rarely saw in them, almost a red shimmer. He growled, uncharacteristically low and savage: "I'm going to *get* those *fuckers* who did this to you."

I might have a dirty mouth, but I most certainly inherited it from my mother. I don't think my father would cuss out a mass murderer. To the best of my knowledge, I was pretty certain I'd never heard him use an expletive in my entire life.

He…wasn't acting like himself. But then, having his only daughter nearly die in a car accident would probably make for a pretty rotten day.

I sat up then, which might not have been the best idea. My head spun, as if I were trapped on some sadistic carnival ride that wouldn't let me off, complete with flashing lights and stars sharpening their points on the corners of my vision. I blinked, tried to swallow. "Dad, it's okay—please don't worry. I'm fine," I lied to him, swinging my bare legs out from under the hospital sheet and over the edge of the bed. In the background, machines began to beep in warning, obnoxious bursts of electronic protest, but I pushed myself up and stood, anyway, trying to prove the point to him that I was "fine."

My father had leapt up the moment I did and was now steadying me with a strong hand at my elbow, but even though he gripped me tightly, it was primarily my own stubbornness that prevented the floor from rushing up to meet me. I ran a hand, wrist hooked up to an IV, through my dirty blonde hair. My hair was down around my shoulders, sweeping against my back in long, lank strands, and I was wishing I could find a ponytail holder somewhere. That was the last thought I had before black dots began to swarm before my eyes.

Even I knew when I was overdoing it.

"So, how cutthroat is that seafood business, huh?" I joked weakly, as I sat back down on the bed. I'd accomplished enough for the moment. I slowly became aware that I was wearing one of those incredibly sexy (ha!) hospital gowns, and I absentmindedly threw the scratchy, starched sheet of the hospital bed over my shoulders, drawing it close as I shivered. "Dad, that guy who rear-ended me... I think he did it on purpose." I breathed out and searched my father's eyes.

Again, something dangerous glittered within his dark brown irises, but he schooled his features, adopting his usual indulgent grin, the one he always got when he was about to say something that would make me furious. Like, you know, the time that he told me I couldn't go to college across the country because I'd "be in danger."

My father has always been overprotective, and never with any sort of *reason* to back it up. It's not as if I haven't proven I can take care of myself. I'm a tough lady, but, in his eyes, I was just never tough *enough*, not to face all of the dangers my father supposed were out there in the world, just waiting to *get* me.

Maybe he had a small point, however, considering the fact that my car was just rammed by a stranger.

"Did they catch the guy?" I asked after a long moment, when my father said nothing, his jaw flexing as he pivoted back on his heels and stared up at the ceiling.

"Elizabeth, sweetheart," said Dad, shifting from foot to foot. He was so terrible at delivering bad news; his mustache drooped a little above his lip.

"Dad, I can handle it," I promised him, softening my voice as I drew the sheet closer. "If the cops didn't catch the guy, I'm sure they will. He's not dead, is he?" I asked then, cold moving over my skin in waves that gave me goosebumps. Yeah, the guy had hit me, but I didn't want him to die for it. I didn't remember what had happened, exactly, after the second impact. Maybe his SUV had flown off the freeway into a guardrail or—

"Sweetheart, I think it's important to start at the beginning." He cleared his throat, throwing out his hands impressively, as if he were on a stage or behind a podium. "As you well know, Grayson Seafood is the envy of the world," said my father then, and I sat back with raised eyebrows. He was taking the long-winded approach, using the very particular voice that he always rolled out at company holiday parties, when he had to make a speech about how *great* the past year had been for the bottom line. And the fishermen and warehouse workers and packers who worked for my dad were usually wasted at that point—as anyone would be at a work holiday party that provided a very generous catered banquet and open bar—and would cheer him through his exhaustive address about how Grayson Seafood was the biggest producer of seafood in the world, and how people across the globe were eating our fish every night, and... Well, you get the picture. Boring, feel-good stuff that would be vigorously applauded while the booze flowed in celebration.

But I'd just been in a car accident. And as the daughter of the founder of Grayson Seafood, I was well-acquainted with just how envied the family business was. A little *too* well-acquainted, considering the number of my father's speeches I'd had to suffer through in my lifetime.

"Dad, what happened to the *driver?*" I asked pointedly. He frowned a little with a sigh; he'd just been getting started, and if there's anything my father loves, it's a nice, rambling speech—but then his lips tightened.

"Well, to put it plainly, the overseas fishing moguls have it out for us, sweetheart," he said with a frown, crossing his arms. "They're targeting me, and since you're my only family, apparently they're targeting *you*, as well."

My father was a bit of a conspiracy theorist, the kind who didn't believe we'd actually landed on the moon, and that the assassination of JFK was some sort of government plot, and that there have been a ton of UFO landings that the Feds don't want us to know about. But this was pushing the envelope a bit too far, even for him.

"Since when is the seafood business taking cues from the mob?" I chuckled, trying to lighten the mood. I grimaced as I shifted my weight, and then I wished I hadn't moved at all. My tailbone was sore—how had *that* even happened? I sighed and leaned back on my wrists, staring up at my father with a long-suffering expression.

He took that as license to continue his speech.

"The seafood business has a long and illustrious history of being just as cutthroat as—" began my father, but then he reinterpreted the look on my face. He swallowed and shook his head. "Sweetheart, you know that we turned profits last year that were almost *double* that of every other seafood company on the planet."

"Dad, I love you—but I hate to remind you that *I'm* not in the seafood business. You are. And I love you very much, and I'm your daughter…but I'm not *you*. So, why would these supposed 'overseas fishing moguls,'" I sighed, making air quotes with my fingers, "be targeting *me*? Frankly, why would they be targeting anyone at all? These aren't perfect diamonds or everlasting oil wells; they're profits made from bulgy-eyed tuna and swordfish," I told him with a shake of my head.

I glanced at the wall clock over his shoulder and felt the icy fingers of dread close around my throat. "Crap, Dad—we have to finish this later. I'm late for practice!" I struggled to stand again, even as the black points began to swarm at the edges of my vision once more. "And if I'm late again, Amelia is going to kill me, and I did just totally survive a near-death experience, so I don't want another *quite* so soon," I told him with as much of a straight face as I could muster.

My coping skills consist of sarcasm and humor. And that's...pretty much it. Which is probably why I've never been able to have a truly serious conversation with any of my ex-girlfriends.

And it's probably why I'm single.

"Honey, you're not letting me *explain*..." My father looked like he was in actual pain as he held out his hands to me with a grimace, waving them to encourage me to lie back down on the hospital bed. "Someone tried to *kill* you today. It was no accident. I really don't think you understand the gravity of the situation, and you're not reacting like you—"

"I'm a big girl, Dad." I sighed, straightening as I stood and winced. The room began to spin, but after a moment, the whirling subsided. Which was about as good as I could expect today, it seemed. "Like I said, you know I love you, Dad. But I think you have a tendency to believe I'm still five years old and need my rocking horse fixed." I breathed out and smiled at him softly, shaking my head. "But the thing is, I'm thirty-three years old," I reminded him with another shake of my head. I squeezed his hands. "And I have my own life, and you need to stop worrying about me, or you're going to develop an ulcer. The guy probably rammed me because of my rainbow bumper stickers or something. He's likely some colossal homophobe hell-bent on ridding the world of the gays." God, I hoped that wasn't true, but I offered my dad a quick smile. "I honestly can't think of a single reason why overseas fishing moguls would even know I *existed*, let alone would try to make me sleep with the fishes. Oh, God, that was such a terrible joke..." I sat back down on the bed, holding my side and taking small, panting breaths. I tried to focus on the problem at hand. "Does Amelia know I was in the accident?"

"The whole orchestra knows. They sent you those flowers," said my father, waving his hand in the direction of a few dozen roses on a side table with an impatient shake of his head. "And the doctors say that if you *take it easy*, you'll still be able to make your concert on Friday."

"I'd better," I groaned, casting my eyes heavenward. "That one piece has been such a bastard, and I've spent far too much time practicing it to just... I mean, I've put in too much work not to—"

"Elizabeth," said my father sternly then. Dad's never been very good at *stern*, and the older I get, the mellower he becomes. So, this was kind of surprising.

"Yes?" I asked heavily.

"Today, because of me, you were almost killed." His eyes were so pain-filled, I wanted to give him a tight hug, but I sat where I was, biting my lip. "And that's... It's unthinkable to me that harm could have come to you *because* of me. It doesn't matter if you believe it or not, but the fishing business *has* gotten vicious these past few years..." He didn't look at me as he spoke. He was examining the ring that my mother had given him years ago, the blood-red garnet flashing with a real, raw fire against the pale skin of his hand under the sickly fluorescent hospital lights. "I couldn't bear to lose you. So, I've taken matters into my own hands." He glanced up at me, his eyes narrowed, his mouth set in a thin, hard line.

Well, that wasn't ominous at *all*.

I swallowed, frowning. "Dad?"

"They're discharging you from the hospital now," he said quickly, glancing back over his shoulder toward the hospital room doorway in that uncanny way he had. No nurse had come by, but somehow he knew I'd be discharged right *now*? That's my dad, psychic extraordinaire. "I'll take you back to my house, not your apartment. I won't hear of anything else—it's closer, and you can rest for a little while, borrow one of my cars until the insurance comes through and you can buy a new one," he said, raising his hand as I began to protest. "And then we'll discuss the measures that need to be taken to keep you safe."

"Measures?" I practically squeaked. I began to shake my head adamantly. "Dad, no *measures*—"

"Ah, Ms. Grayson, it's good to see you up!" said the nurse then, striding confidently into the room with a bright smile. She was very pretty, with curly blonde hair swept up into a ponytail and a wide, comforting smile. I'd just been through a major accident; I shouldn't have been noticing how pretty she was. But I did, anyway. She tapped a pen on her clipboard and flipped through a few pages before glancing back up with another grin. "Let's see if you're all right, and then we'll see about getting you discharged."

"One last thing," said my dad, and he looked even more nervous. "Um…your car was totaled. Smashed like a bug, actually. Remember how I told you about Smart cars being unsafe in accidents—"

"I remember." I sighed, rubbing at the spot between my eyes with my palm. "Smashed like a bug. Just great." My poor, adorable, snub-nosed baby. I'd loved that little car.

But what my dad said next made me forget everything else: "And remember, honey, your violin was in the backseat?"

I stared at him, eyes wide, all of the blood draining out of my face.

"So, it's… I mean, the violin was smashed to splinters," said my father, holding his breath as he watched me carefully.

"My violin..." I felt a lot of things in that moment, waves of raw emotion moving through me as powerfully as a summer storm.

True, as a violinist in the Boston Philharmonic, you tend to own a lot of violins. I had six of them. Or...did have six of them. But only one was concert quality, and that particular violin sang for me like no other instrument I've ever held before.

Losing it felt like losing a limb.

I finally picked an emotion to settle on.

"Did they catch the guy?" I asked again, with a long, slow blink, the kind a crocodile makes before it strikes. That took Dad by surprise. He'd been bracing himself, I think, for a nice long stretch of yelling—punctuated by expletives—from yours truly. That I was calm and reasonable seemed to shock my father, who stood there with his mouth open and slowly shook his head.

"Great," I grunted, as the nurse poked and prodded my middle. I began to grin slowly, a little like the Grinch. "Because I'm going to find that sonofabitch who *destroyed my violin*, and I'm going to kill him with my own two hands."

"That's my girl," said Dad then, with a wide, toothy grin.

The Protector

Chapter 2: Bodyguard

I didn't look like hell. I looked *worse* than hell. Like a cheap, secondhand, microwaved version of hell that had seen much, *much* better days.

I flipped the passenger side visor back up with a grimace, taking slow, shallow breaths because it was still hurting a bit too much to make sudden movements. I had so much on my mind that even as I looked out the car window, I didn't see the old buildings passing us by; I was just thinking of a seemingly endless list of things that Needed To Be Done. For example, I *really* needed to take some more painkillers, and then I had to call Verity's Violin Shop down by the art museum, and I had to make sure that—

"Would mademoiselle like the temperature a bit cooler?" asked Ben, my father's chauffeur, shaking me from my thoughts. He looked a little pained to have me riding in the front seat with him, but the nurses at the hospital seemed to think that sliding into the backseat of a limo wouldn't be good for my stitches.

And, yes, Dad has a town car and a few retro cars, but he *insisted*—much to my dismay—that we drive back to his house in his limo, saying that, in case I was still in danger, other drivers would notice if someone tried to rear-end a limo. Which, I suppose, made sense. It'd be impossible for an assailant to casually rear-end a car as long as an ocean liner.

"No, the temperature's great, Ben," I said, cracking

him a lopsided smile. He still looked uncomfortable, his bright blue eyes surrounded with worried wrinkles, but he aimed his gaze back on the road, flexing his leather gloves against the steering wheel. I tried not to think about the driver of the SUV who'd rammed me; he'd been wearing leather gloves, too.

"So, what's this surprise you have cooked up for me, Dad?" I asked over my shoulder, into the interior of the limo. My father sat in the very center of the leather backseat, his walking cane positioned between his legs, his hands resting on the top of the cane as if he were ready to break out into song. He was grinning widely, and that's the *exact* sort of grin he gave me when he told me I couldn't get my learners' permit until I turned eighteen—and that being driven around was "just as cool" as learning to drive yourself. He was even more overprotective of me when I was in my teens, if that was possible.

So, that sort of grin always worried me.

"You'll see!" he practically chirped.

I sighed and slumped against the seat as we rounded the familiar, graceful curve in the road, and the Grayson mansion came towering into view.

Our family has been in possession of that impressive, sprawling stone structure for about two hundred years, which goes to show you that certain things—like enjoying living in a castle—run in the family. The place has turrets, one of which I took over when I was a kid playing Knights, Dragons and Princesses with the maids' kids. I was always the knight. There are big wooden doors that would look more at home in a castle in Europe than in a mansion outside of Boston, and a verdant garden of red roses. It was June, so the roses were in bloom, big blossoms everywhere, bloodred and sweet-smelling.

As we parked out front on the gravel drive and I opened the door, the wild scent of those roses wafted into my nose as I inhaled deeply. There was birdsong spouting from some of the ornamental trees, and the fountain—

featuring a creepy little naked cherubim with a wry smile and tiny wings—was bubbling happily as the sun shone down, touching me with its warmth.

In short, it appeared as if all was right with the world. And I guess, in some ways, it was. I'd just narrowly avoided becoming goo, smashed between my tiny car and a concrete barrier. I'd say that, all things considered, I was lucky.

But I was also pretty, well, unnerved, because as much as I wanted it to have been an accident, the crash had seemed deliberate, even to me. Which meant that an attack on my life could happen again, something I was desperately trying *not* to think about.

"Mademoiselle should really have let *me* get the door," said Ben, his voice strained as he all but sprinted around the car to help me up and out of the passenger seat while I struggled to stand.

"Ben, you're a peach, and I hope my dad realizes what an awesome guy he has in you," I grunted, sweat breaking out on my forehead as pain rippled through me. Ben's hand at my elbow helped me shift into an upright position. "I'm just not used to having a chauffeur anymore. I'm sorry," I told him, taking a quavering breath. "You've always been too nice to me." I smiled at him fondly.

He returned my smile but shook his head. "Mademoiselle does not look well," he said succinctly, holding onto my elbow as I threatened to fall backwards. I steadied myself, wrested my elbow out of his hand gently, smoothed the front of my skirt, and took a deep breath as my father folded himself out of the backseat and glided over to the both of us, his cane crunching against the gravel as sharply as his Armani shoes.

"I'm fine, Ben," I promised the hovering chauffeur with another smile. I'd known Ben my whole life; this is the guy who'd taken me to every violin practice I'd ever had as a kid, every school concert, and then every string quartet concert when I'd joined one in high school. He'd waited patiently for me during endless music lessons, always had a bit of wise advice or kindness to give the gangly, awkward kid who was way more skilled with music than with people.

"Alice probably has lunch on the table," said my father, and Ben nodded, sliding my crutches out of the limo, handing them to my father, and then hopping back into the driver's seat to take the limo to the garage. My father's hand replaced Ben's, and then he was helping steer me toward the front porch with its marble columns and wide open front door. Alice stood waiting for us, her hands on her hips and her plump mouth in a round O of consternation.

"Elizabeth Grayson, what sort of trouble did you get yourself into *this* time?" she asked, striding forward and all but picking me up as she swung her arm around my middle to steady me and propel me up the stairs. Alice is a marvel: the cook and housekeeper and, now, only maid for my father. She also volunteers at about a thousand charitable organizations, sews costumes for the local children's theater and still manages to find time to garden, her passion. Her long brown hair, now stranded with shocks of gray, was drawn up into the braid that was looped around her head, and she wore her uniform of choice: jeans and a flowy peasant blouse.

"I got into an accident, Al," I told her as she helped me up the last set of steps and into the house itself, my father bringing my crutches behind us. "It wasn't my fault," I amended quickly, as she began to protest.

"Al, can you bring some coffee and possibly a baked good for our recently hospitalized Elizabeth?" asked my father, his mouth twitching into a grin as Alice, again, was about to launch into a tirade after my statement. She opened and shut her mouth, sighed with a very long-suffering roll of her eyes, and turned, bustling toward the kitchen.

"Oh, so you know, that woman's already here! I put her in your study!" Al called, before rounding the hallway corner.

"That woman?" I asked, one brow raised.

My father grimaced, shaking his head, putting a gentle arm around my shoulders as he began to assist me through the foyer. It's an impressive-looking foyer, all black-and-white marble tile, pale blue walls, and Greek busts of attractive women on pedestals. My dad is kind of classical in style, hence the creepy cherub in the fountain outside.

"I don't suppose you'd wait in the hall while I greeted her?" asked my father in a soft murmur as we approached his study. The warm mahogany door was open, and I could already smell the scent of pipe tobacco and the old, deeply comforting aroma of hundreds of books emanating from within.

"I want to know what this is about," I sighed, all of the fight leaving me as the pain began to burn through my muscles again. I felt like an old woman as I considered the fact that, pretty soon, I'd eat a slice of coffee cake and then be able to take my pain pills. They wouldn't come a moment too soon; every inch of my body ached with an intense sort of pain I'd never felt before.

My father sighed for a long moment, too, casting his eyes to the ceiling, probably thinking to himself that there were other parents in the world who didn't have to deal with headstrong kids. "All right," he said then, in a normal tone of voice.

He helped me through the study door, the sunlight spilling through the tall floor-to-ceiling length windows with their many panes of glass, the leather bindings on some of the older books soaking up the sunshine, the antique globe in the corner turning—an odd thing to notice, I realize, but I only caught a glimpse of that, because my eyes were drawn, instead, to the woman who'd set the thing spinning.

She was tall, impressively so, taller than my father, even. She could have played women's basketball. She was muscular, the kind of easy muscle resting beneath her jeans and leather jacket and too-tight red t-shirt that made me think she was a gym rat or maybe a trainer. She looked like she worked for her body, and she enjoyed showing it off, and—I have to admit—I enjoyed looking at it. She had a sharp, angular face that was handsome, devastatingly so, but not beautiful. The lines of her chin, the planes of her face, were too hard, like she'd seen too much pain. A perpetual worry line from frowning too often stood pronounced on her otherwise smooth forehead. Her thick black hair was spiked and curved forward—total butch—and her hazel eyes, brown with flashes of green, immediately glanced my way. There was a small smile on her lips, the only soft thing about her, as she put her hands in her pockets, cocking her left hip in our direction and widening her stance.

God, she was gorgeous. My mouth was suddenly dry as I leaned against my father, taking in this magnetic creature and realizing, again, that I looked like hell.

Great. What a lovely way to meet a devastatingly attractive woman: stitched up and barely alive.

"Ms. O'Connell, it's good to see you again," purred my father, using the tone of voice that piles on the charm like a five-layer cake, the tone he always pulls out when he's at the office. He helped me over to one of the two high-backed leather chairs in front of his too-big carved wooden desk.

Dad straightened and inclined his head, gesturing toward the other leather chair to the woman standing in the corner. Ms. O'Connell. My breathing was coming too fast, almost *panting*, like the reaction a cartoon wolf as he ogles a gorgeous handpainted dame. Who *was* this woman? I didn't usually get so flustered around an attractive woman, but she gave something off I couldn't deny. Or ignore.

Her smile grew, and she stalked over to the chair, flopping down into it with ease. My eyes were drawn to her with a magnetic pull; I couldn't stop staring at her. She had this aura of immense power and grace, like maybe she was a dancer. Normally women who work out a lot have too many muscles to pull off *graceful*. Oh, strong they've got in spades, but graceful is a whole other ballgame.

And this woman was winning at both.

"It's good to see you again, sir. It's nice to meet you, miss," she said, her mouth rolling up lazily at the corners. But there was nothing indolent about her eyes. They seemed to pierce me, pinning me in place as she stared at me. It's as if she was assessing me, and she reached her assessment in a heartbeat or so. She glanced back to my father who sat behind the desk, setting his cane against the side of it.

"Elizabeth, I'd like you to meet Layne O'Connell," he said, nodding to her as he crossed his arms over his chest and leaned back in his leather desk chair. "Layne, this is my daughter, Elizabeth Grayson."

"It's nice to meet you," Layne repeated, one brow up, a wide, easy smile on her lips, the kind that makes you want to smile back. But I was too tense for smiling. There was something going on here, something that—despite the unspeakably attractive person sitting right next to me—I was probably going to dislike.

Let's just say I have a daughter's intuition for when my father is up to something.

"Likewise," I told her, but I was watching my dad out of the corner of my eye. He had his fingers crossed on his stomach now as he leaned back.

"Elizabeth..." he said then softly, delicately, like he was about to tell me a very bad piece of news as he gestured toward Layne, sitting to my left.

Yeah, he was *definitely* about to tell me bad news.

He cleared his throat and then pasted on his most dazzling smile. "Layne is your new bodyguard."

I stared at him flatly, then turned to look at Layne, who was still smiling, but now she was watching for my reaction, her eyebrows up as she rolled her shoulders back, her head to the side. She considered me, a bit of her black hair sweeping in front of her eyes like a female version of James Dean.

I could never have predicted this.

I've got a temper on me, a lovely bit of inheritance

from my mother, and sometimes I can't help my first reaction.

Which was this: "Absolutely *not*," I said, standing quickly, the leather chair squeaking in protest as it was shoved out behind me, its feet scraping against the old wood floor. "Absolutely *not*, Dad," I said, shaking my head emphatically. "Are you *kidding* me?" I practically yelled. I was spluttering, but the anger rippling through me was a pleasant change from the pain, so I stuck with it.

Layne was glancing up at me in amusement, her hazel eyes flashing as she tried to keep the smile from showing on her mouth. And failed.

"Elizabeth, *please*," said my father, eyes round as he gestured quickly for me to take my seat again. An action I had absolutely no intention of doing.

"You didn't even *consult* me. You already *hired* her?" Smoke was practically spiraling out of my ears, but I kept going. "How could you make such an important decision without me? I'm sorry, Layne," I told her then, pivoting on my better leg, the one that didn't have the stitches in the thigh. I stared down at her, my hands on my hips. She lounged back, meeting my gaze with a single elegant brow raised. She could have looked at me like that all day, but I was in no mood to be paying attention to anything below my waist, which was all stirring in spite of myself. "I'm sure you're wonderful," I huffed, "and an excellent bodyguard, but we have no need of your services," I said, all in a rush.

And then I sat back down, because the black pinpoints around my vision were starting to rush back.

"Layne, stay right where you are," said my father, a stern quality beginning to edge his tone. I stared daggers at him, but he wasn't looking at me—not directly. He was looking at Layne.

She shrugged, leaning farther back in the chair. She was lounging like she was at a dance club and not at her new employer's office, a fact I rather liked. But I wasn't supposed to like anything *about* her.

My father knew how I felt about this.

And he'd gone ahead and done it, anyway.

Once, when I was a teenager, my father had insisted I get a bodyguard. I'd refused, with all the drama a teenager can muster. After several long, drawn-out arguments (really the only time I can ever remember my father and I having a shouting match), he'd backed off.

I was already the weirdo in school, arriving with a chauffeur, and having a bodyguard hang around me was going to ruin any chance I had of getting a single friend. And eventually I'd outgrown most of my awkwardness, and I *had* gotten friends. But it would have been impossible to do with a secret-services type person following me around wielding tinted glasses, a serious frown, and a sidearm.

I was, and will always be, grateful for the upbringing I had. I was a rich kid. I know that, in the grand scheme of things, that's more fortunate than most. But I'd had my share of sacrifices, too, my freedom being the foremost of them. Growing up under constant supervision, under lock and key, and being fretted over like you're some sort of emperor's daughter makes you value your autonomy more than anything else in the world.

And, to top it all off, I had wanted, from a pretty young age, to make my own way, and I'd worked my ass off to get where I was today, one of the violinists in the Boston Philharmonic. Which, I'd like to point out, is a really difficult job to earn.

In short, my life was complicated enough without adding a *bodyguard* to the mix. I valued my freedom just a little too much to allow someone to trail me all day, hovering at my shoulder.

"No," I told my father.

"Yes," said my father, his brows raised. "Elizabeth, *please* listen to reason," he hissed then, leaning forward, his eyes flashing dangerously. "You were almost *killed*." Pain passed over his face, and I think he was weighing whether he ought to voice his next words or not. But then he said them, anyway: "And I doubt that a single foiled attempt at murder will stop whoever's after us. There are going to be *more* attempts. Your life is in danger."

I took a deep breath and let it out, and then I tried my absolute best to look at things rationally. My father, of course, was right. I was already looking over my shoulder too much, and the "accident" had *just* happened to me.

"What about you, Dad?" I asked then, a little of the fight gone from my voice. "Don't you need a bodyguard, too?"

"I already have one," he replied mildly, not letting his gaze waver from mine.

"Really?" I hadn't seen any new employees around, and shouldn't bodyguards be with the person they were guarding all the time? But that was neither here nor there. My father had a bodyguard, and he hadn't even been *attacked* yet.

At least, not that I knew of.

I glanced sidelong at Layne.

"I'm looking forward to working with you." She said it in a droll, almost sly manner, and her lips, twitching at the corners, were now completely incapable of masking her insolent expression. She leaned back again, her head to the side, one brow up as she chuckled a little. "I think we'll make a great team," she said, but the words had a bit of a sarcastic bite to them.

I opened and shut my mouth. I thought about the man who'd rammed me from behind, his leather gloves, the lack of any human emotion on his perfectly blank face, as if he felt nothing as he attempted to end a life.

I thought about how he was still out there. How, at any time, he—or others like him—could appear when I least expected it...

"For how long?" I asked, trying to make my voice hard. "For how long would we...require Ms. O'Connell's services?"

The joy—and triumph—that passed over Dad's face

was unmistakable.

"For as long as it takes us to figure out who was behind the attack and bring them to justice," said my father then, shifting his face back to its carefully neutral expression. Layne, beside me, made a little snort at the back of her throat, and I glanced at her, but her expression was unreadable, too.

Bring them to justice? I shivered a little. There had been such a sharpness to those words.

All right, then. Yes, I valued my autonomy more than anything in the world. But I also wanted to keep living the life I'd built for myself. I wasn't ready to die just yet.

"Well," I said, with a very long sigh. "It doesn't seem like I have much choice in the matter."

"Wonderful—just wonderful!" my father sang, clapping his hands together slowly with a triumphant smile. "Ms. O'Connell, I am delighted to have secured your services. I can finally sleep at night again." He leaned back in his chair and breathed out slowly, with a wide grin.

I looked at the magnetic woman sitting next to me.

Layne straightened, her head tilted to the side as she offered me a hand.

She had long fingers, a broad palm, short, carefully trimmed nails. I took her hand. I guess I was expecting a strong grasp, and I think that if she'd shaken hands with my father, it *would* have been strong, the clasp of palm and fingers. But her hold on me was gentle now, as her fingers encircled mine, sliding around my wrist like she was holding something fragile, something that could break.

Her fingertips were so warm, almost hot, as they pressed against my skin.

She bent her head, then. I watched in shock as Layne O'Connell leaned forward at the waist, bent her head, and brushed her warm, soft lips against the back of my hand.

"It will be a pleasure working with you," she said, her voice low, a rumbling growl in the back of her throat, as she gazed up at me through long, dark lashes, her hazel eyes never leaving mine, seeming to shimmer with green over their warm brown.

"I have coffee!" said Al just then, bumping the door with her hip as she pushed an antique tea cart into the room, laden with still-warm blueberry turnovers (which happen to be my favorite) and a carafe of coffee. She had a big grin on her face as she glanced quickly from Layne to me, back to Layne again.

My father stood, still smiling hugely.

And Layne dropped my hand only after a very long moment, too long of a moment for any sort of normal greeting. Her fingers had been so warm against mine.

The softness of her lips against my skin left an invisible imprint that made my blood burn.

Yeah.

Despite my initial reservations, I guess I was looking forward to working with her, too.

Chapter 3: A Better Violin

"You *must* take it easy, Elizabeth—doctor's orders!" my father called from his front porch as I hobbled down the steps, Layne beside me, toward what would be my new car for the foreseeable future: a big black Cadillac something-or-other that sprawled almost as wide as a tank in the driveway, making me miss my sweet little Smart car fiercely.

"I will, Dad," I said for possibly the hundredth time as I smiled tensely back at him, my hand on my side. I had about a thousand errands to run, and time was against me; taking it "easy" wasn't something I could exactly get behind.

It was Thursday. That meant tomorrow was the night of the Mendelssohn concert, and a pretty famous violin soloist (actually, let's be honest: *the* most famous violin soloist on this earth), Mikagi Tasuki, was flying into town for rehearsal to play with us this evening. The rehearsal was, of course, in preparation for her joining us in concert tomorrow evening, and that left me very, *very* little time this afternoon to pick up a new violin.

Which meant we had to leave right away.

If you know anything about string instruments, you know I was certifiable to consider purchasing a new instrument for a concert to take place *tomorrow*. Just like when you're getting to know a person, it takes awhile to learn the ins and outs of every new violin's sound. But I'd been in talks with Verity Olsen, the owner of Verity's Violin Shop, for months now, because it had put me on edge that I only had one concert-worthy violin to my name, and I'd been hoping to get another one for backup purposes.

And finally, Verity had found a violin that she thought would work for me.

I suppose that, if I was held at gunpoint to perform, I had a nice antique violin that could be worthy of being heard with the rest of the string section. But the sound didn't do it for me.

And if Amelia, the orchestra conductor, singled me out, it wouldn't do it for her, either.

The violin is the closest instrument to the human voice (though cellists will tell you that it's the cello; don't believe them for a second). Even if you're not a very musical person, you can hear the difference in sound between instruments. Just like people, they have unique "voices" when played. And comparing my beloved concert violin, the one that had gotten crunched in the back of my car (may she rest in pieces), to my antique violin was like comparing a blueblood Thoroughbred to a petting zoo pony. If you're small enough, each horse will get you where you want to go. But there's a distinctive difference between them.

As I approached the Cadillac, Layne stepped forward smoothly, the passenger car door in her hand as she held it open it for me.

"Uh-uh," I said, folding my arms in what was probably a petulant pose. I shoved my purse strap farther up my shoulder as I shook my head, narrowing my eyes. "*I'm* driving."

She raised a single eyebrow, cocking that narrow hip toward me as she leaned all her weight onto her left leg and placed a long-fingered hand on her waist. My eyes followed her elegant motions as if hypnotized.

"I'm very sorry, miss," said Layne then, shaking her head. "But Doctor's—and your father's—orders state that *I'm* to drive, at least until you're a hundred percent again."

Hot anger rushed through me, and I tried to take a few calming breaths. But the anger still remained.

Here was the beginning of the end of my freedom. This is what it looked like when autonomy was taken from you. It started with little things, like *driving*. I balled my hands into fists. But how could I protest? Yes, I'd finally just taken my pain pills, but the doctor was probably right. I felt utterly rotten. And I still had to get to rehearsal, and hopefully play very, very, *very* well, accident or not.

"Right," I muttered, and Layne opened up the door, her head inclined to me, her lips twitching as she tried to suppress another smile.

I sat down in the passenger seat, holding my purse in my lap.

I felt like a ninety-year-old woman.

Layne sprinted around the side of the car, and then she folded herself easily into the driver's seat, attaching her seat belt and taking a pair of slim sunglasses out of her leather jacket's breast pocket. She unfolded them and slid them on as she started the car.

"So, how long have you been a bodyguard?" I asked her, as she pulled smoothly down the driveway. My father, Al, and Ben waved to us from the porch, and I waved my hand out the window before rolling it up with the press of a button.

"You're my first official client," said Layne with a little chuckle, as she glanced at me out of the corner of her eye behind the shades.

"Oh, really?" The disappointment was evident in my voice. For some reason, I'd assumed she'd been doing this all her life. Maybe it was the confidence she exuded. Knowing that I was the first person she'd ever, well, guarded took the wind out of my sails a bit.

And it made me feel less safe.

"Don't worry," she said, as the gates to my father's estate began to open in front of us. The elegant iron gates clicked slowly on their mechanized runner, and she nursed the brake, slowing as we waited for them to widen. "I'm well-qualified to keep you safe. Your father, as I'm sure you know, hires only the best."

"And you're the best," I said flatly, one brow raised. I *had* just been through a major accident, which would, of course, add to my testiness. But there was also something too smug about this woman. Like she had everything figured out. *No one* has everything figured out.

"Yes," she said lightly, with a slight edge to her tone that brooked no argument.

"Huh." I stared out the window, pursing my lips into a flat line.

"You're a concert violinist, right?" asked Layne then. I glanced at her, and she was smiling at me, but there was a hardness to her eyes.

"Yes," I told her.

"Well, *you* think you're good, right?"

"The Boston Philharmonic thinks so," I said, crossing my legs beneath the dashboard. It was kind of a conceited thing to say, but it wasn't conceit or luck or nepotism that had granted me entrance to the Philharmonic. It was the spectacular way I'd played the violin, the talent that I'd worked thousands of hours to achieve, had—in fact—worked my ass off to acquire. Nothing had been handed to me; I'd had to work every step of the way to achieve my position.

"What makes you qualified to play in the Boston Philharmonic?"

I sat there, stunned by her question. It took me a full minute to respond. "I... I'm qualified because I won the audition years ago," I told her, spluttering.

"Had you ever been in an orchestra before?"

"No, but—"

"Then why did they let you in?"

I stared at her. The anger was starting to cloud my vision, and I was a little worried about smoke coming out of my ears again. "They let me in because I was the best candidate for the job, the best violinist in the long line of auditions they'd heard. They chose me because I was the *best.* I'm damn good at what I do," I told her fiercely.

"Then I rest my case," she said with a smirk, settling back against the seat a little more firmly as she flicked her right blinker on.

"*What* case?"

"Though I've never been a bodyguard, I assure you, I'm the best candidate for the job."

"That's not the same thing at all," I muttered as she turned right, her sure hands gripping the wheel effortlessly, guiding the car onto the next street. I tried not to watch her long fingers flexing over the wheel's surface, her biceps moving under the supple leather jacket. "How did my father find you?" I asked, anger still making me a little terse.

"He found me through a friend of a friend, so he knew that I came highly recommended, and I knew that employment with Mr. Grayson would be a pretty good place to start my career. By the way, where exactly are we headed, miss? I'm just driving in the general direction of downtown right now," she said, lifting her chin to indicate the street.

"Call me Elizabeth," I said serenely, trying not to let her know how curious I was about her. It was hard to swallow down all of my follow-up questions, but for some reason, I didn't want this cocky, gorgeous woman to know that she interested me, or exactly how *much* she interested me. "And we're heading to Verity's Violin Shop, which is by the Fine Arts Museum."

"Gotcha," she said, nodding and taking another turn. Her shoulders flexed again when she made that turn, which is really not something I should have been noticing, and which I was trying really, *really* hard not to. "So, you're in the orchestra," said Layne, which didn't exactly sound like a question, but after a long moment of silence, I realized she was trying to draw me into conversation. I cleared my throat.

"Yeah," I said, worrying at my bottom lip with my teeth. "I really love my job," I tacked on lamely. Wow. I looked like crap, and I was being incredibly inarticulate.

What a great start to this working relationship.

"That's good, that's good," said Layne, glancing in the rear-view mirror as she began to merge onto the highway. "You're luckier than a lot of people. Very few nowadays can say they love their work."

"What about you?" I asked, my curiosity getting the better of me.

She grinned. "Well, technically, it's my first day on the job, so… So far, it's pretty all right."

I swallowed hard and grimaced. "I probably ruined your first day. I mean, I kind of blew up back there. I'm sorry about that," I told her quietly. "I was a jerk. It's just…well, my father's wanted me to have a bodyguard since I was a teenager, and my independence is very important to me. But then there was the whole accident thing…" Oh, my God, I was rambling. I silently cursed at myself and bit my lip to shut myself up.

"Yeah, that had to be terrifying," said Layne, shooting me a sideways frown. "You came out okay, though. You could have been squashed like a grape. Fortunately, you're more like a bruised apple than a grape."

I was laughing in spite of myself. "What happens when my stitches and bruises are all healed up?" I teased her. "Do you have any more fruit comparisons?"

I kid you not: Layne glanced at me sideways, but she was absolutely, positively not looking at my face. "Well, yeah. But I think that's harassment, and it's my first day on the job, so better not press my luck." She tossed her hair out of her eyes and grinned wickedly, keeping her gaze on the road.

Speaking of fruit metaphors, I think I blushed as red as a cherry.

I didn't know what to say. I mean, what *do* you say to something like that? From the moment I saw her, I figured she had to be gay. She was such a butch, an incredibly attractive woman who knew exactly how attractive she was, who prowled like a wolf through the world, confidant and powerful and so magnetic that I couldn't take my eyes off her. But did she know *I* was gay? Was she just guessing, or was she fishing for information? Did she get a vibe from me, or had I been staring at her a bit more than any straight woman would?

Or was she just, you know, harmlessly flirting?

The time for a sarcastic retort or a flirtatious response came and went, and I subsided into miserable silence. I'd wanted, so badly, to say something funny or clever back to her, but this magnetic, gorgeous creature just made me tongue-tied.

Normally, I'm the one flirting with women, flashing a cheeky grin and cracking jokes and being a little inappropriate, but mostly handing out the kind of come-ons that result in me asking the woman out, and the woman usually agreeing to it. This sort of thing—someone acting that way toward *me*—doesn't really happen because I don't allow it to. I'm the kind of person who gets out there and goes after what she wants.

Layne cast me a glance after several moments and cleared her throat. She didn't apologize, only made a sound, and then sighed.

"Look," we both said at the same time then. She chuckled as she turned off the highway. We had to take city roads all the rest of the way now.

"You first," she said, one brow up.

A really insidious thought had stuffed itself into my head, and now I couldn't stop thinking about it. It'd been awhile since I'd been out on a date. I was, sadly, the kind of workaholic that can earn a place in a big-time orchestra— meaning, I was a *compulsive* workaholic. I practiced the violin for about eight to ten hours every single day, and then there were the orchestra rehearsals, and life just seemed to be extra busy lately, which meant that I didn't have time for anything that didn't involve strings, a bow, and sheet music.

And my dad was the kind of person who liked to kill two birds with one really big stone.

"My father," I said, chewing on my lip as I tried to figure out how to tactfully say this. But there wasn't any tactful way, so I went for blunt: "Did he choose you as a bodyguard because he was trying to set me up?"

Layne laughed out loud. She had this rich, velvety laugh that seemed to roll over me, but I was paying too much attention to how red my cheeks were getting to really appreciate it.

"So, I'm, what, a call-girl bodyguard?" asked Layne, wiping at the corner of one of her eyes under the sunglasses as she kept chuckling and sighed. "Oh, my God, that was too funny. No, Elizabeth—your father didn't choose me for any other reason than keeping you safe."

Now I just felt stupid and helplessly awkward. I bristled at that. "I'm sorry," I said, feeling my cheeks redden so severely that I wondered if they'd ever go back to being flesh-colored again. "It's just that my dad is the type of person who would…who would do that."

God, how could I possibly dig myself out of this hole? And she was still chuckling about it, which didn't help matters much.

"That'd be an awfully specific job," said Layne, shoving her sunglasses up onto her head as we hit the city streets. Here the sunshine didn't even reach us; it was getting late in the afternoon, and the skyscrapers and buildings hid the rays of sun completely. Layne cast another mirthful glance in my direction, then shook her head. "I mean, think about it. A bodyguard call-girl for a fishing baron's daughter. I don't know how many people suitable for that role exist in this whole big world."

"I'm sorry if I've insulted you," I said, my words sounding brittle and just the tiniest bit prim. "It wasn't my intention."

"Hell, that wasn't an insult, sweetheart," she said, casting me another sidelong glance. Her voice had dropped about an octave, and a shiver ran through me that I couldn't control. Oh, God, that *voice*. It was pure sex. She chuckled a little at my obvious shiver, and then she was pulling into a parking garage.

She took the ticket the attendant machine spat out at us, and after ascending the very long ramp with all its sharp turns, she parked on the third level. We hadn't said anything more to each other, and I was feeling so frazzled and embarrassed that the moment we pulled into the spot, even before she threw the Cadillac into park, I had the door open and was trying to push myself up and out of the vehicle as I fumbled with my crutches.

It was unreal how quickly she turned off the ignition and sprinted around to my side of the car. I stared at her for a long moment, with the sunglasses perched on top of her head, her hair swept to the side. I stared into those damnable flashing hazel eyes that seemed to never stop shifting color and that also seemed to pin me to the spot with their bold intensity.

"Let me help you," she said softly, as she took the crutches from me and looped a strong hand around my middle, placing my arm around her neck.

She was so strong, the kind of strong that made me think she'd probably won every fight she'd ever gotten into, the kind of strong that is so obvious that you half-wonder if she could bend steel girders around an arm, twisting them into pretzel shapes as a hobby. But she was gentle, too, as she held me about the waist with such a soft touch and helped me limp across the parking garage and to the elevator, taking each step slowly and at my pace.

As I leaned against her, I realized that I was paying an unfair amount of attention to how she felt against me: the firmness of her muscles, her hipbone pressing against mine. There was something out of place in all those sensations, though. I felt a slim, unnatural hardness against her side, close to her breast, in an odd shape.

I went cold a little when I realized it was a firearm.

The elevator *dinged* and opened, and Layne helped me into it, pressing the ground floor button once I was leaning against the back wall.

I stared at her for a long moment. This woman was carrying a deadly weapon—a deadly weapon that she had been hired to use to keep me safe. She tossed her jet hair back, running a long-fingered hand through it before taking off her sunglasses, folding them and sliding them easily into her back jeans pocket.

Layne caught me staring and smiled roguishly, her head to the side as she leaned back on her heels. "I've never been in a violin shop," she said, her smile deepening as she shoved her fingers into her back pockets, too. "I never even knew there was such a thing. Though I guess it's kind of obvious that there'd have to be. But are there really enough people in Boston to keep a violin shop in business?"

"You'd be surprised how many kids take violin lessons," I said, smiling a little after clearing my throat. "And there are actually three string shops in Boston. The other two have cellos, basses, other stringed instruments. Verity's is the only one that deals strictly in violins."

Layne whistled under her breath as she rocked back onto her heels again. "Must be a lot of kids driving their parents crazy with screeching strings around these parts."

I laughed at that. "Sometimes I give lessons. I like kids." I shrugged when her brows went up. "And, yeah, there is a lot of screeching with those bows dragging across the strings, them trying to find the right places for all of their fingers to go, learn the posture. Though the screechy-string stage doesn't usually last long, believe it or not. Kids are quick learners."

"Yeah, well, I don't think there's enough money in the world that would make me put up with that," said Layne with a shake of her head and a chuckle. Then her eyes widened, and her face took on a look of mock horror as she groaned. "Oh, God—I'm your bodyguard. This means that when you do lessons…"

I grinned smugly and chuckled as Layne stepped forward, looping my arm around her neck again as the elevator doors *dinged* and opened up to the ground level. God, she was so hot—not in the metaphorical sense (though, yes, she absolutely was), but more in the body temperature sense of the word. Like, she was almost feverish to the touch.

"I'm not being paid enough if you have to teach kids while I'm around," she chuckled, and I gazed at her sidelong, listening to the deep smoothness of her laugh.

"I'll get you some earplugs before I take on another kid for lessons," I promised her.

"You'd be surprised how good my hearing is, earplugs or not."

We walked across the pavement to the sidewalk outside. Boston in June—it's one of the most beautiful times of the year to come visit our fair city. There were hot dog and taco vendors on the street corners, with the scents from both wafting towards us and making my stomach rumble. Women and men in business suits and kids staring down at their phones lined every corner. College kids sat along the entrance to the art museum as we passed it, writing in their notebooks, or—most often—typing into their electronic tablets.

We walked about two blocks, and by the end of the second block, even though Layne was fully supporting me and all but helping me put one foot in front of the other, I was really feeling the pain.

Finally, thankfully, Verity's Violin Shop came into view.

The shop was in one of the older buildings in Boston, made up of pretty brick and Victorian embellishments, added well after it was built. The sign out front has been hanging above the old metal front door for over fifty years, though it's been repainted many times. The sign looked vintage and beautiful, with its looping "Violin Shop," a hand-painted violin nestled into the words, as if the letters had to grow around the painted instrument.

The front window had several violins on display—

several regular-sized ones, propped up against their cases, and then some extra-small fiddles for the really little kids. The familiar, soothing chime of the front doorbells rang when Layne pushed the door open and held it for me to enter.

The inside of a violin shop has one of the best smells on earth: well-oiled wood and beeswax. I inhaled deeply, and a warm smile came over my face as I spotted Verity behind the front counter.

She was in the middle of stringing a red child-sized violin but stopped the moment her eyes flicked up to meet us. Verity is an impressive woman, with her shockingly (for someone in her mid-forties) white hair drawn back into a smooth ponytail, and her bright blue eyes assessing every situation smartly behind the most retro-looking cat-eye glasses I've ever seen. She was dressed in her usual chic black turtleneck and pencil skirt, black tights and black flats, and as she came around the counter to greet me with a quick hug, her normally smooth and serene features contorted into a grimace as she stared, aghast, at my crutches.

"Oh, honey, what happened?" she asked. Verity's eyes moved to Layne, but she, thankfully, didn't comment on the fact that an extremely attractive, never-before-seen woman was gripping me around the waist and practically holding me up.

"Oh, you know, just a little accident," I smiled wanly at her, but I returned the hug, looping an arm around her shoulder awkwardly. "Sadly, I come with grave news: my violin met with an untimely end," I told her.

Verity stared at me in shock for a long moment, her bright blue eyes wide; then she smoothed down her features again, and she became all business. "Then it's a *very* good thing I have something for you," she said, tapping her finger against her nose as she grinned and rushed behind the counter, into her backroom.

Beethoven's pastoral symphony—his sixth—was being piped through the speakers overhead as Layne helped me to the front counter so that I could lean on it and "stand" without her help. Then, curious, she began to roam through the shop, pausing to look at the back display, an entire wall covered in different violins and bows on pegs, ranging from the standard student model that was only around a hundred bucks to some of the better concert-ready violins in the fifteen-hundred-dollar range...and some much higher than that.

I watched Layne, trying my best to be surreptitious about it. She appeared to be genuinely interested as she crossed her arms and rocked back on her heels, whistling in a low tone as she stared up at a particularly pretty violin. It was plain but burnished so brightly that it seemed to glow. I happened to know that that one was two-hundred-years old, refurbished because it'd been in such bad condition when Verity had gotten hold of it. I'd almost bought that particular violin off of Verity a bunch of times, actually, because I'm a sucker for a violin with a past, but *particularly* a sucker for a violin with a past and a pretty juicy history.

"You know, that one has a story," I said to Layne, leaning heavily on the counter with my elbows as I tried to ignore the pounding in my stitches. Normally, I wouldn't offer to talk up a violin to any random person. I mean, it's kind of nerdy to be so obsessed with musical instruments; I fully admit it. But the way she was looking at that violin—it seemed that she was at least mildly interested.

"Really?" Layne asked, turning back to me. There was a soft smile turning up the corners of her mouth that stole my breath away, and it took me a moment to realize that she wanted me to go on.

Wow, I had to get a handle on this attraction... It was kind of through the roof. I blinked, then cleared my throat, shifting my weight a little as I rested my elbows more firmly on the counter, taking all of the weight off of my leg as I placed my chin in my right hand and purposefully gazed past her. I regarded the violin with a nod.

"That fiddle was made by a traveling music man

about two hundred years ago, up in Maine," I told her, jerking my chin in the violin's direction. "His name was Alfred McNalis, and he was self-taught in the art of instrument-making, and he ended up crafting quite a few impressive violins. He just had a gift for it. And this violin, in particular, was one of his finest pieces. But legend has it that he bargained that violin to the devil to save his life. There was a fire, and the house he was staying in burned down, everything completely destroyed, including everyone else who'd been staying in the house... But old Alfred and his fiddle were unscathed, not a horsehair missing from his bow, not a button out of place on his jacket, and he kept raving while he held up the violin, saying, 'The fire never even touched us.' Later on, the fiddle was badly burned in another fire, but that was long after its creator had died. Alfred was over one-hundred years old when death finally caught up with him, a feat practically unheard of in those days. And everyone says it's because he sold that fiddle to the devil."

"Great story," said Layne with a wink. "Now, how much of that is actually true?" she asked, but she was grinning lazily, indulgently, as she strode over to me and leaned her left hip against the counter, arms still crossed, looking down at me with bright, flashing eyes.

"I...I don't know," I said, gulping at her nearness. This close, the heat radiating off of her was something I could actually feel, even though we stood about two feet apart. "There are a lot of legends surrounding music and musical instruments," I said with a shrug after clearing my throat. "Probably not much of it is *actually* true," I said, all in a rush. "But it makes for a good story, doesn't it?"

"You know, come to think of it, why *are* there so many stories about devils and violins?" asked Layne, her face taking on a quizzical expression as her eyebrows furrowed. "I mean, that song, 'The Devil Went Down to Georgia.' That violin guy who sold his soul to the devil so that he could play perfectly. Stuff like that."

"Because," I said, pushing off from the counter and pressing my palms flat against the wooden countertop. I didn't even think about it as I said, "The violin makes such a beautiful sound that people couldn't explain it any other way than the fact that it must be supernatural. How else could such beautiful music come from something that is, essentially, hollow wood and wire?"

"Beautiful," Layne repeated, but she wasn't looking at the violins when she said the word. Layne's eyes were narrowed as she watched me for a long moment. Her jaw was clenched, and she looked like she wanted to say something to me, but Verity was pushing back through the door again at that moment, a beat-up violin case in hand.

"Sorry it took me awhile to get to. I was storing it in my safe in the back office," said Verity in a hushed tone as she set the case down gently on the counter. She was practically glowing as she leaned forward and murmured, "I think you're going to *love* it, Elizabeth."

Verity always kept her eye out for violins for me. She knew my style, knew what I needed in an instrument, and had a lot of connections in the stringed instrument world. All I knew about this violin was that it was about a hundred years old, and masterfully crafted. She hadn't told me any more than that. She knew that I needed it to play in the orchestra, so the instrument would be of superb quality. But I couldn't have imagined that it would be quite like this.

Many violinmakers have copied one of the most talented violinmakers who ever lived: Stradivarius. You can tell in the slope of the body of the instrument, in the specific curlicues, that it was Stradivarius-inspired. I love a good Stradivarius-inspired violin, don't get me wrong. He was a master, and masters *should* be copied. But I also love a violinmaker who isn't afraid to be himself. The guy who made this violin wasn't afraid in the slightest.

The instrument was of simple construction; there was nothing fancy or ornamental about the body of the violin. But as I picked it up—freshly tuned by Verity—out of the case, I ran my fingers over the strings, and somewhere in the hollow cavity of the violin, a delightful *thrum* answered the sound of my skin connecting to those strings.

I ran my thumb over the strings again, purposefully plucking at them. The cheerful sound of the notes sang vibrantly into the room as Verity picked up the bow from the case and rosined it for me, running the rosin up and down the horsehairs of the bow with the familiar *swish* sound, bits of dry beeswax flaking off into the air. She handed me the bow with a flourish and with the same sort of smile a cat makes after it's devoured the canary.

I held the violin up and placed my chin against it, the movement familiar but also unfamiliar as I learned this new instrument's shape, bending my body in minuscule ways to better connect with it. I held up the bow and placed it gently against the strings.

I played.

I closed my eyes. I listened as the bow *swished* effortlessly across those strings, powered by my hands and fingers as a pure and radiant melody came from the violin, spinning into the air around us like magic. They were so clean, those notes, so pure, that a surge of emotion moved through me, my throat constricted, and almost instantly, tears sprang into my eyes.

I played across the strings, having chosen something simple to test the violin out with—the piece of music that was one of the first I ever learned, the *Allegro* movement from Bach's third Brandenburg Concerto. It's a stunning Baroque piece, almost textbook with all of its dainty, complicated melodies, the kind that you hear and immediately think "period drama," but it has a very innocuous thrum of power beneath it. Don't be fooled. It sounds like something made for kings and queens and court, but underneath the top melody, there's this great passion moving like swift-flowing water below a perfectly calm surface…

There is something hidden in that music, so

resonant that, if you really listen, you find your breathing moves faster, and your heart might just skip a beat, in time with the melody.

I played the final note, finishing the piece and raising the bow off the strings. I was grinning broadly, practically panting. The violin vibrated against my shoulder as I opened my eyes, as if it were something alive and still singing.

I took a deep breath and glanced up at Layne.

Her mouth was slightly open, her lips parted. Her chest rose and fell a little too quickly, and her eyes were wide and shocked, like she'd just seen something she would never be able to describe or explain.

She looked...awestruck.

Suddenly self-conscious, I set the violin down on the counter, clearing my throat.

"It's superb, Verity. I'll take it, thank you. Do you want to send me the bill?"

"It'd be my pleasure," said Verity, glowing herself. "You made it sing, Elizabeth. I can't imagine anyone I'd want it to go to more."

I breathed out, still grinning. "Well, I'm very lucky to have it. It's a treasure. Thank you so much for finding it for me," I said, setting it gently back in its case and affixing the bow into the lid. I shut the case and clicked it closed, taking a deep breath as my fingers pressed against the lid's rickety old plastic. I have a nice wooden case I could put it into, I thought. Something classy enough for it...

When I gazed up at Layne again, her expression had shifted; it'd gone back to being guarded. But when our eyes connected, there was something that flickered behind her gaze: wonder.

"You never disappoint, Verity. Thank you, seriously," I said, hugging the woman across the counter as I smiled widely. She returned the embrace, smoothing a wisp of white hair behind her ear as she nodded at me with a slight shrug.

"It was my pleasure, truly. And I'm really looking forward to seeing that Mendelssohn concert tomorrow. When is Mikagi Tasuki flying in?"

At hearing the famous violin soloist's name, I shuddered uncomfortably and glanced at my watch. "Oh, you know, in half an hour," I groaned, placing the crutches beneath my arms and taking a tentative step back from the counter, leaning on the crutches and my good leg. "We've really got to get going if I'm going to make the rehearsal in time. Verity, you're amazing. I'll see you Friday?"

"Wouldn't miss it for the world," she said with a bright smile.

I waved at her over my shoulder and began to hobble toward the front door that Layne, graciously, held open for me, the violin case dangling from her fingertips. For half a moment, I considered asking her to be careful with the instrument, but then I realized that would be ridiculous; she had to know how much it was worth, and at the very least, she knew it was important to me. She wasn't a careless person. And she did sling it gently under her arm once we were out on the sidewalk again, clasping the case close and tight to her leather jacket as she slid her hands easily into her pockets.

Layne glanced up, far up, and I followed her gaze, past the skyscrapers surrounding us to the deep blue sky, the setting sun in the west making the sky dive to a deep, breathtaking shade of indigo. And farther still above us, a slim crescent of moon made its pale thumbnail imprint on the sky.

Layne glanced up at that moon, and her eyes narrowed as she gazed at it. Then she unexpectedly shuddered a little, like a chill breeze had just touched her. She flipped up the collar of her leather jacket, though the day hadn't suddenly gotten colder.

We walked to the parking garage in unexpected silence.

Chapter 4: Audience

I winced as I heard the dulcet tones of the orchestra conductor, Amelia, yelling at the top of her lungs. Her angry expletives were magnified by the empty balcony seating in the concert hall, making the tiny woman sound like she was an ogre intent on destroying a village with a very large club...and *not* a diminutive orchestra conductor.

We weren't even in the building, but her mood was projecting, loud and clear. It was going to be one of *those* rehearsals.

Great.

"Hey, Liz!" said Bob, our principal flutist, as he stubbed out his cigarette in the brick side of the building and held the back door open for me with a grin. His graying hair was combed back and to the side under a fedora that had a red carnation sticking out of it. He whistled in a low tone and gazed down at my crutches as he tossed his lighter into his suit jacket pocket. "I didn't know the accident was quite that serious. Are you okay?"

"Hey, I've still got all my fingers and toes, so I guess I'm doing pretty well," I joked as Bob continued to hold the door open for Layne, his eyes growing a little wider as he gazed up at her. Bob isn't exactly the tallest guy, but Layne seemed to tower over him in the entryway with all her big-shouldered, leather-jacket-wearing charisma that filled the relatively small space.

"Bob, this is Layne. My dad hired her to...um..." I bit my lip, searching for the right words—and failing to find them as I gestured up at her. "She's helping me out with some stuff," I said, finishing lamely.

Layne flexed her muscles as she took off her leather jacket and draped it smoothly over her forearm, holding my violin case in her other hand. Her red t-shirt was snug around her biceps, and I tried very hard not to stare at the pronounced curves of her chest or her impeccably chiseled abs that the t-shirt accentuated. "Pleased to meet you," she said, offering a hand to shake.

Bob shut the door behind him and came into the hallway with us, shaking her hand quickly. He winced; obviously, she had a firmer grip with him than she'd had with me earlier. "Charmed," he groaned a little, then chuckled as he jerked his thumb down the corridor and toward the concert hall. More of the angry yelling ricocheted down to us. Amelia wasn't just in rare form today: she was on *fire*. "Amelia's been impossible to live with all this week because Tasuki's flying in," said Bob, with another wince as he shook his head at me. "Seriously, Elizabeth, you should have taken a couple of sick days or something. Look at you! You're in crutches, and you *willingly* come to submit yourself to this abuse!" He shook his head and sighed, palming his lighter in and out of his pocket nervously, as if he needed something to do with his hands. "You're such a masochist," he pronounced.

"Not so much a masochist, I promise. I just wouldn't miss playing with Mikagi Tasuki for the entire world. And a little bit of yelling has never scared me off, remember?" I chuckled and continued to hobble down the corridor.

"This is the woman," said Bob, his voice dropping to a stage whisper as he leaned his head toward Layne, "who auditioned when Amelia had *just* gone through four hours of traffic. It's legendary, how angry Amelia was that day. And Liz won the audition, anyway!"

"It's really not legendary," I murmured and shook my head at Layne, who was grinning. "I just really, *really* wanted to be in this orchestra."

"Anyway," said Bob, stopping off at the men's room, "I'll see you out there!" He ducked inside, and I could hear him humming the melody from one of our harder pieces as the door swung shut behind him.

"Nice guy," said Layne with a small smile.

"They all are. Really, everyone in the orchestra is. They're very good people here," I said, pausing for a breather, my hands gripping my crutch handles. "Okay. Well, sometimes family members of musicians in the orchestra come in and watch rehearsal, so having you here isn't really that unheard of. Just take any seat you like out in the audience once I'm set up," I told Layne as we continued along the corridor.

"I'll be as quiet as a mouse," she promised with a wink. And then we were rounding the corner.

The concert hall was extra cold today, I realized, as I hobbled across the stage toward the first row of violin chairs in the string section.

Or maybe it was just Amelia's personality making the hall that much chillier.

Amelia Booth stood an impressive four feet five inches, but not a single person had ever looked at that woman and thought she was small. There was just something about her that towered over you. Maybe it was her out-of-fashion beehive hairdo that spiraled ever upward in a tall cone of brassy red hair, or her shoulder pads under her signature blazers that continuously made her look like she was not, in fact, an orchestra conductor but a football quarterback.

But it wasn't her hair or wardrobe or anything that superficial that made Amelia Booth so intimidating.

It was her larger-than-life personality.

"Ah, Elizabeth, I see that, despite my hopes, your near-death experience has not made you realize the important things in life—like punctuality. Didn't you *literally* see the light?" asked Amelia, one penciled-in eyebrow raised over her thick, Coke-bottle glasses. She was tapping one of her ridiculously high patent leather heels on the wood floor of the stage, and her arms inside of their black-and-white checked blazer were crossed so tightly in front of her, she looked like a caricature of an impatient person.

Layne glanced at me with both of her brows lifted, but I was grinning and shaking my head.

"It wasn't one of *those* near-death experiences, Amelia. Since when have you ever been that lucky?" I teased as I turned around, hopping on one foot and hooking the crutches out from under my arms. Layne handed me my violin case, and I nodded my thanks as she shoved her hands in her pockets, nodded to Amelia, and trotted toward the far staircase that led down to the seating area.

My second in the first string violin section, Tracy, looked me up and down and shook her head, her gray eyes wide as she plucked at her strings and began tuning them. Her long blonde curls were swept up in a messy updo, and her pretty face wasn't wearing any makeup, not that she needed makeup. Tracy would have been gorgeous in a burlap sack half-full of potatoes.

"I've been so worried about you!" she hissed under her breath, resting the violin over her knees as she set up the sheet music in front of her on the stand, clipping it into place. "Seriously, what happened?" she muttered out of the side of her mouth.

"I'm all right. Don't worry," I promised her quietly, fishing my sheet music out of my shoulder bag. "When is Tasuki supposed to arrive?"

"Frederic went to pick her up from the airport," she said. Frederic was our sound and lighting guy, and pretty much everyone in the orchestra agreed that he didn't get paid enough to put up with all of Amelia's demands and idiosyncrasies. But then, we all agreed that *none* of us got paid enough to put up with Amelia—a fact that she herself happily supported. "So they should be getting here soon," she added, adjusting one of her music stand clips. Everyone in the orchestra was supposed to use the standardized binder clips to hold their music to the metal frame, but for rehearsals, Tracy used clothespins that she'd painted flowers onto. She was kind of crafty.

"I'm a little nervous," I admitted, beginning to tune my violin, fiddling with the pegs as I thumbed across the strings and listened to the notes emanating softly from the body of the instrument. "I mean, my violin got *creamed* in the accident, so I just came from Verity's with this new baby."

"I was gonna say—that's a sexy fiddle if I ever heard one," said Tracy in hushed tones as she listened to the notes reverberating in the violin. She wrinkled her nose and shook her head, stray curls flying. "You're brave, though, bringing a new instrument to rehearsal, and especially *this* rehearsal. Amelia's been on fire today. She's so nervous about Tasuki playing with us," she said, grinning lopsidedly at me.

"I think I got knocked in the head in the accident," I muttered dryly. "So it's not so much *bravery* as *stupidity*." Any musician knows that you have to learn the ins and outs of an instrument before you even *think* about publicly performing with it.

Ah, well. Trial by fire.

Everyone filed into place, busily tuning their instruments, leafing through sheet music, and taking sips from bottles of water. Some musicians had started to go exclusively electronic, and—to me—it still looked a little strange to see e-tablets propped up on the music stands. Just as there was that perfect scent of wood and rosin, I would always associate happy thoughts with paper sheet music.

Though, to be fair, when I dropped my sheet music or got coffee stains on important sections, had sheets scatter everywhere, and occasionally completely lost a page or two, I saw the appeal of the electronic route.

Amelia loomed in front of us, nursing an extremely large, cracked blue mug of black coffee as she muttered crabbily into her phone, her mouth twisting from a grimace into something that *almost* resembled a smile. "All right, gang!" she practically sang out as she ended the call, pocketing the thing. "They're in the building!"

Tracy and I exchanged a chuckle and grin. I was pretty certain that we'd never seen Amelia look this happy—*or* this nervous.

I glanced up at the rows of seating. Layne had taken a seat three rows back, now leaning against her plush theater chair, her chin in her hand as she gazed at the stage. Her eyes were bright and focused, and for a moment, I thought she was glancing from musician to musician. But when I gazed up at her, I caught her staring…at me.

I hoped to God that my blush wasn't visible, but I could certainly feel my cheeks redden under her intense stare. Tracy glanced at me and elbowed me a little as she placed her violin under her chin and sketched the bow across the strings. "Who's the cutie?" she muttered softly.

"Oh, you know…a bodyguard," I groaned, glancing sidelong at her. "My father finally did it; he hired one for me. It's because of the accident," I whispered to her as she stopped playing, setting the violin in her lap again with an open mouth. "We think the guy rammed me off the road on purpose," I breathed to her.

"Oh, my God," said Tracy, her mouth rounded in astonishment, but then the entire orchestra was standing—me a little less quickly than the others as I tried to rise without the crutches—as Mikagi Tasuki (and Frederic, carrying her violin case and following close behind) stalked into the room.

As a violinist, I have to admit: I was a bit of a Mikagi Tasuki fangirl—though, really, I think every single person in our orchestra would have confessed to the same thing. Mikagi Tasuki had, after all, singlehandedly transformed violin music from a classical, kind-of-nerdy thing to listen to, to something anyone on the street would say they enjoyed. She'd made violins, for lack of a better word, "cool." Her specialty was fusing perfectly executed classical music with punk, pop and rock, and pretty much everyone from any developed country would say that they knew of her and had heard her music, and had probably danced to a song or two of hers at any recent wedding they'd attended.

I'd never had the pleasure of seeing Ms. Tasuki in person, but she looked much like she had on *The Tonight Show*, which was one of my favorite performances of hers, and one I had in my favorites folder on YouTube. This afternoon, she was wearing all black, her chin-length black hair almost iridescent in the bright lights from overhead. Her dark brown eyes were wide and expressive, and she was willowy and graceful in her knee-high riding boots, knee-length black skirt, and jacket. She paused next to Amelia, glancing at the rest of the orchestra with a small smile tugging at her full mouth.

Ms. Tasuki smiled widely, then, and did a little bow to us as silence fell across the stage. "I'm so pleased to be here," she said loudly, in her heavily accented, but low and charming, voice. The words rolled out over us as she nodded. "I am so excited to be playing with all of you, and I am so excited for the concert tomorrow!"

And my heart, already fangirling, began to soar.

I mean, she *probably* says that to every orchestra she plays with. But Ms. Tasuki seemed so genuine, what she was saying so heartfelt…that I believed she really *did* want to be here playing with us.

Frederic set her violin case down, and Ms. Tasuki had her violin out in a heartbeat, plucking at the strings and tuning them, drawing her bow across them in an effortless, graceful motion.

All of us picked up our instruments, too, and in short order, we began the rehearsal.

So, I've got to be honest: it wasn't my best rehearsal, not by a long shot. Being so close to Mikagi Tasuki had apparently shut down all of the really clever sections of my brain, and that meant that my hands played on autopilot.

Which wouldn't have been a big deal during any normal rehearsal, though I always tried not to phone anything in.

But during *this* rehearsal, though everyone was attempting to do their best, the jagged nerves (which we're all good at managing, usually), caused by playing so close to a star... Well, it was a *rotten* rehearsal. And, yeah, the pressure was getting to a lot of us.

To our great relief, though, *because* Mikagi Tasuki was there, Amelia couldn't exactly yell her head off like she normally would if we'd put in such a bad performance on a regular day. Instead, her face took on a unique shade of red; it appeared as if several of her blood vessels were bursting.

Mikagi Tasuki was, of course, perfection, every note flawless and so passionately played. I'd seen enough of her performances on YouTube and on DVDs to know that she was a world-class performer, strutting and dancing across the stage while cradling the violin to her chin, playing it like it had never been played before. But being able to watch her from behind was a rare treat, too. Not in *that* way (though her rear was definitely gorgeous from an objective, she-is-a-beautiful-woman standpoint), but because she kept throwing little glances and grins back to us, parading across the stage like she owned the place but was sharing it with us, too, cheering us on during the more difficult sections.

After the rehearsal, and after Amelia's face took on a more normal hue, Ms. Tasuki introduced herself to everyone, demanding that we call her Mikagi. Which, of course, proved that she was even more of a class act than we'd thought. When you're a musician, you just assume that pretty much everyone with an ounce of star power is a stuck-up narcissist. But not Mikagi. She was humble, down-to-earth, and shook everyone's hands like she meant it.

I sighed happily and hobbled away towards backstage with my crutches and my violin case dangling from my fingers. Tracy snatched the case up from my hand and walked beside me, carrying her own violin case tucked under her arm.

"That was *euphoric*," she sighed happily, her voice cooing just a little. "Though I think I missed about twenty notes." Her face screwed up, and she sighed. "I didn't even miss that many notes in my first jury test in music school."

"Yeah, well, I think we were all just a little dazzled by playing with Mikagi for the first time. I know we'll be a lot better tomorrow," I told her, confidence noticeably absent from my tone...but I still hoped it'd be true. We certainly couldn't be *worse* than that rehearsal we just stumbled through.

Probably.

"So, anyway," said Tracy, her voice dropping down to a conspirator's whisper as we wandered over to the coffeepot positioned near the coatroom. The pot was slowly spitting out coffee-smelling sludge, which several people stood in line for. "That cutie of yours was making eyes at you during the rehearsal, if you hadn't noticed," she told me with a wide smile, leaning closer.

"Cutie?" I muttered, one brow up after wincing at that word. Then I blanched a little. "Oh, God, you mean Layne. *Tracy*, she's my *bodyguard*," I told her firmly, shifting so that my weight was taken off my bad leg.

"That didn't stop Kevin Costner from hooking up with Whitney Houston that one time, I'd like to point out," said Tracy, chuckling a little as the line for coffee moved forward by a person. The familiar, comforting scent of black coffee wafted into the air, and I realized how thirsty I was.

"You just want me to turn into a Lifetime movie. I can see it coming," I groaned, shaking my head with a chuckle.

"Maybe not *Lifetime* so much as *Showtime*. Don't they have lesbian shows on Showtime? I mean, you were *meant* for your own show." Her nose was wrinkled in that adorable way she got whenever she was teasing me.

"I'm cutting you off from making any more jokes about this," I groaned, rolling my eyes. "My life is not *The L Word*, Tracy. Thanks for *that* stereotype. And I'm not getting together with—"

"That was really good." Layne had one brow artfully raised as she cleared her throat behind me. Tracy had suddenly turned as red as a tomato and was carefully watching the coffeepot with as much concentration as a nuclear scientist gives a test tube. "You're remarkable." Layne's voice was soft, just for my ears as she curved closer toward me, leaning her upper body so that her mouth was inches from my ear. She was grinning wickedly, her hands shoved deep in her leather pockets, her shoulders curving toward me, her whole body in an angle that seemed to point in my direction.

My mouth went dry as I gulped down air.

"You couldn't possibly have heard me. You can't tell one musician from the others in an orchestra; that's the point," I chided her softly, but my lips were twisted in a grin before I could help it. "Tracy, this is Layne, my new bodyguard." I cleared my throat, sweeping a hand toward the gorgeous, brooding woman to my right. "Layne, this is my friend and colleague Tracy Conroy, also a violinist." I indicated Tracy, who was staring at Layne with wide eyes.

"Hello." Layne gave another lopsided grin, her voice going a little deeper as she leaned close, her full lips curving. "You were quite good, too."

Tracy giggled a little and blushed as she held tightly to her violin case, a little like I'm sure she used to do in high school as she held her schoolbooks and was given a compliment. "You probably say that to all the violinists," she murmured in what I'd assumed was a joking tone, but her voice was a little breathy, and I glanced at my friend with wide eyes. She was staring at Layne with the kind of look she got when she was hitting on someone, all pouty lips, leaning her chest forward just a little.

Tracy was straight. Admittedly, she wasn't really arrow-straight, but she certainly liked men an awful lot.

But then, Layne *was* pretty impressive, and when she was training those intense hazel eyes on you, smiling her seductive little smile, and tossing some roguish hair out of her eyes while wearing the hell out of that leather jacket...yeah. I could understand feeling a little flustered.

Like I was, right now.

"You know what we should do?" Tracy blinked as if she'd just snapped out of a trance and grabbed my arm so hard I almost lost my balance on my left crutch. "Oh, sorry," she murmured penitently, helping to steady me with an arm around my shoulders. "I just got the best idea! Why don't we all go out for drinks? We can celebrate Mikagi Tasuki playing with little old us. We can celebrate...your new bodyguard..." She trailed off with a chuckle and inclined her head toward Layne and me. "I'm sure we can think of a bunch more things to celebrate. What do you think?"

I narrowed my eyes and raised a single eyebrow at Tracy, who was trying her best to appear completely innocent with her wide eyes, blinking those long lashes slowly with a soft, neutral smile. Yeah, the innocent act really wasn't working. Either she wanted me to have some relaxed time with my attractive new bodyguard, or *she* wanted some relaxed time with my attractive new bodyguard.

"I'm up for it if you are." Layne cocked her head and regarded me. "If you haven't overdone it, Elizabeth? Are you tired after the rehearsal?"

I hung there on my crutches and shook my head. The pain pills were working pretty well, and I hadn't overextended myself in the rehearsal that day. "Yeah, drinks would be great," I told Tracy with a grin. "At McBride's?"

"I'm insulted that you even had to ask." Tracy chuckled and gave me an absurdly campy wink.

So McBride's it was.

61

The Protector

Chapter 5: Not Really a Date

Fun Boston history fact: McBride's was a lesbian bar long before any of the other gay bars moved into town. It's been around since the *nineteen-hundreds*. How many lesbian bars can say that? Way back then, of course, it was all pretty hush-hush, something that no one but ladies in the know talked about. But nowadays, McBride's wears its pride on its proverbial sleeve. There's a rainbow flag unfurled outside, hung off the side of the building by the front door, and inside, the air of be-whoever-you-want-to-be is as constant as the flowing booze, strobing lights, and insistent, thumping dance music.

As such, while there are a hell of a lot of lesbians here on any given night, there's also a fair share of gay men and everyone else on the queer spectrum you can think of, and a lot of straight people, too, gyrating to the music on the dance floor and ordering as much beer, liquor, and fancy drinks as the lesbians. Because of the mixed atmosphere, it was usually our place of choice after a spectacularly good—or bad—rehearsal, where we went to celebrate, kick back, and relax. And to party, just a little.

"You know, after a rehearsal that bad, I should really just turn in my fiddles and consider a career in housekeeping." Tracy sighed. "Who knows? Maybe I missed my calling." With that, she swung back another shot. She staggered in her chair a little.

We were both getting pretty tipsy. And Layne sat there sober, taking occasional sips of club soda and grinning indulgently at the both of us.

"You don't want to go into housekeeping." I shook my head. "And let's be honest—you weren't nearly as bad as me today. I missed a *lot* of notes. Like, at one point, I played the measure from the next *line*."

"You guys are speaking Greek to me." Layne chuckled, signaling the bartender for another club soda. The bartender, a gorgeous woman with long black hair that curled around her shoulders as if she were about to pose for a shampoo ad, had mostly ignored Tracy and me, fetching us our drinks occasionally, the same as everyone else at the bar, but she sailed right on over when Layne called for her with a bright, dazzling smile, leaning forward so that her chest, quite visible in her plunging black v-neck tank, was propped up on her arms. She breathily asked Layne if she was *sure* she couldn't buy her a shot.

"No, I'm fine." Layne offered a wry grin, twisting her mouth sideways. "But if you want to buy me that club soda..." There was a subtle shift in her body. Before, it'd seemed like she was lounging in the bar chair, like her body didn't have a bone to it and had just pooled into the seat, like water in a glass. Now she leaned forward a little, her lips slightly parted and shimmering, as if she'd just licked them. Her eyes went dangerously dark as her muscles tensed almost imperceptibly, and you were immediately aware of the raw power in her. Suddenly, as I stared at this gorgeous creature, the bar became much, much, *much* too hot for me. I tugged at the front of my sweater, trying to remember how to breathe.

The bartender had apparently experienced a similar reaction: her jaw was almost on the bar itself, and she poured Layne a club soda so fast, the glass nearly catapulted off the counter when she slid it toward Layne.

But Layne caught it with a hand that moved too quick for me to even follow.

I'd had a few drinks at that point, but seriously...she was *fast*.

"Well," said Layne, her rich, velvety voice moving in commanding waves over me. I stared at her and breathed out slowly, conscious of the fact that, when she spoke, my heart rate began to skyrocket. "For what it's worth," Layne practically purred, "I thought you were *both* perfect. You're great musicians and shouldn't be so hard on yourselves."

"There you go again! Liar, liar." Tracy wagged her finger in Layne's face, her speech a little slurred. "Everyone knows it's impossible to hear individ...indi...each musician in an orchestra *separately*." She sniffed and shook her head, slurring her words a little more than she had a few minutes ago. But then, she *was* knocking back the drinks pretty quickly. "You're just trying to be all flirty, I *know* it," she breathed in what she probably assumed was a sexy manner but ended up making her appear a little asthmatic.

I coughed into my drink, but she didn't get the hint that, perhaps, she was being unsubtle.

"Now, see, that's where you're wrong." Layne put her head to the side a little as she leaned forward, crossing her arms on the tabletop, her muscles rippling beneath her skin, visible where she'd rolled up the leather of her jacket. Her eyes flashed as she murmured softly, the words rumbling in her throat: "I have *impeccable* hearing, and I can tell you—you two are good at what you do."

"Ha." Tracy's nose wrinkled like it does when she meets a challenge head-on. "*No one* has hearing *that* good. If you think you're so special, prove it!" she said, waving her hand...which happened to be holding a beer in it. Some of the beer sloshed up and out of the neck, spattering onto the floor. "Tell me what someone in this bar is saying, something you couldn't *possibly* hear. That guy."

Layne glanced past Tracy's shoulder to the man she'd indicated with her sloshing drink. He was about ten feet away, murmuring something into a smaller man's ear. None of us could see his mouth, because the smaller man's head obscured it. They were both wearing tight-fitting t-shirts and skinny jeans, both had ultra-gelled hair, the color of which was hard to see in the dimly lit bar. The taller man had his hand on the shorter man's waist.

I only glanced at the men for a moment, though, because I had to turn back to look at Layne. It was how she was tilting her head, her eyes unfocused but flashing in the dark interior of the bar. Her handsome face took on an intense look of concentration, her full lips open just a little. I stared at her mouth, taking a deep breath and another sip of my martini as warmth began to grow in my belly.

After a heartbeat, Layne's grin returned, her eyes focused, and she tapped the tabletop with a short fingernail. "He's telling his boyfriend that they've had enough to drink, and they should head out to Doctor V's, because it has a better atmosphere for dancing."

Tracy snorted, shaking her head. "C'mon, you can't fool us. 'Fess up: you *so* just made that up."

But then, as we watched, the taller man hooked his arm tighter around the shorter man's waist, tossed a few bills on the bar top for a tip, and ushered his boyfriend past us and right out the door.

"That was just a lucky guess." Tracy sniffed, though her widened eyes told me she wasn't quite sure about that.

I glanced at Layne, my eyebrows raised, and she shrugged a little, sitting smoothly back in her chair, one lazy arm looped over the back of it. Her leather jacket was open enough, and her red t-shirt tight enough, that I followed the path of her chest, and…

Oh, God, she'd caught me staring.

The blood rushed to my cheeks, and I ducked my head a little, taking a gulp of air.

"What about you, Elizabeth?" Layne murmured then. She didn't move. If at all possible, she lounged even more comfortably in her chair, but there was something about her face, about her single raised eyebrow and flashing eyes that made me shift, made me lean toward her across the table, as if she were magnetically tugging me in her direction.

"Yes?" I asked, biting my lip.

Her mouth quirked sideways, and she grinned, that grin deepening into a very wicked smile as she cocked her head a little. "Pick someone for me to spy on," she whispered, lowering her voice into a velvety growl.

I watched her mouth forming those words, a little spellbound, the drink slowing my reflexes and making me forget just a bit that staring at the body parts of my body*guard* was kind of unforgivably rude and inappropriate. I cleared my throat, circling my martini glass with cold fingers as I gazed out across the bar.

I caught the glance of a woman leaning against the bar, talking with two other women. She had short brown hair, stylishly cut, and was wearing a blazer and dress pants, like the two others she was with. She was also drinking a martini, and as I glanced at her, she didn't stop speaking to her companions, but she did raise her glass to me a little, her mouth taking on the tiniest of smiles.

"What about her?" I asked Layne in a stage whisper.

Layne sighed and gazed at the woman across the room. Layne lifted her chin, met my gaze head-on as her lips flattened to a hard line. "She's asking her friends if she should come over and buy you a drink. She thinks you're hot, but she..." Here Layne began to grin again, her mouth curling triumphantly at the corners as she tossed the hair out of her eyes and narrowed them. "She thinks you're with *me*."

"You're just guessing!" Tracy hooted, but she fell silent as quickly as if she'd been stung, because the woman was walking across the crowded bar toward us.

She leaned down toward me, a few wisps of brown hair haloing her face. "Hi," she murmured. She smelled of expensive perfume and booze, and up close, her face showed worry lines around the corners of her mouth as she cleared her throat. "I never do this kind of thing," she said, biting her lip as she stared down at me, "but I'll kick myself for it later if I *don't*—so, I was wondering if I could buy you a drink?"

I stupidly blinked for a long moment. I was so

shocked that Layne could have heard this woman over the loud music, the incessant talking and clinking of glasses. The lady had been *twenty feet away* and *whispering*. I gulped. "I've... I've had enough for tonight, but thank you. That's very nice." I tried to think of some excuse as she began to frown. "I just got into an accident," I said quickly, pointing to my crutches, positioned much like Tiny Tim's as they leaned against the table.

I'd meant the words to indicate that *because* I'd gotten into an accident, I was pretty bushed. But she stood quickly and took a step back. It's not as if I had the *plague*, but she retreated quicker than if I'd announced I was just diagnosed with dysentery, heading to the bar without looking back.

"That was a little rude. She must not like reminders of her own mortality," said Layne snidely, with a shake of her head, but her body language and her smug smile told me all I needed to know. She was very happy that the woman had left us so quickly.

"Okay, so you really *do* have good hearing," Tracy finally admitted, eyes wide. "But, seriously, that was a little spooky. How the hell do you do it? How the hell could anyone *possibly* have that good of hearing? What's your trick?"

Layne shrugged a little, lifting up her club soda and taking a sip. I watched that motion, watched the inherent grace in it, could also see her bicep move as her arm moved. She took off her jacket, then, and I realized I hadn't seen her often without her jacket, and with her jacket now draped on the chair behind her...I was appreciating the view. "Honestly, it's not much of a trick. I just come from a family that has really great hearing. Call it good genes," she said in answer to Tracy's question. But it wasn't really an answer at all.

After another twenty minutes or so of booze and laughter, Tracy glanced down at her watch, bringing it up closer to her face with narrowed eyes when she couldn't make out the time at first glance. "Gosh, kids, I hate to drink and run," she said, yawning hugely and covering her mouth up with her hand, "but I have not *only* a concert tomorrow but a stupid dentist's appointment, like, first thing." She winced and shook her head. "I should reschedule, but..." She trailed off as she blinked owlishly at us and shook her head again. "I think I'm going to call a cab. I can't walk all the way to my apartment," she said slowly, slurring every word as she stood unsteadily.

"Do you want me to call one for you?" I asked, reaching quickly for my crutches. I was a little tipsy, yeah, but Tracy was pretty darn drunk, and I was worried about her and her fiddle getting home in one piece.

"I got this," she said with a wide smile, patting my shoulder. "You two have fun!" she practically sang. She pecked a kiss on my cheek, waved to Layne, and faded into the crowd as she headed toward McBride's door.

Then it was just me and Layne sitting there in the oldest lesbian bar in Boston.

I cleared my throat, taking another sip of my martini.

And I realized that this...*kind* of felt like a date.

But it wasn't. It absolutely wasn't, *obviously*. Because Layne was technically my employee (wasn't she? Or was she my father's employee? *Did it matter?*). Either way, we had a working relationship that sex—or even dating—would vastly overcomplicate.

And did I really *need* more complications in my life right now, when someone had—allegedly—just tried to kill me? Wasn't that complicated *enough?*

I stared at Layne across the table. I couldn't help but stare. It was the way she bonelessly lounged back in the chair, the way she gazed at me with her bright, flashing eyes that could never decide what color they wanted to be, their hazel depths seeming to turn green one moment, sea-blue the next, and then a deep, shimmering brown a heartbeat later.

Their color transformed again as Layne leaned forward, her body language shifting as she curved toward me, her entire body a question mark punctuating an unspoken query.

Her beautiful mouth parted, and those full, perfect lips were going to ask me…something. But then her face closed like a boarded-up house, and she leaned back again, clearing her throat, averting her gaze from me. The moment had somehow come and gone, and I didn't know what had just changed, but something obviously had. "I'm about ready to get going," she said then, quietly. "If you are."

What had just happened? What had she been about to say? Maybe I'd imagined it… But no. That last moment had seemed precious, how she'd curved toward me as if I, for a single heartbeat of time, had a gravity to *me*, too…and I called to her as strongly as she called to me.

"Yeah, that'd be fine," I told her, realizing as I spoke the words that I was slurring them, too. Okay, so maybe I was a little past tipsy. And maybe, just maybe, I'd imagined that moment with Layne.

I stood and tried to grab for the crutches, but I had to grip onto the edge of the table as the world started to reorient itself around me, twirling and spinning like it was a carnival ride that would never let me off.

"I can bring the car to the front of the bar." Layne stood in an instant and put one strong hand under my right elbow. The way her fingers curled around my arm made me lean toward her, but then I was shaking my head, grabbing at my crutches again. I managed to get them under my arms as Layne lifted up my violin case from under the table with a questioning tilt to her head.

"No, no, that's too much trouble to go to. That'd just be silly," I said, as practically as I could under the circumstances. "We can both walk together to the parking garage. And, anyway, the night air in the city always makes me happy." God, did I really just say that? I couldn't put thoughts together long enough to voice them articulately.

"But it's quite a *walk* to the parking garage," said Layne softly into my ear, her warm breath brushing against my skin and making me sigh, my heart beating a little faster. God, I hoped she hadn't *heard* that sigh. "And aren't you feeling it after everything today? Aren't you sore?"

I mean, I was, but the booze was taking care of the worst of the pain. Somewhere in my muzzy head, I remembered a warning label on the pill bottle saying you shouldn't mix the pain pills with alcohol, but I was pretty sure that it was all right if I wasn't driving. Maybe. I blinked again. Layne had asked me another question, but I hadn't really heard it.

"I'm sorry. I'm pretty gone," I finally admitted to her, leaning heavily on the crutches and a little on Layne herself. God, she felt so good against me, her body hard in all of the right places, sculpted muscles beneath the jeans and leather jacket and t-shirt, and soft in all the right places, too... I wanted to touch her.

I wanted to kiss her.

I tried to hang onto the last shreds of commonsense as we eased out of the loud, bass-thumping confines of the bar onto the relatively quiet, chill sidewalk outside. The cool June night air brushed over me, waking me up a little from my stupor as I glanced around at the heavily populated road, covered in brightly lit taxis, cars and buses, and the equally packed sidewalk, swarming with people.

Much to my sadness, a lot of the closer parking garages had already begun to fill for the night—and it was a *Thursday* night! But Boston loves to party any night of the week, so we hadn't bothered to move the car from where we'd parked by the concert hall.

Layne was right: we had a long way to walk, though it was a beautiful night to do it. Layne carried my violin case easily with one hand and placed her other strong, sure arm around my waist, bringing me close against her.

She smelled so good, I realized. Not of cigarette smoke, like the crowd of smokers we'd just passed, or of alcohol, though there'd been a lot of booze sloshing out of various glasses and bottles at the bar. She smelled... Well, it's absurd to describe it like this, but it's the truth, so here goes: she smelled fresh, like she'd just been out for a hike, and there'd been a really brisk, clear wind blowing. She smelled as if all the scents of the forest, of a bright, glorious day, had gotten stuck in her hair and against the warmth of her skin. She smelled fresh, but she also smelled hot, like cinnamon and a dark musk. I could have stood there all day and inhaled the old, sweet leather of her jacket, the musk of her skin, the fresh greenery of a wild ramble, but we were moving through the city—my city—at night, and all around us people laughed and cried and talked, on their way to many different places and experiences, and we couldn't stand there quietly... We had to move with them.

But Layne and I seemed to drift past them all as if we weren't really a part of the crowd. As if everyone else moved in one direction, and Layne, with her warm arm wrapped tightly around me like she'd never let me go, moved in another.

It felt like we were being kept safe in our own little bubble, just the two of us, Layne and me.

That is, until we reached the block with the parking garage.

The crowds had started to thin out more and more. If I'd been paying attention to the time, I would have noticed that it was far past my bedtime, and if I'd been paying attention to the sparseness of the crowds—and, surprisingly, the near-complete absence of people on the recently teeming streets—I would have realized we should probably be progressing to my car a little quicker than we were.

We had to pass a slim alleyway before the parking garage came into view. I'd parked in this garage dozens of times when I drove to the concert hall instead of taking the bus to rehearsals, but I was never around here this late into the evening. The parking garage was a few blocks away from the concert hall itself, which put it in an entirely unfamiliar neighborhood at night.

Which would explain why I never could have predicted what happened next.

If you'd ask me, I would have told you, yes, this was a safe part of town. But it was very late at night, and I guess any part of the city can be unsafe if the wrong people are there.

And the wrong people were there just then.

Like it was a very bad dream or a scene from a dark, gritty movie, two men folded out of the shadows of the building of the parking garage and stood beneath the streetlight, their feet hip-width apart, their heads back, their hoods up. They looked utterly menacing, and as the first one—a big, burly guy with a brown beard—stepped forward, I realized what was happening before the gun came out of his hoodie pocket.

"All right," he said with a quick sneer. "Empty out your purses. Any rings, cell phones, anything of value, give 'em to me. *Right now.*"

My heart was in my throat. I couldn't really breathe, and all I could think about was the fact that I didn't really have anything of value on my person—nothing but my violin, and, really, not that many people in this world would know what that instrument was worth. I wondered if they would shoot us if they knew that we didn't have anything they could take. I wondered what would happen if they became angry...

All of these thoughts came to me in the blink of an eye, because the gunman took a step back just then. His eyes grew wide, and he lowered his gun.

He was staring at Layne.

I looked up at her. I remember how fast my blood was pounding, like we were still back at the bar, and they'd just turned up the bass of an already pretty bass-impressive song, the music thrumming through the soles of my feet and into every inch of my body and bones. The world faded to that deep thumping, and then I understood that the quick, fast bass was my heartbeat roaring through me.

Layne was snarling. Actually *snarling*, her lips drawn up over her very white teeth, her eyes impressively narrowed, and her body posture curling forward. She was a very tall woman, but she seemed to suddenly loom over the two men, which wasn't exactly possible: they were tall, too.

The gunman took another step back, but then his companion shook his head, nudged the gunman's arm. "C'mon, Larry," he said in a strained whisper. "Ask 'em for their stuff again."

It was strange, in that moment, the things that stood out to me. Like how cold I'd suddenly gotten. Like how this second guy didn't have the typical Boston accent but something a little softer and more rounded, almost southern.

And then the hair on the back of my neck stood up to attention as the first guy's eyes widened, as Layne took one step forward.

And the gunman raised the gun and held it at shoulder height, pointed at Layne.

"Back up, bitch," he muttered, his eyes so wide that they were almost rolling in his head.

The gun fired.

There was a scream, but that was me, I realized after a second—*I'd* screamed. Layne wasn't falling backward, like someone who'd just been shot. She was lunging *forward*, and then the two guys were turning and running down the alleyway as if the hounds of hell were on their heels. They were headed back toward the rear of the building, and they were pretty fast, but even with their head start, Layne was hot on their heels.

Layne was so *fast*—impossibly fast, like the fastest track runner I'd ever seen, but somehow even faster than that. She caught up with the gunman in a heartbeat, and then she was shoving down on his shoulder with her hand. It was just a small gesture; it really shouldn't have even broken his stride. But he crumpled to the ground as if his legs had completely given out underneath him, rolling three times over until he rested, possibly unconscious, against the side of a Dumpster, the gun skittering across the ground and thudding up against the side of the building with a metallic clunk.

The second guy glanced back and picked up the pace, his heavy boots thudding against the pavement. He rounded the corner as Layne did, and then the two were lost from my view.

There was a thin, piercing scream, and then a long moment of silence.

Layne strode back around the corner at a quick pace, her shoulders curled forward, her hands in her pockets.

Even at this distance, I took a step back.

Her head was bent forward, and she was wiping the back of her hand across her mouth. She wasn't breathing hard. Her eyes glittered in the darkness, and her entire posture, her muscles, everything…it was intense as she stalked forward. But honestly?

It was also a little frightening.

"Layne," I whispered as she reached me. I clutched my violin case tightly—she must have given it to me before she ran, though I didn't remember her doing it. "Are you… Are you all right?"

"Fine," she said curtly, adjusting her leather jacket's collar against her skin as she growled a little and spat. "We need to call the police, get these men arrested." She took a slim black phone out of her back pocket, dialed 911.

As she turned away from me, I stared at that leather jacket, my heartbeat roaring through me.

There was a ragged hole from the bullet, right over where her heart should be. A hole on her t-shirt, right where her heart should be. There was blood on her shirt, too, bright red beneath the streetlight.

But beneath that hole in her shirt was perfect, unblemished skin.

There was no wound.

The Protector

Chapter 6: The Ring

It rained that night, the unhappy, torrential downpour of a violent June thunderstorm. The wind raged outside my apartment window, making the glass rattle in its casement and driving the raindrops sideways into the glass, but though the storm raged outside, the lightning spearing the buildings around me, all I could think about was the woman in my guest bedroom, her leather jacket hanging on the peg behind the door.

The leather jacket with the hole in it.

I'd been a little appalled when my father insisted that Layne, as my bodyguard, should spend nights at my place, too. I wasn't unhappy really for reasons of my own independence or my own space, though that's what I'd brought up when he'd mentioned it. Mostly, I was appalled that Layne would have no downtime from me.

I had a pretty demanding job that took up all of my time. I really wasn't that interesting of a person to spend twenty-four-seven with.

But Layne hadn't seemed to mind in the slightest. She'd nodded at my father, seated behind his desk with his happy grin pasted across his face because I'd agreed to all of this, and she'd nodded to me with a smile. My father had, of course, brought up the fact that once the people who were after us were brought to justice, I wouldn't have need of a bodyguard, so this arrangement wasn't permanent. He'd asked me to be a good sport, and then Layne had glanced at me sidelong.

"It'll be my pleasure to keep you safe," she'd murmured to me, setting my heartbeat to racing.

And tonight she *had* kept me safe.

Apparently, she'd even been *shot* for me.

And there was not a single trace of that bullet anywhere on her person.

Okay. So where could the bullet have gone? The gunman had shot the gun at point-blank range. That bullet had very obviously gone through the leather jacket—the leather had been intact just moments earlier, and there was no other way to explain that gaping hole in it now. And then there was the gaping hole in the t-shirt, directly over where Layne's heart should be, showing off pale, unmarred skin. Like the jacket, there was no other way to explain the hole in the t-shirt besides the fact that the bullet had gone through it.

And then, of course, there was the blood that had drenched her t-shirt.

How was it possible that the bullet had *not* hit her? But she hadn't said anything about it; she hadn't acted as if she'd been shot. There was no talk about hospitals, *nothing*. Instead, she'd zipped up her jacket so I couldn't see the drying blood on her t-shirt, and she'd smiled at me and asked me about the music we were going to play tomorrow night.

So...had I been seeing things? I *was* pretty drunk... What if she'd had a logo on her t-shirt or something, and it was bright red?

If she'd been shot, she *would* have told me. She would have needed to go to the hospital.

So, this meant...she *hadn't* been shot? Right?

The more I thought about it, the more I realized I must have imagined the red on her shirt being blood. And, obviously, I was pretty damn happy that she hadn't had to take a bullet for me. I was deeply relieved that she wasn't injured on my account. It just didn't make any *sense*, no matter how many different ways I put the pieces together. The gun had been fired at her. The bullet had ripped through her leather jacket. It should have connected with her heart. She very obviously (not that I'd stared at her for hours earlier to confirm this) wasn't wearing a bullet-proof vest under that tissue-thin t-shirt of hers.

And then, of course, I kept coming back to the hole in the t-shirt.

And all that beautiful, bare skin beneath it that was unharmed.

My face burned in the dark of my bedroom as I thought about her skin. As I thought about the fact that that gorgeous woman was a single room away from me.

For a moment, I let my mind linger—but only for a moment. My father had hired Layne to keep me safe, and already, in the first day, she had. She'd been right. She *was* the perfect candidate for this job.

But how had Layne gotten out of our encounter unscathed? And why had the gunman reacted so violently to her? And how had she knocked those guys down? She'd hardly *touched* them.

And the man had screamed…

She'd been so brusque after the encounter, very unlike herself. We'd gotten into the car, had driven the entire way to my apartment in silence, and when I'd shown her the guest bedroom she'd be staying in, she asked me if I was all right. I told her yes, and then she'd practically shut the door in my face.

That had hurt. I'd tried to explain that away, too. She'd spent all day with me, and she'd just been shot at. She was bound to be a little tired and needing a couple of moments to herself. But there had been something flashing in her eyes, something like anger.

I took a deep breath and rolled over, listening to the crack of thunder and lightning outside, listening to the rain beat itself against my window.

When I closed my eyes, I saw Layne grinning at me, her mouth quirked sideways, that wicked grin making her eyes flash with bright fire. But then I saw, too, the look in

Layne's eyes when she'd stared at the gunman.

The hairs on the back of my neck had risen. My skin had gone so cold.

There had been something in her eyes. Something I'd never seen before.

I turned over again and punched at my hot pillow a little with exasperation. I had one of the most important concerts of my career tomorrow and had given a really rotten rehearsal this evening. I *needed* my sleep in order to ensure a better performance.

But there was no help for it.

I *couldn't* sleep.

There was too much going on in my head and in my body, with all of its aches and stitches. I flicked on my lamp with a long sigh and poked around in my bedside table's drawer. No good books to read; the last one I'd finished was on my e-reader, and that had been a week ago, and I hadn't kept the tablet charged. I pressed the "on" button a few times just to make sure, but the same message kept flashing on the screen: "Your battery is dead. Please charge your device." I fiddled with the e-reader's tangled charger cord, also in the desk drawer, and plugged it and the e-reader into the wall outlet behind the table, so at least it'd be charged for me soon.

As I went to shut the drawer, something made me pause.

I didn't have much in that drawer. Some pain medicine, two novels I'd finished a long time ago and should really just shelve in my living room, my e-reader and its charger.

And my mother's ring.

I picked it up and turned it in the light with a small frown. The blood-red garnet flashed, even in the low-wattage bulb from my bedside lamp. My mother had had these rings made for her and my father on their ten-year wedding anniversary. She'd been so happy with them, had wanted to give my father a sweet surprise. I hadn't been there to see it, wasn't even alive at that point, but the way he talked about it... It was a gesture that meant a lot to him, though I never really understood the significance of the garnets, and Dad had never gotten around to telling me.

And by the time I could have asked my mother what they'd meant, she was already gone.

My father had asked me to keep my mother's ring after the funeral. I'd only been a kid, really, but it had meant a lot to me that something so precious had become my responsibility. And even though she was gone... Well, it made me feel that some small part of her was still here with us.

My father's ring was of a more masculine construction, bright silver with high prongs and a very large, square-cut garnet that glittered. He never took it off, so I didn't know if the inside of his ring bore an inscription like my mother's did.

My mother's ring was very different from his. Though it was silver, too, the garnet was a round cut, set in fluted prongs that sort of resembled a tiara from the side. The scrollwork all over the ring was so fine and pretty, very antique-looking, though I knew the ring hadn't been made that long ago—certainly not in the Victorian era, though it looked as if it had been.

And on the inside of the band, words were engraved in a looping script: *Our love is immortal.*

My breath caught in my throat to read those tiny words in the silver, and I brushed the pad of my thumb over the inside of the band as tears pricked at my eyes. I don't remember much about my mother. I remember the way she laughed, like everything was wonderfully funny. I remember the way she looked at my father, like he was the only person in the universe besides me.

It's really sad, I suppose, but I never thought about my mother that much anymore. I was grateful for the fact that she'd brought me into the world, and I'd loved her very much when she'd been alive...but there was nothing much to remember her by. I loved the memory of her, but it was an abstract one: laughter and the way she looked at my dad. I was far too young when she passed away, and I'd given up mourning her a long time ago.

I was, however, very sad for my father. It had been so obvious that she was the love of his life. After Mom died, he'd become extra overprotective of me. Mom had died in a car accident, and it was just one of those things that couldn't have been prevented. That's what an accident is, isn't it? No one's fault, but something's gone terribly wrong.

Still, my father had labored under the belief, all these years, that the accident *could* have been prevented if only he'd been more vigilant. He was obsessed with the idea, actually. So he put all of those overprotective worries on me.

He missed my mother with a fierceness that made my heart ache to witness.

Sometimes I thought about my father never dating, never even looking at another woman since my mother's death, and though it was very sad, and I felt terribly sorry for him…I knew that it was the product of a type of union that was all-consuming. My father and mother had loved each other so fiercely that my father hadn't been able to consider loving another woman since she'd passed. And I had my doubts that he ever would.

Sometimes, I wondered if I could ever settle in my own life for anything less than what my parents had experienced.

I didn't know if I believed in true love, or one person being meant for someone since before they were born. That was cosmic juju stuff that I'd had no experience with.

But if there was such a thing as soulmates, I knew my parents had been that for one another.

My own uncertainties had never stopped me, of course, from dating the women I was physically or intellectually drawn to, and I would continue to date and try to find the woman best-suited to me.

But I wondered if I'd ever be content unless we had a comparable connection to the one my parents had: a bright, fierce, powerful love that could stand the test of time.

And even death.

I turned the ring this way and that in the dim bedroom light as the garnet flashed and winked at me. I didn't keep the ring in my jewelry box, though I probably should.

I placed it in this drawer because I kept meaning to wear it.

The ring was pretty fancy for someone like me, though. I like long, clean lines and a minimum of fuss with my clothing, including a minimum of colors. My favorite color to wear was black, because it's classic and classy, and orchestra members wear a heck of a lot of it. In my downtime, I wore black skirts and black turtlenecks and tights and shoes. I wasn't much like my mother in that regard. She'd loved frilly, fancy, pretty things, the more colorful the better, the more frilly and fancy the better, exactly like this ring. It *was* much too fancy for me. I don't even really like to wear jewelry, could hardly be coxed into the two silver post earrings I wore for performances.

But after the events of the past few days, after all the life-threatening crap that had been happening to me...it kind of felt like a good idea to put on my mother's ring.

Maybe I was being superstitious; maybe I thought this tiny piece from my mother's life would give me a little luck. But, mostly, I just wanted something comforting to hold onto.

If the last few days had proved anything, they'd proved this:

Life throws a hell of a lot of surprises at you. And things you could never, ever predict can change your life forever.

Like an accident.

And a bodyguard.

I held up the ring to the light and took a deep breath

as I stared at the blood-red stone. And then I slid the silver ring down the third finger of my right hand. It nestled there comfortably against my skin, like it'd been made for me, the garnet still flashing in the dull light.

I turned off the lamp. I turned my pillow over to the cool, unrumpled side and placed my cheek against it with a sigh. I closed my eyes, listening to the soft hush of the rain. The storm was dying down, it seemed.

And, unexpectedly and peacefully, the ring growing warm against my skin, I drifted off to sleep.

I woke up to the smell of scrambled eggs and toast slathered in melted butter. The smell was particularly strong because these things were in front of my nose.

Literally.

It was morning, it had to be, because the sun was out, and its bright, warm light suffused my bedroom, spilling over me and my comforter. I opened my eyes and blinked at the sight greeting me. The lamp on my bedside table had been pushed back, and a tray had been placed on the table. The tray, an old wooden one that I usually kept my potted begonia and watering can on, now held one of my china plates heaped with golden scrambled eggs, dark rye toast coated thickly with butter and blueberry jam, and a big, rounded spoonful of cottage cheese heaped neatly on a lettuce leaf.

The lettuce leaf was really what threw me. It was something a restaurant would do, serving cottage cheese on a leaf of lettuce, but, somehow, here it was on my bedside table.

Layne stood in my open bedroom doorway, leaning against the doorjamb with a very smug smile on her face, her arms crossed, her biceps curving just a little as she tilted her head at me. She was wearing a skin-tight *blue* t-shirt this morning, which made her hazel eyes somehow look green. The blue t-shirt, I would like to point out, was thin enough to show off her deeply toned abs, like she was in a commercial for a local gym. Her black hair was combed carefully to the side, and she had on a slim leather wristwatch.

May I point out again that she was standing in my *bedroom*...

I drew the covers a little further up and found myself blushing. I was no stranger to waking up to a woman in my bedroom—and normally, I didn't care what she saw. But Layne...wasn't like that. She wasn't a one-night stand, and she wasn't my girlfriend.

She was my intoxicatingly attractive bodyguard...

Who had apparently made me breakfast in bed.

I was starting to get mixed signals here.

"You don't have to cook for me." The words were out of my mouth before I realized that this was probably not the best first thing to say to her.

I held the comforter to me and painfully realized that I was only wearing a t-shirt and panties, and the t-shirt I was wearing was one from my teenaged years and was therefore pretty ratty. But it held nostalgia for me, which is why I kept it and wore it to bed. It had a picture of Britney Spears on it, the cover of her very first album where she looks all innocent, before her shit hit the proverbial fan. (Also, please don't judge; I'm sure you have one embarrassing piece of clothing somewhere, too. Maybe not *quite* as embarrassing as Britney memorabilia, but still... Then again, maybe it's just me.)

"Eh, I was making myself breakfast, and I thought, why not? Figured it might take the sting out of being held up at gunpoint last night," she drawled, deepening her smirk. Then she lifted her chin, her eyes trailing down my front until they settled on my chest. "So, have you always been a fan?"

Oh, *God*, she *had* seen the shirt. I rolled my eyes and shook my head, drawing up my comforter so far that it rested beneath my nose. "I swear, if you ever bring this up to anyone else, *ever*—"

"You'll...hit me, baby, one more time?" asked Layne, with a low, throaty chuckle that made me blush a few shades redder, and made me realize that she was standing pretty darn close...

Something began to stir in me, uncoiling in my belly as I took a deep breath and bit my lip, trying to figure out a scathing, clever comeback.

"Hey, I don't judge," she said, after a long moment in which I utterly failed to think up a scathing, clever comeback. Layne spread her hands and shrugged as she grinned at me. "Eat up. You have a big day ahead of you."

I shot her a suspicious look, but she was already turning, her hands shoved deep into her back pockets as she whistled "Hit Me, Baby, One More Time" on the way back toward the kitchen.

I stared at those hands in her back pockets. Stared unabashedly, the blush deepening in my cheeks as I realized that I wished *my* hands were in her back pockets...

Oh, *God*, I really needed to get a grip. I bit my lip and realized exactly how warm I was, buried beneath the comforter, and pushed it off, rising and hobbling over to the bedroom door before shutting it with a soft *click*.

Okay, so maybe it wasn't the most *appropriate* thing in the world that my bodyguard had waltzed into my bedroom without knocking (or maybe she *had* knocked, and I was too deep asleep to hear her, I reasoned with myself) and brought me breakfast in bed while simultaneously seeing me in my ratty t-shirt glory. And had my comforter been pushed off of my legs, too? Had my rear been visible to her? God, maybe she'd seen the whole shebang. I blew a sigh and plunked myself back down on the edge of the bed.

Okay, it wasn't appropriate. But hot? Hell, yes.

And she'd made me *breakfast*. In *bed*. Not even my

long-term girlfriends had ever made me breakfast, and I wasn't *dating* Layne.

All right, Elizabeth, *get a grip*.

I took a deep breath and threaded my fingers through my tousled hair. Layne was a nice person, granted. Like she'd said, she'd probably just been making herself breakfast—I'd told her last night that anything in the apartment that she wanted to use, eat, etc., she could—and since she's so thoughtful, she'd figured I might like something to eat, too. It was probably that easy of an explanation. She was making breakfast for herself and made some extra for me. Case closed.

I twirled my mother's ring around my finger and stared at the plate mounded with eggs, cottage cheese and toast. But I wasn't seeing the plate. I was seeing her sarcastic smile as she teased me about once liking Britney Spears enough to keep this t-shirt for nostalgia's sake, and her long-fingered hands shoved deep into those dark jeans pockets over her tightly toned ass.

I leaned back on my hands and let out a very long sigh, the sunshine filtering through the window and streaming over me with as much heat as my blush.

Was she sending me signals, or was she just being kind?

Either way, I couldn't come on to my *bodyguard*.

Could I?

I groaned in frustration and stared at the plate of food again. I scooped up a few of the eggs on a piece of bread and gave them a taste.

They were perfect.

The Protector

Chapter 7: Knock 'em Dead

"I'm going to chew off every fingernail. And then there'll be nothing left," Tracy groaned, holding out her left hand to me. Violinists have to keep their fingernails short, anyway, because our fingertips need to press down on the strings, but Tracy's nails were *drastically* short...and really did look like they'd been gnawed at. Her manicure—a glittery red nail polish—was already ruined.

"Don't be nervous," I told her soothingly. "We're going to do all right."

"Yeah, exactly as we did in rehearsal," she muttered, one eyebrow up as she massaged her temples and groaned a little under her breath.

We were partaking of our pre-concert ritual, which consisted in the both of us getting coffees at the sweet little coffee shop, Thanks a Latte, that was located around the corner from the Fine Arts Museum. Layne was sitting a few booths down from us, talking to my father on her cell phone about "the incident," which was how she was referring to last night's hold-up.

I tugged at the ends of my pure-white sleeves. We were going a little casual this evening in our concert, which was, for me, wearing a buttoned dress shirt and a black pencil skirt with black tights and Mary Janes. Tracy wore the same white shirt but was in a pair of black slacks. Her curly hair was swept up in a sophisticated bun with tendrils dangling prettily around her ears. Mine was in a simple, high ponytail that I kept tugging at because I, too, was nervous.

Tracy pressed her iced coffee to her forehead with a slight groan and sighed. "I really shouldn't have had so much to drink last night, and I *really* shouldn't have gone to the dentist this morning. He filled two cavities. I mean, what was I thinking?"

I chuckled and shook my head with a shrug, trying to keep it light. Since our concert *was* so soon, and I didn't want to throw either one of us off our game, I'd decided not to discuss "the incident" with Tracy, because I didn't want to worry her. And, I mean really—how do you bring up that sort of thing? *You'll never guess what happened last night—we were held up at gunpoint!* I fiddled with the ring on my finger and cleared my throat.

"Layne made me breakfast in bed this morning," is what I finally settled on telling her. Tracy set her drink down on the table between us and raised both of her eyebrows, her hangover momentarily forgotten as a slow smile spread across her face.

"No way! Breakfast in bed, *seriously*? So, was this after a night of wild and passionate—"

"Mind, get the heck out of the gutter," I said, jerking my thumb as I rolled my eyes and shook my head.

"Honey, I think your mind needs to jump *into* the gutter. She's so attractive that not a *single* person has been unable to look at her when they walk past her table," Tracy whispered, leaning forward and tapping a bitten fingernail on the tabletop. "Earth to Elizabeth's lady parts... Come in, Elizabeth's lady parts!"

"I really can't take you anywhere," I muttered dryly and sighed.

"Is it the whole employee thing that's turning you off? It's probably that." Tracy leaned back in her booth. She groaned a little under her breath, her frown deepening. "Seriously, Liz, she's not *your* employee. Your *father* happened to hire her to keep *you* safe. If she keeps you safe on a couple of dates, or—you know—in *bed*, all the better."

I winced at that. All of my misgivings about what

could possibly happen between us started to bubble to the surface again.

"Okay, let's say I do just that," I said with a sigh. "I ask Layne out, and Layne and I get together, go out for a couple of dates, end up in bed. And then what? What if it doesn't work out? What if we fail spectacularly? Does my father, put between the *impossible* rock and the *terrible* hard place of his daughter getting together with the bodyguard he hired for her, tell Layne that her services are no longer required? Does he *fire* her? That'd be pretty shitty. So, say Dad doesn't let Layne go, and we keep working together. Then we're *stuck* together, her guarding me while we sort of try to avoid each other and the topic of dating or sex. She's staying at my *apartment,* for goodness' sake, Tracy. We'd never be able to get away from each other." I sighed, biting my lip. "Just believe me when I say that it would never work, and it's a bad idea to even try it."

Tracy frowned a little and sort of deflated. "I'm sorry. I just thought you were really attracted to her," she murmured.

I am, I thought. *I'm desperately attracted to her.* But I didn't say as much. Instead, I stared past Tracy's shoulder at the intensely magnetic woman sitting a few booths down, her head bent and her shiny, expertly gelled black hair sweeping over one eye as she softly discussed with my father how she saved my life. Like it was no big thing, taking that bullet for me.

And that was *another* thing...

My insides twisted as I wrapped my fingers tightly around my to-go cup of coffee, trying to warm myself so I could stop the slight shiver that traveled down my spine. No matter how hard I tried to put all the pieces together, the simple fact was that I still didn't have any logical explanation for what had happened last night.

When the police had come and we'd given the report, Layne had been so matter-of-fact, but when explaining the circumstances of the evening, she hadn't *exactly* gotten the story straight. She'd told the officer that the gun had discharged, yes, but that it had shot straight up in the air.

I hadn't said anything at the time because I was so shocked at her lie. The gunman *hadn't* shot the gun straight up into the air.

He'd shot the gun right at her *heart*.

It had been dark last night, obviously, and the streetlamps weren't very bright, and she'd folded the collar of her leather jacket just so, so that it wasn't obvious that there was a hole in her jacket.

I'd forgotten that part in the exhaustion and confusion of last night. But I didn't have a logical explanation for any of it.

And, for some reason, I didn't want to question Layne about it. Just the thought of bringing it up to her made me remember the expression she'd given the men last night.

Like she was hunting them.

Layne's brow was furrowed now, and her dark head was bent as she spoke in low tones to my father. Her dark hair was carefully gelled, and there was an attractive little pompadour on the front of her scalp that made my insides twist, made me feel so warm, and made parts of me flicker on. She had such an animal attraction that when she glanced my way, just then, I *felt* my heart skip a beat.

There was something about Layne. Something I couldn't quite place my finger on that had made me spellbound with her from the very start.

Spellbound...but something else, too.

Something that made my insides flutter.

Something, well, dangerous.

Layne ended the call with my father and slid the slim phone into her jeans pocket as she rose smoothly and prowled over to us. Tracy was right; she passed a man in his late forties, wearing a plaid shirt and jeans, and a woman in a gray pinstripe suit, and both of them turned their heads to follow Layne's progression down the aisle in the coffee shop, their eyes wide and glazed as they gazed at her with absolute and apparent attraction. And, I guess, a little lust.

"How are you ladies getting on?" she asked in low tones as she arrived at our table, checking her wristwatch with a quick glance. "Is it almost time to get going?"

"Almost," I muttered, glancing down quickly at my cup of coffee, the steam curling like a beckoning finger out of the hole in the lid.

It was best not to look up into Layne's eyes, because when I did, I wasn't sure about anything other than the fact that I *was* incredibly attracted to her.

And there wasn't anything I could do about that.

Or, let me be clear: There wasn't anything I *should* do about it.

Tracy stood, taking up her empty cup and beginning to chew on another fingernail. "I'm so nervous. I probably shouldn't have had that cup of joe with those two shots of espresso. Now I'm *extra* nervous and shaky, and I kind of want to run a marathon."

"You'll be fine." Layne raised her brows, shaking her head at the two of us. She rocked back on her heels. "You're world-class musicians, aren't you?"

"I mean..." began Tracy, but Layne shook her head with a wry grin.

"No, you *have* to be world-class musicians, or you couldn't have gotten into the Boston Philharmonic. Right, Elizabeth?" she asked. Her voice dropped down an entire octave when she addressed me, and I shivered a little. Hopefully, it was an invisible shiver.

"Right," I responded without much enthusiasm. I lifted up my crutches from where I'd placed them in the booth beside me, and I slid out of the booth, trying to find my balance. Layne was, of course, right there, with a smooth arm around my waist as she helped me stand. "Thanks," I murmured to her, and I made the utter mistake of looking up into her gaze.

She looked down at me with bright, flashing eyes, eyes that shifted color as I gazed into them, eyes that seemed to pin me to the spot. But it was everything about her, really, that pinned me there: those beautiful, full lips that I wanted, more than anything, to taste. That gorgeous line of her jaw that I wanted to trail my tongue across...

God, I had to get it together. Maybe I was just having a logical reaction to being saved by her. Of course you're attracted to someone who saved you from a gunman.

Of course.

But I knew that wasn't the case.

I was incredibly attracted to Layne for no other reason than she was incredibly attractive. And totally my type.

Okay. There. I'd thought it.

And now I had a concert to get through.

I could think about other things later.

Right now, it was showtime.

I hobbled alongside Tracy and Layne as we began to make our way to the concert hall. Layne kindly carried my violin, though I could have managed it myself. When we crossed streets with the congested, Friday night rush hour traffic and all its blaring horns and crazy drivers, she thoughtfully held my elbow firmly. I tried to think over and over that my father was paying her to do these things for me, but that wasn't exactly true. He was paying her to keep me safe from assassins, not to be thoughtful and helpful in day-to-day life.

"Your ticket's at will-call," I told Layne, once we reached the hall and paused outside it in the milling crowds of concertgoers. I glanced up at the brightly lit marquee overhead that declared Mikagi Tasuki was playing with us tonight, and then I glanced at Layne, who was watching me carefully. I smiled softly at her. "I hope you... I hope you enjoy the concert."

Tracy's eyes went wide, and she grinned as she sort of sidled away from us, making her way toward the back of the building and the musicians' entrance.

Effectively leaving me alone with Layne in the crowd of people that were beginning to swarm the building.

"I've never been to a classical concert. Or the symphony... Whatever you call it," said Layne then. Her voice had gone soft, and the usual mix of strength and sarcasm seemed to fade away from her. When she spoke those words, her eyes went a little wider, and her deep smile showed me exactly how excited she was about seeing this. I was surprised. Maybe it was the leather jacket or the tough demeanor, or maybe none of those things, but I had kind of figured she'd be bored out of her wits by this performance.

Maybe I shouldn't have assumed that.

I stared up at her and grinned a little. She returned that grin and handed over my violin case with a nod.

"Break a leg," she said, with one brow raised. "Just not...literally. It'll be nice when you're off those crutches for good, so let's not keep you in them, okay?"

"If I break a leg while sitting in a chair and playing a violin, I have major, major problems," I chuckled at her. In the fading light of the day, and beneath the bright lights of the concert hall signs, she looked so beautiful. She was utterly handsome, yes, but it was a hard handsomeness.

But here, wide-eyed and eager about attending the concert...she'd become truly beautiful.

My heart skipped a handful of beats as we stood close to one another. I didn't know what to say, and she didn't offer anything, so a moment passed by with the fresh, hot scent of her surrounding me, with the bright warmth of her along the length of my body. We weren't even touching, but her warmth crossed the small distance between us and seemed to envelop me.

"I'll be seeing you," I whispered, frustrated at myself that I couldn't think of something more interesting to say. But as I turned, her hand darted out, and her fingers closed around my wrist.

I paused for a long moment, waiting expectantly for

whatever it was she'd been about to say, because she definitely looked like she was prepared to tell me something. Her mouth opened and closed, and something dark moved over her eyes, something shadowed. But then the moment had come and gone again, and whatever it was she'd intended to tell me remained unspoken. Layne shook her head, cleared her throat.

"Good luck," she murmured, and moved away from me. In an instant, she was swallowed up by the crowd.

I stared after her, my heart pounding too quickly, the violin dangling from my fingers that were curled around my crutch.

She'd wanted to tell me something, and from the expression on her face, it was something important. But then she had changed her mind, held her tongue.

What the hell had that been about?

I limped backstage, so lost in thought that I almost ran into Bob, smoking like a chimney outside of the back door.

"I think Amelia's going to have a stroke," he remarked, shaking his head and stubbing the cigarette out beneath his toe. He held the door open for me. "Everyone's got such a case of the nerves—it's crazy!" He followed me in, tossing his lighter into his suit jacket pocket. "Seriously, *I'm* nervous, and I'm not a nervous person. I wasn't nervous at my own wedding, at the birth of my daughters, at the birth of my son, at *their* weddings, at—"

"Nerves are catching," I interrupted his chatter gently as I glanced sidelong at him. "And, come on, it's Mikagi Tasuki. I can understand the nerves."

"No, it's not like that," he said, shaking his head and biting at a thumbnail. I'd never seen Bob bite at any of his nails—*ever*. The guy was a rock, and he was completely unflappable. Just...not right now. It was a strange sight to see. I stared at him, my brows raised.

"What do you mean?"

"I dunno." He shook his head again, a little more

emphatically, and shifted his weight from foot to foot. "I just dunno. There's just...just something in the air today. Something not good."

"Huh," I replied, leaning on my crutch. Musicians aren't nearly as superstitious as theater people, but I have to be honest with you: We *are* pretty superstitious. If Bob—good, steady Bob—was telling me that there was something "not good" in the air today, that meant that pretty much everyone in the orchestra was thinking that exact same thing.

And that was a pretty rotten omen for the upcoming concert.

"I need another cigarette," Bob muttered, and walked down the hallway, back the way we'd come, toward the back door.

Swallowing down my worry, I continued to walk slowly down the hall, limping along with my crutches, my violin case dangling from my fingers.

I found Tracy standing outside the bathroom, leaning against the wall with a paper cup of water in her hands, taking deep, calming breaths. It was a common occurrence to see her doing this before a performance; it was her habit to "get in the zone" for each concert. But today her face was tight, hardly calmed from the exercise. There were deeply etched worry lines on her brow, and she was holding her eyes shut tightly; she looked tense enough to snap.

My cell phone in my handbag began to vibrate. I leaned against the wall next to her, propped one of my crutches between us and fished in my purse for it. The screen was lit up with one familiar, comforting word on the caller ID.

"Hi, Dad," I said warmly, pressing the phone to my ear after hitting the green button. "Are you here yet?"

"Just got here," he said on the other end of the line. I could hear the murmur of voices raised in conversation behind him. He was probably in line at will-call. "I'm so proud of you, sweetheart! Performing with Mikagi Tasuki is such an honor. Almost everyone at the packing plant got tickets!" he chirped. "This is going to be an amazing concert. Knock 'em dead!"

I chuckled and shook my head. "I'll do my best, Dad."

Ever since my very first concert with the Boston Philharmonic, my father had never missed a performance. He always bought front-row tickets, or as close to front row as he could get, and he brought roses for me. I'd like to point out that we do practically weekly, and sometimes twice-weekly, concerts. In the beginning, I was a little embarrassed by his overwhelming enthusiasm. I mean, he gave standing ovations when *no one else did*. But, over time, I came to realize that this was the way my father related to me. He was supremely proud of the fact that his daughter, while not having taken over the family business, loved her job enough to share it, and was pretty good at it.

So he was always there, always supportive. And he called before every performance to wish me luck.

Which made my heart grow three sizes, every single time. I loved him fiercely, and I was really grateful for him. Always.

I was also really grateful that, though Layne had just talked to him about our being held at gunpoint, he hadn't brought the subject up, probably because he didn't want to make me nervous right before my performance.

I ended the call and slid the phone back into my purse as I considered things. I was a pretty lucky woman. Yeah, there was the negative of having been held at gunpoint last night. Yeah, there was the fact that someone had tried to ram my car off the road and, effectively, murder me because my father made a bit too much profit from fish last year—a really rotten motive for murder, if you ask me (as if there's ever any *good* motivation).

But I had a father who loved me…and that made the world a great place, regardless of everything else.

Still, my smile slipped from my face when I glanced

sidelong at Tracy, who was shaking her head, crumpling the now-empty paper cup in her hand as she grimaced and bit her lip.

"Something's wrong," she muttered. I raised my eyebrows.

Granted, the latter half of last night hadn't exactly been fun. But even after all of that, even after being held at gunpoint, I didn't have any sort of bad feeling—just general nervousness about performing with a star of Mikagi's caliber.

Whatever everyone else was feeling, whatever ominousness permeated the air...I couldn't sense it.

"I think we're all just feeding into one another's nerves," I told Tracy soothingly. "Honestly, Tracy, what could possibly go wrong?"

The lights flickered overhead. The sign of five minutes to curtain.

"Crap," I muttered, shoving the crutches under my arms again. "We've got to get going."

"I'm not even *tuned* yet," muttered Tracy, cursing under her breath as she dashed down the corridor.

Then it was just me and my violin and my damnable crutches, trying to hurry down the hallway as quickly as I could. Everyone else was, of course, already in their seats. Leave it to me to be late. I muttered some expletives and kept hobbling as quickly as I could, which I would like to point out wasn't quick at all. God, I was going to catch it from Amelia...

The hairs on the back of my neck began to stand up, the skin on my arms rising into gooseflesh.

There in the corridor, trying my best to make my way quickly to the stage, I had the feeling that I was being watched.

This was ridiculous. I was in an empty corridor, but I was also in a *packed* concert hall. I wasn't even going to dignify that creeped-out little feeling with the response of glancing over my shoulder. The events of the past few days were just making me a little jumpy, that's all.

But then I *did* dignify that feeling, because I couldn't help the instinct. I glanced just a little behind me, ducking my head as I turned.

I went cold.

There was a figure all in black—a black trench coat, no less—standing in the center of the hallway behind me as the lights continued to flicker overhead.

I hadn't been expecting to see anyone, but now, with the shadows and the trench coat and the distance, my heart was in my throat.

"Hello?" I called, cursing myself wordlessly for my shaky voice. "Can I help you?"

The lights came on fully again, and the hooded figure—it was wearing a *hood*, I realized—began to stalk toward me.

It moved so *fast*, the black trench coat flaring out behind it, the hood eerily big and wide, like a monk's hood, but completely shadowed so that I couldn't see a face... The figure seemed to *race* toward me, without its feet really touching the ground.

It stopped right in front of me, taller than me, and even though we were a foot apart, I *still* couldn't make out a face.

The flickering lights steadied overhead.

And then they went out.

I stood my ground. My heart pounding through me, my good leg shaking like a leaf, I still stood my damn ground.

And the lights came back on.

Mikagi Tasuki removed the hood from her head, the trench coat flaring out around her as she stared at me with narrowed, dark eyes, her head tilted to the side a little.

"Ms. Grayson, is it? Violin?" Her heavily accented English was so soft, I had to strain to hear her. I gulped and nodded, my heart still hammering.

She smiled at me a little as the lights flickered overhead again. She had a very wide smile. A very bright smile. But it didn't exactly reach her eyes.

And, for a moment, it had seemed that her eyes had flickered somehow, too, just like the lights...but I wasn't exactly certain what I thought I'd seen behind them.

"I'm sorry," she murmured, unbuttoning the top few buttons of her trench coat as she raised her chin. Her short black hair swept against the back of her neck, reflecting the lights overhead brightly, like every strand of her hair practically glowed. "I am afraid that I am dreadfully late," she said slowly, carefully, as she folded the coat over her arm and watched me with her chin up, her eyes unblinking. "We will go to the stage together?"

"Yes," I managed, taking another deep breath of air. God, I was getting so easily spooked. It was only *the star of the evening* "stalking" me. My imagination was clearly on hyperdrive.

Why had I thought that there was something not quite right about her?

I couldn't really remember now...

My skin still had goosebumps as we began to walk down the corridor together, me hobbling, her striding easily with her long legs, as graceful as a predator; her high heels clicked against the linoleum floor.

We reached the stage just as Amelia's face was beginning to turn the same shade of red as a cherry. Her expression went from pure, potent rage, upon seeing me, to incandescent bliss when she spotted Mikagi. The buttons on her blazer practically popped right off as she puffed up with happiness and pride, lunging at Mikagi to draw an arm around her and propel her toward the stage.

For once, Amelia's rage was perfectly justified. It was *terrible* to show up right when the curtain was about to rise. I should have been in my seat for at least the past half hour, tuning my violin, setting up my sheet music, and focusing on having my instrument ready for the performance—and instead, I'd been getting creeped out down in the hallway.

101

Normally, we don't use a curtain at the concert hall; the audience files in and listens to us warming up, which is part of what makes the symphony so intimate. But because of Mikagi, we'd wanted to make the show a little more...dramatic, I guess, and we'd brought our old red curtain out from storage just for the occasion. This was wonderful, because as I did my best to hobble across the stage quickly, I was shielded from view by the audience.

The billowing red fabric of the curtain shut out the scene of the packed concert hall, but it did nothing to mute the noise. We had soft mood music piped in over the loud speakers as everyone was getting situated, and it was practically drowned out by the ambient roar of murmuring voices and laughter from the audience.

The all sounded *really* excited to be here, and that excitement was catching.

My violin out of my case, held tightly against me, and the crutches left backstage made for an interesting trip across the wood floor, but I managed, limping heavily, to finally get to my seat.

Mikagi got out her own violin, a beautiful black instrument that had probably been custom-made for her (it looked like the kind of instrument a rock star would have), and she began to pluck quietly at the strings, tuning it expertly, a little off center of the stage as she held her head to an angle and glanced sidelong at the orchestra behind her.

We took our places. We held our instruments expectantly.

And the curtains rose as the first note sounded out, mournful and plaintive and sweet, summoned from Mikagi's bow as it dragged almost violently across her violin.

We began to play.

We drew music out of our own instruments, at times mournful, at times jubilant. As the concert progressed, Mikagi strutted wildly across the stage, pirouetting and dancing along to the music that was all but conjured from her violin. I had never witnessed such a beautiful performance in my entire life; she *embodied* the music she was playing. As Mikagi moved, my eyes couldn't help but follow her, even though I was supposed to be paying close attention to my sheet music, to Amelia who conducted us, *and* to Mikagi…but I could really only watch Mikagi.

Somehow, we played flawlessly, all of us. The rehearsal may have been a bit botched, but the concert itself seemed to be going off without a hitch.

During a lull in the string section, I glanced toward the front row. The audience was backlit for this number, and I could make out some familiar faces out there. I scanned the first row, and then the second; I couldn't quite remember where my father said he'd be sitting.

Ah, there he was—in the third row. I listened to the music building in intensity and glanced from my sheet music back toward him.

Huh. That was strange. He was sitting next to a woman, and he seemed to be in deep conversation with her. His face looked clouded, and he tensely whispered into his companion's ear.

She was gorgeous, though I couldn't tell what age she was from my furtive glance. She had long, white-blonde hair that curled around her shoulders. She was wearing a stunning black dress that showed off plunging decolletage.

I wondered if my father had brought a date. If he had, good for him—it was about time. I hoped that's who his companion was, but somehow, I didn't think that was the case. This was a woman who looked really familiar to me; I'd seen her at my father's parties over the years, I realized, which meant that she was probably a colleague of his, and my father would never dream of dating someone in his extremely rich friend group.

The music began to build, and I skated my bow across the strings, closing my eyes as the humming of the violin, the great passion of the melody, began to build in me. All around me were masters of their craft, playing their instruments for all they were worth. Before me danced and played a star of our generation.

I still remember how happy I was in that singular moment…

And then the lights went out, plunging the theater into darkness.

The lights in our hallway backstage were timed with the performances and manually flickered to announce that we'd better have our butts in the chair right that instant before a concert. The lights for the stage and the concert hall itself were run by Frederic, the sound and light guy who'd picked up Mikagi from the airport, and who ran all sorts of odd errands for Amelia. The lights were, of course, supposed to go out at the end of the performance.

But this was in the middle of the last song.

It was pitch black on the stage and in the audience—not even the emergency running lights along the edge of the stage and aisles were on. The audience knew something was wrong, and a frantic murmuring was spreading like a virus across the rows of seating before us. The music had cut off when the lights went out because all of the musicians had stopped playing almost at the same time from the shock of the anomalous darkness. But now a few thrums from shifting fabric against strings or a thumb against harp made for an odd backdrop, and a very eerie soundtrack, to the beginning panic in the audience.

I sat in my chair in the dark patiently and waited for the lights to come back on. It must be something technical. It was bad timing, sure, but there was nothing wrong. There couldn't be anything wrong.

But the lights didn't come back on.

And, in the dark, something brushed against my hand.

I was surrounded by people; of course someone would touch me by accident if they were moving about on stage. The stage was crowded with an entire orchestra's worth of people, you would, in all likelihood, run into someone in the dark if you were trying to make your way toward the exits. I'd had my violin on my knees, and my hands resting against the instrument, but I drew my violin up closer to my chest to protect it in case anyone ran into me again.

But that same feather-light touch followed my hand.

My ponytail at the back of my neck was brushed aside then. Instantly, I was covered in gooseflesh as a skating of fingertips danced down the skin of my neck. I shuddered against that touch, so light, so ephemeral, I wondered if I was imagining things.

But, no, I wasn't imagining it.

I gasped as I felt a cold mouth press against the skin of my neck.

I *couldn't* be imagining this.

I turned my head quickly, bending forward and brushing my hand against my neck, like you do when you're shoving away cobwebs. It was an instinctual reaction, something I didn't even think about. But there was nothing and no one there.

Could it really have been a mouth against me? A *kiss*? I was so confused, and as the hair on the back of my neck stood to attention, I began to feel…well…

Afraid.

Out in the darkness, the furtive voices were completely silenced when a *snarl* echoed around us.

It was a snarl, a snarl like a vicious animal makes. It echoed in the silence, and my entire body shivered.

And then, at that instant, the lights came back on, stuttering and flickering to life.

I turned quickly to look behind me, but there was only Tony, holding tightly to his violin, sitting several feet behind me in the next row of violinists. Tony was sitting there with wide eyes, talking to Emily, another violinist seated next to him, with fear apparent on both of their faces.

There was no one *there* who could have touched me, who could have kissed me. I must have imagined it, the lips against my neck, the caress along my hand. But it had felt so *real*. How could I have imagined something so real? I brushed my fingers up to the back of my neck and grew cold again as they encountered a bit of dampness...exactly as if someone had placed a kiss against my skin.

I furtively glanced around, trying to find and place everyone in the orchestra. But I knew everyone here. They were my friends and my deeply esteemed colleagues, people who would never randomly *kiss* me, and, anyway, everyone was distracted, upset and tense. No one had grappled toward me in the dark.

So, then...what the hell had just happened?

Audience members started to stand and try to make their way to the exits, but they paused as Mikagi strode to the center of the stage. Where had she been? I hadn't seen her when I glanced across the stage a heartbeat ago. She'd completely disappeared...

"Ladies and gentlemen," she said with a wide, gleaming smile, holding up her violin in one hand and her bow in another as she held her arms out to the audience in a gesture of sympathy. "Please return to your seats; it was just technical difficulties. We would now like to give you the finale of a lifetime!"

There was a smattering of lukewarm applause, but at least the audience members were obeying her request, returning to their seats instead of swarming the exits. They even seemed to be warming back up to us as they sat down, the panic from being plunged into darkness forgotten when Mikagi pressed her bow to the strings. People began to applaud her as she started the last song of our set again.

But Mikagi hadn't waited to see if the rest of the musicians were ready to continue. She'd just started without us, plunging headlong into the piece as we were still adjusting our sheet music or taking our own seats. Again, I glanced around furtively as everyone scrambled to accompany her, adjusting their instruments and launching into the song somewhat unceremoniously.

My eyes were drawn back to an incongruous spot in

the orchestra. That was odd. The wind section didn't look normal. I glanced again as I raised my bow to the strings.

Wait. Bob wasn't there.

I stared in shock at his empty seat and missed an entire measure before my body switched to autopilot and kept playing the violin. I wracked my brains trying to think of the last time I'd seen him. Yes, that was right—Bob had gone back outside for one more quick cigarette when I'd come into the building. But surely he'd gotten up to the concert hall since then. Surely Amelia wouldn't start the concert without him; that would be ludicrous. He was our principal flutist. You couldn't have a concert without the principal flutist.

I glanced at Maria, one of our other flutists. Her face was screwed up with concentration as she played her heart out. I hadn't been paying much attention to the wind section in rehearsal, but I remembered that she didn't have much of a part.

It dawned on me with a cold realization that Maria was playing Bob's part.

Bob had not shown up to his chair.

Okay. There was a perfectly logical explanation for this. Maybe he'd had a family emergency, one of his kids had called him, something important or terrible had happened. But unless one of his kids was dying—and I desperately hoped that wasn't the case—I couldn't imagine a strong enough reason that Bob would miss such an important concert.

Dread began to fill my heart as the music swelled around us.

He'd had a bad feeling.

No. That was just a superstition. It couldn't *mean* anything…

I gulped air and swept my bow across the strings. Around me, everyone put their heart and soul into the music.

The crashing waves of sound were silenced as the

last note was played together.

The audience roared in applause. We achieved a standing ovation almost instantaneously as Mikagi glanced back at the orchestra, beaming, sweeping her violin and bow up in each hand and turning back to bow low to the audience.

The orchestra members stood, too, but as I held my violin under my arm, all I could think about was getting off this stage as quickly as possible and going to figure out what had happened to Bob. Figure out where he was, if he was okay.

Why wouldn't he be okay?

The audience began to time their clapping to an insistent beat, practically demanding an encore. We'd prepared one of Mikagi's most iconic songs for this eventuality, "The Dream Suite," and as we began to play the piece—it starts with a mournful bit of strings and builds eventually to something triumphant involving the whole orchestra—I shivered a little as I drew my bow across my violin.

We played through three encores. By the fourth demand for an encore, Mikagi only blew kisses to the audience, bowed low, and the curtain was mercifully dropped.

"Tracy." I turned to her immediately, my heart in my throat as she glanced up at me, her eyes widening at my expression. "Have you seen Bob?" I asked her.

Tracy was grinning from ear to ear, and that expression faltered for half a heartbeat. "Um…" She glanced to the wind section, and then her eyes got wider. "What the hell—he didn't play with us? Where *is* he?"

"I don't know…" I tried to rise, but the multiple times that I'd stood and sat back down after the performance and during the encores had made my leg begin to scream. I needed to get backstage to where I'd set my crutches leaning against one of the walls, but the wide floor separating me from backstage was suddenly looking very daunting, indeed.

Mikagi turned and glanced at me. It was a surreptitious glance over her shoulder, one I might not have even noticed if I wasn't looking in her direction. I caught her gaze and held it for half a heartbeat.

And she came to me, gliding over the floor like she was grace personified, her high heels clicking impressively against the hardwood.

She held her violin and bow effortlessly in front of her. I hadn't had a chance to really appreciate her outfit before, as it'd been under the trench coat, but she looked so flawlessly beautiful this evening, wearing a daring black dress that clung to her upper arms and chest but plunged incredibly low in the back. The collar was a boat neck, and the skirt itself was a very pretty knee-length a-line. It looked like the type of dress that an actress from the forties would wear. With her severe chin-length haircut and her flawless, pale skin, wearing so much black made her look like she was glowing.

Her eyes flashed as she took me in, as she smiled widely at me. "What a lovely concert!" she said, tossing a glance back at the curtain. Then the euphoria seemed to fade away from her, because she was looking back at me, her chest rising and falling quickly as she licked her lips. "Would you...like some help?" she offered, holding her elbow out to me, like she was a gentleman in a top hat, ready to escort me anywhere I wished.

"That'd be lovely, yes," I winced, threading my arm through hers. I held my violin against my body and did my best not to lean on her as we began to walk across the stage. She was a slight woman, but even though I'd wanted to try and support my own weight as much as possible, by the time we reached backstage, I was leaning heavily on her. But she didn't seem to notice. She strode confidently forward, practically holding me up.

"Did you enjoy playing?" she asked me, then. It was a hushed question that she whispered in my ear, her voice a low growl of pleasure. I glanced up at her quickly. Her eyes were unreadable.

"I did, very much. It was wonderful of you to come play with us," I told her distractedly, all in a rush. I should have been deeply flattered that Mikagi Tasuki, world-class violinist, was helping me to my crutches, but, really, all I could think about was Bob.

That was odd… There should have been a clatter of voices, of laughter. When we reached the back hallway, there should have been a hubbub of activity, flowers being delivered, family members allowed backstage, the press…

But there was only silence.

"Oh, my God, Elizabeth. Oh, my God," said Tracy, running up to me and flinging her arms around my neck as she buried her face in my shoulder and began to weep.

There was a stretcher out by the back door. The flashing lights of an ambulance made the corridor glow as red as hell as two of the ambulance crew helped each other lift the body that was lying on the steps up and onto the stretcher, instead.

Even though I was quite a ways down the corridor, even though it was now dark outside, the light from the ambulance and the light from inside spilled over the concrete steps.

They illuminated, clearly, the blood spattering the sidewalk and the steps.

Bob lay on the stretcher as they buckled him to it. As they drew a sheet over his face.

I went cold as ice, my heart in my throat.

"He's dead," Tracy moaned, dissolving into sobs against me.

Chapter 8: Trust

It's hard to describe what it's like, staring at a murdered man's dead body. Especially when the murdered man was someone you knew, someone you cared about, someone who showed you all of the five-hundred photos from his Caribbean vacation every year, beaming over the pictures of his wife and kids—even though they were all grown up—because they were the most important parts of his life.

Someone you shared jokes and coffee with, someone you worked closely with. Someone you'd known and laughed with and shared parts of your life with for years.

And now he was dead.

Bob was dead.

I think I was in shock as I stared at the grisly scene before me. We were far enough down the corridor that extreme, close-up specifics evaded me, but the blood was still so evident on the concrete steps, on the door, no matter how far away we stood. There was too much blood.

Tracy sobbed against me so hard, I was almost pushed off my crutches. Absentmindedly, I brought an arm up to her shoulder, tried to rub my hand in small, soothing circles against her as she wept, but I was a million miles away.

The corridor, though it was full of people, was eerily silent.

There were several police officers down by the door, talking in low, hushed tones with Amelia, who had her arms folded and a stony expression on her face, and a few men in plain clothes, suits, jackets, staring down at the blood with frowns. I guess they were detectives. One of them, an older man possibly in his fifties, with a graying handlebar mustache and bright blue eyes, stepped forward then, edging past the blood to stand in the center of the hallway as he cleared his throat.

"Folks, if you'd indulge me..." he began, his voice booming. "I'm just going to ask you a few questions. I realize you were all just up there—" He pointed with his pen to the ceiling, and to, presumably, our concert hall. "—playing your little hearts out, and I realize you're tired and want to go home after a job well done. But this'll only take a moment."

"Elizabeth!" I turned just in time for my father to fold his arms tightly around me and pull me close. He smelled so comforting, like his expensive cologne and coffee, that I buried my nose in his shoulder, and, for a moment, I was worried that I'd lose it, start crying and never stop. But I took a deep, quavering breath, and then I stepped back from my father's tight embrace.

"Hi, Dad," I said woodenly as he searched my eyes, gripping my shoulders tightly with strong hands and holding me out at arm's length, as if he had to look me over to make certain I was still there, still standing right in front of him.

Still alive.

In the back of my head, an odd thought surfaced: his companion that I'd seen him talking to in the concert hall, the beautiful woman with blonde hair, was no longer with him. Maybe they hadn't even come together, had only been talking together because they knew each other.

"I'm all right, Dad," I told him quietly when he drew me in for another embrace. "But Bob..." My voice quavered on his name, and I took another deep breath.

"We need to get out of here," said my father flatly, in a strong growl that brooked no argument. "You've been through a lot these past few days, and you need to rest."

I was about to protest a lot of that: I could take care of myself, it wasn't *me* who'd been murdered, I was fine, and, anyway, we'd been told to stay put for questioning. But then the man who'd told us to wait to be questioned, the man with the large handlebar mustache, strode up the corridor and stopped beside us.

He was just as tall as my father, which meant that I felt a little dwarfed as I stared up at him.

"Mr. Grayson!" the man practically boomed, holding out a hand for a shake. "I'll be damned—been seeing a lot of you lately."

"Chief Potter," said my father with a wide smile, taking the man's hand and shaking it briskly. "Chief Potter, this is my daughter, Elizabeth, she's a violinist in the orchestra," he said, pride dripping off every word as he put a hand at the small of my back.

Out of the corner of my eye, I saw Layne striding down the corridor toward us from the direction of the concert hall. She had her hands shoved deeply into leather jacket pockets, and she was glowering fiercely, power radiating off of her as she practically stalked down the hallway of bright lights, past confused, milling groups of orchestra members and the families and friends of the musicians who'd rushed backstage to congratulate us on a job well done...

To be confronted by all of this.

My father and the chief were discussing something in low, muted voices, their heads bent together, and the chief toying with his phone, flipping through brightly glowing screens and obviously in the middle of a private conversation. Tracy had gone to get a drink from the water cooler, situated between the restrooms, and was talking (and occasionally sobbing) with a few more of our violinists. I cast a glance over my shoulder.

Mikagi Tasuki, who'd been with me just a mere moment ago, was nowhere in sight.

Layne reached me, curling a hot hand around my

upper arm, her nostrils flaring as she stared down at me with flashing eyes.

"Are you all right?" she asked hotly, her voice low and aggressive. I shivered under her intense gaze and angry tone, my brows furrowing.

"I'm all right," I told her as I searched her face. "Are you?"

She didn't seem to be. Layne, in fact, seemed incredibly agitated as she shifted from foot to foot, leaning the weight back on the balls of her feet as she scanned the milling orchestra members with a quick frown, taking a deep breath, her head tilted to the side a little, as if she could sniff out the trouble that had caused all of this.

"Yeah, yeah," she said quickly, waving her hand with dismissal before raking long fingers back through her jet-black hair, upsetting her carefully gelled strands and causing a few of them to stick straight up. But she was too distracted to notice as her eyes darted through the crowd, and she stepped closer to me, her fingers tightening on my arm.

"Thanks, chief," said my father with a broad smile as he took a backward step from the officer, holding out his arm to the both of us. "We've been cleared to go, Elizabeth, Layne, so let's get a move on."

"Cleared to go? But I haven't been questioned," I began to protest, but my father widened his eyes, shook his head almost imperceptibly as Chief Potter turned from us and began to stride toward a milling group of cellists.

"We're cleared to go," said my father again, his brows up. He had the same look on his face that he always got when he was playing poker with me and he'd just bluffed terribly.

But I was too shaken up to argue, and who really wants to be questioned by the police? So, in a daze, my father and Layne helped me hobble away from the blood-spattered steps and up through the concert hall, to take the same exit as our audience.

The night outside was warm and muggy and devoid of stars.

And when I closed my eyes, all I could see was the blood of my friend, his too-white hand falling out from under the sheet the ambulance driver had tried to pull over him.

I couldn't stop shaking.

My father wanted us all to go back to the Grayson mansion, have a couple of cocktails to relax and order about two tons worth of pizza. Which, in theory, sounded like a great idea, and was a very sweet offer, but I was too shaken to eat anything (and, trust me, after witnessing so much blood, pizza sauce starts to look a lot less appealing), and I needed some time after the performance to wind down.

I needed some time by myself.

But, of course, "time by myself" now meant "time with Layne." I couldn't be by myself, even if I wanted to.

There were so many unanswered questions. I'd gone my whole life without witnessing or being the brunt of much violence, and then in the span of a couple of days, I'd been rammed from behind, held at gunpoint, and a friend of mine had been brutally murdered. My father had told me the chief was definitely considering it a homicide; it couldn't have been a suicide, he'd said. I knew that, logically, none of these horrific events were connected. They were all just random acts of violence.

But didn't it seem odd that they had happened so close together?

So, Dad went home, and Layne and I drove back to my apartment, where she helped me up the stairs to my front door, through it, and then I immediately hobbled to my couch and collapsed on the old blue cushions, lolling my head back against the pillows and staring at my perfectly neutral tile ceiling that seemed so pristine, so calming, after the terrible moments of the night.

But when I blinked or closed my eyes, I could still see the spatters of Bob's blood, how dark they looked against the cool gray of the concrete...

"Here," said Layne, pressing something cold and icy into my hands. It was a bottle of craft beer she'd pulled from my fridge. She was flipping the cap up into the air— had she just pried it off with bare fingers before she'd handed it to me? She seemed to be full of surprises.

"Thanks," I muttered, and put the cold mouth of the bottle to my lips. This beer was supposed to taste a little like blueberries, and it actually did. I took a couple of gulps, letting it fizz all the way down my throat and blossom coldly into my stomach. It made my thoughts, dangerously looping on Bob's body and blood, calm down just a little.

I watched as Layne sat on the couch beside me, sprawling backwards with her legs spread in front of her, one foot propped up on my coffee table in the perfect picture of relaxation. She had another craft beer in her hand, and—as I watched—she flicked the cap off of the bottle like it was a pop tab. She took a very long gulp of the beer, and with a long sigh, she leaned her head back against the top of the couch, staring at my ceiling, too.

"I'm sorry about your friend," Layne told me then, in a low, husky tone.

I'd thought I was numbed to everything, that I could feel nothing but that cool detachment after the image of Bob's blood had been burned into my brain forever. But the gentleness in Layne's voice seemed to open up a floodgate inside of me, and slowly, quietly, hot tears began to trace down my cheeks, plunking softly against the fabric of my shirt as I took another long sip of my beer, my heart opening up to a great ache that almost made me double over with the sudden pain that seemed, at once, unbearable.

I didn't know how to respond to her. I didn't have

to; she wasn't waiting for me to make a great big speech about Bob or even tell her thanks. I could have said nothing, but I needed to speak, just then, or the ache inside of me would crush me.

"He was just a really good guy," I said simply. It seemed to encompass everything I could ever have told her about Bob, anything I could have come up with to eulogize him, and the sad, small words lingered between us, sinking into silence.

"Do you want to talk about it?" she asked me quietly.

I shook my head almost immediately. No. No, I didn't want to talk about it.

I wanted, more than anything, to stop thinking about the blood, about my friend…about how he was dead.

After a very long moment of silence, Layne cleared her throat. "It's been a hard couple of days. When's your next…" She spun the hand not holding the bottle of beer in the air as she searched for a word. "Practice?"

"Rehearsal," I said automatically, biting my lip as I picked at the edge of the beer's label with my thumbnail. "We have rehearsal on Sunday morning for the Sunday matinee concert. Sometimes we get Saturdays off—'free Saturdays,' we call them—and tomorrow's a free Saturday."

"Really?" asked Layne, her head to the side. I was suddenly aware that her shoulder and arm were pressing against me, that her hip and thigh were against mine, too, and that everywhere she touched me, my body tingled with her warmth.

Somewhere, deep inside of me, I felt warm feelings begin to circulate, slowly beginning to ease the tremendous ache in my heart. I shouldn't have felt anything but sadness right then, I knew, but she was so warm, so close, her muscles sculpted beneath the thin fabric of her t-shirt…

I was beginning to realize that I couldn't help some of the ways that my body reacted when I was close to Layne O'Connell. It was all pure instinct.

"...did you have plans for tomorrow?" asked Layne, and I realized I hadn't been paying attention to what she was saying, only paying attention to her body and all of the places it touched me. I swallowed, trying to focus, realizing my face was hot and flushed, my cheeks especially too warm. I took another pull at the beer, trying to clear my head from the cobweb wisps of desire that had begun to form in me so quickly.

Honestly, it usually takes more than half a beer to get me drunk. What was wrong with me? I sighed.

"Did you have plans for tomorrow?" Layne repeated, grinning sidelong at me as she turned the beer cap over and over in her long fingers, like she was running a coin over her knuckles. I shook my head as I took another sip.

"No, nothing," I told her, one brow up. What was she getting at?

"Well," Layne said then, drawing out the word long and low as she worked her jaw to the side and stared at the ceiling again, leaning her head back against the couch. "You've been through quite a lot these past few days. It's kind of been a rough week. So, how would you like a day off?"

I chuckled dryly at that, shook my head a little. "Don't you know anything about musicians?" I found myself teasing. "We *never* take a day off. It's in the contract—practice from sunup to sundown."

"All right, all right, suit yourself," Layne said, flipping the cap into the air with a smirk. "But all work and no play..." She trailed off into silence as she took a drink.

My curiosity got the better of me, and she knew it would, judging by her cat-who-ate-the-canary grin. "Why do you ask?" I finally said.

"Because I thought you'd like to get out of the city for a day," she told me mildly, brows raised. "You know, it's *spring* in Massachusetts. Aside from fall, obviously," she grinned widely, "it just so happens to be the prettiest time of the year around here. And I thought you might want to take in the scenery or something. You know…have a little fun."

I stared at her. "Well…what exactly did you have in mind?"

She leaned forward a little, her head tilted as she turned to consider me. My heart began to beat a staccato rhythm against my ribs. "Do you trust me?" she said with a soft, velvet smile.

I nodded, trying to remember how to breathe. Her face was so close to mine that if I leaned forward just a little, too, I could kiss her.

Did I want to kiss her?

Oh, God…I wanted to kiss her.

In one smooth motion, she folded herself upright, her beer bottle at her lips again as she drank down the last of it. "Good," she said with a wink, stretching her arms overhead. "If you trust me, then you'll find out what I have planned tomorrow. Good night, Elizabeth," she told me. And then she turned on her heel and—without looking back—stalked toward her bedroom with long strides.

I sat alone on the couch with my half-finished beer, trying to calm down my heart.

And trying not to be desperately disappointed that she'd gone.

And I hadn't had the time to work up the courage to kiss her.

The Protector

Chapter 9: In the Wild

"Realize that I'm on crutches," I reminded Layne for, possibly, the tenth time that morning. And what a morning it was.

The day had dawned uncharacteristically gray, with looming, angry-looking storm clouds along the horizon, up and over the ocean. But even with the threat of rain (or, rather, the threat of a torrential downpour), we'd still gotten up, showered and dressed ("wear something comfortable and outdoorsy," Layne had warned), and we were now on the road, heading north up the coast. Well, after we'd stopped at a Starbucks for coffee *and* coffee cake (it was my day off, after all), and then we'd driven along the coastline, keeping the ocean to our right.

"I *know* you're on crutches," said Layne soothingly, taking another sip of her coffee and making a face like it'd burned her, screwing up her nose with a shake of her head as she set the paper cup back into her cup holder. "By the way, I think they served us lava, not coffee. I'm going to need reconstructive surgery on my tongue."

"Well, normal mortals usually wait for it to cool," I teased her, blowing into the hole on my lid as I watched steam curl up in an inviting spiral.

For some odd reason, she stiffened a little at that, circling the steering wheel tighter with her fingers, the knuckles standing out against the black of the wheel.

I frowned, cleared my throat. "And, anyway," I continued as her face relaxed a little, "I just have this terrible feeling that all of this is leading up to you taking me hiking, and I wanted to remind you that I'm on crutches and can't exactly power over the trails like I normally would."

"Do I look like the kind of woman who forces hikes on others?" she asked, arching a brow and casting a sidelong glance at me. A grin tugged at the corners of her mouth, and her devastatingly handsome eyes—flashing more blue and green than brown today—seemed to sparkle with suppressed laughter.

"I mean…" I waved my hand in her direction, taking in her entirety. She was wearing her leather jacket, as usual, today, but it was paired with stone-washed jeans and a t-shirt with a screen-printed face of Marilyn Monroe. Layne's jet-black hair was teased upright. Honestly, she looked like she'd recently escaped from a time machine from the eighties. "You're not *exactly* the hiking type," I amended. "But I know there's lots of hiking to the north of Boston—"

"Uh-uh. No guessing," said Layne, holding up a finger and practically shaking it under my nose. "You said I could surprise you, and I'm damn well going to do just that."

"I said I *trusted* you," I corrected her, placing my coffee cup back in its holder near the vent. "*Not* that you could surprise me. Who knows where we'll end up?" I had one brow raised, but I was still teasing her.

Across the distance between us, Layne casually offered her hand, palm up, to me. It was the kind of gesture you make when you want someone to slap you five. But somehow, I didn't think that's what she was going for. I realized that my face was red almost immediately as I questioningly placed my hand, palm down, on hers.

Her fingers wrapped around my hand as if they'd done it a thousand times before. Layne held my hand tightly, squeezing with a gentleness that made my knees melt. Thank heaven I wasn't standing.

The heat of her palm, the softness of her skin, was far too intense of a sensation.

"No matter what," Layne said softly, her velvet

voice pitched in a low growl that sent a shiver down my spine, "I'll keep you safe," she whispered. "So, don't worry."

My breathing was coming too fast when she let go of my hand. I rolled down the window of the car, just a crack, so that the chill air over the sea could rush into the car and blow against my face just a little, cooling down the blush. I took great gulps of the salt breeze and tried to forget how hotly her palm had burned against mine, how soft her fingers had felt entwined with my own, like our hands fit together, puzzle-piece perfect.

My heart beat so loudly against my ribs, I was certain she must be able to hear it, my pulse racing through me and my ribs practically vibrating from the thud of my heart in my chest. And she did cast me a sidelong glance, her brows raised, but maybe it was because the air in the car was getting much colder since my window had been rolled down. I rolled it back up slowly and took a deep breath.

Only people without a pulse would *not* be attracted to Layne O'Connell. She was funny and sarcastic and ridiculously graceful and intense and more handsome than my eyes and heart (and other body regions) could grasp. There was such a deep, magnetic pull to her; your eyes *had* to find her in a crowded room and follow her movements, because her body tugged your gaze in like the sun holds the earth in orbit.

Part of me wanted to tell Layne that I *was* incredibly attracted to her, and then take it from there. Part of me wanted to make that first move. But I wasn't certain if Layne was attracted to me. She treated me like everyone else that I saw. So, if she didn't find me attractive or return my feelings in any way, shape, or form, I really didn't want to make a fool of myself in this working relationship.

And, let's be honest, it *was* a working relationship. I'd been truthful when I told Tracy my reasons for not pursuing Layne: it would be such a mess if, after all, Layne had feelings for me, too, and then the relationship failed, and we were stuck together whether we liked it or not. She, effectively, worked for me, and that made things so much more complicated than they would normally be.

But there were…other issues. Other reasons that I hadn't told Layne how I felt about her. I couldn't have put them into words, exactly, aside from the fact that, sometimes, Layne felt dangerous to me. There were too many unanswered questions surrounding her.

Still, a little mystery can be incredibly captivating.

I cast Layne a sidelong glance. She had her chin up, her shades down, and a wry smile tugging at the corners of her lips.

I couldn't so much as *look* at her without my heart flip-flopping all over the place, my breath coming a little faster. I promise, I'm not this hopelessly smitten around most women. And even if I feel attracted to someone, I'm much more smooth about it…usually.

But when it came to Layne, that all went out the window.

I wondered how much longer I could go without telling her I was attracted to her.

If she kept grabbing my hand like that, squeezing it, and promising to keep me safe, my best guess was…not very long at all.

Soon after that, we arrived in Gloucester.

I hadn't realized how long we'd been on the road, but it had apparently been an hour or so since we left Boston proper. For awhile, we'd driven on the highway surrounded by thick green trees, their branches tossing about since the storm over the ocean was picking up speed and bringing the wind with it. But then the trees parted, and the ocean had come back into view.

I was pretty familiar with Gloucester, because it's where my father has one of his biggest shipyards and one of his largest seafood plants on the east coast, so he often brought me on trips he took to them, guiding me into the airport-sized packing plant that I really should have been disgusted by, even as a kid (fish guts *everywhere*). But the men laughed and whistled while they worked, telling each other dirty jokes while they threw around halves of tuna and crates of shrimp, and it's kind of odd to say that shipyards and packing plants are comforting to a kid...but they had become that way to me.

The little seaside town of Gloucester has been known for its brave fishermen since the pilgrims sailed over on the Mayflower. It also has the saddest history of shipwrecks and men lost at sea. One of my father's own ships, the *Pretty Godiva*, was lost at sea about fifteen years ago, full of Gloucester fishermen. One man was drowned; the rest were rescued. Whenever I come here, see the storm-washed fronts of the houses along the main street that wraps around the little bay, I'm reminded of what the town has lost.

It's not as bad as all that, though. Gloucester is a bustling little village with a thriving tourist industry now. Even though the skies were still threatening inclement weather, big, gray clouds rolling over the sea, the main street that ran along the bay with its two famous statues was bustling with tourists.

Because of the traffic, we drove slowly past the statues of Gloucester, one after the other, and I watched the people clustered around them taking pictures. There were the most people, of course, around the very recognizable "They That Go Down to the Sea in Ships" statue of a fisherman in all his rain gear, holding onto a steering wheel for dear life as an invisible storm threatens his invisible ship. Fewer people, but still a crowd, had gathered around the slightly less recognizable statue of the woman and her children, waiting for her fisherman husband to come back from sea.

But Layne wasn't headed toward the bay. She turned the car away from it and kept going along the road that wound up toward Rockport, the next town over.

"I grew up in Gloucester," said Layne suddenly, her

125

voice unusually quiet. I glanced at her in surprise. She was staring out the front window at the red light we were stopped at, her eyes soft and a little misty. "My dad worked in your dad's packing plant, believe it not, after a scare out on one of the boats." She accelerated when the light turned green.

"Your father was a fisherman?" I asked, my curiosity piqued.

"He was on the *Pretty Godiva*," said Layne, casting me a sidelong glance. My brows rose, too.

"The ship went down in the spring," I murmured, remembering all of the details as if it were yesterday. I'd been a teenager, and my father had taken the loss extremely hard. I still remember him weeping brokenly and openly behind his desk, his face buried in his hands after he'd had to tell the wife of the fisherman who hadn't made it that he'd been lost at sea. My father was a sensitive, strong guy, and he was never ashamed to weep, but I'll never forget the sound he made that day. He was as distraught as he was the night of my mother's funeral, when he thought I couldn't hear him weeping.

"The ship went down in the spring," I repeated after licking my lips, my mouth suddenly dry. "The ship sank completely, and the fishermen aboard had to stay afloat in the wreckage on the ocean's surface for six hours before help could get to them, because of the storm."

"Yeah," said Layne curtly, her jaw working as she cleared her throat. "He survived that. But it affected him pretty bad. PTSD, the doctors said. He couldn't go back out on the boats. So, then he went to work at the plant for your father instead of fishing. The ocean... I mean, it's kind of cliché, but it's true: the ocean was dad's life. After that, he was never the same. I mean, he still had his sense of humor about stuff, but he started drinking." She breathed out for a long moment through her nose. "He's gone now. He died last year."

"I'm so sorry, Layne," I said quietly. I didn't even

realize I was doing it until my hand was halfway across the space between us, but then I just went ahead and placed my palm against her arm gently.

She half-smiled at me as she shook her head. "No, honestly, it's all right. Wherever he is, I'm sure he's happier than he was those last few years. He had pretty bad survivor's guilt. But, yeah," she said, clearing her throat and nodding her chin out the window at the rows of salt-worn houses. "I grew up here. Down that street, actually. The little blue house on the corner."

I looked out the window at the tiny blue house, some of its shutters missing, and its darker blue door so worn, it looked like it was original to the house and hadn't been repainted since. It looked too small for even two people to live there comfortably. The street itself was pretty broken up, potholes and chunks of pavement making it look hazardous to drive down, and toward the end of the bend in the street, there were a couple of kids running, a big black dog tight on their heels, its long fur straight out behind it as it ran with the kids.

"Anyway," said Layne with a tight smile, "I didn't bring you here to show you my old house, I promise. I have a few tricks up my sleeve yet. I want to show you something. One of my favorite places."

The way she said it, the passion that ran through her voice in those few words, made my heart skip a beat again. It had already skipped a dangerous amount of beats that morning because of Layne, so I was beginning to feel a little lightheaded. I took a great big gulp of coffee as I turned Layne's story over and over in my head.

Rockport is pretty close to Gloucester up the coast, and that's where I thought we were headed. But a few miles before the town center of Rockport, Layne slowed down a little. The highway between the two towns is so dense with trees, I often imagined, when I was a kid, that this is what the "new world" must have looked like when the pilgrims stepped off the Mayflower, this wild and impossibly green

127

place. Now that I'm a little older and have a bit more history under my belt than I did when I was seven, I know that this isn't really what New England looked like to the pilgrims.

But it's pretty damn close.

Layne pulled into a strange little parking lot I hadn't even seen on the right. The spit of parking lot was situated in a grove of tightly packed trees that seemed to tower over us. Overhead, and rolling in off the ocean, the clouds were growing darker still, darker than I'd thought possible.

As dark as night.

Layne rolled to a stop by the far corner of the lot, threw the car into park and pulled the keys out of the ignition. She stretched, rolling her shoulders as she turned to face me. "Welcome to Dogtown," she said, sweeping her hands in front of her to take in the densely packed underbrush and the trees that stood shoulder to shoulder.

I'd only heard the name before, and never really with any sort of definition to go along with it. I peered through the underbrush, a frown tugging at the corners of my mouth.

"Is this when you tell me that we're going hiking?" I hazarded after a long moment of seeing absolutely nothing but choked underbrush and crowded trees.

"Well," said Layne, drawing out the word again as she opened her car door. "Not *exactly*." She was grinning mischievously as she stood up and came around the side of the car in an instant to open my door for me. "I'll help you around," she promised, and then she reached into the car after I undid my seat belt. She reached in much too close, her face an inch or so away from mine, and for a full, startled heartbeat, I wondered if she would kiss me. But, no, her eyes were pointed down. And then there was an arm under the backs of my knees, and an arm around my waist...

And Layne was lifting me out of the car. And holding me. And carrying me. The sort of carrying that usually happened to damsels in distress, or Victorian women who had fainted because their corsets were too tight. The kind of carrying that a groom usually did to a bride half his size, to usher her over the threshold of a house. Not that it mattered with Layne. She was stronger than most men, or, really, a lot of men *combined*, it seemed.

So, she stood there, outside the car, toeing the car door shut gently with her foot. She stared down at me with a wide grin and held me tightly and gently both, cradling me in her arms like we'd done this before.

"This is a little undignified," I managed to say. Really, I was doing my best not think about her grip around my waist, or how my arm had gone up and around her neck like it was absolutely meant to be there. Or how her hand was against my thigh soundly and securely, like she was never, ever, ever going to let me go, her palm burning hot, even through the fabric of my jeans.

"Undignified, maybe," she said, her mouth set in a sideways smirk, "but easy for you to see some pretty amazing things instead of hobbling around on those crutches and probably reinjuring yourself something fierce? Definitely."

"Hey, miss, I like hobbling. It may be slow, but it gets me where I want to go," I bantered back. Layne was already taking long, easy strides across the patchy gravel of the parking lot, still holding tightly to me. I felt like I was floating on water. "And...what the heck is Dogtown?" I asked, after clearing my throat.

"How can you be a Boston native, born, bred and raised, and not know about Dogtown?" she asked mournfully, shaking her head. "Don't worry." She grinned then, hefting me up a little as the gravel path began to change to one made entirely of the overgrown grass, patchy and tall as meadow weed. "You'll find out what it is today."

I waited patiently for her to continue as she navigated up a pretty steep, grassy hill. I realized that even beneath the overgrown grass, weeds, and wildflowers, there were still a few patches of gravel. This place kind of reminded me of how the world looks in a "Life After

People" special.

"So, way back in the day," began Layne, clearing her throat and taking on a storyteller's tone, "and, I mean, we're talking...sort-of pilgrim era, is where this story starts." She reached an even part of the path that leveled off and stood still for a long moment. The trees overhead curved their thick, leafy branches down toward us, and it felt a little like we were in a forested tunnel. Or, you know, a fantasy novel, and elves were about to start singing up in the trees somewhere. I stared up, entranced by the intense, woven greenery overhead.

"So, back then, people settled in Gloucester and Rockport," continued Layne, ducking under a particularly low-hanging branch that brushed along my arm with leafy fingers. I shuddered against her and picked an acorn out of my hair. "And most of the people who settled in those towns were fishermen and merchants and traders. But there were, of course, also farmers who wanted to make their living working the land. And this is way before grocery stores," she chuckled, winking at me. "People needed vegetables—they couldn't live off of a diet consisting only of fish or trapped game. So, some folks moved inland from the towns along the coast and started a settlement that was farther from shore, far from the ocean storms that would've wreaked havoc on fields.

"These people built homes, tried to till the ground. The *problem*," she said, jutting her chin forward, "is that—as everyone now knows—New England soil isn't necessarily conducive to farming. Since it's *full* of *rocks*."

Ahead of her, rising between the trees like sleeping beasts, came a host of boulders, some as tall as Layne, some twice as tall, towering above us. I stared up at their gray, jagged enormousness with an open mouth.

"They tried to farm *here?*" I asked, indicating the boulders with my free hand. They really looked like elephants, dozing on their sides in the forest. "Didn't they see all of these when they got here?"

"Well, yeah, but you know the people who settled around here were true New England folk. They were almost as stubborn as those boulders," laughed Layne. "So even though they *knew* it'd be challenging, they still thought they could conquer the land. They tilled and tilled, broke their plows and backs, but hardly any crops came out of the rocky ground. And over the course of a few years, with no success at all, most of even the most stubborn people gave up and moved back to Gloucester, Rockport, or kept going further inland toward western Massachusetts. Some went to other portions of this brand-new world, where they thought they might have better luck.

"And then came the Revolutionary War. Over time, the town began to…change," said Layne, her voice dropping to a velvety whisper that sent a chill up my spine. Especially since the sky had suddenly gotten a whole lot darker. The brooding storm clouds were moving in quicker now, the wind picking up and creaking the branches overhead eerily.

"All that was left of the people who had settled here," said Layne then, pausing at the crest of another hill to take in the stony, verdant view, "were a few of the most obstinate and poorest women. And a whole lot of dogs. See, when the men went to fight in the wars, they left big dogs to protect their women and children. And, of course, those wars had terrible casualties, and most of the men—poor farm folk who had never been taught how to fight or kill, and wouldn't have small chance at getting out of any war alive—never came back.

"So, some of the dogs went wild, and some of the women kept their dogs for protection. And because there were so many packs of dogs around, wild or otherwise, people started calling this place Dogtown. But, you see," said Layne, a smile tugging at the corners of her mouth, "people started to come up with a whole heck of a lot of rumors about this place, too, since it was a place full of just women. And a rumor started to circulate—unsurprisingly, when you consider where we are in Massachusetts, so close to Salem—that the town was full of witches. Of shapeshifters. Of lesbians, even," she laughed a little, and I realized I was staring at her with rapt fascination.

I had to bite the hook she was dangling in front of me. "Well," I said slowly, carefully, "were any of the rumors..." Overhead, thunder began to rumble from far away. "I mean, were any of them true?"

"Hmm..." Layne exhaled and set me down gently, so that I was putting all of my weight on my good leg and leaning against her. We stared out at the dense trees, and as my eyes adjusted to the gathering gloom, I began to realize that there, among a particularly dense copse of trees, rose a very old stone wall, created from long, flat stones heaped on top of each other, and with a sharp stone border along the top made from pointed bits of shale stacked on their sides. The skin on my arms began to rise into goosebumps. I wondered how old this wall was, wondered if it might be from the original Dogtown. It probably was.

"The best rumor," continued Layne, one brow raised as she watched my expression, "was what ended up *happening* to the women in Dogtown."

She had me now, hook, line, and sinker. She was also holding me tightly so that I could stand upright without my crutches, and the intense warmth and closeness of her body was making my good leg as limp as a noodle. I gazed up at her beautiful, changing eyes, now mostly brown against the verdant greenery of the woods. Her long, lean body was pressed in quite a lot of the right places against mine; my heart began to beat at a faster rhythm.

I took a long, deep breath, trying to steady my erratic heartbeat. "What happened to the women in Dogtown?" I asked, a playful smile tugging at my mouth.

"Well, the history books agree that, with all of the conditions stacked against them, they probably all died of starvation, disease... Bad winters," said Layne, her head tilted to the side as her gaze shifted from me and peered out, into the trees. Her voice took on a deeper, darker tone: "But we don't know for sure. No one knows for certain what happened to the last stubborn women here. They did all disappear without a trace. Odd, when you consider that bodies should decompose, that there should be skeletons..." She gazed back down into my eyes intensely, searching them. "But there was nothing. They were just...gone."

A chill breeze picked up in power, and I shivered under Layne's intense gaze.

"There is, of course, a legend about Dogtown. It says that, on one full moon night, all of the women came out of their houses and stared up at the sky," Layne whispered, ducking her mouth close to my ear, close enough that her hot breath made me shiver against her. Her palm was planted firmly on the tree behind my head, and her body was leaning against me, her other arm wrapped around my middle.

"And, together, on that night of nights, the remaining women of Dogtown threw back their heads and *howled* at the moon. And together, they transformed into sleek gray wolves and ran off into the wilderness together, finally free of all of the bad luck of this place, finally free to be together.

"But according to the legend, they didn't always remain wolves. Only once a month, during the full moon, did they take on their beastly forms, but the rest of the time, they looked just like you do: human."

I paused for a long moment, searching her face. "Werewolves," I finally murmured, one brow raised as I watched her.

Layne nodded almost imperceptibly, her wild eyes flashing.

All around us, the wind had grown into a monster, rushing through the trees and making them creak and groan. Branches thrashed overhead, and leaves, twigs and other flotsam were beginning to rise all around us, hurled about by the mighty forces of the gale. But it was as if Layne didn't even notice. She leaned against me, over me, and with her strong, feverish body shielding me from the beginning of the storm, I felt—and was—perfectly safe.

Just like she'd promised I would be.

She was hot against me, physically hot to the touch, and I found that, in that moment, I was moving on instinct. Maybe it had been her story, about women who were wild enough to become wolves if left to their own devices. Maybe it was her nearness. But either way, I found then that my hand was rising and that I was powerless to stop it. My fingers curled tightly around her belt, my fingertips drifting under the edge of her shirt.

They met with the heat of her skin, the softness of it, with the ripple of muscles on her belly that seemed to shiver against my touch.

I shivered against her, too, staring up into her eyes as my lips parted, as a rush of air escaped me. She was regarding me with wide, dark eyes that were full of longing; my body responded likewise.

I arched back my head, stood up as tall as I could on my good leg, and I brought my mouth to hers.

Her lips were feverish, so hot that their temperature contrasted brightly with the cold wind—unusual for a June morning—that roared around us. And for a single, perfect moment, her mouth met mine every bit as intensely, opening and drinking me in like she'd wished for this moment as much as I had. Her hand against my waist held me tighter, pressing down with ferocity, and then she was pressing me fully against the tree, the bark biting into my back, but I hardly even noticed that, because her hips were hard against mine; she was standing between my legs, and I hooked my fingers into her belt loops and pulled her to me, holding back a moan as her hand pushed up under the edge of my shirt, her hot fingers raking over my skin, the world spinning and...

Layne stopped. Her mouth went hard against mine, and she took a single step backwards, licking her lips, her hand stilled against my back, her gaze planted somewhere above my right shoulder. She took another step back completely. She was no longer touching me.

I was left to hold myself up against the tree, my legs still spread, from where she'd stood between them, my center aching. I felt disheveled and more upset than I wanted to be.

"What is it?" I asked, tugging at the hem of my shirt and pushing my braid back over my shoulder with a frustrated shove.

She shook her head, raking her long fingers through her carefully teased hair so that it stood up in all directions. She pushed her hands deeply into her jeans pockets, shrugging her shoulders forward, her gaze still distant and not looking at me.

"I can't," was all she said, as simply as if it were written in stone.

I felt my face redden, flushing hotly. I tried to stand tall on my own two feet, but since I couldn't put any weight on one of them, it didn't come across as cool- and detached-looking as I'd intended. So I just leaned against the tree heavily, feeling its coarse bark at my back.

My heart hurt as if it'd been crushed beneath her boot. I hated that.

"Why?" I asked, trying to make my voice even. But it cracked at the end of the word as I pressed my full weight against the tree's solid bulk and tried to take a deep breath.

She shook her head, her eyes steely as she rocked back on the heels of her hiking boots. "I just... I just can't. I'm sorry, Elizabeth."

The words were cold, and they made me angry. No explanation. I wasn't even worth an explanation.

My mind spun through everything I knew or thought I knew. Maybe she was already with someone—though I would have assumed I'd have heard of her. Maybe she wasn't attracted to me in the slightest. Maybe she didn't want to date the daughter of the guy she was working for, the woman she was trying to keep safe. Maybe she didn't want to get involved with someone who people were trying to kill. Maybe a million things, but without any sort of explanation, I couldn't know, or even guess.

I felt desperately embarrassed, made worse by the fact that desire was ripping through my belly, a red haze of lust and longing making it difficult for me to see.

I blinked, rubbing the back of my hand angrily across my eyes. "Sorry," I bit off curtly.

She looked surprised at that, and she shifted her gaze back to me, away from the spot she'd been staring at over my shoulder. For a moment, something flickered in her eyes, which were now a deep, dark brown that seemed to have an odd sort of depth. She swallowed audibly, shook her head again, and leaned back on the balls of her feet, bowing away from me.

"Elizabeth, I..." She worked her jaw, glancing upward, as if the words she was searching for were written on the dark, brooding storm clouds overhead. When her gaze came back down to earth, her eyes had taken on a hard glint as she looked at me. "There are things you don't understand," she said softly. Then she fell silent and watched me.

"Things I don't understand," I repeated, my voice brittle. "Really? Like what, Layne?" I asked, the words coming out knife-sharp. "What could I *possibly* not understand? What is *obviously* too far beyond me for me to comprehend?"

"That's not what I meant," Layne snapped, and then she pursed her lips together, her eyes flashing dangerously. "It's going to start storming soon," she said, raising her voice as a particularly epic burst of lightning touched down, crackling probably a mile or two out to sea—but still, the shadow of the lightning bolt burned behind my eyelids when I blinked, and I considered that the storm was going to hit shore much sooner than I had expected.

But I wasn't done with this. Not yet. It was too important.

"No," I said impetuously then, drawing myself up to my full height and shaking my head. Frustration coursed through me hotly. "What is it?"

For a long moment, I wondered if she'd actually tell me. Her gaze softened almost imperceptibly, and the same look came over her face as before, her brows furrowing, her eyes becoming gentle and concerned. I remembered that expression. She'd been about to tell me this important thing a few times in the past few days, something *so* important, something so absolutely and completely essential...

But just as quickly as her gaze softened, it hardened again, her lips curling down into a deep frown, and she shook her head. "I'm sorry, Elizabeth," she said, almost formally, with a curt bow to her head. "But I'm not at liberty to discuss this."

She sounded like she was addressing a board, not speaking with a woman she'd just kissed passionately.

I'd never felt so embarrassed, humiliated, or more stupid in my entire life. There was no way that I could extricate myself from this situation with a scrap of dignity left intact.

Dignity and humiliation aside, however, I was simply and plainly hurt. She'd wanted to kiss me; she'd kissed me with so much fervor that it had melted every bone in my body. That kiss had been everything I had ever dreamed of, when I imagined kissing Layne O'Connell. But in my dreams and fantasies, the kiss hadn't ended like this.

I'd felt attracted to Layne from the very first moment I'd met her, like we were two opposing magnets, pulled together by forces we couldn't understand or control. And then, when she'd kissed me, for a single, pure moment, I'd known that all of those things I'd felt? *She'd* felt them, too, and she answered them with a fervor that matched my own.

But for some reason, some *inexplicable* reason, none of this seemed to matter, because Layne wouldn't tell me what was keeping us apart.

"Please take me home," I managed to say, my voice cracking. But the lightning and subsequent rumble of thunder overhead hid the break in my words.

"Of course," said Layne, avoiding my eyes, a pained cast to her own, her jaw set as she turned.

Overhead, the heavens opened as she lifted me in her arms easily, if I were weightless. The rain was cold and hard, and it beat against us while she effortlessly carried me back to the car, unspeaking.

Chapter 10: Third Time's the Charm

We drove home in complete and excruciating silence, the windshield wipers dashing back and forth at full speed, trying to make the view even partially visible. But the wipers could do little to combat the onslaught of gale-force rain driving into the front of the car as if it were hellbent on pushing us off the road. I didn't know how Layne was seeing out that window, but I was too numb to care, looping over the kiss, over how much she had seemed to want me, and then her subsequent—and unexplained—refusal. I was too upset to consider anything else. And, anyway, the rain and the explosive thunder rumbling around us made it impossible to talk, even if we wanted to.

When we got back to my apartment building, Layne parked the car on the street and helped me hobble inside, then to the elevator, down the hall and through the apartment door. We were drenched, leaving a wet trail behind us. But still, exhausted, and with the both of us resembling drowned rats, I rounded on her with as much strength as I could muster.

"I think it would be best," I said coolly, as I'd practiced it in my head about a thousand times on the last leg of the drive, "if you took the afternoon off."

Her eyebrows rose. I think whatever she'd been expecting from me, it wasn't this. She shifted her weight, narrowed her eyes. "I'm your bodyguard," she growled, as if I wasn't already painfully aware of that fact. "I don't get the afternoon off unless your father permits it. Which, I hate to point out, he hasn't."

Perhaps she didn't mean for that antagonistic edge to be in her tone, but it was there, all the same.

"Well, I'm your client, aren't I?" I hissed between clenched teeth, my hands balled into fists at my sides to keep them from shaking with emotion. "Which means that if I tell you your afternoon is off, it's off." I opened the door and pointed to her bedroom. "So, come in, get a change of clothes, and go enjoy yourself." What would have been far too petulant to say—but what I mentally added—was this: *since you obviously don't enjoy your time with me.*

Her face had taken on a stony expression, and she hadn't budged a muscle.

"I'm sorry for the inconvenience, Ms. Grayson," she said, every inch the professional, her voice practically *oozing* civility. "But I was hired by your father to keep you safe, and that's what I'm going to do."

"It's not raining poison in here. Or teeming with armed men," I said, my tenuous grasp on my own civility snapping. "I don't want to see you right now, Layne. Take the fucking afternoon *off*."

She winced, but I held my ground, my heart twisting in me at her pained expression.

"Fine," she said, drawing herself up and setting her jaw, her eyes flashing in the darkened hallway. "I'll be back tonight."

"I can't wait," I murmured.

Layne turned on her heel, and she stormed back down the hallway. She hadn't come in for a change of clothes and would probably get pneumonia from the unseasonably freezing rain. I was about to call after her to stop, but then I was too angry to voice anything.

So I slammed the door.

But I didn't get any sort of satisfaction from it. I'd seen her hunched shoulders. She had maintained her coolness in front of me, the calm exterior, but for a fraction of a second, that mask had slipped, and genuine pain had been made evident, her body curling forward as if she'd been kicked in the stomach.

I pressed my back against the door as I covered my face with my hands, pressing the heels of my palms against my eye sockets, willing the tears to stay inside of me and not spill.

But I began to cry, anyway, big, fat tears that ran down my cheeks with abandon as I felt my heart cracking inside of me with an acute pain I was fairly certain I'd never felt before in my life.

What a terrible day. What a horrific day. I wished I could wipe it from my memory forever.

How could I have been so stupid?

I took a ragged breath and shook my head, pressing the heels of my hands harder against my eyes as a wracking sob escaped me, and I sunk down a little against the door, my good leg shaking. What if, this entire time, she hadn't been attracted to me at all, and I'd just hurled myself at her like I was desperate? And maybe I *was* desperate, just a little, but it was desperation for *her*. There was something about her that made my blood run hot, that drew me to her, and I couldn't explain it away, and I couldn't stop it from happening. I knew, in that honest moment with myself, that each day that passed I was falling more in love with Layne O'Connell.

And, God, how I wished I wasn't.

There are things you don't understand, she'd said. What could I *possibly* not understand? I knew I'd drive myself crazy if I went over and over and over every moment of the morning again, but I couldn't help myself. Had my father made Layne sign a contract that said she wouldn't date me or sleep with me? Was Layne already with someone? Was I simply ridiculous to have hoped she was attracted to me, too?

My thoughts looped over the sudden and intense passion she'd shown me with that kiss...followed by her extreme shift into cool detachment. How she kept saying, "I can't." What did that mean?

All of my worst fears about things not working out between us, fears I'd expressed to Tracy, had occurred without anything nice to remember the experience by. We hadn't dated; we hadn't gone to bed. We'd simply kissed, and now it was as bone-achingly sad and terrible as if we'd done all of those things, and it had gone bad in the end, anyway.

I took up the crutches from the side of the door where I'd left them, and I pulled myself up. Then I used the crutches to hobble over to the couch. I sat down, not caring that I was pretty drenched and my couch would now sport an Elizabeth-sized wet spot.

I undid my braid and ran my fingers through the long, dripping strands of my hair and tried to think about anything that could take this painful weight off of my chest, could remove the pain from my heart. I contemplated, briefly, having a nice, long, hot shower, ordering pizza, and then watching about two dozen of my favorite comfort movies, or practicing for the concert tomorrow in my pajamas, but all of those actions required a tiny bit of effort on my part, and it was infinitely easier to stay sprawled on the couch and feel utterly and completely pathetic and sorry for myself. Which, I finally decided, was exactly what I would do.

Which was, of course, exactly when there was a knock at my apartment's door.

I wondered if it was Layne, back already. But she had a key to my apartment, and for some reason, I didn't think she'd knock, not even after the argument we'd had. But maybe it *was* Layne. I really wasn't expecting anyone else. Maybe she'd come back to apologize, to tell me that it had all been a mistake, that there had been, in fact, a silly reason for breaking off the kiss. Maybe she'd come back because she wanted to kiss me *again*. Maybe she'd push me against the wall in the entryway and...

Before I could get too far along in the fantasy, I

stopped myself. I knew I was torturing myself now. I shook my head, feeling my cheeks grow pink at the very thought of Layne pressing me against anything, and I struggled to get up. It probably wasn't Layne at the door.

And it wasn't. Through the peephole, I saw a woman in what looked to be a dull gray jumpsuit with the apartment company's logo, Stellar Suites, embroidered on the lapel, along with a name tag that read *Sheila*. The woman was a little shorter than me, with bright red hair that was carefully pinned to her head, and an astoundingly pretty face: full lips, high cheekbones, and almond-shaped eyes that were a sparkling green. She was carrying a toolbox.

I threw the security latch back and opened the door.

"Hello," said the woman, her smile deepening when she saw me. "Are you Ms. Grayson?"

"Yes," I said, finding myself returning her smile, though mine felt a little strained. Still, I had to smile because hers was purely infectious.

"I'm Sheila. I'm from Stellar Suites," she said, her brows furrowing a little as she pointed to her lapel. "I'm so sorry, but there seems to be a leak coming from your kitchen pipes, and it's affecting your neighbor downstairs. I know this is terribly inconvenient on a Saturday, but I really must get that leak fixed. Could I come in for just a little while? I'll be quick." She held up her toolbox and grinned again. "I promise."

"Oh, of course. Don't even worry about it," I assured her, hobbling backward and holding the door open.

"My goodness, are you all right?" she asked, stepping smoothly through the door and cocking her head to the side as she took in my foot. I was holding it above the ground a little; I'd failed to grab my crutches from the couch.

"It's nothing. I was just in a little accident." I shrugged, shutting the door behind her. I was suddenly acutely aware of the fact that I was dripping and that I was standing with no great balance on one foot, wobbling as if I'd had one beer too many. "My kitchen's over here…"

Since I'd left the crutches behind, I now found myself hopping on one foot in the general direction of my kitchen, praying with all my might that I could remain upright.

My face, I figured, probably looked like I'd just had a really good cry, all splotchy and red. It certainly felt that way.

This day really couldn't get any better.

I hobbled for another step, but then I was stopped by a hand on my shoulder. "Please, let me help you," said Sheila softly, and a firm, strong arm was around my waist, her hand against my stomach, and she was propelling me toward the kitchen.

Normally, a pretty woman holding me tightly around the waist would do an awful lot for my morale. But I found, strangely, that I wasn't really in the mood for this sort of thing, as friendly and helpful as it was. Also, I was *soaked*.

"I'm all right," I managed, flashing her a smile as I disentangled myself from her arm. I paused beside the couch, leaning over and fishing up my crutches from where I'd left them, precariously tossed against the right couch arm and next to that enormous wet spot.

"Of course," said Sheila, her bright, wide smile staying firmly on her face. Wow, she must use a lot of whitening strips to make her teeth that damn…white. They could probably be seen glowing from *space*. Or maybe she was a model in her spare time. She *was* ridiculously beautiful, like the kind of beautiful you see on television, in the movies or in magazine ads. She was too beautiful, really. Like she was Photoshopped. I'd never been more aware of how I looked, the fact that I was dripping a puddle onto my living room rug, that I'd just cried a river, and that I'd never felt more sorry for myself in my entire life.

Not the best time to have a model-gorgeous repairwoman stop by on a surprise house call. My confidence was currently in need of life support.

"The sink's through here," I said, hobbling toward the kitchen again, then, with my crutches, Sheila following close behind.

She was actually following *very* close behind. When I paused again, her free hand actually brushed against my rear.

I probably wouldn't have even noticed that if her hand hadn't *remained* on my rear for about a minute.

"Uh…" I said, trying to sidestep her. It was such an odd moment. She wasn't wearing gloves; it was her bare hand against me, which meant that she *must* have known what she was doing. But when I turned to glance at her, her eyes were wide and innocent.

Though maybe her smile *had* taken on a tiny bit of a mischievous slant.

To be perfectly honest, it kind of felt like a porno was about to break out in my kitchen. Wasn't it the stereotypical setup? A devastatingly attractive woman came to "fix" a "leak," but really came to get it on with the apartment's inhabitant... Wasn't that the totally cliché start of almost every porn movie? A repairwoman or a pizza delivery woman or something like that?

But it wasn't exactly an *attractive* feeling I was getting from this woman, oddly enough. Yes, she was beautiful, *dazzlingly* beautiful, with the stray curls of red bouncing along her perfect skin and gently sculpted cheekbones, the way her jumpsuit strained against her chest and hugged her hips tightly. But there was something off about her smile, the wideness of it, like she'd pasted that grin on the first moment she'd gotten up in the morning and had kept it on, and now it was causing her face strain. But she kept smiling, anyway.

"So," I said, my brows furrowing together when she didn't move toward the sink, her hand *still* on my rear end. I hobbled to the right, and her hand fell away from me. I felt so flustered that, for a long moment, I didn't even know what to say, but then I gestured toward the sink. "There…it is. The sink."

"Oh. Oh, yes," she said, her smile not faltering for a second as she knelt down and deposited her toolbox by her left knee. I was actively relieved that she wasn't touching me anymore. She gazed up winsomely and practically batted her eyelashes. "I'm sorry to ask this of you, but do you, uh…have a drink of water?"

I blinked. "Yeah, sure. I mean, there are glasses in that cabinet there," I said, nodding toward my glassware cabinet. "And, I mean, the sink's right there. Help yourself."

But she didn't move from her position, kneeling on one knee in front of me. Her hand was still gripping the toolbox handle, and her smile—her really *creepy* smile, I was now realizing—hadn't moved a fraction of an inch, had, in fact, grown *wider*, it seemed. In horror movies, someone who smiles this much is usually about to kill you in fun and interesting ways, just before the opening credits roll.

I stared at her for a long moment. Maybe she'd just had jaw surgery or something, and she wasn't very good at moving her facial muscles yet. I inched past her just a little. My apartment kitchen is kind of tiny, and when I moved past her place on the floor, I had to brush my body against her, my left thigh connecting with her shoulder in a much more intimate gesture than I would have liked.

Her hand snaked out and grabbed my wrist. It was as if she hadn't even *moved*, the gesture was so quick. Now she was kneeling there and holding tightly to my left wrist, her fingers encircling it like steel bands, still staring up at me with a wide, bright smile that made her eyes look a little cold…

This was so…strange. Her teeth… They hadn't looked quite so pointed before. I stared down at them, feeling my heart begun to thunder inside of me. Something was wrong.

Very, very wrong.

"You are Ms. Elizabeth Grayson, yes?" asked Sheila, the words coming out soft and clipped as her unblinking eyes pinned me to the spot.

"Yes," I muttered, trying to tug my arm out of her

grasp.

It was as if her hand was made of solid steel. The fingers were completely immovable.

I glanced down at her fingers, clasped tightly around my wrist, and then looked back up at her face.

"Good," whispered Sheila, her smile widening, a feat I'd imagined would be impossible. "It's nice to know I have the right person."

She drew me closer to her, a little bit like a fisherman reeling in a catch. I'm not a weakling, but I couldn't move her fingers an inch, couldn't twist out of her grasp, and she was squeezing her fingers so tightly around my wrist now that it was beginning to hurt. White-hot pain sprouted from my wrist as she twisted my arm then, a cruel expression beginning to overtake the smile.

"I think you should leave."

The words were a dark, rumbling growl; I knew that voice. There, in the entrance to the kitchen, stood Layne. She was still just as wet and disheveled as I was, but there was something about how she stood there, her body angled toward us and a sneer of anger on her face, making her lips go up and over her teeth...

Layne's shoulders curled forward, but not in dejection anymore. They curled like she was carrying a huge weight on her back, and she was about to throw it off, perhaps violently. Her leather jacket seemed to be too small for her muscles, and for a long moment, there was a pulse of heat and power coming from her form that radiated across the short distance of my kitchen, rolling over both Sheila and me in one dizzying wave of aggression.

The repairwoman let go of my hand, standing in one quick, jerky motion, like she'd just been bitten.

"I'm sorry," she said softly, wide eyes glued to Layne, hands spread in front of her, her palms up in the universal gesture of please-calm-down. "I think I have the wrong apartment."

Layne took one step forward, Sheila took one step

backward, and then Layne, who'd had her head bent, lifted her chin, raising her gaze and staring at Sheila.

From somewhere far away, I heard a gasp. *I'd* made that sound, I realized in a detached sort of way, like it was someone else making it, not me. Because this moment? It felt like a dream. It didn't feel real in the slightest.

Layne's eyes were no longer brown with flecks of green and blue.

They were as red as blood.

"Get…" she whispered, the words shimmering in the air like they were carved of solid ice, "…out."

Sheila stayed frozen for a long moment, her entire body quaking, and then she bolted faster than I thought any human being could move, past Layne and out of the kitchen and through the living room, and the door slammed shut behind her, making the walls of the apartment shake.

Layne stared at me, her nostrils flaring, her eyes narrowed, and her hands clenched into such tight fists at her sides that it looked like she was braced and holding back a falling wall. But she was just standing there in the middle of the entrance to my kitchen, still as wet as she'd been when she'd left, just moments before.

But now, the air seemed to flicker around her, like waves of heat were radiating off of her body into the colder air.

"Did she hurt you?" said Layne, getting each word out with some difficulty. I stared at her, knowing that my heart was beating too fast, but this time, it wasn't from attraction.

It was from fear.

There was something strange about Layne, the Layne who was standing in my kitchen right now, completely different from the Layne who'd walked down the corridor a handful of moments before.

This Layne was dangerous, I knew.

"What's wrong?" I managed, the words small and hardly audible. I stared at her tense form; she shook for some reason, shook like she was holding back an avalanche, a mountain, a moon, with only herself between the object and something she was trying to protect. I cleared my throat, tried to make my voice stronger. "What happened to you?" I asked.

She shook her head, growled a little under her breath, swallowed. She took a very long breath and visibly straightened, raising her head again, relaxing her shoulders to curve downward instead of hulking forward. Her hands went flat against her thighs, and then she assumed a more relaxed position, sliding her hands slowly and carefully into her leather jacket's pockets.

When she raised her gaze to me again, her eyes were their normal, captivating hazel.

Had I imagined the red? But, no, I'd *seen* it. I'd *seen* her eyes, and they were *red* like *blood*. But they weren't red anymore; they looked as if they'd never been red. I had to have imagined it...

I leaned against the sink, suddenly drained of the energy to even hold myself upright. The adrenaline that had been pouring through me left as quickly as it'd come, and now the distance to the couch, someplace that would hold me while I slumped down onto it and curled myself into a ball, seemed practically overwhelming.

I tried again: "What *happened* to you?" I asked, my words soft in the space between us, but there all the same.

I really needed some answers.

But it didn't seem like I'd be getting them anytime soon. Layne simply shook her head at me, stepped forward smoothly. As if she knew how exhausted I was, she scooped me up and carried me, just as she had on our hike earlier today, back to the couch. I didn't protest. With her overly warm body tight against mine, I avoided thinking about what had happened earlier, in Dogtown, about the kiss she'd stopped.

I thought, instead, about the Layne who had stood in the entrance to my kitchen just moments ago, the Layne with her lips up over her teeth, the red eyes...

"I forgot the car keys," said Layne simply, as if that was any sort of rational explanation for why she'd come back to the apartment just in the nick of time to stop…what? What had that repairwoman been about to do?

Really, what had happened here? My intuition told me that woman had been intent on harming me, and Layne had, by her presence, saved me...

But my instincts were also telling me that there was a lot more going on under the surface of things.

Layne crossed to the little table by the door and scooped her keychain up from the bowl there. She turned to look back at me over her shoulder.

"Keep the door locked. Don't let anyone else in," she said, one brow up and a grin tugging at the corners of her mouth. "Though I don't think anyone else will show up."

She almost looked smug.

"What the hell?" is what I managed to say, then. It seemed to encompass everything I was feeling quite nicely.

Layne grinned, shrugging her shoulders, and with that gesture, sloughing off the last of her tension.

"I hope you know that I'm not going to let this go—not until I get some answers," I told her, as she shut the door behind her.

"I didn't think you would," she muttered, right before the door clicked shut, leaving me alone in my apartment, confused, a little afraid, but mostly angry that something unspeakably strange had happened, and I had no explanation for it at all.

But I was sure as hell going to get one.

Chapter 11: Instinct

"Who the hell *is* Layne O'Connell, Dad?" I asked, trying to keep my tone steady as I held the cell phone tightly and narrowed my eyes. "I mean, *really?*"

"She's your bodyguard!" said my father cheerfully on the other end of the phone. It was early Sunday morning, and every Sunday morning, my father went into the office, made a good, strong cup of coffee, and created a game plan for what he would tackle in the coming week in the company. I knew I was interrupting some of his prime working time, but—to be frank—I didn't give a damn today. For some reason, I felt that my father and Layne were pulling the wool over my eyes, and I was sick of it.

There was something going on, and I needed answers. Now.

"So, some strange repairwoman came into my apartment last night, and I think she had a nefarious plan," I said, waving my arm about as my voice cracked. "Seriously. A *repairwoman*. But, somehow, *magically*, Layne knew that there might be trouble and sort of just *appeared* out of nowhere to save the day, but not as the Layne we know! Nope!" I was practically shouting now. "She had *red* eyes, Dad."

"You must have been seeing things, honey. People don't have red eyes," said my father indulgently, smoothly steamrolling right over what I'd been about to say next. "Elizabeth, shouldn't you be getting ready for your concert?"

"I *am* ready for my concert," I replied hotly. "And

you are evading my questions."

"Elizabeth, sweetheart," said my father with a sigh, "I want you to go to your concert and have a wonderful time. I want you to forget about all of the fishing moguls that are currently making your life—and, I'd like to point out, *my* life—a veritable living hell. Go play your music, sweetheart. Do what you were born to do."

If he was gearing up for one of his inspirational speeches, the kind that he always gave his plant workers, he had to know I was in no mood. I sighed for a long moment, pressing a fingertip to my forehead to stave off the headache that was beginning to pound in my skull. My father had started to throw the words "fishing moguls" at me anytime anything was a little—and you'll have to forgive my pun here—fishy. And I wasn't buying it any longer.

"Dad," I said then, my voice small. I went for broke: "I just want some answers. People are trying to kill me, and I don't know why."

His voice swelled with emotion. "Honey, I'm doing everything I can to make certain you're safe, okay? Please believe me, sweetheart, I'm doing *everything* in my power. There's nothing in the world that I want *more* than to keep you safe. They're after *you* because of *me*. And that's unforgivable. I'm going to make it right."

There was so much rawness in his words. I knew them to be true. My father loved me with all of his heart, and he *did* want to keep me safe.

But I knew my dad through and through—and there was something he was keeping from me. Had, perhaps, been keeping from me for a long time. His answers were too evasive, his voice taking on that certain distant quality that he used when he told me what he'd always called a "white lie" to keep me in the dark from something that might hurt me.

I twisted my mother's ring on my finger absentmindedly, staring down at the garnet glinting in the morning sunshine that streamed through my kitchen window. I would never forget that he'd taken on that distant tone the morning of my mother's funeral. His eyes couldn't meet mine that entire day, always looking over my shoulder as if he were waiting for my mother to stride into the house behind me, waiting for her to come back from the grave, as if she'd never really gone.

I shivered a little and sighed.

"Is Mikagi Tasuki going to play in the concert with you guys this afternoon?" asked my father mildly. I could hear papers shuffling on his desk and his laptop making the boot-up sound. I knew he wanted to get on with his work, and I should really run through today's concert pieces one more time. My fingers were practically itching to pick up the violin.

"No, she's not playing," I said, pouring myself another glass of orange juice and setting the pitcher back in the fridge. "Mikagi's supposed to fly home tonight, but we thought she would come to the concert to watch."

"That's great, sweetheart," said Dad, his mind obviously millions of miles away. "Hey, are you coming over for dinner tonight?" We usually had Sunday dinner together, if we could swing it.

"Well, yeah, but, more importantly, what are we doing for your birthday on Wednesday?" I asked, my lips pursed as I took a sip of juice. "Celebrating on a weekday is always so disastrous. Let's be honest: you're always thinking about fishing projections, I'm thinking about the new piece of music I'm working on for the Friday concert. We're too distracted. So, I was thinking why don't we celebrate your birthday next weekend, instead? Say...Saturday?"

"Sure!" said my dad in his far-off voice that meant he was looking at reports and no longer listening to me.

"I'll talk to Al about it," I said with a grin, invoking the name of his housekeeper, who would make certain he didn't miss his own birthday celebration. "I love you, Dad," I told him.

"I love you, sweetheart," he said, and meant it.

I ended the call and set my phone on the counter, next to my glass of juice, glancing over my shoulder at the shut door to my guest bedroom, where Layne was evidently still sleeping. She'd come home late last night and had entered that room, and she hadn't left it yet. I wanted to talk to her about what had happened yesterday, but that was going to be a long, involved conversation, because there were two things, really, that we needed to discuss.

One: How the hell had she known I was in danger?

And two: What the hell was happening between us?

I smoothed the front of my skirt, took a deep breath and tried to imagine the way the talk would go. But I couldn't, really. I'd been trying to coach myself on how to open up each of those conversations all night—and I didn't get much sleep.

As if she knew I was thinking about her, Layne opened the door to her bedroom.

Instantly, the hair on my arms stood to attention, I had to suppress a shudder, and my heart began to beat like I'd just narrowly avoided a head-on collision with a semi. She was wearing plaid pajama bottoms and a white tank top, her hair sticking up in every direction, as if she'd slept on it and hadn't even run her fingers through it yet. Her eyes were half-lidded and sleepy, but even sleepy, she exuded power. She wasn't wearing a bra under that tank top. And it was kind of an old, threadbare tank top, the kind that gets gauzy with excessive wear and is slightly see-through. I stared at her and tried not to, feeling my cheeks flush bright red. I leaned back against the counter, ducked my head down, stared at the tile floor of my kitchen.

Her feet shuffled into my view, and I had to stifle a chuckle.

Layne O'Connell, the sexiest and most captivating woman I'd ever met…was wearing white bunny slippers.

"Hey, don't knock 'em—they're really comfy," said Layne with a companionable growl as she glanced from my face down to her slippers, and then back up again. She stifled another yawn as she pulled open the fridge door and stared at the shelves as if she was looking for the lost continent of Atlantis. "Are we *really* out of milk?" she finally groaned.

It was such an incredibly idyllic scene, the kind of thing that would happen to an old married couple, or to two women who were dating and were ridiculously in love and had just had a rather passionate morning and were now famished. This sort of banter wasn't what sprung to mind when you thought of a single woman's Sunday morning conversation with her bodyguard. I tried to quell the ache in my heart but failed to, swallowing and shaking my head.

"We've been out since yesterday, I'm sorry to say." I shrugged. "I usually make my grocery store runs on Sunday."

"We should put milk down on the list, then," said Layne with a nod and another yawn. She shut the fridge door and stretched overhead, rolling her back and her shoulders in the most graceful undulation I'd ever seen.

My mouth went as dry as a desert, and my heart began to experiment with its own rhythm section.

"I…I don't shop off of a list," was the first somewhat articulate thing I could think of to say. "I just buy…whatever looks good at the store…" I trailed off, because Layne was staring at me, her mouth open a little, and her eyes as wide and shocked-looking as if I'd told her the sky was green and the moon really *was* made of cheese.

"You don't shop off of a grocery list? I mean, are you human?" she asked, her mouth still parted. Paired with her sticking-up hair, the expression looked unbearably…cute. I never thought I would use that word to describe Layne, but no other word fit in that moment.

Layne shook her head, her jet-black spikes swaying as she walked over beside me, reaching past me to grasp a pad of paper and pen that I kept in my wire bill rack, next to the toaster. Then her hand came to a standstill, palm flat on the counter as she stared down into my face, searching my

155

eyes with her own brilliant flashing ones. Today her hazel eyes were more bluish, like the bright blue sky outside my kitchen window.

She was so close, and she was so warm. Even though our bodies weren't touching, the heat coming off of her radiated across the little space between us, making me shiver from the sudden change in temperature.

Layne placed her other hand on the countertop to my right.

I was boxed in between the counter and Layne, her arms around me but not touching me as she stared at me, her face unreadable.

My heart ached so much, I felt crushed by it as I stared up at her perfectly impassive gaze. She searched my eyes, her lips pursed, the corners of her mouth tugging down gently into a beautiful frown.

"We can't do this, Elizabeth," she finally growled.

But she didn't move an inch.

I didn't even think. "What's *this*?" I asked her, pain sharpening my words. "What are we doing? And why can't—"

Her hands moved so quickly that, if you'd ask me, I would have told you that they had been gripping my waist all along, her hot arms along my sides, wrapping around me as if she'd conformed her body to mine a hundred times before. But, no, this was only the second time she'd held me so tightly, like she was afraid I'd disappear right in front of her, like I could dissolve at any moment into nothingness.

She held me like she was doing something wrong. Like she was about to get caught.

But like she had to do it, anyway.

Her stomach against my stomach, her hips against my hips, her breasts against my breasts—the heat and sensation from it was dizzying, but not nearly as much as the closeness of her mouth to mine, as much as the intensity in her gaze as she stared down at me before kissing me so tightly, I forgot how to breathe.

You ever have one of those kisses? You've wanted it for so long, and you've imagined it so many times, but imagination can only do so much. And then the kiss happens, and it's so much better than anything your imagination could have come up with. The kiss is so perfect, so savage and powerful and beautiful, that you forget everything else: how to breathe, how to stand, how to feel anything other than the connection that makes you not a single person but this perfect tandem thing, and you're one body, not two. You're so connected that you have no real knowledge of where you begin or where she ends. You're just one together.

Yeah. This was one of those kisses.

She held me so tightly against her that I felt that drowning people, dragged up from the sea and tasting air again, must feel like this, feel so saved and inherently safe. She savored me not in a soft, sweet kiss, but in a powerful devouring of me, her mouth hot against mine.

But let's be honest: I devoured her right back.

For the first few seconds, I was in pure, blissful shock. But that didn't last long. My body responded to her not only with every instinct I possessed, but with all the raw want and need that I'd been torturing myself with since I first met her. I was leaning against the counter, and—frankly—I was leaning against her, so I didn't even have to worry about maintaining my balance with my bad leg.

All I was, in that moment, was that kiss, was that connection to Layne O'Connell, the woman I had been drawn to, driven to, from the first moment my eyes met hers. We were meant to be drawn together, I knew. There was something ancient and instinctual about how much I wanted her. I could never have predicted that want. If you'd asked me even a week before that moment, I would have told you I wasn't even sure two people *could* be pulled to one another like this.

This wasn't purely physical attraction. This was the attraction of one heart to another, two hearts beating together in the same perfect rhythm.

I would never have believed I'd be saying it, but there it was, as plain as day, and I have to say it if I'm being truthful: This was a *soul* attraction. And I wasn't even sure I believed in souls.

It all happened in an instant: her body against mine, her mouth devouring mine…all in a single, perfect moment. And then Layne pressed her palms flat against the countertop again, and she bent her neck, placing her forehead against my shoulder as she breathed quickly, panting against me.

"We…can't…" she growled, her breath hot against my skin, her body wherever it touched mine making every atom in me spring to attention. I was no longer shivering. I knew what I wanted.

And it was her.

"I don't understand," I managed to tell her, burying my mouth in her hair, inhaling the scent of her deeply, that beautiful, rich aroma of wild air and the remnants of cologne. Even the scent of her drew me in. "I don't understand," I repeated, as she bent away from me, and it was my turn, this time, to grasp her waist. And I did. I held tightly to her as she stared down at me with wide, upset eyes, frowning so deeply now. "But I don't *care*," I told her, the words breaking as she took a step away from me. "Layne, don't…" I said, as she took another step back, and I stood, leaning against the counter, and she stood, several feet away from me, no longer touching me.

But though there was no physical contact, I could feel something stretch between us. Something that felt like a bright line between our hearts.

She had to feel it, too. Didn't she?

"I don't understand," I repeated woodenly, but she shook her head, running her fingers through her hair.

"There's too much," she said. She searched for the words, rocking back on her heels as she curved her shoulders forward, like she'd been punched. "There's too much keeping us apart, Elizabeth," she finally managed, her voice a low, aching growl. She ran a hand through her hair again, shaking her head, her eyes so pain-filled that everything in me called out to comfort her. But I stood where I was. She cleared her throat, brought her gaze up to mine. "There's so much at work here… It's bigger than just the two of us. There's...too much keeping us apart," she repeated.

"What the hell is that supposed to mean?" Pain made my voice soft, strained. "Is it because you're my bodyguard?"

Layne shook her head and kept shaking it, rubbing at her arms as if she were cold. Again, she leaned back on her heels, curling away from me. "Please believe me," she said then, her words a quiet growl. "You wouldn't want me if you knew everything about me."

"That's ridiculous," I said instantly. I already knew: there wasn't anything that Layne could tell me that would make our connection any less. I wanted her, felt bound to her, and there was something deep and instinctual that made me feel that way. I *knew* she was a good person. Whatever she thought I'd hate about her...she was wrong.

"Give this a chance," I told her softly, gently. She looked like a wild animal about to run, and I used my most soothing tone, holding out my hands to her. "You feel something between us too, don't you?" I asked, trying to placate her, even as she took another step backward.

"I'm sorry," she said, and her eyes held me as if I were pinned into place. "But I can't do this."

Raw pain began to flow through me, and I took a deep breath. I'd learned long ago that I couldn't get so upset right before a concert. It would mean the loss of my focus, and then I'd mess up during a piece; it'd become my worst nightmare on stage, me missing entire measures of the music, the swelling violin cut short because I'd lost my place. I couldn't do that. I was a professional, and the concert was mere hours away.

But we needed to figure this out.

"I don't know what you're talking about, that there's stuff keeping us apart." I squared my jaw. "But we're going to discuss all of this in detail later. And we're also going to discuss," I said, taking another deep breath as Layne's nostrils flared, as her frown deepened and her eyes narrowed, "about what exactly happened yesterday with that repairwoman and your arriving in the nick of time to save me from certain doom."

"No," said Layne, one brow up, "we're not going to discuss it. It's not *open* for discussion."

It took me a full moment to process what she'd said. My hands were clenched into fists now, and I folded my arms in front of me, lifting my chin, but before I could say anything, she spoke again.

"I'm sorry, Elizabeth," she said, and for a moment, her confidant demeanor faded, and I saw the pain in her face. But then her expression shifted back to stony immovability. "There's nothing more to talk about. We both have jobs to do, and we're going to do them well. I have my orders. And you have yours."

"And what are mine, exactly?" I asked, my voice sharp.

Layne lifted her chin, holding my gaze for a long moment…and then she glanced away from me, strode back to her room with her long, predatory legs.

She didn't even look at me as she growled back over her shoulder two simple words: "Stay alive."

Chapter 12: An Invitation

"Why won't Layne sit with us?" asked Tracy, glancing behind me at Layne, seated several booths back, staring down at something on her phone with an angry, brooding look on her face. Layne sat hunched in the booth as if, at any moment, she was going to crumble her phone in her hands. "We don't bite," said Tracy a little wistfully.

"Yeah, well," I muttered, poking my straw up and down in my frozen coffee as I gritted my teeth, "I guess you'd say we're having a kind of…off day."

The atmosphere in the relatively empty Thanks a Latte coffee shop was a sleepy one. There was one kid off in the corner, typing furiously on a laptop with big headphones lost in his curly brown hair. Other than him, Layne, Tracy and me…the shop was deserted. Not unusual on a Sunday afternoon, but I sort of wished there was a general hubbub going on to distract me from the fact that Layne and I hadn't spoken since that intense moment in my kitchen.

Layne had driven me to the coffee shop in stony silence, had situated herself in that booth and hadn't moved a muscle since. She was far enough away that she couldn't hear our conversation, but close enough that, if something bad broke out in the sleepy little shop (highly, *highly* unlikely), she could spring into action. In other words, she was doing her job to the letter, and absolutely not a bit more.

"Honey, people who *date* have off days," Tracy told me with a sniff and a shake of her head. "I'd like to point out that you guys aren't dating." But then her gray eyes got wide, and she leaned forward with a huge grin, planting her palms open on the tabletop as she slapped it. "Oh, my God, or *are* you? Did something happen—" Her voice in the empty coffee shop practically echoed, bouncing off the coffee-brown walls, and I grimaced, waving my hand. But Layne didn't raise her head when I stole a surreptitious glance over my shoulder. If anything, she stared with an even fiercer frown down at her phone.

"No, no, nothing like that," I said with a frown of my own and a shake of my head. I pressed a palm against my forehead, wishing I'd thought to remember to take a pain pill. I'd run out of the course of pain pills for my leg, sadly. "Can we talk about it later? Maybe go out for drinks or something?" I asked hopefully.

"On a Sunday? Oh, honey, if you want to go out drinking on a Sunday, I think you have it bad," said Tracy, leaning forward and searching my face. "But seriously, are you okay? You've been pretty quiet. What's wrong?"

"Nothing a night with my best friend and a whole heck of a lot of booze can't cure," I promised with a smile.

"I want to go out with you, I really do," said Tracy, her head to the side and her eyes narrowed as she sighed. "But I...think I have a date."

I stared at her in surprise, momentarily distracted from my own problems. "Wow, really? That's wonderful!"

"Yeah," she said with a wrinkle of her nose. "Don't get so excited—trust me, I really don't think it's going to be that great. I'd ditch him and the whole thing to go out drinking with you, but I was set up by Phyllis, and, well...you know Phyllis," she muttered, intoning the name of our primary harpist. Yes, I did, in fact, know Phyllis—and she'd never forgive Tracy if she ditched a date that Phyllis had set her up with. "So can I take a rain check?" asked Tracy, checking her watch and standing, grabbing her to-go cup. "Come on, we don't want to be late."

"All right," I said, both to the offer of the rain check and getting out of the coffee shop. I took up my cup, too, and when I stood, grabbing the crutches from the booth beside me, Layne, those few booths down, stood, as well, rolling smoothly up and stretching overhead, her leather jacket and shirt lifting to reveal a line of her skin and a peek of her ridiculously sculpted abs.

I hated that I glanced at them, and I hated that that simple glance awoke that same want and need that I'd been busily trying to squash for the past few hours. Seriously? A mere inch of skin, and I was ready to throw myself at her?

I didn't want to be that desperate. Connection or not, I wasn't going to beg Layne O'Connell to be anything more than what she already was: my bodyguard. But still, as Layne finished her stretch with a yawn, as she raked her fingers through her hair unthinkingly…it was a difficult promise to myself to keep.

What I wanted, what I wanted so fiercely, was something that Layne was refusing to allow to happen. So, what was I supposed to do? Fight for her against herself?

Layne stopped me as we walked past. Well, Tracy walked past; I continued to hobble. I'd been promised that I'd only need the crutches for another day or two, but I was already very sick of them and wouldn't miss them when they were gone.

I waited a long moment for Layne to say something. Her jaw was working, and she was refusing to look at me, instead planting her gaze somewhere over my left shoulder so she wouldn't have to look me in the eye. "I'll be in the audience," Layne finally told me stiffly.

That rankled me. If there's one thing I didn't want, it was Layne watching a performance as if it were an obligation. "You don't have to," I pointed out, gazing up at her with a frown. "Why don't you go—I don't know—catch a movie or something?"

Layne's eyes narrowed. "But—"

"Look," I sighed, "I'm with everyone in the orchestra the entire time. I don't go out for a smoke like Bob. He was alone when he was attacked, and trust me—in the orchestra, I'm never alone. I'm surrounded by people. I'm safe," I told her. What I didn't put into words, but what was slightly obvious from my tone, was that we needed a little time apart. That it would probably do both of us a world of good.

I was frustrated and crabby and heartbroken and shaky now, because I'd downed two frozen coffees on an empty stomach. What a terrible combination before a performance. What a terrible sensation to be staring down someone you had deep feelings for.

"Maybe," was what Layne said then, sliding her hands deep into her leather jacket's pockets.

I didn't look at her as she leaned a narrow, gorgeous hip against the table, gaze smoldering and burning into me, finally, as she turned her attention on me. She gazed down at me for a long moment, but now it was me who couldn't meet her gaze, because I was too frustrated, and I was afraid I would say something angry that I'd regret. So I turned away, and I continued after Tracy, out of the coffee shop, leaving Layne alone.

But I could feel her gaze burning into my back. I could feel her gaze on me as palpably as if her warm fingertips were brushing over my skin.

I was so angry at her for not discussing what kept us apart.

But I was angrier at myself for wanting someone so much. Wanting someone I couldn't have.

On the way to the concert hall, Tracy fell into step alongside me, shifting her cup to the other hand as she pulled her phone out of her purse. "These Sunday matinee concerts are so damn stupid," she huffed, half to herself, half to me. "Hardly anyone shows up to fill those seats unless we have a big name playing with us, because everyone's recovering from church or at dinner. We really need to talk to Amelia about shifting the concert's start time to later in the afternoon. Maybe four-ish."

She held the back door of the concert hall open for

me, and I gingerly shuffled over the concrete steps that, I noticed, were no longer stained with Bob's blood. But I couldn't help seeing the blood in my mind's eye when I looked down at them.

Tracy continued to ramble on about concert times as I glanced back at the steps with a long sigh. Bob had really loved the Sunday matinees. His kids usually came to them, and it made him really happy.

The investigation was underway on Bob's murder. There were just, unfortunately, very few leads to go on. No one had seen Bob outside of the concert hall when he was supposedly killed; there were no security cameras in the vicinity, no evidence left at the scene of the crime, not even a fingerprint or a tissue sample. Oddly enough, it was all a mystery.

As far as a motive for his murder, Bob was beloved by pretty much everyone who knew him. There was no obvious reason that anyone would have murdered him. It could have been a random murder, but it was such a gruesome one... None of it made any sense, and according to the rumors, the police were becoming frustrated by all of the dead ends.

We walked down the hallway toward the stage, and I wondered idly who we'd get to replace Bob. As we drew our instruments out of their cases, tuning them subtly, listening closely to the strings, I kept glancing at the wind section. It seemed so empty without him. Bob was a funny guy. Usually, for Sunday matinees, he wore a top hat that his kids, long ago, had decorated with ribbon. It had become a sort of hallmark of the Sunday shows. It was such a silly thing, but not seeing that top hat in the wind section... There were dozens of times each day that I realized that Bob was really gone. But it hit me particularly hard at that moment.

Amelia was in rare form, barking orders about something or other, when I saw a movement backstage. It was almost as if a shadow fluttered around the corner, but the slight movement drew my eyes, nonetheless. And there, standing in the center of the hallway, wearing her coat with her hood up, was Mikagi Tasuki.

And she was staring straight at me.

She caught me glancing her way. And then she tilted her head and beckoned me forward.

What the hell?

I looked sidelong at Tracy, but she was doing a quick, quiet run-through the scales—not something orchestra members usually do, but I knew that it was her ritual calming exercise before any concert.

I stood as quietly as I could—orchestra members were still coming and going at this point—and hobbled across the stage toward the back hall.

"I don't have long," said Mikagi the moment I got close enough to hear her throaty whisper. Her eyes were narrowed as she gazed at me, and she wrinkled her nose. "You're in trouble."

"Excuse me?" I said, leaning against the wall with my shoulder. This really wasn't what I'd been expecting her to say. Frankly, I hadn't even been expecting her at all. When I saw her, dressed all in black, from her Mary Janes to her tights to her dress and hooded jacket, I realized she looked exactly like the person I'd seen on all those music videos, parading around with her violin, playing her heart out. But this wasn't the Mikagi Tasuki I'd thought was a great star. She wasn't at all how I imagined her.

She stared at me with unblinking eyes.

"You're in trouble," she repeated, lifting her nose and grinning at me, her eyes practically twinkling. "But you play well. It'd be a sin to lose you. Don't trust anyone, all right?" she asked me, her head to the side.

"What are you talking about?" I asked her, mouth open. The time for politeness was over.

She leaned forward, her smile deepening. "Trust me when I say we'll see each other again," she said. I straightened at that, frowning. And then Mikagi Tasuki walked past me, trailing her fingertips over the back of my neck.

Exactly like…during the concert…

My jaw dropped open, and I turned to ask her if it had been *her* who'd kissed my neck in the darkness of the unlit concert hall—

But somehow, impossibly, Mikagi Tasuki was no longer in the corridor.

She was gone.

I limped back to my chair in a daze. What the hell had she been talking about, *trust no one*? It was a bad line from untold numbers of movies, and it didn't actually *work* in real life. And what did she mean that I was in *trouble*?

The concert passed by as quickly as a summer's breeze. As much as I wanted to be wholly consumed by the music, I found that my attention kept drifting, looping back onto painful subjects that not even the hum and vibration of the violin could quell. There was too much for me to think about. Mikagi's warning. Bob's murder. The attempts on my own life. Layne's red eyes. Okay, let's be honest: everything else about Layne. Layne herself.

As my bow swept across the strings in the last song of the afternoon, I found myself staring at my mother's ring as it drew close to my face and then away, borne in a rhythmic back-and-forth by my bow, from the music that I made with my new instrument. The violin sang in my hands, the strings vibrating with life and music, and the ring's garnet flashed in the overhead lights. I guessed that little superstition that I'd had about the ring keeping me safe wasn't very accurate. Bad things, very bad things, had happened since I'd put it on. But that's all it had been: a silly superstition. It still made me happy to feel my mother's ring against my skin, the reminder that somewhere in this world, good things really *had* happened. My mother and father together had been wonderful.

As the music swelled around us, my heart skipped a beat.

The connection that I'd felt for Layne… I

wondered if my father had ever felt that for my mother.

The music ended, and I was still turning that new idea around and around in my head as we held our instruments, drawing out the last note. There weren't many people in the crowd, but the ending applause was warm and robust, a few of the older members actually standing and applauding enthusiastically. I grinned at that, resting my violin's base on my knee. It was another concert done, and—despite my thoughts being in a million places at once, despite Mikagi's warning—it was a concert done well.

The audience members exited their seats and poured out of the hall, and, as I gathered my things, I felt the hall empty behind me. I'd swept my eyes over the attendees, and I hadn't seen Mikagi; she must have left.

As the orchestra members began to pack up, I felt a gaze on me, and when I was folding up the last of my sheet music, I saw a hand wave from the edge of the stage. I glanced up, eyes drawn to the motion, and then my eyebrows furrowed. The beautiful woman with long, wavy blonde hair who stood at the foot of the stage looked familiar. She was also staring straight at me, her friendly grin deepening when she saw me glance up.

"Elizabeth Grayson?" she called out to me. I nodded and stood a little unsteadily, hopping across the stage toward her.

I remembered why I'd thought she was familiar now as I drew closer. This had been the woman sitting with my father at the concert with Mikagi Tasuki, I remembered now. As I got closer, able to see the shape of her face, I inwardly sighed. Drat. This was Magdalena Harrington, a friend of my father's. That's why she'd seemed familiar at the concert, too.

It's not that she was forgettable, but my father had a lot of high-powered friends, and they ran in the same crowds and cliques. Magdalena, like many of them, always came to my father's large New Year's party, and I only remembered her name because I'd thought it was very pretty when I was a kid.

I'd also thought, when I was little, that she was one of the prettiest women I'd ever seen. She hadn't changed much over the years, which I thought was criminally unfair. She had long, white-blonde hair that flowed over her shoulders in elegant waves, and her petite form was encased today in a gorgeous, rich plum dress that was sleeveless, timeless with its boat neckline and attractive shade of purple. She smiled up at me as I approached the edge of the stage, her impeccably made-up lips stretching into a pretty, ruby-red curve.

"How are you, sweetheart?" she asked me then, leaning forward and enunciating the term of endearment as if she'd last talked to me a week ago, not a year ago. She'd always been a little overly familiar with me, I remembered. I saw her once a year, and I hardly ever talked with her, often forgetting her name, but she was a colleague of my father's, and I tried to be as polite as possible to any of my dad's friends, even if they seemed a little fake.

"I'm doing fine," I told her with a smile. "How are you, Ms. Harrington?" There was always that second of terror after I used a name with Dad's friends that I'd remembered it wrong, somehow, and that would be an almost unforgivable faux pas among the elite who believed, utterly, that the world revolved around them. But her smile deepened even further, and it seemed I was in luck. This *was* Ms. Harrington, after all.

"I'm delightful, just delightful," she said, clipping the words smartly. "Now look, dear," she said, wasting no time to get to her point. "Your father is turning sixty this week. Sixty! That's a big number worth celebrating, and several of his old friends got together... Well, we're throwing a party for him tonight," she said, leaning forward, her bright eyes unblinking. "I know it's dreadfully short notice, but do you think you could attend? He'd love that so much. It wouldn't be a proper surprise party without you! You know how much you mean to him."

This, I began to realize with slow, cold dread, was going to be one of the most bone-crushingly boring nights of my entire life. It wasn't that I didn't want to make an appearance at a surprise party for my father. That was a very sweet idea, and it had been very nice of whomever had taken the time to organize it. But it was going to be a bunch of extremely rich people being pretty snobby with each other, my father keeping the peace between old rivalries, and everyone acting super-nice to me and asking about the orchestra, but it would all feel extremely pretentious, because of course they didn't care about me or the orchestra, and most of them were only at the party to put in an appearance so that they could be seen to somewhat care for my dad.

To be fair, there would be people at the party, too, who were my father's genuine friends. But I'd been to enough of these stale, mind-numbing functions to know that there were many *more* people who went to these sorts of things to look good than those who actually cared about what they were attending.

So, yes, God—it would be boring. It would be dull and involve a lot of drink-holding and trying to be polite while swallowing my nausea at the casual mentions of millions of dollars being thrown around, so that they could try to outdo each other in the richest pissing contest imaginable.

But this was for my father. And I would go because I loved him.

"Absolutely! It sounds great," I told her, in what I hoped to be my most sincere voice. I glanced down at my wristwatch. "When is the party?"

"Well," she said, with a frown and a sympathetic, embarrassed chuckle. "Would you believe it's within the hour, actually? Dear, I know this is dreadfully short notice," she said quickly, when I blanched. She put on her most soothing expression and checked her own wristwatch, a gold number with diamonds inset around the face. "And I really wish I could have given you more notice, but I was only informed of it myself just this morning by Jerry. You know Jerry, right?"

I didn't, but I shrugged, glancing backward at my violin and somewhere metaphorically miles away. Leaning against the far wall in the back hallway were my crutches. I was getting pretty tired standing on only one foot. The crutches, of course, wouldn't look good against the clothing I'd have to wear for such a function.

"I didn't bring a change of clothes," I began, realizing that I would need a cocktail dress to attend this thing, but Magdalena shook her head, her smile deepening.

"Don't even worry about it," she tsk-tsked. "You look stunning. What you're wearing is perfect. It's a casual get-together." I grimaced at that. I was dressed in a pencil skirt and a really nice blouse; the outfit was hardly casual. "We just wanted to surprise your father, show him a good time," she said, inclining her head toward me with a wide smile. "Please tell me you'll do it? It won't be the same without you!"

She was pretty insistent—and she was right. It wouldn't be a big thing for me to show up; it was what a daughter should do to support her dad.

"Well, then, I guess I could come," I said, hoping my voice was still even a little bit enthusiastic. I glanced out across the now-empty seating area. Layne had obviously taken me up on my offer to go see a movie. She'd come back here afterward, though, wondering where I was. I'd have to text her so she didn't think I'd been kidnapped or something.

"I just have to get my violin and my bag," I told Magdalena, straightening. "Oh," I said then, realizing that Layne had the car. I grimaced again. At this point, it just sounded like I was coming up with a million excuses not to go, which wasn't really true. It just seemed that there *were* a million little things that were stacked up against my going. "I don't have a ride. I'm afraid I—" I began, but again, she cut me off as smoothly as a knife.

"My dear girl, I came in a limo big enough for the both of us, I assure you," she said, her eyes glittering. It was a classless thing to say, but when people have enough money, even classless things sound a little classy to them. I bit my lip and sighed again, nodding.

"All right, just let me get my things," I told her, hobbling back across the stage toward my violin.

Magdalena waited patiently at the edge of the stage, examining her perfect nails while I gathered up my violin, placed it in its case, and then grabbed my crutches and my purse.

I air-kissed Tracy on the way past her. "Good luck on your date tonight!" I told her, squeezing her arm.

"Thanks. God, I'm nervous," she said, fanning herself with a stack of her sheet music. She leaned a little closer to me with a grimace. "The way Phyllis was describing this guy—I mean, he might be really nice. This could *actually* be a good date, but I don't want to get my hopes up."

"Don't worry," I promised her with a small grin. "You're going to be fine. And get your hopes up. I mean…isn't that what life's for?"

She gave me a funny sort of look as I grinned sidelong at her and shrugged. "I'm going to be spending the rest of my evening at a birthday party for my father," I told her, then. "So maybe it's good that we took that rain check for drinks. Maybe tomorrow, yeah?"

"On a Monday night? God, you're killing me," she grinned and winked. "And, yeah, I'll probably—hopefully—have a lot to talk about tomorrow." She wrinkled her nose again, but she looked a little excited.

I grinned. "A lot of good, surely."

"Yeah, I like that. You're positive." She grinned at me, and then I was hobbling away from her. I met Magdalena at the edge of the stage stairs.

In the back of my mind, I'd tried to figure out things to talk about with Magdalena on the limo ride over to…well, wherever the party was being held. But I really didn't have much of a head for dull, pointless conversation and couldn't think of a single subject that would be good fodder for small talk with someone I hardly knew. I seriously hoped that Magdalena could carry the conversation, that she was still the talker I remembered her being.

And she was.

Once we were seated in her limo, which had waited, parked illegally out front with a very bored-looking driver thumbing through his phone and leaning—actually *leaning*—against the post that warned people not to park there since it was a fire lane, Magdalena launched into a soliloquy about how her various stocks were doing, and how my father and she had a little rivalry going about something—something stock-related, I think; my eyes had glazed over before we'd reached the first traffic light.

I was tired. Actually, that's not an accurate word: I was *exhausted*. And I was frustrated. I wanted to sit down with Layne and understand why, exactly, she thought we couldn't be together. But we were both too stubborn, it seemed. She wouldn't discuss it, and I wouldn't let it go. My mind looped over the terrible recent events. I thought about the repairwoman who had been about to do...something to me. I wasn't certain what. Had she been after me? And where, exactly, do you hire a hitwoman these days? Especially one who's willing to dress up as a plumber?

My mind wandered to the kiss in Dogtown. It wandered to the kiss that morning in my kitchen. It wandered to Layne's flashing eyes, her sarcastic smile, the way her hands felt, fingers curling around my waist...

Layne. I snapped to attention somewhat guiltily and cleared my throat as I pulled my phone out of my purse. "I'm sorry, Ms. Harrington, I have to text my...my friend," I said with a slight grimace as I tried to find a word for her. "She was supposed to pick me up after the concert," I explained, holding up my phone, "and she's probably worried about me."

"Of course," said Magdalena, her smile deepening.

But as I unlocked my phone to send a message, the screen was already lit with a text from Layne. I frowned a little as I brought it up.

ran into a friend going to bar to catch up left car for you see you tonight

I blinked and read the text a few more times, just to be sure, feeling a little lightheaded. Layne had left me to drive the car back by myself. I took a deep breath. Well, I'd wanted more autonomy. And I was the one who'd told her to go see a movie. To leave for the afternoon. She didn't have to be around me all the time. And, anyway, I was going to this party, so she wouldn't have been able to be "on duty," anyway. It would have been too obvious that she was my bodyguard if I'd brought her to the party, because I certainly couldn't bring her as my date, considering the disaster of that morning.

But still, even with all of these perfectly logical thoughts swirling in my head, there was a thick twist of foreboding in my gut. Maybe Layne hadn't really run into a friend; maybe she was just sick of me asking her to disclose secrets she wasn't comfortable telling. Either way, to simply leave the car for me to make my own way home wasn't very Layne-like. Something was up. Something having to do with not wanting to be around me, probably. My heart flip-flopped as I read the text again, and then slowly, carefully, I locked the screen and slid the phone back into my purse.

Also, Layne always used punctuation and capital letters when she texted me. Maybe she was a little drunk? This wasn't like her at all...

I frowned and tried to stifle a sigh.

"Trouble in paradise?" Magdalena, seated across from me, practically purred.

I glanced at her, brows furrowed, but her smile remained firmly in place, and she crossed her legs, leaning back against the plush leather seats of her limo with a deepening smile.

"No," I said, clearing my throat. The word sounded weak, even to me.

"Ah," said Magdalena, nodding knowingly, but not looking convinced. "You just... You looked *distressed* is all."

I took a deep breath and let it out slowly and steadily, resting my suddenly damp palms flat against my thighs. "No," I repeated. I carefully slid a mask of a smile on, realizing it was probably as fake-looking as could be, but not really caring anymore. "So," I said, clearing my throat and desperate to take the focus off of me. "Where is this party being held?"

"At my mansion," said Magdalena with a shrug, carefully rolling her shoulder and letting a perfect wave of white-blonde hair fall behind her, against the seat. She glanced out the tinted side window, her blood-red lips pursed. "Your father hasn't been by in a while, and I think my new remodel will really impress him. I can't wait to show it off."

My brows furrowed again, piecing together the little I knew about this party. "But..." I began, biting my lip. "Did you say that Jerry was throwing the party?"

Actually, now that I thought about it, hadn't she said she was unaware of the party until that morning?

"Oh, well, you know Jerry," she chuckled smoothly, her grin widening. "His head's just full of stuffing! So very scattered. I mean, seriously, if the party wasn't at my place, it'd never happen."

"Ah," I said, leaning back in my seat.

I don't know why, but the hairs on the back of my neck were standing to attention, my skin felt a little cold, and I had begun to feel overall...uneasy.

Not that Magdalena Harrington would inspire comfort on the best of days. She was the kind of woman who had obviously fought, tooth and nail, for everything she'd built her vast empire of stocks upon. It was because of the hardness to her facial expressions. Don't get me wrong: she was absolutely gorgeous, and she had a beautiful face.

She was utterly beautiful in the kind of way that most women would envy, a flawless, perfect sort of beauty that's uncommon to see in real life. But even with her beauty, her eyes glinted with hard edges, and her smile was one of the most insincere I'd ever experienced. Her legs looked as if they were made entirely of muscle and sinew. She must have had a great personal trainer.

And her outfit was impeccable. There wasn't a hair on her head out of place. She didn't strike me as the type of woman who lazed around the table on Sunday morning with the paper, still in her pajamas. She struck me as the type of woman who wore a power suit one hundred percent of the time, lived in the office, ate protein bars out of her desk, and took odd but complete satisfaction out of giving someone a terrible performance review, eating them up in a few perfectly placed, savage words.

As if she knew I was considering her, Magdalena's eyes blinked slowly at me, and her smile deepened as she uncrossed her legs and crossed them the other way in one easy motion, lounging farther back in her seat as she tapped her red fingernails on her skirt, plucking away an invisible speck from the fabric. "So tell me, Elizabeth," she murmured, her words low and velvety as her lips curled, "how is that new bodyguard of yours working out for you?"

I went cold instantly—how could she know I had a bodyguard?—but she tilted her head to the side, reached out and with freezing fingers, and patted my knee slowly. "Don't look so shocked, dear. Your father found Layne O'Connell through me, after all," she chuckled. "And I realize you want to keep it all hush-hush. But don't worry." She leaned forward a little, the smile unwavering. "Your secret's safe with me," she told me in a stage whisper.

"Oh. Ah…" I trailed off, trying to compute the fact that this meant Layne probably knew Magdalena. They didn't really strike me as compatible people. "How do you know Layne?" I asked then, my curiosity getting the better of me.

"I knew her father," said Magdalena, glancing down at her nails again with a small frown, as if she'd just noticed that her blood-red nail polish had a tiny chip on the pinkie nail. "Temperamental fellow, who Layne takes after quite a bit. Moody. Aggressive. Perfect bodyguard material, though," she said, her head to the side when she glanced back up at me. "Once she decides that you're worth protecting…" She trailed off, raising her brows. "Well, I think she'd stop at nothing to keep you safe. Good musculature, very strong. Yes, she's great bodyguard material."

For some strange reason, I didn't like the way Magdalena was talking about Layne. Like she was some sort of commodity, like a nice new designer purse or designer dog. Mentioning her *musculature*. And, frankly, I couldn't imagine Magdalena having even the most cursory knowledge or acquaintance with a hardworking fisherman, like Layne's father.

I was about to ask how she knew him when her face brightened, and the limo slowed down. "Ah, perfect timing… We're here!" she chirped.

Out of the tinted windows of the limousine rose a very sizable mansion. It was actually a little bigger than my father's—which was, apparently, something that you were judged on in these types of well-to-do circles. Yes, they actually compared the sizes of their mansions. I glanced up at the sprawling, five-story, turreted house. It looked pretty old, like it'd been constructed a hundred years ago, if not more, with Victorian brackets curling along the doorways and arches. It was a lovely house, built of thick, red stone blocks and wide windows with diamond-paned glass. It was close to the street, and nearer to Boston than my father's house, so there wasn't any room for a lawn out front.

Magdalena's driver pulled up to the edge of the curb, threw the limo into park and ran around the side quickly to open the door for us.

When the door was open, Magdalena unfolded her

long legs and rose out of the limo effortlessly, glancing back at me with a small, unimpressed frown as I tried to grapple with my violin case, my crutches and my bag, and was the exact opposite of her: graceless and a little clumsy as I attempted to angle my crutches under my arms and still hold the violin case without banging it against the side of the crutches. Magdalena seemed to grow impatient with my efforts; she leaned down and peeked back into the limo, offering me a hand with a wide smile that she pasted on a second too late for me not to glimpse her deep frown.

"Thanks," I managed, and, despite the fact that I didn't want to accept her help—there was something about her sneer-turned-smile that made my stomach sour—I leaned forward and took her proffered hand.

She was still as cold as ice.

She was so cold, in fact, that it felt like her skin was burning my fingers with frost when she closed her hand around mine, grasping it tightly and pulling me up so quickly I felt like I'd flown into a standing position.

"James," said Magdalena to her driver, "take her things, please." And then, with an apologetic smile, Magdalena leaned a little closer to me after dropping my hand. "Can I help you in? Those look a little unwieldy…" she murmured, her face full of fake concern as she held the crutches out to me as if they were more than a little repulsive to her. Her nose wrinkled while glancing down at them.

I took a step backward, trying to gain balance on my one good leg as my thoughts whirled. She was as freezing as Layne was hot to the touch. I stared at her, brows knit together, but she took a step forward then, laughing as she secured a frozen arm around my shoulders and helped me toward the red stone steps. "I really have to talk about getting that air conditioner fixed," she said, still laughing like it was the funniest thing in the world, when it was really just awkward and uncomfortable.

There were ten steps leading up to the front door. I counted them, because steps were still pretty difficult to navigate with the crutches. And Magdalena's help wasn't actually all that helpful. By the time we reached the top of the steps, I was shaking from how cold her skin was against me. The cold was insipid, had seemed to burrow into my body, taking up residence in my bones and my blood. It was that deep type of cold that makes you wonder if you'll ever be warm again.

"James," said Magdalena coolly to her driver. "Can you get the door?"

As he moved past us, I was struck by the fact that, on this relatively sweltering day—the chill of Magdalena aside (and the inside of the limo, whatever she might say about the air conditioning, had actually been warm)—he was wearing leather gloves. He unlocked the front door and held it open for us, staring straight ahead. I couldn't make out his eyes from beneath the glasses, but I had this weird thought that I knew him from somewhere. He looked familiar. I couldn't shake the strong feeling that I'd seen him before...

As we passed from the sunny day into the cool darkness of the entryway, it felt strange. The warmth of the day faded away and was replaced by the insipid cold as my brain kicked into overdrive, trying to shake the bad feeling that had been growing within me on the entire limo ride here.

But the bad feeling didn't leave. Instead, it deepened.

And it dawned on me with sick, stark realization, just as Magdalena ushered me into the foyer and the door was shut behind us.

James, the man who had driven us here in the limo, looked *exactly* like the man who had rammed me from behind. It was an odd thing to remember, the features of the man who hit you, but I'd seen his face in the rear-view mirror one split second before impact, and that face was one that, if I lived to be a hundred, I could never possibly forget. His face was forever outlined in the darkest corners of my mind and appeared in my nightmares, dreams in which I was driving a car, and then suddenly the car was spinning out of control and hitting the guardrail. I'd been rammed from behind, over and over again...

I turned back, horrified, gulping down air, but Magdalena's arm was wrapped too tightly about my shoulders, and I couldn't glance back. Her grip was overly familiar, and as I politely tried to disentangle myself from her grasp, I stopped trying to look behind me and looked forward at the impressive entryway.

And I stopped cold.

My very first thought was that this couldn't possibly be real. That maybe I'd had another accident, and what I was currently experiencing were the odd hallucinations and half-dreams that come with being knocked unconscious. But no—Magdalena's cold arm around my shoulders brought me back to reality with a crash when she tightened her grip.

What I was seeing *was* real.

The entryway was beautiful. Perfect, really. It was classical in design, with Roman columns and a bright, sweeping oaken spiral staircase that led up to the second level. There were old paintings on the walls, taller than a person, with gilt frames around bored-looking men and women in Victorian garb and very large hats. There was a bust of Beethoven by the entrance to another open room that had an antique piano in the very center of it upon an oriental rug. The tiles underfoot in the entryway were black and white, gleaming.

But none of that mattered. It faded into the far reaches of my consciousness, like it was sketched in, or the background of a painting.

Because the only thing that mattered was Layne.

She was wearing her white tank top and jeans, but that's where the normalcy of the moment ended. Because Layne was standing spread-eagle between two of the Roman columns. There was silver rope tying her arms to each column, and her ankles.

And she looked wounded. There was bright red blood flowing from her nose, from one ear, and from a gash in her head that appeared fresh and jagged, ugly on her handsome face. She also had two gashes along her neck that slowly and almost silently dripped blood onto the pristine black-and-white marble floor.

She was staring across the space between us with a grimace, staring into my eyes with such vibrant intensity that I took a step backward and collided with Magdalena. Realization came over her face at the exact same moment that it came over mine.

The spell of horror and silence was broken, and I found my voice.

"Layne," I whispered, and then I was yelling my head off: "Layne!" Her head bowed forward like she'd momentarily lost her strength, and then it raised, and her eyes flashed with fire as she took in the sight of Magdalena's arm clamped around my shoulders, and me suddenly struggling against her. Because I *was* struggling—but Magdalena didn't let me go.

Instead, Magdalena's hand darted up, and then it was deep into my thick hair, tugging my head backward. My violin case fell out of my hands with a *thump*, along with my bag and crutches, and when she pulled me backwards, I crumpled, screaming in agony as her other hand darted out and gouged the wound in my leg that had been carefully stitched and partially healed. She dug her fingernails through my skirt and deep into the wound like they were daggers.

"Be quiet," said Magdalena companionably, and then she dropped me, crumpling to the ground, and left me writhing on that beautiful black-and-white tile as she clicked forward in her high heels and stood with her hands on her hips in front of Layne, who hung limply between the columns, staring at Magdalena with unreadable eyes.

Magdalena clucked her tongue, shaking a head and wagging a finger at Layne as a bright smile spread across her face. "Really—and after you gave my girls such a fright, too—you were *so* easy to bring in," she purred, and quicker than I could imagine anyone being able to move, her hand darted forward and slowly, caressingly, she traced her finger over the blood on Layne's neck in a long, sensual motion.

Was I in an episode of *The Twilight Zone?* Through the haze of pain at having my wound torn into with wickedly sharp nails, I clutched at my leg, and I stared at the bizarre scene in front of me.

I watched, my eyes widening, as Magdalena brought that bloody finger away from Layne's neck, and then slowly, carefully, as if she were tasting a dollop of whipped cream, she licked the blood off her fingertip.

Layne stared at her, breathing slow and long and deep in her gut, taking Magdalena in with those complicated eyes, her gaze unwavering, glittering in the darkness of the entryway.

"Disgusting," said Magdalena mildly, licking the blood off her lips with a long sigh and shaking her head. "But then, I've always found the blood of *animals* repulsive."

Layne began to breathe heavily, the silver ropes holding her up creaking as sweat sparkled on her forehead. She gazed at Magdalena through the jet-black hair that had fallen in front of her eyes, then lifted her face further, tilting her chin up. Her voice came out like a croak: "What are you going to do with Grayson?" she asked slowly, carefully. "Hold her for ransom?"

Grayson? Me? What the hell was she talking about? Frustration eating through the ache, I managed to pull myself up to one knee, grabbing one of the crutches and propelling myself to my feet with a series of awkward tugs of my leg.

"What the hell is going on?" I asked then, my voice a little shaky but loud enough to get Magdalena's attention.

She turned a little, leaning back and pivoting on her left heel, her head cast to the side as if she were a puppy trying to understand a difficult command. "I'm sorry," she said, shaking her head and wagging a finger at me. "But you're to be seen and not heard, young lady. This is your final warning."

"Elizabeth, don't," said Layne quietly. Her face was serene and cool; she even had a small, arrogant sneer on her lips as she gazed back at Magdalena, but the sheen of sweat on her forehead had grown more pronounced.

She was in tremendous pain.

I took a step backward, and then another one, angling toward the door as I felt for my phone in my pocket. It was a tiny, half-formed plan, but I was going to dart outside, press 911, and hope that someone picked up before Magdalena caught up with me. But the plan disintegrated before I could even put the first step into action. James walked through the door at that moment and closed it quietly behind him, standing impassively and staring straight ahead, his sunglasses making it impossible to see his eyes.

And out of the shadows, as if this were an odd reunion, stepped the repairwoman, rounding one of the Roman columns. The name stitched on her jumper had been Sheila, I remembered, as she smiled at me that creepy, fake smile. Her teeth were razor sharp, all of them, like a nightmare. She wasn't wearing a jumper anymore but black slacks and a pretty black cardigan that was buckled around her waist, her hair pinned perfectly in place, incongruous with her horror-movie mouth.

I glanced from James to Sheila. And then I stared at Magdalena with wide eyes, my heart racing inside of me.

"Unfortunately, my dears, I didn't call the two of you here today for my own amusement," Magdalena said, her head tilted to one side again as she grinned at me, too widely and smugly. "I'm afraid it's taken long enough for this to happen, what with the idiocy of those beneath me." Both James and Sheila visibly winced but stood to attention again, staring forward, their shoulders back as if they were soldiers and Magdalena was their general.

Magdalena stalked toward me, her heels clicking on the floor. I stood my ground the best that I could, my good leg shaking beneath me but still holding me up. I didn't know what to expect—a blow? I braced myself, waiting for impact, but when Magdalena reached me, she simply stood in front of me, smiling widely.

It was then that I realized that *her* teeth were pointed, too. Sharp and glittering in her mouth like diamonds, her incisors fanged.

I took a deep breath. My entire body was shaking now, but I still managed to stand, still managed to glance over Magdalena's shoulder at Layne, hanging between the Roman columns like she'd been beaten and hung up to die. I shuddered, my heart aching, wishing I could reach her, aching to touch her, comfort her. I stared Magdalena down.

"Is this some kind of sick joke?" I managed weakly, my words growling in my throat.

"No, no joke," said Magdalena with a soft chuckle. "It isn't, dear. Well. Maybe it is a *little* funny." She leaned forward, and she searched my eyes with her own wide, unblinking ones that narrowed as she tilted her head back. Then she laughed, laughed like she'd just been told the most hilarious one-liner. It was bizarre, and my heart rose into my throat.

But her laughter stopped just as suddenly, and her incisors, right in front of me, as I *watched*, grew longer. Sharper.

"Hold still," she said quietly, her eyes glittering.

"Magdalena," Layne growled out into the perfect stillness. She choked out the word, blood dripping over her lips as she shook her head, panting. She leaned toward us, against her ropes. "Magdalena, *don't*. There's no reason for you to do this. You know that a ransom makes more sense. It'll get you exactly what you want, anyway, without..."

She trailed off as Magdalena paused, paused and turned to look inquisitively at Layne. My heart was pounding so quickly in my chest, and I still half-believed that this was a dream, even as I heard the soft drips of Layne's blood falling to the marble floor, even as I watched

Magdalena's fangs glitter in the half-light of the entryway.

But I couldn't fully convince myself that I was dreaming. I was in too much pain. This felt too real, too hard, too horrible.

Magdalena, with her long, sharp fangs, looked just like a...

I took a deep breath, my blood running cold.

"Vampire," I whispered into the stillness.

Somewhere, far away, I could hear the general commotion of Sunday afternoon traffic in Boston. Somewhere, a cabbie (probably) laid on his horn, and the tinny sound of it echoed in the streets. But here in the unnaturally cold, dark entryway of this stone mansion, my breath came out in front of me like a ghost as I sighed out, and the sound of blood dripping was the loudest thing in the room. The world was bustling far away. The world was safe far away. And it was not safe here and now.

Magdalena turned a little, her eyes bright as she gazed back at me with her unnaturally wide smile. "Yes," she said, like she was speaking to a very small child. "*Vampire*. What's so terribly funny about all of this is that you're hearing it from me, dear," she said, grinning wickedly. "And not from your own father."

"Magdalena," said Layne again, keeping her voice steady and low. "He'll give it to you if you give Elizabeth back in exchange, unharmed. You know he will." And then she said, softly, the world desperate, "*Please.*"

"Ah, but that's where you're wrong," said Magdalena, steamrolling right over Layne's words and smiling without a single trace of warmth at Layne as she took a step toward me, her high heels making a smart click against the marble. Magdalena held out her hand to me, her blood-red nails long and glinting in the rays that drifted down through the wide, diamond-paned windows far above us. "I don't want it as a *gift*. I will take it as it was always meant to be taken. With brutal, violent force."

I had no idea what they were talking about. But

Layne was standing there, tied to columns, bleeding all over the pretty floor, and Magdalena—a woman I'd known since I was a kid—was sprouting teeth a vampire bat would envy, and I was trying to stand upright and failing, because the pain from my wound was making it difficult to see straight...and everything, just then, seemed impossible, and vastly over my head.

Through the thin fabric of my slip and skirt, blood began to seep, leaking down my leg. Great. I took a deep, lightheaded breath, and I hung on for dear life to the courage that I drew from...somewhere.

"What about my father?" I asked then, drawing myself as tall as I possibly could. I held my head up defiantly as Magdalena took a few steps closer, with a wide, bright smile.

"It's *because* of him," she said slowly, carefully, "that I'm going to kill you."

My blood roared through me as I glanced past Magdalena at Layne. Layne hung there, between the columns, but she held herself up, her chin lifted and her jaw set. Her head was raised in arrogance; there was a hard glint to her eyes, and even as the blood gently *plinked* off her neck and her forehead and her face, she held my gaze unwaveringly, with bright, glittering eyes.

Where the silver ropes cut into her hands and ankles, it looked as if her flesh was burned, blood seeping down from the wounds there. There was so much red in the sterile black and white of the room.

"Elizabeth," said Layne slowly, carefully, gritting her teeth together from the pain. "*Run.*"

"There's nowhere for her to run *to*, silly girl," said Magdalena, as she glanced with mild interest back at Layne. "And it's all your fault that she's in this predicament, anyway, so this should be even more enjoyable, to *kill* her in front of *you*."

Magdalena reached out between us, and she brushed her fingertips over my skirted thigh, bringing up her now red fingers to her mouth and licking my blood off of them with her pink tongue, holding my eyes as she did so with a wide, wild grin.

"Don't you *touch* her," Layne snarled, and she jerked forward, pulling at her restraints.

A few things happened then, all at once. Just like yesterday in my kitchen, just like when we were held up at gunpoint a few nights ago, power and heat seemed to radiate off of Layne in a big burst of energy. Sheila and James both took a step away from her, staring at her with trepidation before resuming their stony looks.

And the ropes creaked ominously, the Roman columns actually shifting. They were solid marble and *huge*. It wasn't possible...

"I'm afraid I'm too old for your tricks to work on me, Layne, dear," Magdalena purred, turning back to me and licking one of her still bloody fingers slowly as she considered me. "And I have to tell you that this ends now. I'm tired of waiting. And I've been waiting so long..."

Magdalena reached for me. Like a snake, her upper body darted forward too quickly, encircling my waist with one arm and my shoulders with another, her thin arms as strong and sinewy as steel cables. She threw back her head, and somehow, impossibly, her sharpened teeth grew even longer as she licked them, as she breathed out in euphoria, her eyes rolling back in her head.

And behind Magdalena, there came a thunderous growl.

It was as if there were an earthquake. But that's impossible; there are never earthquakes in Boston. But still, the two Roman columns that were flanking Layne seemed to start to waver, back and forth, back and forth, as Layne lunged against them and the constraints that bound her to them, the silver ropes—*metal* ropes, I was beginning to realize—screaming in protest. Layne lunged forward again and again, blood dripping from her wrists, from her ankles, but Magdalena ignored her utterly, held me tightly, and breathed out again.

Magdalena lowered her head down as sensually as if she were about to kiss me, but she went past my face, past my mouth and brushed her lips against the skin of my neck, her cold mouth making a violent shiver move through me as fear, cold and insistent, filled me entirely.

There was a bright blossom of pain so intense and piercing against my neck. I felt myself falling backward into darkness.

And somewhere, as if from far away, there came a...howl?

It was low and deep and guttural, perhaps the most animalistic, savage thing I'd ever heard in my entire life, and the howl itself seemed to enter me, shaking me to my very bones.

I fell hard against the floor, my body thudding against the cold marble as if I'd fallen from stories above, not a few feet, and I saw stars, but, somehow, miraculously, I didn't black out. Confused, and with the planet spinning beneath me, I pushed myself up to my hands and knees, even as my leg buckled beneath me in a riot of exquisite pain. I lifted my head, blinked about a hundred times and tried desperately to understand what I was seeing.

Because this is what I *thought* I was seeing:

Magdalena was pinned to the floor on her back, thrashing and snapping her too-sharp mouth up at what was pinning her.

Which was a wolf.

The wolf on top of Magdalena was as tall as a horse, with a shaggy silver-gray pelt that shimmered in the half-light of the entryway, and a large, lupine head that tapered down to intense sharp, white fangs that were now very much exposed and snapping at Magdalena's face, just as Magdalena was comically snapping up at her. The wolf's big paws were pinned against Magdalena's shoulders, claws digging into the exposed skin there, and the wolf's bushy white tail curved over them both.

I stared at the scene in horror, my heartbeat thundering through me.

But everything seemed to stop when the wolf gazed my way.

Her eyes were hazel. As I watched, the deep brown seemed to shift right in front of me to red.

I looked to the Roman columns.

The silver ropes swung from them, limp and torn at the ends, empty.

Layne was gone.

I pieced everything together, even as the wolf turned her attentions back to Magdalena. Magdalena, despite the fact that she was small and lithe, screeched in protest, and had the strength to throw the wolf off of her, using her thin arms to push against the shaggy beast's chest as if the wolf weighed no more than a small dog.

The wolf leapt backwards and landed upright on four paws, still snapping her teeth, and when Magdalena rose to her feet, the wolf and the woman squared off, the wolf growling savagely, all of the silver hackles on her back raised, and Magdalena crouching, snarling herself, teeth supernaturally long and wickedly sharp as they flashed in the light.

James and Sheila were nowhere to be seen.

Pure adrenaline pumped through me as I backed away from the wolf and Magdalena. I lifted up my right crutch, realizing I was close enough to hit the woman in the back of the head. I'd often wondered, before this moment, if circumstances were terrible enough, whether I could harm another living being. But as Magdalena snarled an inhuman sound at the wolf, an inhuman sound that made every single hair I possessed stand on end and a violent shiver move through me, I didn't even think about what I was doing. I hefted up the crutch and let it swing through the air with all my strength.

After all, I'd never considered what I might do against an opponent who wasn't necessarily *human*.

The crutch connected with Magdalena as if she were a brick wall and bounced off of her, the impact roaring through my arms and making me drop the crutch as I fell to one knee, crying out. My wound twisted and opened. Magdalena remained standing in front of me as solidly as if I'd brushed a feather against her. So instead of falling to the side unconscious, like I'd hoped she would, Magdalena turned to face me, deepening her smile, which looked freakishly terrible with her red lips and her long fangs. She raised an arm with sharp nails as if to backhand me.

The wolf stepped between Magdalena and me with a deep, guttural snarl.

"You can't protect her anymore," the vampire hissed. "She is going to die, and I'm going to make you watch. And then I'm going to kill *you*—"

But the wolf had leapt forward, and in a single, terrible instant, her large jaws clamped firmly around Magdalena's neck.

There was a snapping sound.

Magdalena crumpled in a bloody heap to the ground, looking for all the world like a life-size doll, and the wolf sprang to the side, landing heavily on her paws. The wolf stood there for a long moment as she licked her blood-flecked snout. The beast breathed out, shaking herself.

Magdalena made a bubbling, wheezing sound; then she fell completely silent.

The wolf lifted her lupine head and gazed at me with those big red eyes. Eyes that, as I watched, changed from red to hazel...a beautiful, familiar hazel.

My breath came fast in my throat, my heart roared blood through me as I said, in the smallest voice, "Layne?"

The wolf hung her head, her eyes leaving my gaze. And, as I watched, the wolf became smaller, the nose shorter, the fur seemingly growing backwards, into skin that looked remarkably human...

And then there, kneeling on the ground in front of me, was a bloody, battered Layne, naked and dripping blood from the wounds in her neck, on her wrists, on her ankles.

Beside her, the heap of body that had once been Magdalena twitched.

"That won't hold her long," said Layne gruffly, rising and picking up some stray clothes that, as she moved into them, I realized were hers. It took her only a moment to get dressed again, and then she was striding quickly toward me with only the slightest of limps as she left a trail of blood drops behind her. She held out a hand to me, letting out a deep breath. "Elizabeth, we have to go."

I winced away from her as she reached my side. But Layne didn't seem to notice, or she might have, because she set her jaw and then shook her head slightly, leaning down and picking me up again, just like that day in Dogtown, her warm arms encircling me.

Carrying me, she stalked past Magdalena toward the front door.

But she paused before she opened it. She leaned down a little and, shifting me in her arms, she picked up my violin case.

The Protector

Chapter 13: The Choice

It must have been an odd sight, a bloody woman carrying another bloody woman down the street, their clothes disheveled, Layne's hair matted and her arms and legs leaving a trail of blood behind us. I clung to her neck and concentrated on breathing as the wound in my leg finally seemed to seal. But if we looked strange, or like some sort of nightmare vision, at least there weren't many people out to see us, and we made it to the parking garage without incident, other than an old man staring at us from a cafe chair, folding his paper in front of him, his mouth open and his eyes wide, as if he'd seen a ghost.

We didn't say anything to each other until we were safely in the car, the doors locked, peaceful silence falling between us.

"Elizabeth..." began Layne, taking a deep breath and tightening her hands on the wheel, the keys still in her jeans pocket and not in the ignition. There was so much dried blood and grime on her hands. I stared at them and blinked. "I'm...very sorry you had to see that," she whispered then. And she glanced at me, her eyes dark and pained.

"I just... I don't understand what's going on," I said, my voice breaking. "Was she... Are you..." I didn't know how to put everything into words, and my broken syllables hung in the air between us.

Layne bit her lip, shoving a blood-caked bit of hair out of her face. She shook her head. "I can't," she said simply. "It's at your father's discretion to tell you. Or not."

"Tell me *what?* What are you talking about? Why does everyone keep bringing up my father?" I knew I was nearing hysterics, but if I didn't get answers, and soon, I didn't know how much more of this I could take.

Layne's cell phone, from her pocket, chirped.

"Your ring tone sounds like a chickadee?" I asked her incredulously. With a sheepish grin that was absolutely incongruous to her bloodstained face, Layne tugged her phone out of her pocket and pressed it to her ear.

"Yes, sir. She's safe. Right away," she said between pauses. She glanced at me as she ended the call, and then she carefully reached across the space between us and took up my left hand, threading her dirty fingers through my dirty fingers, both of us bloody, but her warm skin against mine so comforting in that moment that I shuddered a little, a tiny bit of my tension leaving me.

"Your father wants to see you," Layne said finally, searching my face. "And I think he's going to tell you."

"Tell me what?" I asked miserably.

But she shook her head and started the car.

The drive to my father's house passed in a blur. When Layne pulled up to the building, there was no one to greet us on the porch, the wind making the baskets of pansies that hung from the columns swing back and forth against the ominous, graying sky.

When we walked into the entryway, there was no one there waiting for us, no Al with her cart of tea and baked goods, no Ben with his driver's cap on backwards and a big grin on his face. The room was empty and cold.

Layne had helped me hobble up the stairs and into the house, but now, again, she picked me up effortlessly, and I made no protest. Through the long hallways, she carried me, until we'd reached my father's study.

The massive wooden door was shut, and Layne set me down gently against it. She lifted up her hand, and once, twice, three times, Layne knocked lightly on the door.

From the other side came my father's voice, impossible to read. "Enter," he said quietly.

Layne paused for a long moment, her hand still folded and resting against the door. She didn't reach for the doorknob but stayed, her hand against the wood, closing her eyes and taking a deep breath as she lowered her face, bit her lip.

I turned to her, like she contained a gravity that I had to answer to. She was so close, so warm. Blood still dripped down her face, and she was probably in so much pain, but still, *still*...she turned, lifted her chin, and Layne stared deeply into my eyes with her own flashing ones, her jaw set in a hard line.

"Elizabeth," she said simply, softly. I'd never heard her voice so quiet. "You know now. About me. But you *don't* know," she whispered, searching my face, "about yourself. You don't know..." She swallowed, and then she was actually blinking back tears. She rubbed the back of her hand angrily over her right eye, shaking her head as she growled deep in her throat. "I'm sorry," she said then, and the two words sounded so broken.

I wasn't entirely certain what had just happened. I wasn't certain what I'd just seen. It seemed surreal. Impossible. But here I was, and here Layne was, and we were standing together. Broken and battered but whole and somehow, impossibly *alive*, and we were together.

I moved purely on instinct when I put my arms around her shoulders and tugged her closer to me. I didn't think as I stood up on my one good leg, on tiptoe, and pressed my mouth against her bloody one.

She tasted salty and warm, metallic and feverish. But we kissed, anyway, the two of us, pressing tightly against each other because we'd both been through hell that afternoon.

And I supposed now that I knew her secret.

Even if I didn't know mine yet.

Layne broke away from me, her strong arms around

my waist as, again, she bent her handsome head and pressed her forehead against my shoulder. She breathed out brokenly, choking down a hoarse sob, tears standing clearly in her eyes. "When you go into that room," she whispered, "your father will tell you everything." She said the words so softly, so brokenly, and my heart ached inside of me. "And it will *change* everything," she said.

"It won't," I told her fiercely, but she straightened, stiffened, shook her head. She rolled back her shoulders, and she took one step forward, past me.

And slowly, Layne opened the door for me to my father's office.

I clenched my hands into fists, but I couldn't put off the inevitable. I took a deep breath and stepped inside the study, Layne sliding in after me.

Alexander Grayson sat behind his desk. The desk I used to use as an imaginary ship when I was little. Now, he sat there, pale as a ghost, face contorted in worry, and he stood quickly, coming around from behind the desk to gather me in his arms and hug me tightly.

"You're not all right," he said, staring me up and down and taking in the blood leaking down my leg, dripping from my thigh. "You're *not* all right!"

"Dad, I'm fine. I'm fine. Please don't worry—I'm okay," I told him, patting his shoulder and trying to take deep breaths. I was losing a lot of blood and starting to feel lightheaded, but I considered that the least of my troubles. Instead, I plopped down in one of the chairs in front of his desk and gazed up at my father with a frown. "Now…please. What's going on?" I asked simply. My voice sounded so tired.

He glanced sidelong at Layne, his eyes widening when he took in her appearance, and then my father—my incredibly sweet father—pulled out the other chair for her, which Layne gratefully took, depositing herself down in a heap of limbs, resting her head on the back of the chair and groaning as she stared upright at the ceiling, as if she felt no need to ever get up again.

My father folded his hands nervously in front of him, and then he cleared his throat. "I'm going to say this as simply as I can," said my father then, leaning back against his desk as he looked at me with grave eyes, all traces of nerves gone, and resignation apparent. "Elizabeth, sweetheart, you need to know... You almost died today because of a promise I made to your mother."

I watched him, my heart starting to turn inside of me, even as I twisted my mother's ring on my finger.

"Your mother died because she made a choice," said my father then, his face contorted in pain. "She had that choice. She asked me to keep that from you, to spare you from it. To let you live a normal, happy life. And you have, Elizabeth, haven't you?"

"I don't understand," I whispered.

"This is so much harder than I thought," he groaned, threading fingers through his hair and rubbing at his chin. He gazed at me thoughtfully. "Elizabeth, your mother died because they were trying to get to *me*. I couldn't protect her, and she was killed."

I stared at him. "She was killed...by the fishing moguls?" I managed weakly.

"No," he said, and then my father gazed down at me with such a sad expression, I could feel his heart breaking from where I sat. "She was killed by vampires."

Hearing the word made me feel sick. And though my dad was a funny kind of guy, I knew that he absolutely, positively wasn't joking.

"I'm a vampire, sweetheart," said my father with a small shrug and a wince. "And for many, many years, I have kept that fact from you. And I have kept from you that I am also the leader of the Nocturne Council of Boston. Which means that I'm the leader of this whole area. And that others don't particularly like it, and have been trying to oust me for a very long time. They got your mother, because your mother didn't want to...to change, to become like me, and because she was human, she was an easy target." He gazed at me meaningfully for a long moment.

"What are you saying?" I whispered.

"They won't stop until I am destroyed. And now they have discovered that I have a weakness. They think it is easiest to destroy me through...well, you. Your mother made me promise not to tell you the truth. She wanted a normal life for you, and I respected that. But now that you've almost died...I hope she forgives me." My father crouched down in front of me, searching my face. "Elizabeth," he said softly. "There's only one way to keep you safe now."

Layne glanced at me, a single tear running down her cheek, across her clenched jaw and falling onto her arm, mixing with the blood there.

"I can change you, sweetheart, and you'll be safe forever," said my father, searching my face. "I can turn you into a vampire."

Chapter 14: Inevitable

"You can turn me," I repeated, my mouth suddenly dry, "into a vampire?"

Dad flicked his gaze from me to Layne, but she wasn't looking at him—she was staring at the floor, her jaw clenched, her hands dangling from the arms of the chair, drops of blood falling from her long fingers onto my father's lush rug.

"This is all...a little hard to swallow," is what I realized my mouth was already saying before I could even think about it. I sounded a little high pitched, and—if I'm being honest—a tiny bit hysterical. "Dad, how in the world are you a *vampire*? Aren't they just... Aren't they only in books and movies? And...and chocolaty breakfast cereals?"

My father blinked at me, and then he was actually laughing, but it was a small, nervous chuckle, and it didn't last very long; he leaned back on his desk. "Believe it or not, that's kind of offensive, honey," he said with a wince, but I shook my head adamantly.

"You've *got* to give me a better explanation than this," I told him fiercely, swallowing. "I was almost killed by a woman with sharp teeth, a woman who had Layne trussed up to some columns with metal rope, Dad. She *kidnapped* me. Why is this *happening?*"

My father sighed for a very long moment, a finger to his brow, like he was trying to think up a solution to this problem, but that solution was not forthcoming. But then he sank down in front of me again, crouching right before my chair, his arm on his knee as he held my gaze.

And when he smiled at me now…

Well.

He had fangs.

I stared at my father, and I felt the world drop out from under me.

These were actual fangs in his mouth, not the nice, normal, *human* teeth that he'd been sporting a moment ago. No, these were the kind of fangs that Magdalena had when she was trying to bite me. Teeth so long and wickedly sharp that they could tear through anything.

They could tear into human flesh. And those teeth were in my dad's mouth. My *dad*.

It was true. I sat there, and I stared at my father's pointy incisors as the realization that this was all *real*, and all *really* happening to me hit me with the finality of a massive semi careening out of control. There were no more "rational" explanations I could use to dismiss all of this; I could attempt no more convincing to my brain.

My father crouched in front of me with fangs.

He was really a vampire.

And that meant that everything I thought I knew had just been blown apart.

"You're a vampire." My voice was dull as I spoke those words, and he nodded tiredly, standing up and buttoning up his suit jacket again smoothly. "You're a vampire," I repeated, as he leaned back against his desk, casting a sidelong glance at Layne.

"And your bodyguard…" he remarked dryly, folding his arms in front of himself, "is a werewolf."

"Yeah." My voice managed to croak out that word, then was a teeny, tiny bit sharp for the rest of it: "I figured that out when she transformed into a wolf to save my life."

But the pained expression on my father's face took all of the sharpness out of me in an instant, and I was suddenly on my feet (or, you know, *gradually* on my feet. My thigh was still bleeding, my wound—freshly opened—

needed to be restitched, and on top of all of that, it had been one *hell* of a day, so "suddenly" was going to be out of my vocabulary for little awhile), and I was hopping over to him on my good foot, wrapping my father tightly in an embrace. As always, Dad was cold, literally cold, when I hugged him tight, the cold radiating through his suit jacket and into me and making me shiver from the chill. He'd always been this way, and my entire life, he'd explained it away as having poor blood circulation. Which, laughably, I'd always bought.

But now I knew that he was cold to the touch because he was a *vampire*, and that kind of shook me to the core. Because if my father was a vampire, what the hell did that mean for everything *else* out of fiction books and fairy tales?

"So, wait a second. Are aliens real?" I asked weakly, and my father chuckled, holding me out at arm's length.

"Let's not get ahead of ourselves there, Scully," he said with a wink, and then his face took on a more serious cast as he inhaled deeply. "I know this is all very overwhelming, sweetheart," he said, searching my gaze, "but I was very serious about changing you into one of us. You don't understand... The political climate has been eroding, and—"

"Political climate?" I cleared my throat. I assumed he wasn't talking about presidential races or political parties.

"I am the leader of the Nocturne Council of Northeast America," said my father, as he lifted my chin, holding me in his sights. "And this means that I have a tremendous amount of power at my disposal. Power that some undesirables would stop at absolutely nothing to attain."

"Whoa, whoa, back it up, Dad. How are you the *leader*?" I asked him, searching his gaze, too. I wanted to know everything, but he was already shaking his head, his lips pursed.

"I'll tell you sometime. I'll tell you the whole story," he promised. "But right now, you have to know that things have been changing recently. Magdalena wants to take my leadership, and she will take it by force. She knows now, absolutely, that if she gets to you, I will be weakened, and she has come into enough power very recently to make good on her threats. She will be relentless in her attacks against you, and unless you are a vampire yourself, you are completely vulnerable to those attacks.

"As a human, she could do anything she wanted to you… She has demonstrated that she is cunning, that she was capable of luring you to her house, that she was capable of subduing Layne—"

At that, both Layne and I started talking at once, drowning out my father, and he raised his hands, his eyes wide.

"Ladies, please," he said, and his voice was very tired. "Layne, I know that you did your job superbly. I am not faulting you on that at all. Instead, I am very humbly in your debt. If you had not stopped Magdalena, my daughter wouldn't be alive right now. I am forever grateful to you. But Magdalena did get hold of you and was able to subdue you for a short amount of time, and perhaps next time, with even more men and women at her disposal, ready to die for her at a moment's notice, she might actually succeed in not only capturing you, but killing you, as well. And as for you, Elizabeth," he said, turning his heavy gaze on me, "the next time Magdalena sees you, she will not dwell on theatrics or waste any time. She will kill you outright. Instantly." His voice took on a pleading tone as he leaned forward. "I can't keep you safe anymore. You *must* change into a vampire, sweetheart." My father frowned deeply, sadly. "Or you will die."

I'd sat back down a moment ago because my leg was killing me, and in my haze of pain and exhaustion, I couldn't hold myself up, but now I sagged farther back into my chair, feeling the weight of my body…and the weight of everything that was yet to come. I took a deep breath, and I leaned my head on the chair, and I stared up at the ceiling of my father's office.

I'd stared up at that ceiling perhaps a million times before. When I was little, my father would bring me into this office to comfort me about my mother's death, and to scold me when I'd been bad (which, as a neurotic, straight As, anxious kid, wasn't that often), and I'd always stared up at that ceiling then. It was comforting, looking up the bookcases that towered around me, that had stood in this room since long before I was a born, and—I was assuming—would be here long after I was gone.

They usually brought me a sense of peace, of permanence, with their old, dusty books. Even the ceiling comforted me with its dull, antique white surface. It was something soothing, calming, something that was always there.

But nothing seemed capable of soothing me tonight.

"It's...it's impossible, that decision," I finally told my father, straightening in the chair and holding his gaze as I sighed out. "I... Dad, I just can't. Not right now. I'm bleeding. I'm exhausted. I almost just died..." There was still so much adrenaline racing through my body that, when I glanced down at my hands gripping the chair arms, I realized they were shaking uncontrollably. I gripped a little harder. "I can't do this," I told him, swallowing. "Not right now."

My father's jaw tightened, and his eyes flashed. Then he lifted his chin, and he gave me his most disapproving frown. "Elizabeth, you have to know that if you don't make this decision right now, you're in grave danger. I can't keep you safe, and that means that, at any moment, you're susceptible to attack. And that is unacceptable."

"Grave danger? I'm here. I'm safe," I told him, but my father glanced over his shoulder at that moment, out the window, his eyes narrowed further, as if he'd just heard something.

Dad had several windows in his study, windows that were just as tall as the bookshelves, and they looked out onto his prize rose garden, with its well-manicured rows of prize-winning rose bushes. It was nighttime now, and the moon was directly overhead, which cast the rose garden in a romantic, lovely glow. I'd looked out on that rose garden so many times, and those beautiful rows of rose bushes had never made me feel anything but happy. The garden was a lovely place.

But when I glanced out the window now, following my father's gaze, I was filled with dread.

I was beginning to realize that vampires move very quickly and stealthily. They could attack rapidly, moving much faster than a human being could ever dream of moving. Right now, there could be vampires out there, out in that pleasant rose garden, lurking in the shadows. I wouldn't see them until it was much too late. Even if I was surrounded by people who loved me and cared about me and wanted to protect me…all it would take was one heartbeat, a vampire moving in an unexpected way, reaching me before the others could move…and then it'd all be over.

If my father was nervous about my safety, perhaps he had every right to be.

I sat there, the hairs on the back of my neck rising as I took a deep breath.

I knew, then, that I was really in danger.

"This is ridiculous." I buried my face in my hands and shuddered a little, trying to quell my tears. God, I wanted to cry; the adrenaline needed some sort of outlet, but I knew that if I started to cry now, I wasn't going to be able to stop. Being kidnapped, seeing Layne tied to those columns, seeing the vampire's body, her broken neck, all that blood… Knowing that the vampire, even *with* her broken neck, was going to come back to life… It was just too much for me. I needed a release, but I also needed all of my wits about me. So I took another deep breath, and I blinked back the tears.

"Dad," I said then, lifting my face and letting out that deep breath slowly. "What are my options? *Are* there options?"

Layne, apart from arguing with my father for that one moment, hadn't spoken a single word since we'd entered my father's study. She sat in the chair, slouched unhappily, her fingers gripping the chair arms, too, and she would occasionally glance my way, but her face was hardened into a mask that was incredibly difficult for me to read. Her eyes were haunted, hunted, and sad, and I didn't know what was going on in that head of hers. But when I glanced sidelong at her now, she lifted her chin, and her flashing eyes met mine. And then she glanced back up at my dad.

"Mr. Grayson, sir," she said, her low voice quiet as she let out a long breath, leaning forward in the chair. "Elizabeth's right. This is… This is too big of a decision for her to make right now. She needs time to understand what she's getting into."

My father stood straight and tall, and sorrow passed over his face as he nodded to Layne. He turned to me. "Elizabeth, you must know that it is inevitable, your changing into one of us. You are not safe if you do not change, and whether your mother wanted you to know or not, now that you *do*, you must also know that it is your birthright. You can follow in my footsteps, sweetheart," he said, his voice so soft I almost didn't hear the last few words.

"I…I know," I told him, my voice quiet. "But I can't do this. Not right now. I need…time. Time to come to grips with everything. Time to…" I tried to search for the right words. "Dad, I know nothing about being a vampire. I don't know anything about *any* of this. My whole world was just turned upside-down."

My father pushed off from the desk, nodding quietly. He had his chin in his hands, and he stroked his little beard, as if that was helping him think. Layne said nothing. She'd sat back in her chair again, and she was staring moodily down at the floor, her jaw clenched, her eyes flashing, and her face filled with pain. That much I could read easily. Layne had said, in the corridor outside my

205

father's study, before we kissed, that what my father was about to tell me would change everything between us. And, obviously, learning that my father was some sort of vampire king (that's what I'd gleaned from his information so far) was pretty overwhelming.

But it had nothing to do with Layne.

Did it?

Finally, my father cleared his throat, and he crouched down in front of me again, his elbow on his knee as he held my gaze. "I understand," he told me quietly. "And I know what to do."

I raised a brow, but then he was standing smoothly again before I could ask him specifics, and he stepped aside as he cleared his throat, gesturing toward the back of his office. "Tasuki, can you please come here?"

And out of the shadows, from the far corner of my father's office, the darkness where the single lamp on his desk could not penetrate, came a hooded figure wearing a stylish black coat with a large hood that I would recognize anywhere.

It was Mikagi Tasuki, the most famous violinist in the world. And she was in my father's study...

Why?

Mikagi removed her hood with gloved fingers and stood tall beside my father, burying her hands in her coat pockets and rocking back on her tall heels with a wicked grin on her face. "Hello, Elizabeth," she said, her thickly accented voice warm as she cocked her head a little, her grin deepening. "I told you we would meet again."

In the chair beside me, I could feel Layne stiffen, and when I glanced sidelong at her, I could see that her lip went up and over her teeth, very similar to the snarl of a wolf.

Oh, yeah. Because she *was* a wolf.

Wow, that was going to take some getting used to.

"What are you doing here, Ms. Tasuki?" I asked her, surprised, but she started shaking her head immediately.

"If we are going to be seeing more of each other, you must call me Mikagi," she said, in a tone that brooked no argument.

"Um...okay." I flicked a glance at my father. I'd be seeing more of her?

"Mikagi Tasuki," said my father, raising a brow and gesturing to Mikagi, "is...one of us."

"One of..." My eyes began to widen, and then I glanced at Mikagi again.

When she smiled at me this time, her grin wide, her incisors were pointed, sharp.

A vampire. Mikagi Tasuki, the most famous violinist in the *world*, was a vampire.

That...would also take some getting used to.

"How...why..." I began, but Mikagi was already chuckling, a warm sound that made me glance her way. When she looked at me again, her eyes were warm, too.

"Questions, questions," she said, shaking her head with finality, "but you do not have time to ask them. We must go now."

"Go?" I asked weakly, but Layne was already standing, and when she glanced at Mikagi... Well, it certainly didn't look like there was any love lost between the werewolf and the vampire. Mikagi returned Layne's frown with one of her own, her dark eyes flashing with animosity.

"Mikagi is going to be traveling with you and Layne tonight, sweetheart," said my father with a small smile as he placed his hand on my shoulder. "If you do not want to change into a vampire tonight—I understand that's a big decision to make, and I want you to be able to make it with all of the information you need—then you need to go somewhere safe. So Mikagi and Layne are going to be taking you to that somewhere safe."

"I owe your father a favor," said Mikagi, her head tilted to the side as she stepped forward smoothly, moving between Layne and me as my father stepped back from us. "And I will repay it this way. How badly are you hurt?" she asked, looking me up and down.

I was much too tired, and heaven knows I'd lost a lot of blood, but I was apparently not tired or wounded enough to stop from noticing that Mikagi's eyes on me...they lingered.

Not for the first time, I wondered if the kiss against my neck when the orchestra lights went out...that kiss in the dark...

Had it really been Mikagi?

I began to blush. After everything that had happened tonight, there were some universal truths that were starting to make the blood move a little quicker through me. And one of them was that I'd been a Mikagi fangirl since the moment she came on the international music scene, with her violin music that brought everyone together...

And she was currently giving me the once-over. Well, possibly. And I had intense feelings for Layne, feelings that I would never betray, not even if there was the possibility of anything between Mikagi and me—which there was probably *not*.

But if your music idol was making eyes at you...well, it was bound to make you blush. So I was blushing *profusely*, and when Mikagi sank down in a crouch beside me, the black skirt of her dress and long coat swirling out around her as she settled in place, I gulped down a little air as she leaned forward, her hand hovering over—but not touching—my thigh.

"I think I need new stitches," I told her, wincing as Mikagi glanced down at her hand over my thigh...and then she brushed her fingers against my leg. It was a very gentle movement, and there was hardly any pressure beneath her hand, but I blanched as the pain from that simple touch ricocheted through my body so violently that I almost passed out, white stars poking at the edges of my vision with great insistence.

"*Don't*," came Layne's voice, menacing and with a

great growl, but Mikagi raised a single brow after quickly removing her gloved fingers from my thigh and glanced over her shoulder at Layne.

She gave Layne a look then that made my blood—previously rushing hotly through me—run cold.

It was a look of such disgust, her mouth turned up cruelly at the corners as she sneered at Layne. Mikagi rose smoothly in one graceful motion, and then she was standing almost nose to nose with Layne.

"Sit, dog," Mikagi murmured, her cruel grin deepening. "And heel."

Layne and Mikagi in that moment, squared off as they were, their hands curling into fists at their sides, looked like they were about to fight...but then my father's voice broke through the tension.

"Mikagi." I glanced up in surprise at my father. I don't think I'd ever heard his voice sound so stern. Mikagi, however, was unimpressed and grinned over her shoulder at him, her incisors pressing against her lower lip.

"I will protect your daughter, Alexander," she said, and smoothly, lifting her chin. "You have my word." And then she bent down to me, and in one seamless motion, I was picked up in gentle arms, and she was carrying me exactly as Layne had done. I peered over Mikagi's shoulder at Layne, Layne who followed after the vampire with her mouth set in a thin, hard line, her eyes flashing as she balled her hands into tighter fists but followed the both of us, anyway.

"Take care of yourself, Alexander," said Mikagi over her shoulder. "I swear, I will keep her safe."

"Dad?" I said, and Mikagi stopped, turning so that I could look back at my father, my father who stood, leaning against his desk like he was exhausted, his entire face wracked with so much worry that my heart broke for him. "Where...where am I going?" I asked him, my voice small.

My father straightened at that, and he tried his best to offer me a reassuring smile. "Somewhere safe, sweetheart. Somewhere with people that I would trust with my life, who will protect you no matter what."

"And *where* is that?" I persisted, as he stepped forward, crossing the distance between us to press a kiss to my forehead.

"To Maine," he said, and he nodded with finality. "You will be safe in Maine, in Eternal Cove. At the Sullivan Hotel."

Chapter 15: Road Trip

I couldn't remember the last time that I had left Massachusetts, and I certainly couldn't remember the last time I went to Maine. Working in the Boston Philharmonic Orchestra was a dream come true, but it also meant that I had to work tirelessly to remain at the top of my field, and that required practice every day, tough concert schedules. I didn't really have time for vacations.

I wanted to get out, do things…but time passed, and I kept working and living for "someday." And now someday was apparently today. I just never thought it would come about quite like this.

Mikagi and Layne stopped at my apartment first so that I could pack my things. Which put me in a pretty strange mood, to be honest. Because as I was looking around at my sparse apartment, my apartment that I'd lived in for so many years, I realized that this might be the last time I was seeing it through human eyes.

Or it might be the last time I ever saw it at all. Since I could be murdered at any moment, apparently. A fact that, no matter how hard I tried to focus on the task at hand, was never far from my mind.

We were taking the sports car that Mikagi had rented when she arrived in Boston to drive up to Eternal Cove (whatever that was; I'd never heard of the place). So space was at a premium, and my packing options were pretty limited. I couldn't take my other violins, as much as I wanted to. I settled on the violin I had just bought as the one musical instrument I would bring along, leaving it by the apartment door so that we wouldn't forget it.

I dragged my little suitcase out from the closet with Layne's help and filled it with my clothes while Layne stalked into the living room to have a word with Mikagi: a low, *tense* conversation, growling arguments between them filtering into the bedroom and making me pack all the faster. I couldn't hear what they were saying, but the tone was angry. How in the world did Layne and Mikagi know each other, and why was there this much tension between them?

We were only at my apartment for a few minutes, since I packed in record time. Soon I was ready, and we had to leave. Mikagi and Layne didn't say it as Layne picked up my suitcase and violin case, and Mikagi picked me up again, but I was assuming that they were worried one of Magdalena's people would see us at the apartment and attack…or even that Magdalena herself would appear and come after us. Which, of course, made the hairs on the back of my neck stand upright, and made me hurry probably faster than I should have as I packed.

I was still losing a lot blood, blood that dripped on the carpet as Mikagi turned, carrying me through the apartment door and into the corridor.

Once the violin and my suitcase were in Mikagi's car and I was seated in the passenger seat, Layne sullenly lounging in the backseat next to my violin, Mikagi glanced sidelong at me.

"All right," she said crisply, turning the car on with the touch of a button. "We need to get you stitched up before we leave. Can't have you bleeding on the rental," she said, with another sidelong smile.

We made a quick trip to a doctor that my father had on retainer, a really nice older gentleman with a handlebar mustache, who stitched up my thigh in his home's living room (still wearing his bed clothes; we'd obviously woken him). He did the work with minimum conversation and didn't even ask me how my stitches had become ripped out, for which I was very thankful. I was so exhausted and so in pain that I couldn't think of a good excuse. If he'd asked me, I would probably have just said "vampire," which wouldn't have been the best response, even if it was the truth.

The whole time the doctor was working on me, I watched Layne carefully. She hadn't spoken much to me at all since leaving my father's study, and I didn't know what to make of it. Obviously, Mikagi and Layne didn't see eye to eye on something and were antagonistic toward each other, but there was something else going on. Layne leaned against the far wall, her hands jammed deep into her jeans pockets, her shoulders curling forward, and her usually spiked hair flattened a little and drooping over her face. She was in profile to me, and I could see the downward sweep of her beautiful, full lips. She gave me something to concentrate on as the doctor stitched up my leg. I looked at Layne, and I felt my heart ache, rather than my thigh, and I didn't know what was bothering her...but I wanted to soothe it.

When the doctor was finished, he wiped his hands on a floral towel and handed me a bottle full of pain pills with a small smile. "Just in case," he told me with a wink, and I tossed them quickly into my purse, not wondering—or caring—where he'd gotten them. My thigh was so hot with pain that I was nauseated; there had been several moments during his stitching when I thought I would black out. But I had held Layne in my sights as something lovely to concentrate upon, to prevent myself from fainting.

The doctor had slathered my wound with something to numb it, but even through the numbness, waves of dizziness kept pounding against my head, sweeping over me.

"And the final thing? What Alexander discussed with you?" asked Mikagi when the doctor turned to her, wiping his hands again on the now-stained towel. The doctor gave her a blank look, and Mikagi turned her hand in the air, searching for the English words. "The excuse," she finally said.

"Ah, yes, I'm sorry," said the doctor, and he got up, heading over to his desk, situated in front of the window. It was an old rolltop desk, and he opened it, grabbing a piece of paper from inside. "This should help," he said, and he handed it to me.

I glanced down at the note and realized what I was looking at. It excused me from work for seven days, citing "extensive injuries" that needed time to heal and that would be exacerbated by concerts and practice. I wouldn't have to work for seven days... Injuries and vampires who wanted me dead aside, I was actually upset that I wouldn't be performing for so long. It was the longest I'd ever gone since I'd signed on to the orchestra.

"Seven days will be enough time for you to make your decision," said Mikagi, taking the paper gently from my fingers, folding it and sliding it into the breast pocket of her coat. Then she nodded her thanks to the doctor, picked me up gently in her arms, and turned to go. Layne, still standing in the shadows of the living room, stepped forward then, her eyes narrowed and challenging.

"I can carry her," said Layne in a tone that was only a little bit nicer than a growl, but Mikagi wasn't even looking at her.

"You need recovery, too, wolf," Mikagi murmured as she moved past Layne, exiting the doctor's mansion and making her way to her car.

"Yeah, wait. Layne, you need stitches, too, don't you?" I asked, as Mikagi set me in the passenger seat again, and I glanced up at Layne, my eyes wide. Layne held the passenger door open when Mikagi tried to close it, and Mikagi simply shrugged, moving back from me so that Layne could crouch beside the car, staring at me with her burning hazel eyes, so close that I could touch her easily...and I did, though I was nervous about it. I reached up, and I very gently—my fingers trembling—moved a wisp of hair behind her right ear.

Layne shuddered at that brief contact, and I did,

too. The connection that had been growing between us was getting bigger, brighter, stronger, and though there was so much left unsaid, so much pain in her for something I didn't quite understand...it didn't matter. Layne turned and gently, gently, she placed her cheek against the palm of my hand, her eyes closed. She breathed out, a great sigh of sadness, and when her eyes opened to me again, there was such pain in them that I gasped out a little.

"Did you need to get stitches?" I repeated, brushing the pad of my thumb over her warm cheek. Layne took another deep breath, breathing me in, her cheek pressed against my palm, but then she straightened a little, and our connection was broken.

"I'm all right," she told me, and she held out her wrists to me, showing the wounds that I'd definitely seen before now, where the metal had cut into her skin...but as I stared down at her wrists, I gave a little gasp.

The wounds were still there, but they did not look at all as they had a few hours ago. Instead, they appeared as if they were nearly healed. In some spots, she was completely healed.

I glanced up quickly to her face, and Layne shrugged. "Werewolves heal faster than humans," she told me gruffly, but she seemed glad to see my smile when I gave her one, a tired smile, but a smile, nonetheless. She reached out, and she took the hand that had touched her, the hand I was holding in my lap, and she squeezed it gently. "Please don't worry about me," she whispered, searching my face.

"She may look healed, but she still needs recovery time." Mikagi's tone was clipped as she slammed the driver's side door behind her, situating herself behind the wheel and rolling her shoulders back, like she was getting ready to play a performance. "Get in, wolf," she said, one brow up. "We have miles to go. You can rest while I drive."

Layne looked like she was going to say something about how *she* should be the one driving, but then her full tiredness seemed to come over her face, and she nodded, climbing into the seat behind us and leaning her head back against the seat, stretching her legs sideways in the car.

"You said…at the doctor's house…" I cleared my throat. "We're only going to be gone seven days?" I asked Mikagi and Layne. I glanced in the backseat of the car at the werewolf who raised her head and held me in her sights for a long moment, her jaw tense. But it was Mikagi who answered.

"Your father has high hopes that, surrounded by vampires, being shown what it is to be one, you will then decide that you wish to become a vampire quickly. He hopes that you'll change sooner rather than later," she said, casting me a sidelong glance.

"It's not a question. Once she meets the Sullivans…she'll change," said Layne quietly from the backseat.

And her voice, as she spoke those words, was filled with so much regret that it broke my heart.

"It's my decision to make," I began, but even as I said it, I knew—and everyone else in the car knew—that I was expressing false bravado.

"With all due respect, Elizabeth, there is no reason in the world to put off becoming a vampire," Mikagi said as she revved her sports car out onto I-95. Wow, we were leaving the city a lot faster than I'd thought. I figured I'd have a little bit more time to say goodbye to Boston. I stared out at the bright buildings as we passed them, feeling my heart rise into my throat.

"I mean, I hear what you're saying," I told Mikagi then. "But…it's *becoming a vampire*. I don't want to offend you—I have no idea what's offensive to vampires," I told her truthfully, "and I don't want to say anything that would be hurtful…but vampirism can't possibly be all sunshine and rainbows. You're a *vampire*. You drink *blood*. Don't you? Isn't that what Magdalena was about to do to me?" I asked her, covering my throat with my hand as I shuddered a little, remembering.

Mikagi wrinkled her nose and shrugged a little. "Don't you eat meat?"

"What does that have to do—"

"Same thing," she said with another shrug. "Blood is better, because we usually don't kill what we're drinking from."

"I...don't think that's the same thing at all," I began hastily, but Mikagi was glancing sidelong at me again, and her dark eyes were flashing dangerously.

"Elizabeth," she said, and her tone was very firm, "being a vampire is *phenomenal*. You are very fast, very strong... You become something like...a superhero. Yes, you hunger for blood, but that hunger can either control you, or you can fight through it and become stronger. And once you fight through that hunger...nothing can stop you."

"That," said Layne from the backseat, her voice a low growl, "is a gross oversimplification."

"Says the wolf," Mikagi snorted, passing a semi that was going too slow, the engine revving dramatically. There weren't that many people out on the road, but then, it was late at night. I watched the center lines in the highway whiz by, and I began to feel sleepy. I'd already taken some of the pain medication, and that—paired with whatever the doctor had put upon my leg to numb it—was starting to make me feel a little better, the pain throbbing much less insistently.

And though my mind was churning with questions, though terrible things had happened to me tonight, I began to fall asleep.

Before I drifted off, I reached between the seats, and I felt around behind me, searching for Layne's hand. As if, instinctively, she knew what I wanted, she threaded her fingers through mine, her hot palm against my own immensely comforting.

"Sleep," she murmured, leaning forward between the seats and brushing her lips against the side of my face as I glanced back at her, leaving a soft, lingering kiss on my cheek. "I will keep you safe," she growled. And I knew it was a promise.

Mikagi drove us into the night, and I slipped away into dreams, holding tightly to the werewolf who had saved my life.

I woke up with a start as I felt the car begin to decelerate. My entire body was stiff; every movement brought pain. I opened my eyes, blinking and looking across the dashboard, surprised to see that the sun was rising up and over the edge of the horizon.

It was morning. I'd slept through the rest of the night.

Mikagi was pulling off another highway, onto more rural roads, trees rising all around us, and she turned to smile at me as she slowed down a little more. "You've only been asleep for four hours," she said, raising a brow when I glanced at her, surprised. "Don't humans need more rest than that?"

"I think I'm good," I told her, straightening in my seat and stretching. I winced at the aches that the stretch could do nothing to alleviate. My shoulder was twisted from holding Layne's hand behind me...which she was still holding. I glanced back at her, and my heart rose into my throat, my aches and pains completely forgotten for the moment.

Because Layne was fast asleep, resting her head back against the seat and pillowed against my violin case. Her thick black hair—normally spiked forward in her trademark devil-may-care style—drooped even more now and fell in front of her eyes so that, in this moment...she looked completely vulnerable. Her hard exterior had melted away to reveal the softness beneath. I'd never seen her look so open, so gentle, her full mouth soft, not set in a hard frown or a sarcastic smile. The frown lines on her forehead and around her mouth were softened, and she looked so at peace. It broke my heart, because there was dried blood on her face, on her scalp, on her wrists, blood from the wounds she'd received for trying to help me... Though as I stared carefully at those bloody areas, I realized that there were no actual wounds beneath them anymore.

Layne had fully healed in the night.

I watched her breathing steadily for a long moment, and I tried my best to stay right here, in the present, with her here near me, but I couldn't. I was wracked with guilt, because I knew that the blood was there because of me, wounds or no. Because of me, Layne had been captured by Magdalena. Who knew what pain she'd endured before I arrived last night? She'd had so many wounds, blood dripping down her face, her arms, her legs, when I walked through that front door. If I lived to be a hundred, I knew that I'd never forget that scene, forget the pain that had flashed across her face, forget that she'd been tied to those columns with metal ropes, terribly hurt because of *me*. Layne was simply hired to keep me safe... How did *torture* fit into the job description?

It was as if Layne knew what I was thinking about, knew the guilt that was racing through my heart, because her eyelashes fluttered on her cheeks at that moment, and she began to wake up. The very first thing she did when she opened her eyes was set me in her sights. Her eyes seemed bluer today, the light of the rising sun reflecting off of them as she glanced to the front seat—and to me. She smiled a little when she saw my face, and then her gaze flicked down to our hands, still entwined.

"Hello," she said, her voice gruff with sleep, but soft, too. "Did you get some rest?" she asked me, searching my face.

"I did," I told her, peering over the seat back at her and returning her smile in spite of myself. "Are you...okay?"

"Never better," she promised, letting go of my hand to stretch overhead with an impressive yawn. She settled back into the seat, and she ran a hand through her hair, making it stick up in all directions. She leaned forward a little, and she looked like she was about to tell me something, her face soft and open, but a minute passed, and she didn't speak. Instead, she glanced at Mikagi, and her expression hardened. "How much longer?"

"It's been four hours," said Mikagi, flicking her gaze to the rear-view mirror. "We're almost there."

"Great," said Layne, sprawling back in the seat again. She didn't sound enthusiastic at all.

We were driving through a small town now, but since I'd been looking back at Layne, I hadn't noticed any town markers when we'd passed them. I wondered if this was Eternal Cove, and when we drove past a bookstore with a hand-painted wooden sign proudly proclaiming it *Eternal Tales*, I assumed we were here. Nervousness flooded through me, and I knew that four hours of sleep after such a harrowing night really *wasn't* enough. I wished that I had at least a cup of coffee in me before I had to face this.

Whatever "this" was.

"What...should I be expecting?" I asked then, clearing my throat.

Mikagi laughed, and she pressed her foot a little harder down on the gas as we began to climb an impressive hill, thick brush and tall trees lining either side of the steep road. The car was a powerful little beast, but even it had trouble with the angle of the hill. I was flattened back against my seat, and put in mind of a rocket launching.

Mikagi lifted her chin, flooring the gas pedal, and the sports car tried its best, but we were still going pretty damn slow. "You should expect," she began, "to find yourself around people who are exactly like you," she told me then, and she gave me a sidelong glance, a shrewd one as she narrowed her eyes, her mouth turning up at the corners.

"What does that mean?" I asked, but she shrugged.

"You'll see."

Layne made a noise from the backseat, and when I glanced at her, I realized that the sound she was making was a growl, a deep, intense rumbling that seemed to make my seat vibrate. Or maybe that was the car, still trying to climb the hill.

"She is *not* exactly like them," said Layne, but Mikagi did not reply.

Between the seats, Layne reached out to me again, and I took her hand, squeezing it tightly. I was so nervous, the kind of nervousness that had blessedly never touched me before a performance, the gut-deep kind that was sickening me with worry.

But I didn't have to wait long.

The steep hill flattened out suddenly. Apparently my body expected a roller coaster-style drop, because the adrenaline was pounding through me faster than my heartbeat. But there was no drop-off at all.

Instead, we were driving on the flat top of the hill and spreading before us was a monstrous building that I assumed was the Sullivan Hotel.

It was an enormous red stone building on the edge of a cliff face. If you knew vampires existed, you would probably assume they lived in a place like just like this. The building stood several stories tall and had two big columns out front. The sun was just rising, but in every window, a candle burned. The architecture looked gothic in style, even with its big, blocky features, and with a sprawling stone driveway and parking lot, with the sun rising, the ocean waves rolling and edged with light, the whole sight was impressive, beautiful, even though the structure was made of blood-colored stone.

My heart was in my throat. We were here. And I was about to meet more vampires.

When Mikagi pulled into the parking lot (there were hardly any cars parked in it, so it seemed like we had the place to ourselves), turning off the car, I could actually feel the anxiety rushing through me, making my pulse pound harder. I flexed my fingers, still held by Layne. As if she knew what I was thinking, she leaned forward, reaching out and gently curling her other hand around my upper arm, her fingers resting against me and radiating warmth into my skin, even through the shirt.

"Forgive my mood," she murmured to me, and I glanced back at her in surprise. "This place is full of vampires," she said then, and her tone was begrudging, "but it is also full of good people. I have not met them, but I have heard stories of them, and all that I have heard makes them the exceptions to the rule."

"What rule?" I murmured to her.

Layne's eyes were stormy as she gazed at me. "Most vampires want humans dead, Elizabeth. But not the Sullivans."

Mikagi snorted at that and pocketed the keys in her coat before opening the driver's side door. "The Sullivans are human sympathizers," she said with a little laugh. "So you will get along great with them, being human yourself."

Layne raised a brow, but she squeezed my arm gently once more for comfort as she let go of my hand, and then she was opening up her door, too, taking my violin case with her as she left the seat. When Mikagi came around the side of the car, Layne pressed the violin case—not too gently—against Mikagi's chest. I could hear the *twang* of the strings from inside the case as it jolted between the women.

"I'll take her in," Layne growled. Mikagi looked like she was about to argue, her face curving instantly into an angry frown, but then she glanced at me—I was staring up at Layne hopefully—and she sighed.

"Suit yourself." Mikagi shrugged and moved to the back of the car to get my suitcase out of the trunk.

"Listen," said Layne as she opened the passenger side door, crouching down to my level, the gravel crunching beneath her shoes as she leaned forward with intensity. "There are treaties in place here at the Sullivan Hotel and grounds that mean no vampire can harm you. But you need to know that the Sullivan Hotel is full of vampires, both good and bad. Regardless, you are safe here...so there's nothing to worry about. I just...I know you're worrying." She said the words passionately as she held my gaze, her own fierce eyes burning with sincerity. "I want you to know the truth, but I also don't want you to worry anymore."

"Layne..." I began, but then Mikagi was back, my violin case dangling from her fingers along with hers, my suitcase held in her other hand. She lifted a brow at the two of us, and I undid my seat belt. Layne put her arms under my legs and around my back, and then she was lifting me effortlessly.

"Does...does anyone know we're coming?" I asked then, staring up at the enormous red building like it was something that loomed out of a horror movie. Mikagi moved past me to walk ahead of us, her A-line black skirt moving animatedly around her slender legs, and she was nodding.

"Your father told me that Kane knows we're coming. And that's all that matters. She's the one who owns the hotel. Kane Sullivan," said Mikagi, shooting this last bit of information back over her shoulder coolly. "Come on."

Layne followed Mikagi, holding me against her tightly, but with gentle hands. I had my arm wrapped around Layne's shoulders, and I lay my head down there, pillowed against her. I closed my eyes as the sun, on the very edge of the horizon, was lost from view into a darkened cloud bank.

There would be a storm today, I thought, as I closed my eyes to the lightning flickering along the horizon.

I had to admit, it was the perfect atmosphere to meet some vampires.

When we walked into the foyer of the Sullivan Hotel, I stared up in surprise at my surroundings, suddenly on high alert. Straight ahead of us was a ridiculously steep staircase. I mean, "staircase" was a generous term for what I was looking at. The steps ascended at such a treacherous angle that it was steep enough to be a ladder, but with wide rungs. I couldn't imagine any normal human being (without rock climbing gear or a death wish) actually being able to ascend it. To the side of the staircase was a sprawling, antique desk with a wall of keys behind it, and stretching out from either side of the desk and staircase were two hallways, lined with walls full of well-lit paintings. The floor beneath us was a checkerboard of black and red.

I saw all of this in an instant, because what my eyes were immediately drawn to was not the architecture or the floor.

My eyes were drawn to a person. A woman.

Who was, I'm assuming, a vampire.

She stood beside the front desk with her hand resting lightly on the old wooden surface. Her chin was lifted, her long, white-blonde hair was pulled up into a high ponytail, and her skin was so pale that it was almost translucent. She had very high cheekbones, and with her full mouth drawn into a soft frown, her face took on a sad look. She was wearing a men's suit, the black tie pulled snugly to her cream-colored neck, and shiny black leather shoes.

But what really drew in my gaze was her eyes.

I had never seen eyes so blue in my life. They were a type of blue that was almost incandescent, as if her eyes were glowing from within.

And there, too, resided so much sadness.

She was handsome in the same way Layne was, with a magnetic presence that drew your gaze. But even in my very first glance of this woman, I knew that she possessed a great heartache. It wasn't obvious or apparent in her body language—she held herself tall and strong. But there was something about the expression of her face. There was sorrow there, under the surface.

It broke my heart to see it.

"Kane," said Mikagi, her voice clipped as she pulled

up short in front of the tall woman. "This is Elizabeth Grayson, Alexander's daughter. And the wolf I was telling you about."

Kane's jaw worked to the side a little as she glanced at Mikagi, and her eyes—pale and bright a heartbeat ago—flashed. "This is neutral ground, Ms. Tasuki," she said, and when she spoke those words, my eyes grew wider. Her voice, like Layne's, was low, but there was a very subtle power there. She did not have to growl to put weight behind her words. Rather, they were whisper-soft, but the depth of them almost made the floor shake beneath us.

Mikagi actually straightened, glancing back over her shoulder with her own eyes narrowed. "That is Layne O'Connell," she said then, begrudgingly.

The woman stepped forward then smoothly, a soft smile making her frown disappear—but just barely. "Ms. O'Connell, Ms. Grayson, it is good to meet you both. I am Kane Sullivan, and this is my hotel," she said, spreading her hands and glancing up at the structure that rose around us. "You are welcome here, welcome to stay as long as you will."

Layne, stiff and tense beneath me, relaxed a little, and she nodded to Kane. "It's good to meet you. Please call me Layne."

"Call me Elizabeth," I echoed, and though I was holding tightly to Layne, I took my right hand down awkwardly and held it out to the vampire. "It's a pleasure to meet you."

Kane's smile deepened, and she took my hand and shook it gently, wincing as she glanced down at my thigh, hidden beneath my skirt. The dressing on the stitched wound had leaked through, and though my skirt was black, it was still obvious that there was blood on it. "Your father gave me a very cursory explanation last night as to why you were coming to the Sullivan Hotel for sanctuary," said Kane, her voice low as she gazed at me with concern. "Are you all right? We have a doctor here in town should you require aid."

"She got patched up. She only needs some rest," said Mikagi, stepping beside Kane and staring down at the blood on my skirt with her eyes narrowed. "Do you have a room prepared for her?"

"Of course," said Kane, and gestured down the left hallway. "Please follow me."

Layne did, and she walked beside Kane so that it would be easier for me to hear her. Kane was very soft-spoken, and with her low voice, it was sometimes hard to make out what she was saying unless you were directly beside her. Now that the introductions were out of the way, Kane's face had taken on that same sad quality as before. I wondered what had happened to her to make her so forlorn.

But Kane was also curious, and she asked the first question. "You were attacked by Magdalena, yes?" Kane glanced sidelong at me. When I nodded, her jaw tightened further, and her face hardened. "I am sorry," she said, and she sounded like she meant it. "Magdalena does not represent what a vampire is, and I hope you won't judge us all based on her merits."

"I don't know what to think," I told her honestly, my voice soft, too. Kane nodded.

"It's a fair assessment. Your father hopes that I and the others here can change your mind about what it means to be a vampire, but that's a tall request, Elizabeth," she said, and she smiled again at me, a smile that didn't quite reach her eyes. "I was not given a choice when I became a vampire, and this entire situation, your being given a choice to change or not is, to put it bluntly, unusual."

"My life right now is...kind of unusual." I was laughing lightly, and when Kane glanced at me, she chuckled, too.

We ascended a staircase that was broad, with nice, regular steps, quite unlike the staircase at the front of the building. When we reached a landing after a few floors, Kane unlocked a big mahogany door to our right with a skeleton key, then pressed that key into Mikagi's hand.

"I'm a phone call away," she promised. "When Elizabeth wakes up, call for me, and we can introduce her to the rest of the Sullivans."

The rest of the Sullivans? I didn't know what that meant, but the four hours of sleep really hadn't been enough, and drowsiness was trying to draw me back to dreamland. When Layne crossed the room, setting me down on the bed, I couldn't help it. I closed my eyes, and—feeling truly safe for the first time since the attack—I fell asleep immediately.

The Protector

Chapter 16: Love and Truth

Pain brought me back, pain that lanced up through my thigh into the rest of my body, pulsing in time with my heart.

I opened my eyes and sat up groggily, putting my hand to my forehead. The shadows were long and lean outside, and the sky had taken on a burnt-orange hue. I was assuming it was around sunset, which meant that I had slept the entire day away.

The very first thought I had was that I was starving, and I needed to eat something in order to take my pain pill, and I needed to do that right away, because I hurt so much. But then the animal side of me, all concerned with food and pain, faded away, and I realized where I was.

And who was lying beside me.

I was sitting up in bed, but a comforting, hot weight of an arm was draped around my middle, holding me tightly. I glanced to my side, and my heart rate increased—not from the pain, but because it was Layne lying beside me. Layne, who was fast asleep but still gripping me as if she was never going to let go.

If I had thought she'd looked vulnerable while asleep in the car, then I hadn't realized how truly vulnerable she could appear. There was a softness to her face, to the smooth, sculpted line of her forehead, her mouth open a little, her breath coming and going gently, like she was perfectly relaxed. Oh, she always acted relaxed, lounging on chairs and leaning against walls with sarcastic smiles, but anyone who looked at her would know that she could get up from that chair or push off of that wall in a heartbeat, moving across the room with a predator's skill.

She may have been a werewolf, and I may have seen her transform with my own eyes...but, here and now, the predator was gone, replaced instead with a woman who, in sleep, reverted to a person who had never seen blood or pain or sadness. A woman who, despite all her scars and sad memories, could still be soft. Could still be gentle. I experienced this gentleness when Layne touched me. When she looked at me, there was an immense amount of compassion, of kindness. There was...love, when Layne looked at me.

And there was love on her face, in her expression now, as she dreamed.

I glanced around the room surreptitiously, but it appeared as if we were alone. Mikagi must have gone somewhere. So it was just Layne and me, and though I wanted her to sleep more, get her rest, I also needed to talk to her about what had happened between us last night.

I wrestled with that decision for a long moment: should I wake her, or should I let her sleep? But in the end, I didn't have to choose. Layne's eyelashes fluttered against her cheeks, and then she was opening her beautiful eyes and glancing up at me.

For a full moment, the softness remained on her face, but then Layne sat up, too, looking around the room as I had to see if Mikagi was still here, and the softness left her immediately, replaced by a guarded restlessness. Only when she saw that we were alone did she relax again, lying back down against the pillows. The bed that we were lying on was enormous, a king size, and though there was a lot of room, we'd both somehow, in sleep, drifted naturally together, our bodies melting against each other under the covers.

"How did you sleep?" Layne asked me, her mouth turning up at the corners as she glanced at me with soft eyes. I nodded, lying back down beside her on my side so that we faced one another, almost nose to nose.

"Good," I said, wrapping my arm around her waist and drawing her to me. "And you?"

"Good," she repeated, searching my eyes. There was worry in her expression now, and though my arm was wrapped around her tightly, Layne had not put her arm around my waist again after waking.

"Listen, Layne," I said, and I wasn't sure what to say, so I let the words pour out, hoping that they made sense. My heart was aching too much to be delicate about this. "I...I don't know what's going on between us, but I'd really like to talk to you about it. You said, before we went into my father's study last night, that he was going to say something that would change everything between us. But he... I mean, he said a lot of things. That I have to change into a vampire," I said, feeling my cheeks flush at how dismissive of my current predicament I sounded, but I didn't have time to beat around the bush. "But that... That doesn't have anything to do with you. Unless you hate vampires, and...and wouldn't want to be with a vampire," I whispered, watching her face carefully. "So, why were you upset about what he had to say? Why are things weird between us now?"

Layne's eyes flashed with pain, and she was already shaking her head before I'd finished. "You don't understand," she began, and then she breathed out. "Look, it's not so easy as all that," she whispered. "There is a history between your kind and my kind, a history that is as old as the human race itself."

"'My' kind? I'm not a kind of anything. I'm just human," I reminded her gently, but she kept shaking her head.

"That may be true right now, but soon you will no longer be human. The human part of you will fade away, and you will become a vampire. You will be bitten, and you will change. And when you do...then you'll understand."

"Understand what?" I asked, and some impatience

was clear in my voice. "I understand that I have feelings for you. I've been drawn to you from the first moment I saw you in my father's study. My heart leapt up inside of me," I whispered, and I reached out between us and took her hand. I spread her warm fingers between mine and then tugged her hand closer to me, placing it over my heart, pressing her palm against the bare skin there, my buttoned blouse pushed aside. Layne's eyes widened, but I held her palm steadily, pressing down, and then she softened against me, her fingers hot over my skin, over my heart. I took a deep breath. "I knew you, and I knew that I was drawn to you. And if you feel the same way, then that should be enough."

"I want it to be," Layne whispered, and her voice was hoarse as she held my gaze. I realized, shocked, that there were tears at the corners of her eyes. "But my kind and your kind can*not* be together." She was emphatic. "For thousands of years, thousands upon thousands of years, there has been an understood hatred between vampires and werewolves. It's just the way it's always been."

"I don't hate you," I told her fiercely. "And when I become a vampire, that won't change."

"And I don't hate you," she repeated, holding my gaze, "and that won't change when you become a vampire. But it's so much bigger than us, Elizabeth. It's so much bigger. Someday," she said, as I began to protest, "you will inherit your father's position as the leader of the Nocturne Council. It's a group of *vampires*. And I'm getting really ahead of myself here, but if your girlfriend or your lover or your...or your wife," she whispered, her voice cracking on that word, "is something that they despise, they will never take you seriously, and you will fall. And you can't just *abdicate* as leader of the Nocturne Council. They will hunt you down, and they will kill you. You will never be safe, even if you *are* a vampire. You must know this. You must know that to be with me would seal your end."

I stared at her for a long moment, trying to believe what I was hearing. "But that's... That's just common prejudice. Vampires against werewolves, a race against a race. How does that make any sense to anyone?"

"Prejudice never makes sense," said Layne quietly. "Hatred for someone based on the color of their skin or what god they worship or who they fall in love with. It's all baseless, because in the end, the person that you're prejudiced against is something that you fear. Not because they can hurt you, but because they are different from you. That is one of the oldest human faults—one that my kind and your kind have never evolved past." There was pain on her face as she held my gaze. "Humans and vampires and werewolves will never evolve past it, Elizabeth. To be with me would destroy you. And that means...you can never be with me."

"Don't," I whispered then, and my voice was shaking.

Layne's eyes widened as I drew her closer, as my fingers curled around her hips and pulled her tighter to me, but her body acquiesced, and she drew her hips snugly against my own, wrapping her arms around me finally. "Don't," I repeated again, and I held her gaze, feeling my heartbeat flutter against my ribs with anxiety, but not even caring. This was too important.

She was too important.

"You have to listen to me, okay?" I said, and my voice was still shaking, but my words came out strong and clear. "I don't care about the history or how long this has been going on. I don't care that I'm going to become a vampire and that you're a werewolf. It's ridiculous. This is all *ridiculous*. I didn't sign up for this. I mean, what if I don't even want to become my father's successor?"

"I don't think that you get a choice, or—" began Layne, but I pressed a finger to her mouth, and though her eyes flashed, she stayed silent. My finger against her hot skin was so sensual that it almost made me shudder, but I didn't allow myself to.

"For a moment," I whispered to her, "forget about

233

everything else but us."

Layne's mouth downturned into a soft frown, but she nodded once, and I removed my finger from her lips. But I didn't take it straight away. Instead, I caressed the side of her face with my fingers, tracing that one fingertip down her mouth to her strong jaw, to the hot skin of her neck. Against me, Layne shivered just a little.

"Obviously, I don't know anything about my own kind. About vampires," I told her, my mouth dry when I said the word, drawing a circle over the skin of her neck and reveling in the heat of her against me. "And I don't know anything about werewolves. I'm in way over my head," I told her, sighing with a nervous chuckle. "But right now, I don't care about any of that. I'm going to have to care in, like, an hour. Whenever Mikagi comes back," I said, and when I spoke her name, Layne's eyes flashed—but she remained silent. "But right here and now, it's just you and me. And isn't that enough?"

Layne took a deep breath. For a brief moment, she looked uncertain. She looked as if maybe, just maybe, I'd gotten through to her. But then sadness fell over her face once more. "We were born and bred to be the embodiment of Romeo and Juliet," she murmured to me. "That doesn't bother you? It doesn't worry you?"

My mouth turned up into a smile, even as I tried to maintain a serious expression. "You're really going to bring Romeo and Juliet into this?"

Layne held my gaze, her own intense expression unwavering. "The similarities are striking," she said, raising a brow. "You were born into a family of creatures who hate what I am, and—"

"But Romeo and Juliet were kids who had no power by themselves, who had no ability to make their own decisions, because their families controlled them," I told her quietly. "And we're *not* them. We are two strong, grown women who know what we want in this lifetime, and know that we can have it, if we just try hard enough."

"It's not so simple," Layne warned me, but then she stopped talking when she looked at my face.

"I may have just gotten my stitches torn out by a vampire...and I'm kind of incapable of standing on my own right now," I told her, trying to suppress my smile—trying and failing. "But I still consider myself pretty damn strong. I worked tooth and nail to get that orchestra job, and I worked tooth and nail to become as good as I am at the violin. I've practiced for thousands upon thousands of hours for my career. My entire life, I've fought for what I wanted, for what I dreamed about..." I took a deep breath and held Layne's gaze. My voice cracked, but I kept going, emotion making my words thick. "And if it's what you want, then I want to fight for you, too."

For a long moment, Layne remained silent, her deep, hazel eyes searching my gaze, my face, her brow furrowed as her expression softened. I thought she wasn't going to reply at all, but then her eyes widened, and she was leaning forward.

Layne brushed her hot fingers along the side of my face, tracing patterns of heat there, and she was suddenly holding my chin, cupped tenderly in her hands, drawing herself closer, drawing me closer so that the two of us met, our mouths connecting.

Layne was so hot against me, hot to the touch, and when she kissed me deeply, my skin felt like it was on fire, burning over me and through me. So much had happened over the last few days that I hadn't really allowed myself to think much about what was happening between Layne and me, but now I let the emotions flood through me. Heat poured through my body, waking every inch of me, leaving me breathless.

I held Layne close, gripping her hips with my fingers, hard, pressing myself against her as we kissed, as I tasted her. When I breathed out against her, I moaned a little, and that's when she climbed over me, straddling my hips in one smooth motion. Her dark hair brushed in front of her eyes and against my face as she drank me deeply. I was nowhere but in that moment, then, and I wasn't thinking about anything else but her, us, how our bodies were coming together. I'd wanted this from the first moment I saw her, even though I could never have articulated it then. There was a connection from that first moment, a line that stretched between us, and now it was taut and singing, just like a violin's string, humming with something bright and beautiful, a single note of love.

I kissed her deeper, working my fingers around her leather belt, tugging at her to press her center down against my hips, and Layne's fingers were at the buttons of my blouse, swiftly undoing the first one—when we both heard a sound from the other side of the room. It was a throat being cleared.

Mikagi was entering the room, tossing her black coat onto an antique, high-backed chair in the entryway and shutting the door behind her, leaning against it with a smug smile. "Oh, am I interrupting something?" she asked, and her thick accent did nothing to mask the sarcasm in her words.

When Layne glanced up at her, still arched over me, still straddling me, she growled a little, her lips going up and over her teeth as the growl emanated from deep inside of her. Mikagi shrugged and crossed the room to her own little suitcase that had been set on top of the old mahogany dresser. She popped it open, not even glancing our way.

"The vampires want to meet you, Elizabeth," she told me, as she riffled through her suitcase. "You should get ready." Mikagi took up yet another black dress (I was fairly certain that everything she owned was black) and snapped out the wrinkles, shutting the suitcase with a few clicks as she glanced over at the two of us. "You should get ready *now*," she reiterated, emphasizing the word. Then she ducked into the little bathroom to get changed, shutting the door behind her.

Layne glanced down at me, the fire still burning in

her eyes, but more subdued now. "I don't know if—" she began, but I shook my head, I drew her face down to me, and I kissed her once more. It was a gentle kiss, a soft kiss, and I hoped she'd remember it.

"Don't think about anything but this moment," I told her when we surfaced for air again. "Just...try to stay here and now. In the present. We'll figure everything out when we get to it, okay? But I want to try. With you," I told her, searching her face.

Layne looked down at me, her elbows on either side of my head, her hands buried deep in my hair, and she gently stroked my cheeks, my forehead, with her thumb, tracing her fingertips over and over my skin. Her jaw was tight, and when she nodded, it was almost imperceptible. But she *did* nod.

"It's crazy, is what it is. A soon-to-be vampire and a werewolf together," she said, her voice low as she breathed out. "I don't know if it's going to work out."

"Give it a chance," I told her, without skipping a beat. "Give *me* a chance."

She held my gaze for a long moment before moving, and I could tell that her entire body was tense. But she nodded, and again it was almost imperceptible...but she did it.

"Always," is what she murmured before she leaned down, brushed her mouth against my own, our lips meeting in something soft and real. Layne lingered for a long moment against me, kissing me deeply, before she slid off of me, being very careful not to touch my injured thigh. And then Layne was standing beside the bed, running a hand through her hair in frustration and adjusting her clothes, straightening her shirt over her chest, drawing the hem down and around her hips.

We'd been too tired to change into anything resembling bed clothes last night and had just fallen into bed wearing exactly what we'd worn yesterday, but that meant I was wearing what I'd worn to my orchestra's concert, and I was pretty damn uncomfortable. I'd slept in my bra, too… I was going to have the *worst* crick in my back and shoulders. I desperately wanted to change into some fresh clothes, but I was met with a pretty interesting conundrum: what did you wear to meet vampires?

We didn't have much time to consider, so I opted for a fresh black skirt and white blouse, locking myself in the bathroom after Mikagi vacated it. I struggled to change my clothes, hopping on one leg and sitting on the edge of the old clawfoot tub as I fumbled with the skirt, but I refused to let Layne into the bathroom to help me get dressed. It was just the principle of the thing. I wanted the first time that she saw me naked to be sexy, memorable, not another checkmark on her list of chores concerning me.

It was awkward and difficult, but I managed to get the skirt on and zipped up, and the blouse buttoned, and then I was hobbling out of the bathroom on my crutches. Mikagi and Layne were both by the door and ready to go. I guess Layne had changed in front of Mikagi, because she was wearing her leather jacket, another tight t-shirt (this one a bright blue), and skinny jeans that showed off her muscled legs so well that I immediately felt my cheeks redden when I gave her the once-over. But she was giving me the once-over, too, and when I glanced back at her face again, she was grinning like a—well, a wolf.

"You'll take all day to get there if you walk around using those things," said Mikagi, wrinkling her nose and waving her hand at my crutches. "I must carry you. Or I suppose the wolf could do it. Which will it be?"

"Layne?" I said instantly, and Mikagi snorted, not even glancing back as she stepped forward and opened the door to the room, holding it open for us. Layne took the crutches from me and set them gently against the wall, and then she was picking me up effortlessly, her arms sliding into place behind my knees and at my back as she lifted me up off the floor and into her arms.

"Are you ready?" she asked me, her voice low and

gruff, and I nodded, my heart in my throat.

"As ready as I'll ever be."

Obviously, I knew that I was meeting a bunch of vampires, and that would probably make anyone nervous, but it was all so much bigger than that. Last night, my life hadn't just changed irrevocably. My father had told me that he was sending me here, to the Sullivan Hotel, to keep me safe. But also to show me what being a vampire was like.

And I had no idea what to expect.

Layne followed Mikagi and carried me down the broad hallway, the red-and-black tile clicking beneath her shoes. There were bends in the corridor, and we went up another spiral staircase, but eventually, we found ourselves in front of a large oak door. The wide door frame was carved all around with flowers, and cherubs (which, admittedly, looked a little creepy), and from inside the room, there came the sound of women's voices and laughter.

Mikagi knocked loudly at the door three times. And the laughter and voices ceased instantly.

"Come in." The words echoed from the other side of the door, and they sounded familiar. I remembered Kane from this morning, and though we hadn't spent that much time with her, her voice was very distinctive.

Again, Mikagi opened the door and held it open for Layne, gesturing us forward stiffly with a frown painting her pretty features. Layne moved past Mikagi, and then we were swallowed up by the dark room.

The hallway we'd just come from was bright, even though the sun had already sunk below the horizon; antique lamps lit the corridors, and chandeliers sparkled overhead. But the inside of this room was smoky and hazy, and there was hardly any light at all. In fact, one of the only sources of light was the fire roaring behind the grate in the fireplace on the other side of the room.

Layne stepped inside, and Mikagi folded in behind her, shutting the door and essentially dousing us in darkness.

It took a long moment for my eyes to adjust to the

dimness, and in that time, there were muted conversations happening around the room, women speaking in low voices. When my eyes finally did adjust, Layne had carried me over to a brown, antique leather loveseat positioned against the far wall and near the fireplace, and she was setting me down onto it gently. Her eyes were narrowed when she gazed at me, and she brushed her fingers over my shoulder before she stood at attention and leaned against the wall beside me, folding her arms in front of her and surveying the room of women with narrowed eyes.

Kane had been standing beside the fireplace, her hand on the mantle, when we came into the room, but she approached us now, crouched in front of me easily, gazing up at me with her blue eyes full of concern. "We are happy to have you, Elizabeth, but did you come here straight from your room? You must be hungry. Shall I have something sent up from the kitchens?"

"I'm... I'd like to just meet everyone first," I said carefully, and Kane nodded like she understood, patting my leg with sympathy twice before standing and gesturing behind her.

"Welcome to the Sullivan Hotel, Elizabeth," she said sincerely, gazing down at me with a soft smile. "I am most pleased to introduce you now to the rest of the Sullivans, my...'sisters,' for lack of a better word."

Around me, several women stood or sat, all of them gazing at me with interest, their eyes bright and engaged. Kane walked up to the woman nearest to her and nodded.

"This is Dolly," Kane said, waving to the blonde woman with springy curls, wearing a red vintage dress that flared out around her waist like she was on an episode of *I Love Lucy*. Dolly waved at me enthusiastically, bouncing in place so that her curls sprung around her head.

"This is Jane," Kane said, indicating the woman who stood next to Dolly, a sour-looking lady with strong, muscled arms and a blonde pompadour. Jane gazed at me with a frown, then turned away, pulling Dolly aside and

240

whispering something into her ear, effectively ignoring me.

"This is Mags," Kane continued, gesturing to a tall, black-haired woman who had curves for days and a very wicked smile. Mags, also, was apparently not that impressed with me, because she sneered a little, then turned back to the conversation that she'd been having with Jane.

"This is Luce and Cecilia and Victoria," Kane said, indicating the three women who were sitting on the couch on the other end of the room. Luce, the woman on the far left of the sofa, had long, wavy brown hair and wore a silver armband. She nodded kindly to me with a bright smile. Beside her on the couch sat Cecilia, a woman with long brown hair that had been swept up into a bun on the top of her head. She wore a dress shirt and a very loose-fitting blue tie, and she was leaning forward, her elbows propped on her knees, deep in conversation with Luce—but she also nodded to me before continuing the conversation. The last woman on the couch, Victoria, gazed at me with dark eyes that flashed brightly, putting her head to the side as she gave me a once-over, her bright red lips curling up at the corners. She had deep black skin, and her gorgeous hair hung loose in tight curls around her head. She was currently filling out the curves of a breathtaking red dress that made my heart skip a beat. She gave me a little wink, then leaned forward and put her arm around Cecilia, rubbing her back a little, like Cecilia had just been given a piece of bad news, and she was comforting her.

"This is Branna," Kane said, nodding to the close-cropped, brown-haired woman who was standing next to her. Branna had gentle eyes and a soft smile, and—like Kane—she was also wearing a men's suit, with a smart bowtie at her throat. Branna grinned brightly at me, folding her arms in front of her.

"And this is Tommie," said Kane, gesturing last to a black-haired woman who sat across from me in an antique, Victorian-looking chair. Tommie had her ankle on her knee as she leaned back in the chair, and she tipped her fedora to me, her green eyes raking over me, then ending back up on my face as she gave me a sly, sexy smile. She was wearing straight-leg black pants, a dress shirt, and a green tie that complimented her eyes damn near perfectly.

"All of the women before you," said Kane, gesturing to the room at large, then, "are vampires. We each came to vampirism in different ways, but while you're here, we hope that you'll ply us with questions to help you reach your decision." Kane leaned against the wall again and was about to say something else when Tommie spoke.

"The decision," she said, rising from the chair, her low voice smoky and electric as she took a pull on the cigarette that was dangling from her lips, before reaching up with long fingers and flicking the ash off the end of it, "is that there *is* no decision." She pinned me in place with her bright green eyes and chuckled. "It's obvious. Become a vampire. It's the best decision you'll ever make."

I stared in surprise at her. "Why do you love being a vampire?" I asked then, and Tommie shrugged, rocking back on her heels as she stuck her hands deep into her pockets.

"That's like asking what you enjoy about breathing," she said, her mouth turning up at the corners into a sarcastic smile. "I'm faster, stronger, better than my human counterparts. I'm practically a god. I have nothing to fear."

The brown-haired woman, Branna, if I remembered her name correctly, came to sit beside me on the loveseat. She moved gracefully, like she was a part-time dancer, and though the loveseat was very narrow, and though her hip brushed against mine, I felt nothing but sincere kindness coming from her as she leaned forward, placing her elbows on her knees as she glanced sidelong at me.

"Tommie makes it sound like it's a very easy decision, a no-brainer, as it were," she told me, and her voice was just as warm and gentle as her eyes when she shook her head. "But I must tell you that it's not so simple. It's perhaps the most important decision you'll ever make, one that will change your life irrevocably, and the course of your future forever. Like Kane," she said, gesturing up to Kane who leaned against the opposite wall now, lighting a cigarette with a silver lighter from her pocket, "I was not given a choice in becoming a vampire. I was forced to become one, my body choosing for me. Your situation is unique in that you get to make the decision yourself, so I understand why Alexander sent you here."

"Branna, she doesn't exactly have a lot of *time*," muttered Tommie, breathing out a ring of smoke into the air. "You'd better tell her."

"Tell me what?" I asked Branna, my heart in my throat as I turned to look at her.

Branna shifted uncomfortably on the loveseat and cleared her throat. "We don't want to worry you, Elizabeth," she said, searching my gaze, "but perhaps you don't have as long as you hoped for in order to decide."

"You mean, I'm not staying here for seven days?" I said, my voice sounding shaky, even to me. What was she talking about?

Branna nodded. "Your father called us again today while you were asleep. Things are…happening, back in Boston. Perhaps a bit more rapidly than any of us would have liked."

"The Nocturne Council in Boston is starting to see a little…upheaval," said Kane, taking a deep pull on the cigarette. "We were hoping that this wouldn't happen for a little while longer, but time is, unfortunately, not on our side."

"It's running out," said Tommie, raising a brow.

"Running out? Listen," I said, holding up a hand. "I appreciate, very much, your letting me stay here and—I'm assuming—your protecting me from vampires who would like to suck me dry." My mouth was twisted as I said this last part, but the three arguing women in the corner had actually stopped talking, and everyone was watching me now, some with wide eyes, some with smirks. In the case of

Tommie, with a genuine smile. When I glanced sidelong at Layne, I saw her leaning against the wall beside me, her hands deep in her pockets, her shoulders curled forward...but giving me a soft smile of encouragement. So I kept going. "If you could just explain exactly what's going on succinctly, I'd really appreciate it," I said with finality, rubbing my wet palms on my skirted knees.

Kane glanced sidelong at Tommie, who toed the chair she'd recently occupied over to her. Kane sank down into it then, crossing her legs and holding the cigarette between her first two fingers. She let it dangle over the edge of the chair as she rested her hands on the upholstered arms.

"Well," she said, and her low voice broke when she chuckled a little, "succinctly, we're vampires, and your father is, too. He is leader of the Nocturne Council in Boston. The Council has far-reaching power and control over the vampires in this section of the country. All of the northeast, basically," she said, taking another pull of her cigarette. "As you can imagine, this means that people who are less scrupulous than your father would like to take his power for themselves. Magdalena has recently come into her own, and she is gathering momentum among the vampires. She wants to challenge your father for leadership of the Nocturne Council, and she—rightfully so—assumes that if you're out of the picture, it will weaken your father, assuring her place as leader of the Council."

"That's terrible," I said, all in a rush. "But...but why? Why all of this?"

"There are two types of vampires, Elizabeth," said Kane gently. "The type of vampires who, like ourselves," she said, gesturing around the room, "think humans are important and worthy of life and protection. And then there are the vampires who, basically, think of humans like..." She took a deep breath. "Well, like cattle." Kane grimaced. "Vampires who would like nothing better than to take all humans and lock them up, feeding on them when necessary, making vampires the dominant species on this planet and humans, for lack of a better word, enslaved to us."

I stared at her, my mouth open. "That's...that's not possible," I began, but then I shook my head. I clearly didn't know what was and wasn't possible since, up until yesterday, I'd never even known vampires were real.

"Magdalena has been gaining power among the ranks of vampires who think like she does. Your father does not think that way, of course, and she's positioning him as 'weak' among her followers," said Branna, seated next to me. She sighed for a long moment, shaking her head. "If Magdalena came to power in Boston, that would start to change things. Fast."

"There's never been a vampire with her views in control in North America," said Kane, taking another pull on her cigarette. "But if someone like Magdalena took power, the structure of society would begin to crumble. Vampires would come out into the open. And they would rule, killing any and every human they pleased."

"There are laws put into place among vampires so that type of thing doesn't happen. And, if it does, it's punished," said Branna, glancing at me. "But if Alexander is no longer in power, there will be no one there enforcing those laws, and every available human becomes nothing more than a blood bank. It would be a sort of Armageddon for humanity. A sort of...end of the world," she said, her full lips downturning into a frown. "So you see that Magdalena must not rise to power. If she challenges your father for leadership of the Nocturne Council, she *must* fail."

"How has this not happened before now? If there are so many vampires who think like this, who want humanity to be subjugated," I asked, swallowing, "how has the human race survived this long?"

"Because there aren't, truly, that many vampires in the world," said Kane, uncrossing her legs and leaning forward. "We've been in hiding, which I don't mind at all. None of us does. If we overtook the world, it would be because we had ruthlessly murdered and oppressed humans in order to do it. And that is not anything worth having," she said firmly.

"But not everyone thinks like that," said Tommie, tucking her hands deeper into her pockets and giving me an appraising glance. "*You* might not even think like that," she said carefully, shaking her head, "when you become one of us."

"I would *never* think that humans deserve to be enslaved, murdered..." I spluttered, horrified. "That's something a *dictator* would think. An evil person—"

"Hate begins as something small," said Branna then, gently, clearing her throat beside me. "The vampires who wish for humans to be used like cattle—they didn't start out believing that, either. They were all human once, too, and it's very difficult to turn against something that you once were, or that you've come from. Hate was born and bred inside each vampire, fed by others who hated. Hate was perpetuated and spread, like a disease, among them."

"This hatred did not grow overnight. It's been festering in vampires for some time." Kane looked up at me, and her brilliant blue eyes were flashing.

"If it's been there for so long, I can't imagine that vampires haven't tried to gain control of the world before," I said, emphasizing my point again, but Kane tilted her head to the side as she stared at me, her eyes narrowing.

"It did happen once before. Magdalena has been trying to get to your father for a long time. She almost succeeded once."

I stiffened at that, my entire body tensing as I turned to fully look at Kane. I didn't ask her to explain herself. Her eyes were wide when she glanced at me, and she was sighing.

"Your father didn't tell you?" she asked, and when I shook my head, she sighed again, her full mouth flattening into a thin line. "Trust Alexander to leave the hardest tasks to me," she murmured, leaning back in the chair and crossing her legs. She placed her forehead in her hand and thought long and hard for a moment. Then she looked up at me with her shockingly blue eyes. "What do you know of your mother's death, Elizabeth?" she asked, her brow furrowed in concern.

My mouth had suddenly gone very dry. "I... Where are you going with this?"

"Your mother was killed by Magdalena," said Kane solemnly.

The Protector

Chapter 17: The End of Normal

Everyone in the room had fallen silent; the smoky space was so soft, so hushed that you could have heard a pin drop. Or the sound of a single tear striking fabric. Which is what happened then. Because a single tear made its way out of my right eye, traced its way down my cheek and chin and fell, glittering, to the fabric of my skirt on my lap.

"That's not possible," I said then, as nicely as I could. "My mother died because of a car accident."

"Your mother's car was rear-ended by one of Magdalena's goons," said Kane slowly, carefully, holding my gaze. "She was pushed off the highway, into oncoming traffic, and the car was decimated. She was rushed to the hospital, but she died that night. I remember," she said with some finality, "because I was visiting the Graysons at the time. I was there when your father begged your mother to let him change her into a vampire to save her life." Kane exhaled heavily. "I was there when she refused."

My entire life flashed in front of my eyes at that moment, not because I was in any imminent danger, but because everything I'd always believed, or thought I knew, was proven false. I remembered the many, many times my father lamented about my mother's accident. I remembered the hundreds of times that he'd blamed himself for it. I remembered, at the funeral, the look he'd had on his face as he watched the pallbearers lower the casket into the ground, the misery and abject pain that flashed in his eyes.

It now made sense. So much more sense.

I remembered how my father told me, just last night, that my mother had died because she'd chosen to. She'd made her choice, he'd said. And now I needed to make mine.

"Magdalena—she did this to gain control? She killed my mother...for what? To weaken my father?" I asked, and my voice was shaking, but my words were loud and clear.

Kane nodded, taking another pull on the cigarette. "Magdalena thought that, with your mother out of the way, Alexander would crumble and relinquish control of the Nocturne Council easily. But he knew the stakes if he stepped down as leader, knew that he could not let Magdalena have his seat. So he did the best he could, he kept his allied members of the Council close about him, and he carried on. And then he did everything he could to keep you safe."

"Okay. So...why hasn't Magdalena hasn't come for me sooner?" I said then, licking my lips nervously. My hands were in fists on my lap, and I don't think I'd ever been more tense. "Why hasn't she tried to kill me before now?"

"She was, of course, punished for what she did to your mother," said Branna then, glancing sidelong at me. "And much of her power was taken from her, and her allies abandoned her. It has been many years since she was able to gain allies again, allies who believe that she will make good on her promises this time and be able to gain control of the Council."

"Promises. Like the promise to annihilate my father. To gain control of Boston and all of the vampires by any means necessary," I said, my voice flat and low. The vampires surrounding me nodded, and when I glanced up at Layne, she wasn't looking at me; she was staring down at the ground, her jaw flexed, her eyes dark.

"That simply can't happen," I said then, lifting my chin. "We can't let that happen."

"Obviously," said Tommie, folding her arms in

front of her. "My question is—what are *you* going to do about it? Magdalena has been biding her time. She's been amassing allies and power, and she won't make the same mistakes twice. She's very angry," she said, one brow up.

"I don't… I don't know what I can do about it," I told her truthfully. "I just know that my father needs help. And I know that *I* have to help him." I swallowed. "I…I think I need to become a vampire."

Kane dropped the cigarette onto the floor and stepped down onto the lit ember of it, grinding it out with the heel of her shoe slowly. "It's too much to take in all at once, everything we've just told you," she said kindly, her voice soft and sympathetic. "I'm sure it hurt a great deal to hear. I would ask you to please sleep on it, and then we'll meet again in the morning, and you can make your decision then. No decision this big should be made in haste," she said quietly, leaning forward and placing her elbows on her knees as she pinned me down with her bright blue gaze. "Do you agree, Elizabeth?"

I took a deep breath. I tried not to think of my father, all alone in Boston, facing off against Magdalena. "Is Dad all right?" I asked then, and Kane was nodding.

"He has his friends on the Council surrounding him. He's going to call an emergency meeting tomorrow night to discuss what to do with Magdalena, but Magdalena will be present, as will all of her allies. And I have no idea how many vampires are on her side." She paused, considering. "I have a bad feeling that Magdalena will take that moment to reveal her true power and try to destroy your father…" she trailed off, watching me carefully.

"Well, then I have to be back in Boston tomorrow night to help him," I said simply.

Kane nodded once. "Frankly, your father is going to need all the help he can get, if what I suspect is true. I am assuming," she said solemnly, "that Magdalena has been able to get quite a few of the Council members on her side this time."

"It only takes four hours to get to get to Boston from here," Mikagi piped up for the first time since arriving in the room. She was sitting at an ancient card table, playing an animated game of Solitaire with herself. She gathered all of the cards off the table from their neat lines and began to shuffle them again. "I can get you there even faster," she said with a wicked smile as she flipped the cards neatly in the air and set the deck back down onto the table.

"That's settled, then," said Kane, rising smoothly. I rose, too, or tried to: I had to push off of the loveseat arm, but I teetered on my one good leg until Branna, lightning quick, was standing beside me and gripping my elbow surely.

"Thanks," I murmured to her, and she smiled warmly at me, glancing over her shoulder at Layne, who had pushed off from the wall and was looking at me with worried eyes, her jaw clenched.

"It's my pleasure. But I'm sure your lover would rather be doing this job than me," she said with a little chuckle as she stepped away, gesturing to Layne. "Ms. O'Connell," she said, her head tilted to the side as she offered my arm to the werewolf.

Lover? Was it that obvious? I smiled in spite of myself, in spite of all the dire news I'd just heard, and I glanced over my shoulder at Layne.

I'm guessing that Layne didn't have much experience with vampires treating her like an equal, especially considering what she'd told me about vampires and werewolves hating one another since the dawn of time. She gazed at Branna with wide eyes, surprise evident on her face, before she stepped forward, nodding uncertainly to the vampire.

"Thank you," she said gruffly, then wrapped her arms around my waist so that I could lean easily against her. And I did, feeling the warmth of her, the heat of her, radiating through my clothes and my skin, into the very deepest parts of me. I looked up at Layne, and I wrapped my arm around her middle, holding her close as I leaned on her.

"Now," said Kane, spreading her hands, and though there was still sadness evident in her eyes, she did her best to smile, and nodded to me. "Tomorrow is coming soon, and tomorrow everything changes. But right now, I want the rest of the night to be a celebration. A celebration of your visiting us, Elizabeth, and a celebration of your humanity. And of what you might become. We've come together—now let's make the most of it," she said, her bright blue eyes glittering.

Branna nodded, glancing eagerly at Layne and me as she swept her brown hair out of her eyes, raking her fingers back through her gelled hair so that it stuck up at odd angles, making her look even more endearing. "I'm almost afraid to ask—I know it's frightfully rude—but we *do* have one of the best violin players in the world beneath our roof...*and* a violinist from the Boston Philharmonic..."

Mikagi, still seated at the card table and balancing the chair back on its two legs, let it fall with a *whoosh* and was standing before Branna had even finished talking. She was grinning from ear to ear.

"I'd love to hear the both of you play," Branna said, all at once.

"Let's get some food for our guest first," said Kane, and she stepped forward, clapping Branna on the shoulder gently as she glanced my way. "Are you in the mood for some breakfast now?"

I laughed a little. "Breakfast at night? Sure, why not?"

"I'll get it sent up from the kitchens," she promised, and then she crossed the room, picking up a beautiful crystal decanter of alcohol from a table by the door. She swirled the liquid in the glass and raised it in a toast to the assembled women. "Now, let's drink."

Tommie was looking at me curiously, and when Mikagi walked over, Tommie wrapped an arm around her waist and drew her aside, leaning down and whispering into the vampire's ear in a pretty sensual way, her mouth against Mikagi's skin. Mikagi was stiff next to Tommie, but she flicked her gaze over to me when she thought I wasn't looking. I glanced up at Layne with a smile for her, but she was frowning, watching Tommie and Mikagi talk.

"What is it?" I asked her quietly.

"Nothing I can't handle," she said, but the words sounded dull, wooden, and the concern on her face told me that this clearly wasn't the "nothing" she claimed it to be. But she didn't elaborate, instead lifting me up again gently and carrying me over to the sideboard where Kane was pouring crystal glasses full of the liquid and setting them in a neat row on the table.

"Brandy," she told me with a raised brow and a small smile when I looked at the glasses with trepidation. From this angle, and with the low lighting in the room, I'd half wondered if she was pouring blood out of that bottle.

"Oh, good," I managed, but when I took the glass from her, I felt a bit embarrassed.

"We can eat and drink just like you can," said Branna, coming up behind us and taking another glass. She swirled the liquid in it, glancing down into the crystal tumbler and smiling a little. "We just don't crave food, and we don't need to eat. We often do it out of habit. Or just to enjoy the food itself."

"And blood?" I asked her, swallowing a little before taking a sip of the brandy. It was good brandy, but I knew that if I drank a lot of it before eating, I was going to get tipsy quickly.

Branna shook her head. "Contrary to popular belief, vampires don't *need* blood. Though there would be vampires out there who argued me on that point, and viciously. But, no, we don't need human blood to survive."

"Then why drink it?" I asked, downing the rest of the contents of my glass. I handed it back to Kane, and she filled it up quickly, handing it right back, though she didn't seem to be paying attention to the action. Her face was very sad when I glanced sidelong at her, and she was staring off into the distance, holding her glass over her heart like she was remembering something.

"Because it's wonderful," said Tommie, her brow raised, as she came up and took a glass of brandy from Kane, too. "When you have your first taste of blood, Elizabeth—you'll see. You'll see why vampires want it, desire it...take it. It's not right," she amended carefully, pinning me to the spot with her bright green gaze, "but you'll understand."

I didn't say anything and drank the contents of my tumbler quickly again, so quickly that the liquid almost burned my throat. But I gave the glass back to Kane, and she filled it for a third time, handing it back to me with a raised brow.

As I took the glass from her, I heard a brief *ding* from my phone. It was wedged into my bra, beneath my blouse, because I hadn't wanted to bring my purse if Layne was carrying me around, and I really didn't have any pockets in my skirt or blouse. Layne set me back down on the loveseat, and I fished my phone out, looking at the text.

It was from Tracy.

Date went really well, thought you'd want to know. He's super nice. Heard you weren't feeling well. Miss you at rehearsal. Are you okay?

I bit my lip and texted back quickly: *I'm fine, just needed some time to get better. Glad the date went well. Details?*

Layne took a glass of brandy from Kane, too, and she leaned against the wall, glancing down to me before taking a sip of her drink. "Who was that?"

"Tracy," I told her. I started to get overwhelmed as I sat there, as I felt the weight of my phone in my hands and thought about how blissfully normal that text had been. Tracy's date went well. She missed me in the orchestra. Normal, everyday stuff that I'd always taken for granted.

What was going to happen when I wasn't human anymore? What was life going to be like, feel like?

255

"Penny for your thoughts," said Layne, crouching down next to me. I smiled at her, but the smile wavered a little on my lips. Her sharp eyes noticed that, of course, and she put her head to the side, leaning on the arm of the loveseat. "I know you're worrying, but please don't," she said, and she reached across the space between us, taking my left hand in hers and squeezing it gently before threading her fingers through mine. "Everything's going to be okay."

"Is it, Layne?" I asked her, my voice soft. I gulped down air and stared down at my phone with eyes blurry from unshed tears. "Because… I mean, everything I just heard, it pretty much sounds like it's not okay at all."

I'd had a couple of glasses of brandy, and it was already starting to make me feel drunk. I wanted to relax back into it, let myself go and just have one last evening of normalcy (or as close to normal as I could get right now), but I was too tense as I stared down at my phone with blurry eyes.

Considering everything I'd just been told, the future was starting to look…bleak.

"Elizabeth," said Layne gently, and when I glanced at her, gazing into her bright, hazel eyes, the depths of them multicolored, beautiful, I felt myself relax, even though I didn't really want to. I felt my entire body ease as she gripped my hand, as I felt her warmth seep from her skin into me, soothing me as she held me.

"You told me that we should try, right?" she asked quietly, searching my gaze. "You said that it was worth it. This. Us."

"It is," I told her, and my voice sounded strong, impassioned, in spite of the sadness rising inside of me. "You're worth it," I told her, gripping her hand just as tightly as she was gripping mine.

"Then that's all that matters," said Layne. "You, me, us. We'll keep your father safe; we'll keep Boston safe; hell, we'll keep humanity safe, if we have to. But we can only do that if we're in this *together*. If we're fighting side by side. I believe in this. I know you do, too. Together, we can do it. But only together."

When she finished speaking, her eyes were glittering with emotion, and I felt my heart swell inside of me. I reached out, and I cupped her face with my hands. She was on one knee beside me now, and as I held her face and searched it with my gaze, memorizing every line and curve—her full mouth, those beautiful eyes—I felt my skin warm from hers, and I knew she was right. I knew, just like I knew from the very first moment that I met her that there was something between us, something powerful that I couldn't name, but that simply was.

"You're right," I told her, and my voice cracked with emotion. "This is all... This is just overwhelming."

"Your whole world is being turned upside-down. It'd be overwhelming for anyone," said Layne, and she gazed deeply into my eyes. "I've only known you for a small fraction of your life, Elizabeth. But in the time that I've known you, I've witnessed your tenacity. If anyone can deal with all of this, it's you."

I took a deep breath. I centered my gaze on her. And the tension that I was feeling eased from my shoulders, through my body.

"We'll get through this," said Layne, her voice low and strong. "Together."

I nodded and wrapped my arms around her shoulders, drawing her to me for a tight embrace, feeling the warmth of her body permeate my own. We stayed like that for a long moment, the vampires moving about us, talking in low tones or laughing. It was like any other cocktail party you might imagine, but there were so many subtle things different about it. Tomorrow morning was going to change everything, and Layne was right: I believed, firmly, that we could get through this together.

But right now, I had no idea how we were going to do it.

There was another chirp from my phone, and I

leaned back from Layne, glancing down at the phone to see that I'd just gotten a new text from Tracy. I smiled in apology at Layne for being distracted as I scooped up the phone and unlocked the screen to read the text.

Police are saying Bob's death was definitely a murder, but they've got nothing. No suspects, no motive, no murder weapon. I don't mean to worry you, but I thought you'd like to know where it all stands.

I swallowed, Layne stiffening beside me as she read the text, too. I shut off my phone's screen and slid it back under my shirt and into my bra as I realized something. Then I was clearing my throat and glancing across the room to Kane, who was talking in low tones to Branna close by. Kane knew so much about my father and the state of things with the Nocturne Council. Maybe she'd know about this, too.

"I'm sorry to ask you this, Kane," I said, and Kane turned to me again, drawing a cigarette pack out of her suit jacket pocket. She tapped the pack, taking out a cigarette, and she lit it up, the flame brightening her face for a brief flash as she glanced at me quizzically. "But...do you... Does anyone know what happened to my friend, Bob Huller? He was the principal flutist in the Boston Philharmonic," I said, my mouth suddenly dry again. "And he was murdered last week."

"Bob," she said, her head tilted to the side as she considered the name. "Was that the man who was killed outside the concert hall?"

"Yes," I whispered.

Kane shook her head, flicked the ash off the end of the cigarette. "Bit of bad business, that," she muttered. "Magdalena drank him dry herself. And then bragged about it to some of our contacts," she said, her mouth going into a thin, flat line.

My hands curled into fists in my lap, but then Mikagi was beside me. She'd moved so quickly, and she sat down gracefully on the loveseat beside me, spreading her skirts wide so that they were partially on my thigh.

She had a glass of brandy in her hand, and her cheeks, usually so pale, were brightly flushed as she glanced at me with sparkling eyes and a wide smile.

When Branna had seated herself beside me earlier, even though our thighs were touching firmly (the loveseat was very small), there had been absolutely nothing sexual about the contact. Now, as Mikagi leaned forward, brushing her thigh against mine, her hip against mine, her shoulder and arm against mine...I wasn't so sure.

"I was trying to stop her, Elizabeth," said Mikagi then, pinning me in her sights. When I glanced at her in surprise, she chuckled, swirling the brandy in her glass. "Do you remember? When I met you in the hallway of the concert hall that night?"

"Yes," I told her, feeling a chill come over me.

"Magdalena had come for you. She was going to kill you, and once you were dead, she was going to make sure that your father found your body. But the moment she knew I was there, she changed her plan, and out of rage, she killed your friend Bob. I kept you safe. She knew not to attack when I was there. If it wasn't for me, well...you'd be dead."

There was a growl beside me, a low, thundering growl that seemed to reverberate into the very marrow of my bones, and when I glanced sidelong at Layne, she was no longer gripping my hand, and her eyes were no longer soft and gentle; they were ferocious, flashing with sparks of fury as she curled her hands into fists, sinking back onto her heels in a crouch beside me. "I was on my way. Magdalena would never have gotten to her," she began, but I reached out, placing a calming hand on her chest, and shook my head. It didn't stop her from continuing to growl, but at least she relaxed a little beneath my touch.

"What, is there a vampire Facebook, and she updated her status about killing me?" I asked bitterly, but Mikagi laughed a little beside me and took another sip of brandy.

"No. But I am friends with one of her friends. Which is how I knew," said Mikagi, leaning back in the loveseat. "Vampires are very…close. And there are a lot of vampires on the Council who are still undecided as to where they intend to place their loyalties," she said, one brow up.

"That's…terrifying," I said, taking a deep breath. But then I glanced at Mikagi—Mikagi who had saved my life. I didn't doubt that Layne was trying to make her way to me that evening, but no one could have ever suspected that I wouldn't have been safe when I was surrounded by so many people. I smiled at Mikagi. "Thank you," I told her sincerely, and Mikagi sank back against the loveseat, taking a very long drink from her glass and looked smug. When I glanced back at Layne, I was surprised to see a frown of jealousy come and go quickly across her face.

There was a knock at the door to the room, and Kane crossed over to the door and answered it. "Ah…a breakfast for you, Elizabeth," she said, taking a tray of food from a woman on the other side and shutting the door behind her with a murmured thanks. It was a silver tray with a silver-domed lid, and beneath the lid was a stack of pancakes, a stack of waffles, a bagel with butter and cream cheese, and a glass of orange juice.

I thanked Kane and then ate as much as I could while Tommie, Dolly, Mikagi and Victoria started a game of cards (what game it was, I wasn't quite certain), and Kane brought me another glass of brandy, sitting beside me and watching the card game with a sad look in her eyes. Branna offered me another glass of brandy…

And that's when the events of the night started to get a bit fuzzy.

Chapter 18: The Duel

Branna seemed to have been waiting for me to finish eating, because when I was done, she appeared out of thin air. She was holding three violin cases, their handles dangling from her fingers—one was mine, one was Mikagi's, and the third...

"It's mine," said Branna, handing my violin case to me, then glancing down at hers with a smile, lovingly caressing the surface of the case. "I play the fiddle, too—though not with the talent you two possess."

"I am looking forward to seeing this talent," said Kane, sitting down in the Victorian chair across from me. She lit up another cigarette, and though she gave me an encouraging smile, there was something morose about her features. I wanted to ask her about it, wanted to ask if she was all right, but Mikagi was already beside me and opening up her case, so I followed suit.

Mikagi and I took out our fiddles, setting the cases on the card table to do so. I wasn't that strong on my one leg, but Mikagi reached out when I lost my balance and leaned heavily on the table. She wrapped her arm tightly around my middle.

"I can hold you while you tune it," she said mildly, but I smiled wanly at her and tried to disentangle myself from her grasp. There was something about the way she was touching me; it was more intimate than she'd dared touch me before. I couldn't tell you exactly what made me think that. Maybe it was the expression on her face. But I felt a little uncomfortable.

"I'm good, thank you," I said, and she shrugged.

"Suit yourself." She removed her violin from the case and started to pluck at the strings, adjusting the notes and strumming at them, listening carefully.

Layne appeared at my left elbow, and again when I looked up at her—I really couldn't be imagining it—there was a flicker of jealousy in her expression. "Where do you want to play?" she asked me, and I glanced around at the empty, antique folding chairs that had been drawn up to the card table.

"Right there," I said, indicating the nearest chair, and Layne helped me to it. I sat down on the edge of the chair, and I tuned my violin, watching as Layne walked past Mikagi. Well, rather, she *stalked* past Mikagi, giving her an angry glance. Mikagi snorted, raking her bow across the strings and lifting her chin as she listened to the set of notes that emanated from the violin, as if she didn't have time to pay attention to Layne.

It was obvious that the two of them didn't like each other, but I wasn't, at that point in time, aware of *why*. I had a lot on my plate, obviously, but if I'd been a bit more sober that night, and if I'd been a bit more aware of my surroundings and the people I was with, I might have noticed sooner that there was more than a casual rivalry going on between Mikagi and Layne.

But I didn't. Instead, I tuned my violin as thoroughly as if I were about to perform on the stage. Because any performance you make is important. It was something my very first violin teacher had drilled into my head. Mikagi and I finished tuning at the same time, and she prowled over to me, holding her violin by its neck and her bow in easy fingers.

"Ready?" she asked, and I glanced up at her, resting my violin against my shoulder.

"What do you want to play?" I asked, as the other vampires in the room, and Layne, fell silent, watching the two of us expectantly.

"Do you know 'The Devil Made Me Do It'?" she asked, and when she grinned the challenge at me, I could see that her incisors were pointed.

"The Devil Made Me Do It" was Mikagi's first world-famous song. It was an original piece, done in a classical style, with an almost impossible range of staccato notes that had to be played with a lightning swiftness. It was an incredibly difficult song.

But, being the big Mikagi fangirl that I am...I'd learned the piece.

"Yeah," I said, and the drink that was currently rushing through my veins made me give her a cheeky grin in return when I lifted my bow to the strings. Mikagi watched me, and there was a flash of something odd behind her eyes. Something that I couldn't quite place.

We began to play.

The first few notes of "The Devil Made Me Do It" were a tease. They're long, drawn out, supple, as you bend the bow over the strings, coaxing out the notes like you'd caress the skin of a lover with your fingers, soft and teasingly...but then, almost immediately, the bow dives to the lower register of notes, your fingers dancing so quickly across the strings that they blur, your bow darting back and forth as you draw from your violin such a cacophony of notes that it sounds like chaos...*almost*. But not quite. There is an order and a reason to every note, and you begin to hear the dissonance of the music at the exact same time that the crescendo starts to build.

Every toe in the room was tapping in time to the music, because it was so damn infectious. Mikagi had, of course, written the song and performed it to massive audiences countless times. I'd learned the song and played it for my own amusement, so there was going to be a disparity in the level of confidence each of us had. But I'd also had a little too much to drink at this point, and the caution that normally affected how I played the violin had been thrown to the wind.

I played my fiddle with almost violent abandon as I closed my eyes, as I *felt* the music surging through me, through my arms, my fingers, the violin singing on my shoulder and on my chest and against my chin like it was a living, breathing part of me. Connected to me but also separate from me, and I was bringing it to life. The music surged through my heart not in some metaphorical way, but really and truly, vibrating from the box of the violin itself, through my bones and muscle and into my heart.

In the middle of that first song, I opened my eyes. I didn't look down at the violin or my fingers dancing across the strings or the bow. Instead, I looked out into the room. The vampires sat, some rapt with attention, like Branna, eyes shining, and Kane, pure emotion making her face appear pained, a single tear falling from the corner of her right eye and tracing its way across her pale cheek. Some others, like Tommie, were animatedly talking to each other, listening to the music but unmoved by it...which was perfectly all right. As a musician, I knew the truth we all do—that no one piece of music is for everyone. One song is meant for some people and will move them to tears, like Kane. But that one song will not create the same reaction in someone else. They have their own song that will move them so much that their heart will hurt, just from hearing the first few notes.

The trick, as a musician, is to find the people in the audience who are moved by your piece and watch *their* reactions.

But my eyes were searching for someone specific. I wanted to see what Layne thought of the piece. And I saw her standing there by the entrance to the room, leaning against the door frame with her shoulder, her hands deep into her jeans pockets as she watched Mikagi and I play. The set of her jaw was hard, and her breathing was fast, but when I gazed at her eyes then...well, I almost missed a note or two, my bow quaking in my hand in a minuscule way, causing the note to linger a tiny fraction longer than it should have.

Layne was gazing at me with eyes that were dark, dark with want and need and lust, yes... All of those things were present on her face as she licked her full lips, as she lifted her chin up, raking her dark hair out of her eyes and pinning me to the spot with her gaze. But there was something more behind her gaze than sexual desire.

There was so much more.

When Layne looked at me, it didn't matter that I was already pretty much drunk at that point; it didn't matter that my bow was skating across my strings faster than it had ever moved before, borne by the need to impress my peers (which was a pretty strong need for me in that moment, whether it was right or not), but also because I wanted to impress Mikagi—and I was fairly certain I was succeeding in doing that. It didn't matter that I was playing with my idol. It didn't matter that I was giving the performance of a lifetime, pure emotion pouring into every note I played because of everything I'd just learned...and because of the fact that, tomorrow, I was going to be irrevocably changed.

None of that mattered.

Because the only thing I cared about in that moment was that Layne was there, watching me. That she was gazing at me across the smoke-filled room with a look that could have cut through stone, her gaze so powerful that it seemed to slice the air and pierce me through; it was a physical thing that I felt in my heart, in my soul. The pain medication was rushing through me, mixed with the booze (in a far-off place, I remembered that I wasn't supposed to drink while medicated), though everything else about that moment was a bit muzzy, I could see, and knew to my bones and back that Layne was looking at me like I was the only woman in the entire world.

And it filled me with love, a sensation that rushed through me so quickly that I felt lightheaded.

The brandy, mixed with the euphoria of playing with Mikagi and of Layne watching me so intensely—it filled me, and I played harder, faster, better. I could sense Mikagi beside me speeding up on a song that she, herself, had written, because I was outpacing her.

Playing faster doesn't necessarily mean that the song is better for it, but this song had been created for the speed and agility of the musician, and it shone when pushed faster and harder. I look back on it now, and knowing that I was drunk, the piece was probably far from perfect. I remember it as perfect, though, and I'm still proud of how passionately I played as Layne watched me.

We moved together, Mikagi and I, climbing the mountains of notes and reaching the ultimate peak of the piece at the same time, our violins vibrating and thrumming with delight in our hands as we teased out the heights of that final note, holding it for what felt like a blissful eternity.

A cacophony of applause and cheers broke out as we finished the song with a flourish, holding up our violins and bows. Mikagi and I exchanged a glance, both of us grinning hugely, and I bowed to her from my seat. She bowed, too, holding her violin in front of her, and when she glanced up at me she gave me a soft smile.

Though we played other music that night, I would be hard pressed to remember the pieces. I know that Mikagi and I played together beautifully, the both of us urging each other on, challenging each other, our precision and feeling merging in ways it never had for me with any other violinist. I think that anyone listening would have said it was obvious that Mikagi was the gifted of the two of us, but I'm proud to say that I held my own as we dueled.

After a few classical pieces, Kane held up a hand and grinned sidelong at Branna, who was leaning forward in her seat on the couch, her eyes wide and tear-filled, her face rapt with attention.

"Branna," Kane told Mikagi and me, her voice low but warm, "is an excellent fiddle player. And I would love, so much, to hear her play with you."

Branna's cheeks flushed as Mikagi crossed the room

to hand Branna her case from the card table. "Yes, play with us. Come, I want to hear you. And we could use a third."

Branna was going to say something else, but when she looked down at the case, she broke out into a smile. "If you insist," she said, standing, and there was an infectious excitement in her voice. Branna took her fiddle from the case and began to tune it. It was obvious, even though she wasn't standing close to me at that point, that the fiddle was very, very old. I was assuming at least three hundred years, possibly four hundred. It had been handmade by someone, and it was rough, but the craftsperson had seen a fiddle and understood music, knew how to make an instrument that would sing with a voice that would move people to tears. I knew that just from how Branna plucked the strings as she tuned it. The sound that came from the hollow body of the violin made me breathless.

Still, the person who had made the instrument was more focused on the sound than the appearance, so the body of the fiddle itself was battered, folk quality. But I knew, more than most people, to never judge an instrument on superficialities.

And when Branna put her bow to the strings to tease out those first few notes after tuning, my heart actually skipped a beat.

Mikagi whooped, and then she lifted her violin to her chin, and she was playing along with Branna immediately. Those first few notes evolved into a lively Irish reel, and though I didn't know the notes, I was able to follow along, joining in to play a bass line. Branna strode over to the two of us, playing, and then, with an adorably impish look on her face, and turning in one graceful movement...she began to jig.

I laughed in delight. It was obvious that Branna had done this many, many times before, and as I watched her feet expertly execute the jig, her bow and strings never missing a single note as she played the hell out of that fiddle, Mikagi began to dance around her, too.

Mikagi couldn't jig, but she'd made a name for herself with her on-stage theatrics; she always danced along to the music she was playing. So she began to sort-of jig as she whirled around Branna, hopping in time to the music gracefully, and I chuckled again as the two of them began to duel with the music.

Branna would lean forward at the waist, and Mikagi would lean back, and then Mikagi would lean forward, and Branna would lean back, their bows skating across the strings as if the strings were on fire. As I watched, some of the horsehair on Branna's bow began to snap from the pressure and the speed, as did Mikagi's, curling up on either side of her bow as the two slayed their strings.

Branna's hair, an arrangement of gelled locks that had resembled a tiny pompadour, was coming undone, strands falling around her face as she played so quickly and expertly that—well, was it my imagination, or were her strings actually *smoking*?

I picked up my own pace, trying to keep up with the two of them as Mikagi and Branna danced around each other, but it was a lost cause. I conceded and kept playing the bass line of the jig as Branna and Mikagi reached a crescendo that made my heart pound inside of me as I drew my bow back and forth, trying to match them.

The final note was one of triumph, and when Mikagi and Branna raised their bows in salute to each other, ending the song, the other vampires in the room were on their feet, applauding so hard and cheering so loudly that the entire room was filled with the happiness of that sound. I lifted my bow and waved it in the violinist's salute, and when Branna glanced back at me, her face was flushed with excitement, and a grin split her face from ear to ear.

Mikagi looked back at me, and she was smiling, too, laughing in delight. Her cheeks were flushed from her drink, and her eyes were glittering with the type of triumph you can only feel after playing a piece of music, and playing it in such a deeply soul-satisfying way that you've never felt more alive.

I've felt that way more times than I can count. It's why I'm a musician, why this is my deep, abiding passion...

But there was something more in Mikagi's gaze when she glanced at me, her cheeks flushed, her dark eyes wild, her incisors descended.

There was something there that—if I'd been paying attention—I would have recognized for what it was. But I wasn't paying attention. I was flushed myself, and the booze was racing through my veins, making everything seem bigger and brighter and better, somehow.

But I know now that Mikagi was looking at me with longing, as clearly and brazenly as Layne had been regarding me earlier.

Branna clapped me on the back with enthusiasm, pressing a wine stem into my hands and offering a toast to me for my performance. Everything was getting very muzzy, and I set my violin and its bow back in my case, and Branna was bringing a chair closer to me to talk shop, excitedly asking me where I'd gotten my fiddle.

"Verity's Violin Shop," I told her proudly, and Branna's smile was big as she leaned forward.

"I've been there! She's lovely. I bought a fiddle from there last year. Has she gotten anything new?"

"Several really good fiddles are in her shop right now," I said, then glanced around the room. "Layne went with me, and there's one in particular she liked. It has a story…" But I trailed off, frowning a little. Layne was nowhere in sight. "Kane, do you know where Layne went?" I asked as the vampire walked past me, wineglass in hand.

"She said something about your room." Her brow furrowed. "And that she'd be back soon."

"Oh," I told her, and then I offered up a weak smile. I knew it was the brandy doing the thinking for me, but after performing like that…well, I'd really wanted a kiss from her. I'd wanted to be in her arms. It was passionate and made my blood pound to play music like that, and I'd played with my idol, something I couldn't believe I'd done, something I'd *dreamed* of doing. Yes, playing with Mikagi in the orchestra had been tremendous, but to play side by side with her, and with Branna, too, who was such a superb musician—it had been an out-of-this-world experience.

I wanted to share the moment with Layne. But she wasn't here.

"Where did you get your fiddle?" I asked Branna then, taking a long gulp of my drink. I set the empty stem back on the card table and stared at it a bit confusedly. How many times had Kane refilled my glass at this point? I'd lost track.

"I made it when I was a kid," said Branna, wrinkling her nose and glancing shyly at me. "Kane and I grew up in Ireland, long ago, before we were both changed—and I was passionate about music even then. I saw someone playing a fiddle in my village. We didn't have many fiddles around, so I asked him if I could look at it, examine it, and I did... And then I made that violin."

"Are you kidding?" I asked, slurring the words, but Branna shook her head. She most definitely wasn't kidding and seemed to be delighted by my enthusiastic reaction. "Did you have to, like, soak the wood and stuff?" I asked. My head felt heavy, and, admittedly, I was still a little unclear as to how violins were made.

"Yes!" Branna exclaimed, then glanced down at the tabletop, her modesty making her blush again. "It wasn't that hard," she said quietly.

"Oh, my goodness, I'd *love* if you made me a violin," I said, and when she glanced up at me, her eyes wide, I patted her shoulder. Or, at least, I tried to pat her shoulder, but I missed the first time around. I felt so *good* at that point. "I'd love that!" I kept saying to her, until Kane walked past again, this time with her head low, in a deep discussion with Tommie.

"Kane looks really sad," I told Branna, and—I've got to say right now—that if the drink hadn't made me so bold, I'd never have made such a brash assessment out loud.

It wasn't my business whether Kane looked unhappy or not, but my heart ached with sympathy whenever I looked at her, and I wanted to understand why. I lifted my brows and glanced at Branna, and she leaned back in her chair, putting her hands behind her head as she stared at the tabletop uncomfortably.

"Yeah, she's been...sad for a long time," said Branna then, lifting her eyes to meet mine. "Her lover died a long time ago in a fire. And Kane's never forgiven herself for it."

"Oh, my God. That's terrible." I covered my mouth with my hands.

Branna shrugged and bit her lip. "That's one of the prices of living as long as we do. We carry our tragedies with us for an unnaturally long time."

I glanced up at Kane, who was still deep in discussion with Tommie across the room, her hands in her suit pants pockets, her shoulders curling forward and her brow furrowed with concern. Right now, the sadness wasn't as apparent on her face, but when she turned to say something to Dolly, who'd run up behind her animatedly, wine sloshing out of her wine stem, there was softness there, but then the sadness came again, almost imperceptibly, and she stared at the ground for a moment, her jaw tight.

I was about to say something else to Branna when someone tapped my shoulder with soft fingers that lingered against me.

I looked up at Mikagi, and when I saw her gazing down at me, I grinned. I hadn't had a chance to congratulate her yet on how well she had played, and I laid it on thick: "Mikagi, you are... You are so *good*! I mean, I'm sure you know that, but... It was so *amazing* to play with you, seriously! A dream come true!" I told her, and when she crouched down next to me, I gave her a totally awkward, terrible hug. I actually leaned so far forward in my chair that I fell *out* of the chair and into her lap as she crouched back on her heels on the floor.

But Mikagi had been, apparently, expecting me to

271

do just that, and she caught me easily, standing with me in her arms, as if this were a perfectly natural progression.

"Do you want to get some air?" she asked mildly, one brow raised. "You look flushed, Elizabeth."

"Yeah, good idea," I slurred to her, and after I said goodbye to Branna, Mikagi was moving through the vampires and out of the hazy, smoky room, into the corridor. The hallway was darker now, the chandeliers overhead dimmed. And it was late, I realized, as Mikagi walked past a grandfather clock that only struck once, for one o'clock in the morning.

"The Sullivans built their hotel on a cliff face that overlooks the beach. Would you like to go down and see the ocean? It's an almost-full moon out. Very beautiful," said Mikagi, and her mouth was turning up at the corners mischievously.

I didn't know where Layne was, but I didn't see the harm in going down to the beach with Mikagi. She'd promised my father that she'd keep me safe, just as Layne had promised, and I did trust her. She was a good person; we were becoming friends. Besides, I couldn't remember having ever strolled the shores of Maine before, and I was pretty excited about it.

"Yeah, let's do it. It'll be fun!" I practically sang, kicking my one good leg in her grasp, and Mikagi chuckled, adjusting her hold on me so that she was gripping me a little tighter to prevent me from bouncing out of her arms.

"You don't hold your drink very well," she said mildly, and I was laughing, wrapping my arms around her neck.

"No." I wrinkled my nose. "I'm a lightweight. But it's okay. I've got stuff…things… I don't know. Stuff, tomorrow," I said drunkenly. "And tonight, I don't want to think about anything."

"I can understand that," said Mikagi, nodding. "Just for tonight, things can be however you want them to be." And she looked at me curiously when she said that, but

I was staring up at the impressive ceilings overhead; this one was painted with art deco-style stars.

Mikagi carried me through hallways and down stairs, and we were finally out in the fresh air of that sultry June night. It wasn't nearly as hot out as I thought it would be because the ocean was right there, cooling the land, but still—I unbuttoned the top few buttons of my shirt and fanned myself.

"It's so hot," I murmured as Mikagi began to carry me down a path that was carved into the cliff face, leading—I assumed—to the sea. Spellbound, I watched the ocean rolling, the breakers pounding against the rocks. I breathed in deeply, tasting the salt on my lips, and I tipped my head back against Mikagi's shoulder and stared up at the beautiful stars overhead. There were so *many*. Eternal Cove was far enough away, evidently, from any of the major cities in Maine that light pollution was nonexistent. I could see the spangle of the Milky Way far, far above me, that rush of white and stars merging together, and it made me breathless.

"It's so beautiful," I exhaled, and Mikagi chuckled, carrying me across the sand toward the shore.

"The night is beautiful and hot... This is true," she teased me, her dark eyes flashing with merriment. "What else is it?"

"Salty," I said, licking my lips and laughing. "Very, very salty."

Mikagi set me down on a piece of driftwood. I was grateful to take off my flats and sink my feet into the sand, wiggling my toes and sighing happily. If my thigh hurt from my wiggling, I didn't feel it. The booze had numbed everything.

Everything except...

"I wish Layne were here to see this," I sighed.

Mikagi had seated herself beside me, and she peered at me now, her mouth downturned. "Surely you don't see a future with that wolf."

"I...I do," I began, but Mikagi was already shaking

her head.

"You shouldn't waste your time with that dog," said Mikagi, one brow raised as she leaned against me. "You are not a vampire yet, Elizabeth, but you are meant to be one. And you are meant to be with someone who is your equal, someone just like you…" She trailed off, and despite my inebriated state, I suddenly realized how close Mikagi was to me: that her arm was wrapped tightly around my waist, that she was drawing me toward her with a strong arm, her mouth a mere inch from my own…

"Mikagi, what—" I began, but I didn't get any farther.

Because Mikagi was kissing me.

Her kiss was so much different from Layne's. Her mouth was cold against me—so cold that I shivered when she pressed her lips to mine. It was strong, this kiss, insistent and demanding, and if the circumstances had been different, if she had come to me at an earlier point in my life, I would be kissing her right back, wrapping my arms around her neck, drawing her close. I had been in love with Mikagi's music for as long as she'd been making it. I respected her as an artist deeply, and to be able to play with her tonight had been pure magic.

But all of that wasn't so important anymore. Because as much as I respected and admired Mikagi, and as much as I loved her music, I didn't love *her*, and I never could.

Because I loved Layne.

That sobering fact was as clear as the stars overhead, and I pushed against Mikagi's shoulders—gently, but with insistence.

She broke off the kiss, her mouth open, her lips wet, and she stared down at me with narrowed eyes. "What is it?" she asked, and then her voice was angry. "Is it about that dog?"

"She's not a dog," I said carefully, then drew in a deep breath. "Layne and I are in love."

Mikagi snorted. "You can't be in love with someone like her. You are *heir* to your father's seat on the Nocturne Council, Elizabeth. You cannot be with that wolf if you expect to maintain the position."

Shaken, I stared at her. "You're wrong," I told her emphatically. "I...I admire you. Please don't misunderstand me," I said, spreading my hands on my lap, "but I love Layne. I *love* her. I loved her from the first moment I saw her, and that *means* something."

Mikagi rolled her eyes. "Love. I didn't peg you for a sentimental." Then her voice became hard again. "No one will take you seriously as the Nocturne Council leader if you have that dog at your heels. And *then*," she said heatedly, "everything that your father has built will crumble."

Too drunk to hold back at that point, I was shaking my head, curling my hands into fists. "I don't *care* about any of that," I slurred. "I never signed up for *any* of this. I don't even know if I *want* to be a leader." I gulped down air. "I don't even know if I want to be a *vampire*."

Mikagi stood, brushing off the back of her skirt with short, sharp movements. "If you were with me," she said, anger making her words just as sharp as her motions, "you wouldn't be laughed at."

I stared up at her, and nothing was clearer in that moment: "Let them laugh," I told her simply. "I love Layne, and no matter what happens, I am going to give our relationship a chance."

Mikagi crouched down beside me, and for a long moment, she didn't say a thing. The salty wind blew across the sand, ruffling her straight black hair, and her dark eyes held something unfathomable. Then she reached out, and she gently brushed an errant wisp of hair out of my face and behind my ear with freezing fingers. Her hand was so cold against me, her fingers like ice against my skin, but I didn't shiver. Instead, I stared her down just as fiercely as she stared at me.

"You must make your own decisions, Elizabeth,"

she said, one brow raised, letting her hand fall back to her knee. "But once you realize what is best for you, you'll know that you should be with me."

I was about to protest, but at that moment, the hairs on the back of my neck started to stand on end. I turned, because my entire being was begging me to do so, in the same instinctual way that you would keep a predator in your sights if you were at the zoo, staring at lions through the bars.

I turned, and Mikagi turned, and there, on the path that led down to the ocean from the hotel, stood Layne.

Chapter 19: Playing with Fire

Layne strode toward us down the path carved into the cliff face at top speed. Her head was bent, her eyes flashing, practically on fire, and Mikagi actually took a step back when the werewolf finally reached the sand.

There was something feral about Layne in that moment, something that reminded me of the night with the gunman: he had backed away from her, too, his eyes wide with fear, even though *he* was the one holding the gun. Even though Layne was completely unarmed.

Layne then, as now, seemed raw, potent. There was power radiating off of her in waves, a deadly power that projected ahead of her, rushing toward us with so much strength that I felt it physically, a tangible thing, as if she were directly in front of me, towering over me, though she was still at least fifty feet away. I don't know how to describe the sensation, even now, other than to compare it to a wall that was pushed ahead of her, a wall of white-hot energy that you couldn't ignore. You had to step back, move out of the way, or you'd be crushed by it.

"*Tasuki*," Layne growled when she was close enough to us that her voice could carry across the distance. That's when she finally paused in her approach. Her hands were in fists, her shoulders curled forward, and I realized as I was staring at her that this was exactly how she'd looked when she was about to transform into a wolf. I'd only seen it happen once, but that was something I couldn't ever forget.

Still, though the energy waves pulsed from her, and

though she looked aggressive, angry, I stood (well, sat) my ground, perched on the edge of the driftwood, staring muzzily up at the woman who had saved my life, the woman I was falling in love with...

The woman who, standing there on the beach, looked like she was about to become a monster.

"Layne, what's going on?" I asked, and I cleared my throat, trying my best to stand. But I was drunk, and I began to fall to the side, slipping in the sand, losing my balance in an instant.

Mikagi was right beside me, and she reached out and caught me smoothly, her arm tight around my waist and pressing me against her side, but this action caused Layne to growl again. I pushed gently off of Mikagi, raked my hair out of my eyes, and took a hop forward on my good leg, putting up my hands in a soothing gesture—or, at least, what I hoped would appear soothing.

"Layne, what the hell?" I said succinctly. "Everything's okay. Please calm down."

"She *kissed* you," said Layne, and her lips were drawn over her teeth in a snarl.

I blinked, then sighed, nodding. "Yeah, she did, but I told her to stop, and she also did that. Immediately." I glanced back at Mikagi, who was standing there with her arms crossed in front of her and a sneer on her lips. But, to her credit, she did nothing else to provoke Layne. "There was some miscommunication between us...or something like that," I muttered to Layne, shaking my head. "Maybe I sent the wrong signals. And Mikagi is awesome—"

"Thanks," Mikagi muttered dryly.

"But she's not you. I'm falling in love with *you*. Not Mikagi. So, please, seriously... Put the wolf away."

Layne's snarl, her forward-leaning body, her fists, her entire being appeared to pause for a moment, and she stared at me with wide eyes, relaxing just a little as she considered my words.

"Elizabeth's telling the truth," said Mikagi, her brow

rising higher. "Despite all of my protests that it's the *worst* idea for her to be with you, she wants you, anyway." Mikagi shrugged now, glancing at Layne with a sideways smile. "So, congratulations, wolf. You got yourself a vampire."

"I'm not a vampire yet," I muttered, as Mikagi stalked past me, aiming toward the path that led back up to the Sullivan Hotel.

"Tomorrow, you will be," she shot back over her shoulder. "So enjoy your last night as a human." And then, with her arms wrapped around her as if she were staving off the cold—even though it was a warm night—Mikagi walked up the path, her skirt swishing about her legs. Soon, she was lost from sight.

Layne stared at me; she looked as if the wind had been knocked out of her sails. She drooped, her fists uncurling at her sides as she worked her jaw, taking a deep breath. "The two of you were sitting so close together, and... And she kissed you, and I..." Layne sighed for a long moment, then stood a little straighter, raking her hand back through her hair in frustration. "I thought..." Layne took a deep breath. "I thought that, when she kissed you, you wanted it, too. That you wanted *her*."

"No," I said, and I hopped forward, curling my fingers into the lapels of her leather jacket to keep myself upright. I leaned against her. "I have feelings for you, Layne. I meant what I said earlier. I want to give this, us, a chance."

"I'm sorry. I'm sorry," she repeated, searching my eyes, then groaning a little. "God, I just behaved like such a *wolf*."

I grinned at her in spite of myself, shaking my head. "Yeah, well, you can't help what you are."

"Yes, I can, and I should," said Layne, and she sounded so earnest. "I'm sorry. It's just... Mikagi sort of got to me. She'd been talking to me. Before. On the drive up to the hotel," said Layne, raking her fingers through her hair again. Usually so self-confident, her voice was softer now, more subdued. And her eyes looked troubled. "And she was saying how it'd be in our best interests to forget about each other. Because of the whole werewolf thing. I mean, I'm highly aware of the fact that two vampires together—that you and Mikagi together—would please the Council, and that if I was with you, I'd put you in danger..." She trailed off and searched my face. "And I was really angry when I saw you with her, but I kind of wondered—I couldn't help but wonder—if maybe she was right all along, and—"

"Layne," I said, drawing out the single syllable of her name. I sagged against her, feeling lightheaded, the booze rushing through me. Every inhibition I possessed seemed to launch itself into the wind and vanish. "*Layne*," I repeated, and then I drew myself up as tall as I could, standing on the tiptoes of my one good leg, and I tugged on the collar of her leather jacket, tugging her face down to mine.

"I love you," I repeated, "werewolf or not. Vampire or not. Alien or not—"

Layne laughed, the velvety sound filling the night air. Behind the two of us, the surf pounded against the beach over and over again, a rhythm as old as time; overhead, a million stars shone brightly, twinkling along to the the music of the spheres. There was salt in the air, sand on my toes, and I realized that I had never been in a more romantic setting in my life...

And I realized, too, that this was all I had. Here. *Now*. The present moment. Tomorrow, everything was going to change. Tomorrow, I would have to help my father maintain his leadership of the Council. There would probably be a fight with Magdalena and her followers.

And before all of that, I'd have to Change into a vampire—bright and early.

It...was going to be a busy day.

So I dragged Layne to me, and she put her arms around my waist, and I stared up into her changeable eyes, and I felt my entire body come alive.

"I have no idea how to show you that I'm falling for you," I told her then, taking a deep breath. "But I'm going to damn well try."

And that's when I found myself kissing her.

I kissed Layne with so much fierceness that, in that moment, you'd be hard pressed to tell which one of us was the wolf. I tasted the heat of her, the fire of her, as she opened her mouth to me, darting her tongue into my mouth as if she'd been waiting for this moment, this signal. Like this kiss was keeping her alive. She drank me deeply, gripping my hips so tightly that I wondered if they were going to be bruised tomorrow—and then realized that I didn't care if they were.

I didn't want to wait anymore for something good to happen.

I wanted something good to happen right *now*, damn it. And I was going to make it happen—if that's what Layne wanted, too.

The heat of the moment rushed through me, filling me with a red-hot want. I drew in a deep breath, and then I took a step back from Layne (more of a hop, really), pinning her to the spot with my gaze.

I lifted my chin. "Let's do this," I murmured to her, and I let go of her, reaching up with my fingers until I felt the fabric of my blouse beneath my palms. Then slowly, carefully, I found myself unbuttoning my blouse. I bit my lip, watching her chest heave as she stared at me, watching her breathing hard as she watched me with dark, wanting eyes, following the path of my fingers with a hungry gaze. But then she glanced back up at the path that led to the Sullivan Hotel with a small frown.

"You want to do this…right here?" she asked, and then she was stepping forward, and her fingers were tracing their way over the buttons of my shirt, following the path of my hands and undoing the rest of the buttons so quickly. I struggled out of the shirt, peeling it over my shoulders and down my arms, letting it flutter to the sand, and then I was stepping forward and tugging at her leather jacket, pulling it down her shoulders and over her arms insistently.

"You're really fine with doing this here? On the beach?" she asked me, and her lips were curled up at the corners, and one brow was raised.

"Layne O'Connell," I said, using my best stern voice, as I pulled at her jacket in exasperation, "you're a *werewolf*. You should *want* to have sex in the wild, right?" I paused. "Right? Was that offensive? Sorry, if that was offensive—"

"Elizabeth..." said Layne, and then she was laughing out loud, peals of laughter that rang out around us as she shrugged a little, letting me take her leather jacket off. Then she took the jacket from me, and, heedless about the sand scraping the leather, she set it down, spreading it out like a chivalrous knight.

"Are you sure this is what you want?" she asked me, her voice a low growl as she drew me down beside her. The desire in her words was enough to make me melt, inside and out. I was already so wet, every bit of my body and heart longing for her touch, that as I sat there on the ground, panting, I couldn't tell her "yes" fast enough.

But I tried, anyway.

"Yes," I told her, and I was pulling at her t-shirt, tugging it up and over her head. It flew to the side, falling to the sand, and then I had my fingers at the edges of her gray sports bra, intent on getting rid of that in a heartbeat.

But Layne had ideas of her own, and she took my wrists gently—but very firmly—pushing my hands down into the sand on either side of my hips with a tempered strength. My breath hitched in my throat as she knelt between my legs, as she arched over me, and I found myself leaning back down onto my elbows, spreading my legs wide as I drew them up, bending my knees to rest my feet flat on the sand. I was able to ignore the pulsing pain in my leg as I drew my knees up, but I did wince a little when I realized how much I'd pulled my hurt thigh back, the pain arcing through me in that instant with an unwelcome crackle of electricity.

Layne paused, her brow furrowed, gazing down at me in concern. "What is it?" she asked, her voice low, her fingers stilled on my stomach, over my bare skin.

I growled in frustration—the pain was already gone—and lifted my face toward hers. "It's just my stupid leg, don't worry, it doesn't bother me," I told her, dragging her down on top of me breathlessly. I wrapped my one good leg around her middle, and though she glanced sidelong at the wound on my thigh, made visible by my skirt pooling around my hips now that I was lying on my back, she didn't stop. Layne placed her hands on either side of my shoulders in the sand, her hot mouth at my neck.

Thank God she didn't stop...because I'd had no idea, up until this moment, *exactly* how much I needed this.

Exactly how much I needed *her*.

I'd wanted her in the forest at Dogtown, when she had pressed me up against that tree, her mouth hot against my own, my entire body alive with a desire I couldn't remember having ever felt. I'd wanted her so very many times since we'd started working together, from the very first moment I met her, seeing her face in profile for a heartbeat in my father's study and feeling my own heartbeat quicken deep inside of me. I remembered the heat that flooded through me when Layne had joked with me about fruit in relation to my chest (something I would never, ever forget, and would, in fact, tease her unceasingly about forever). I'd wanted this for so long, wanted *her* for so long, and it was finally happening. *We* were finally happening.

And that made this moment, one of a small handful I had left as a human, that much more poignant and precious.

And let's be honest: it was hot as hell.

I had my fingers wrapped around her leather belt as Layne made a trail of heated kisses down from my mouth, across my jaw, down my neck; I hissed against her, feeling the warmth of her lips on that curve of shoulder and neck, her teeth against my skin, nipping me just enough that I moaned, trying to find release by pressing my center down on her hips. But she was still arched above me, and there was no release to be found, because she was purposefully keeping herself from me, high above me on her knees. I groaned against her in frustration as she bit me again, a perfect, little bite on my shoulder as she traced her hot palms up my arms, the fire of them burning over my skin, until she came to the straps of my bra. She hooked her fingers beneath them and pulled the straps down in tantalizing slow motion, the heat of her fingertips and the fabric coasting over my skin eliciting from me a powerful shiver.

I was on fire.

I breathed out, glancing up at Layne. Everything felt heightened in that moment, and though I was drunk, my memory captured sensations: the sand bit into my elbows, the leather was cool but warming beneath my skin. Layne was between my legs, her jeans brushing against the skin of my thighs, her hazel eyes staring down at me with a brightness I'd never seen in them before. Her face, above me, was framed by stars, and the sound of our breathing, of my soft moans, was undercut by the *shush* of the sea. I reached up, curling my fingers around her neck and brought her down to me for another kiss. This was a moment that was special, that was electric. This moment was everything.

Layne did kiss me, and fiercely, as she traced her fingers over the slope of my stomach and side, up and up to my breasts and the tops of my bra cups, and she gently skimmed her sandy hands over my skin. There was enough friction that this felt delicious, and I moaned again, trying to press my center against her, pulling her body down to me with my good leg and bucking up against her.

She chuckled then, her mouth against my neck, the vibration of her voice dancing over my skin, and that's when she pressed down on me, letting her hips connect with me.

She was still wearing jeans, and since my skirt was hiked up around my hips, it was just my panties between me and that exquisite pressure, which she gladly gave. I hissed against her, wrapping my arms tightly around her shoulders as she began to slowly pump her hips up and down, pulling my bra cups to my waist, effectively pinning my arms to my sides as she leaned over, brushing her black hair over my chest, teasing its satin softness over my exposed skin. I shivered beneath her, and that's when she glanced up at me with a wicked smile, bent her head and licked my right nipple.

The wetness of her mouth made me shiver against her, but then her mouth was at my breast again, and this time it wasn't a sweet, soft lick—she devoured my nipple, laving her tongue across the peak, twisting it and tugging it with her teeth and biting down in a way that made me squirm beneath her. My fingers, hooked into her belt, began to undo the belt slowly; I arched underneath her, my eyes closed as pleasure burned through me.

Yes, I was drunk. Yes, it was very, very hard for me to manage the clasp of her belt, my fingers slipping every time they tried to undo the buckle. But I was still thinking clearly. In fact, I felt as if I were thinking clearly for the first time in a long time. There was nothing between Layne and me except a little bit of clothing (and, if I had anything to say about it, that impediment would disappear in a matter of moments). Our hearts pressed together, I whispered her name into the dark, and in that moment, the uncertainty of tomorrow couldn't touch me.

Only she could.

"Layne, yes, there," I hissed out as she trailed her fingertips over my stomach, over the skirt hitched up at my waist, and along the band of my panties. There was still that bit of fabric that separated the two of us, but she traced her fingers over it, too, and down, down, over my clit, over my open, wet center; I moaned against her, gripping her shoulders, scratching her skin. Desperate. Wanting.

"Please," I murmured, and she pushed the fabric of

the panties away from my opening with her thumb, drifting her fingers over my wetness, her breath hitching as she seemed to realized how wet I was. I dug my fingernails into the muscles of her arm, pulsing my hips down, aching, wanting.

And then her fingers were inside of me.

Her thumb brushed over my clit as she entered me, sliding her fingers through my wetness like silk, curving up and into me with controlled power, and my hips rose up to meet her as I gritted my teeth, trying not to use my wounded leg to start the rhythm. I filled my hands with sand, twisting beneath her, crying out as she bent her head and licked my neck, as she captured my mouth again with her own, pulsing her hand in and out of me with such an exquisite rhythm that my entire body asked in that moment: asking for more, harder, faster. I let go of the sand and wrapped my arms around her neck once more as she kissed me. I trailed my dirty hands down her back, across her sports bra, hooking my fingers in the edge of it again and pulling it up and over her shoulders, tossing it away to the sand.

In that moment, I had clarity as the pain in my leg twinged. In a perfect world, I would be on top of her, soon, just like she was on top of me. I wanted her like that, had dreamed of that moment…but I was hurt, and my leg wasn't going to allow me to kneel between her legs. So I was going to have to get creative. I knew my limits, and I knew what I wanted…and I knew that somehow I was going to make those two things converge.

I'd figure out a way.

Her body rose over me in the dark, but it wasn't *that* dark. There was a moon and many, many stars to see by. To see *her* by. She pumped her hand in and out of me, moving through my wetness, her mouth open, panting, and as I stared up at her in the dark, I couldn't help but see her hard nipples, tightly peaked, the small curve of her breasts. I reached up, tracing my sandy hand over her right breast, feeling the satin smoothness of her skin, feeling the hardness of her nipple beneath the pad of my thumb. She increased her rhythm, began to move in and out of me faster, harder.

"God, yes," I groaned again. My entire body *felt* the yes-ness of what she was doing, felt the pleasure she was drawing out of me with two fingers and a thumb, in and out of me and again and again upon my clit; waves of a beginning orgasm were crashing over my body just as hard as the waves beat the shore. I felt the power and rhythm of those waves, felt the power and rhythm of Layne's fingers inside of me, of her mouth against my own, of her arm wrapped around me, holding me, caressing me, everything growing better and bigger and brighter as she coaxed from me an orgasm unlike any I had ever felt before.

When I came, it was shattering, the sensation of weightlessness, of rising above the earth and becoming one with the stars. I'd never felt *this* good, *this* right, and as wave after wave of ecstasy pushed its way through me, I shuddered, calling her name, saying "yes," whispering into her ear so that she growled against me, satisfied as she played me like a fiddle, drawing out that one, perfect note as long as the instrument could bear it. And I *could* bear it; I could bear it all as my head flung back against the sand, as I felt shattered and remade.

"God," I finally murmured when I was capable of speech again, my heartbeat fluttering against my chest so fast I kind of wondered if it hadn't sprouted wings, beating against my ribs like it wanted out. Layne was still on top of me, her hips still rising over mine, between my legs, and her fingers were still inside of me. She grinned wolfishly at me then as she drew them out, and then she kissed my mouth softly, almost questioningly, her grin gone.

"What?" I asked her when she drew back, when she looked down at me with wide eyes, still full of want, but also longing and hope, all at once.

And love. There was so much love evident in her expression, in her face, in her eyes, a warmth and tenderness that transformed the hard lines of her face, the frown she normally wore, to something soft and good. It took my breath away.

"I just want to remember you like this," she told me then, gripping my left hip with one hand and tracing the other across my face, her fingertips creating hot patterns as she smoothed a strand of hair behind my ear. "I want… I want this etched in my memory forever. This," she growled, and she placed a kiss on my stomach, her mouth hot against my skin, "here," and she placed a kiss between my breasts as my breathing quickened, "*now*," she whispered, and she placed a kiss over my heart, her mouth wet.

My heartbeat was now thundering inside of me, and I drew her up, pulling on her shoulders until she was directly above me, her body a perfect mirror to my own as she arched in the darkness.

"The moment's not over yet," I promised her fiercely, and strength was beginning to build in me again, because I knew that I wanted her just as much as she'd wanted me, the need for her burning through me as brightly as the sensation and heat of her skin against my own.

My fingers were at Layne's belt buckle again, and I cried out in triumph (I actually said "ha!") when I finally got the damn thing undone. I slid the leather out of her belt loops and flung the belt away into the sand, immediately tracing my fingers over the waistband of her jeans as I tried to unbutton them. I fumbled at the button and zipper, the drink still racing through me and making this much harder than it had to be, but I got them both undone, to my credit, and then I was shimmying the jeans down over her hips. But her legs were too long, and with how she was crouched there, I knew I couldn't pull them off by myself, not without putting pressure on my leg to sit up.

So I thought about it for half a heartbeat, and then my solution came to me, burning through me with heat as I considered it. Layne raised a brow as I grinned wickedly up at her. I sat up on my elbows on the sand again, putting my head to the side as I regarded her. "Take them off," I told her then, gesturing with my hand to her jeans, pooling down around her hips now. Layne sat up, crouching between my legs and back onto her heels, her smile bordering on wicked, too, as she glanced down at me, her breath already coming fast.

The moon was almost full out, and it really was beautiful, how the silver light spilled down all around us on the sand, turning the beachscape that looked so picturesque in waking hours, with sunshine pouring down onto it, into a silver paradise. The moonlight was so bright that it illuminated everything almost perfectly. There was enough light to see by, and that's what made my heart skip a beat.

With my gaze, I traced the perfect curve of her neck and shoulders, down to the gentle slopes of her muscled arms, the contours and muscled planes of her belly, the perfect curve of her breasts and those hardened nipples, the way she clenched her jaw as she watched me looking at her... Every little part of this moment stood out in detail, and I drank it all in as I cocked my head, lifting my chin; I stared at her in defiance, then.

"Take. Them. Off," I repeated, and my voice was low when I spoke the words, and powerful. Layne lifted her own chin, a challenge flaring in her eyes as her grin deepened.

"I don't usually take orders," she growled, arching over me and tracing her short fingernails over my thighs, careful to avoid my wound. I was shivering on the inside—God, it felt so good; *she* felt so good—but I didn't let it show. I breathed out.

"You work for me, don't you?" I asked imperiously, my heart thundering inside of me, my breath coming short as I murmured the words. Layne raised her other brow, and she stared down at me in genuine surprise. I felt the flush of desire race over my skin, and I pushed up from my elbows onto my hands now, sitting fully, almost close enough to kiss her.

I didn't feel *physically* powerful because my thigh was

throbbing. Normally, I'd be on top of her, pushing her down onto the ground, my hands at her wrists, my mouth hot against hers while she smiled against me. I wanted to take her in bed with strength and confidence, take her so that she growled my name, panting under my touch and begging for release. I wanted to be strong as I moved over her...but I didn't have the luxury of physical strength today.

But I could be powerful in other ways, and we could do this together. If she was into it.

And she very much was.

For a long moment, Layne didn't respond to me at all, her eyes flickering with something I couldn't quite place as she watched me carefully. There was heat in her gaze, and her eyes were dark with longing, and when she took a deep breath, lifting her chin again as she stared at me with a small smile, I could feel my breathing increasing, and knew I was already wet again, and that was just from a single *look*.

I could feel the tension between us crackling as she stared at me long and hard, and the electricity dazzled between us as she considered my words.

But then she nodded once, twice, and she was whispering: "Yes, ma'am." Her voice was low, and her grin was so wide, she was almost chuckling as she tried to control it, biting her lip and forcing her mouth to flatten into a neutral line. She rose up onto her knees, pulled her pants over her hips and down her legs easily, and then she was setting them beside her. She knelt back in the sand, crouching on her heels, her hands flat on her thighs as she watched me with glittering, dark eyes, her mouth a little bit open, her lips wet...her breathing fast.

Lust roared through me as I tipped my head back a little, watching her through my long lashes. I let my eyes stray over her body now, carefully memorizing everything. I lingered there, looking at her, admiring her physique, her toned muscles, her round, small breasts and the soft, tantalizing curve of them as they rose and fell as she breathed. I loved the dichotomy of her, the strength and fierceness of her muscles and the softness of her breasts and skin, the heat of her entire body and the fire in her eyes as she watched me watching her, watched me trace her body with my gaze, her breathing coming faster for it, her hands curling into fists on her thighs, even though I felt that she didn't want me to see what my gaze was doing to her.

She wanted to be impenetrable. But, for me, she wasn't.

Layne's back was stiff, straight, and as she stared at me, I saw the wolf in her eyes, the animal that rose there, all raw and wild as she stared me down. I saw the fierceness that was Layne O'Connell, and I wanted her so much in that moment, I was undone.

"Come here," I told her, and I laid back down on her leather jacket, my head pillowed against the softness of the sand as she rose over me, placing her hands on either side of my shoulders. "No," I whispered to her, and I gripped the elastic band of her black boy shorts, the only piece of clothing she wore. I pulled her up so that she rose higher over me, her hands on either side of my head now as she arched overhead. "Yes," I repeated, and I wrapped my arms around her middle, and I drew her down to me. "Right there," I told her, whispering the words over her skin as I lifted my chin and I took her right nipple into my mouth as if I were tasting fruit on a branch.

She tasted so much sweeter than fruit.

Layne moaned over me, drawing her face down to look at me, her eyes dark, darker than the night sky that rose over us, spangled with countless stars. I wrapped my arms around her tightly, feeling the searing heat of her skin against my palms, against my skin, feeling the heat of her in my mouth, her nipple against my tongue, my teeth, the softness of her body so hot against my own. She tasted salty, but when I inhaled as I bit down gently on her nipple, I smelled the scent of forests, the scent I knew as Layne: of the wildness of trees and mountains and never-ending wilderness. I drifted my fingers down her back, feeling the ridges of her spine beneath her skin, her muscle, drifting my fingers lower and lower until they had followed the curve of her side, of her hip, and then her thigh, tracing my hand around the front of her leg until it dipped between her legs.

I moaned against her then, arching beneath her, my blood starting to thunder through me so much quicker, my heart pounding. She was *so* wet, dripping, aching because of *me*. She groaned as I touched her there, tipping her head back so that her face was looking to the stars; I stroked my fingers gently, gently, over the velvet softness of her center, so hot, so wet, because we were moving together.

All of this did something to me, and though I had been sated just a moment before, a now-familiar fire was already roaring through me, just because I was touching her. The scent of her rose around us as I drew my fingers back and forth over her center, never entering her, just touching her, my thumb brushing her clit again and again, drawing out a moan from her that was exquisite. She wanted it so badly, and I wanted to give her what she wanted, wanted to give it with every fiber of my being.

And what happened next *really* happened, I promise.

Because I gazed up at her as I felt the molten heat of her center, as I traced my fingers across the very core of her being. I gazed up at her beautiful head flung back, her full lips parted, her eyes closed as she tilted her head to the glory of the night sky, her body arched so beautifully over me she might as well have been a sculpture.

And then, flashing past her face, high, high above us, out in space, crescendoing to Earth...came a shooting star.

It was brilliant, that pulse of white light that flashed past her far above, in the heavens, and it took my breath away. All of it took my breath away. The beauty of Layne, arched above me, the beauty of her wetness on my fingers, her breast in my mouth, her hot skin against my own. The beauty of that moment, of the flash of heavenly fire far above us, merging with Layne's profile in the night sky so that, in that heartbeat, she became something heavenly, too… All of it would forever be imprinted in my heart. Always, it would remain there. Always, this moment, one of my final moments as a human, tangled together with my lover on the sand, hearing the surf pound the shore, feeling the hot skin and limbs of the woman I loved merge with mine.

I loved her, I knew, as I touched her, as she shivered against me, as I reached up and captured her left breast with my mouth, feeling the heat of her sear my lips and tasting the salt of her skin.

When I was a child, I made wishes on stars. It's what you do: you see a shooting star, and you make a wish.

But as Layne moved with me, and I with her, we became inextricably twisted together on the beach, and I wasn't quite sure where she ended and I began. As she began to shiver and shake against me, as I drew pleasure out of her like I was playing the final note of a symphony…I knew that there was no need for me to make a wish. Because I didn't need a thing.

My wish, after all, had already come true. My wish was a person, and she was wrapping me in her arms, holding me close and kissing me like I was the only other creature in the whole wide world.

Ahead, the stars swung low in the night sky. Below, the sea sighed against the shore as Layne sighed against me, wrapping me in her arms so tightly, it seemed as if she would never let me go.

And, in that beloved moment of my memory, she never does.

The Protector

Chapter 20: Dying to Live

The first thing that I became aware of was the pounding in my skull, a throbbing rhythm.

Great. A hangover headache.

I couldn't remember the last time I'd had one of these. I knew the amount of alcohol I could hold before getting drunk, and I usually stopped myself in plenty of time, because I *really* don't enjoy hangovers. So why hadn't I stopped myself last night, before I drank too much?

I sat up, my hand to my head, and I blinked groggily as I took in the scene before me. For a long moment, it didn't make any sense—because I was staring at the rising sun. This wasn't a picture of the sunrise on the hotel wall or on a television screen. Nope. This was the real sun rising over the ocean.

We weren't in the hotel room; we were outside. On the beach. The events of the night flooded back to me all at once as I glanced down at my middle, at the arm gripping my bare waist—and I grinned in spite of myself, resting back on my palms on the sand.

Wow. So, last night had been...something else. *Spectacular* was the word that came to mind. And after everything that had happened, we just hadn't had the strength to climb back up the cliff path to the Sullivan Hotel and our hotel room. Rather, we'd remained on the beach, our bodies entangled as we dreamed the night away. We'd slept together on top of Layne's leather jacket, not that the jacket had helped shield us from the inevitable invasion of sand...which was *everywhere*. I blinked muzzily again, reaching up and putting my hand to my head as I stared out at the sun cresting over the horizon and the brilliant blue ocean, a miracle of nature right in front of my eyes.

I'd grown up in Boston, and it's true—I'd seen my fair share of sunrises over the Atlantic. Ocean sunrises are always beautiful, but for some reason, that day, with my lover's arm gripping me in sleep, her long lashes trembling as she dreamed, her full lips open and her breath coming softly, slowly, while she lay so peacefully beside me...I realized that this was the most beautiful sunrise I'd ever seen. I know that's hyperbolic, but it really was.

The sun was ascending into a thick gray cloud bank on the edge of the horizon, so soon I wouldn't be able to see the sun at all. I had the feeling that it would rain later on in the morning. But right now, the sun turned the clouds a burnished orange, with golden rays streaming out, and a touch of purple higher up in the sky.

I could feel Layne's fingers flex against my stomach, and I lay back down, pillowing my aching head on my arm as I turned toward her, nose to nose.

The wind that blew over the sand was cold, but I hardly noticed. I tugged my skirt back down around my hips (one of the only pieces of clothing I was still wearing) and watched Layne sleep.

I was filled with so much emotion: love, excitement, happiness, even though I knew that today I would end my humanity and become something else. I was aware of that fact, but that's what made the fleeting moment more precious. Soon, I would no longer be human. And I didn't know what the world looked like on the other side. I had no idea how vampires perceived reality, and it was a terrifying thought—the notion that I was about to, willingly, dive headfirst into a brand-new, alien existence.

Still, here and now, I had a handful of final moments as myself. And as I lay on the sand next to Layne, I realized that there would never be enough time to do everything I wanted to do, to see everything I wanted to see. My humanity was coming to its close, and was I content with what I'd accomplished? With how I'd lived my life?

It was an existential moment for me, and I didn't know the answers to those questions. So, overwhelmed with love for Layne, and a sudden, piercing feeling of loss, I sat up again, staring down the beach.

I felt compelled to go see the water. Just one last time.

Though I didn't have my crutches with me, and though my thigh was hurting terribly, I found my bra and shirt that had been flung across the sand, and I disentangled myself from Layne and scooped the clothing up, shaking the sand from them and putting them back on. I was crawling on my hands and knees to do this, but I was close enough to the piece of driftwood that I was able to help myself up onto it by crawling, then turn around and use the driftwood to propel myself fully upward.

My leg ached, but I put weight on it, anyway, as I made my way across the beach. It was only a little weight, but the searing pain caused me to hiss out through my teeth as I glanced back at Layne, still sleeping so peacefully. I hated leaving her there, even for a moment, but I knew I'd be right back. I just wanted to…

Well, I didn't know exactly what I wanted to do. But, overwhelmed with the finality of what was about to happen to me, I was too filled with nervous energy to sit still, lying on the sand. I knew I wanted to at least go see the ocean through my human eyes, as sentimental as that sounds. And I didn't want to disturb Layne. Not yet.

It couldn't have been easy for her, knowing that her lover was about to become something that, for centuries, had been at odds with her kind. The situation was bad. Dire, even. We were individual people, and we were going to determine our own futures, yes. But there was so much history behind us. Awful history. I didn't even know the half of it. But Layne knew.

I was troubled as I limped to the water. I wanted the cool salt sea to wash over my feet, to make me feel grounded, because I certainly didn't feel that way right then. I wanted to be confident in my decision, wanted to feel brave. And, to some extent, I did.

But as I finally reached the little waves lapping up on shore, as I stepped into the water, feeling it wash over my feet, I gasped out loud at the coldness of the ocean. It felt good, bracing, to be washed with that cold water, and as I shivered, wrapping my arms around myself and staring out to the sea and that beautiful, rising sun, I took a deep breath.

Far, far away, the sun was rising over the edge of the world. It was impossible not to feel very small. After all, there was an enormous star, the sun, right in front of me, which was pretty damn big just by its lonesome. It spun in the middle of the galaxy, in the middle of the universe. I felt a perspective shift as the chill water washed up to my ankles, as the cool air—extra cool for a summer morning—ran over my skin. My thigh was pulsing in pain, but I tuned that out as I thought about last night, as I thought about Layne.

I stood there and let the water wash over my skin as I took big gulps of the salty air and just let myself pause for a moment. But I was so lost in thought that it was only a pricking at the back of my neck that clued me in to the fact that something was amiss.

You know that feeling you get when someone is watching you from across a crowded room? You can feel the person's eyes on you, even though you haven't spotted them yet. It's unsettling, disorienting, and that's what I was feeling now.

I shook off the sensation. After all, I was alone here with Layne. But when I turned to look back, gazing up the shore toward where I'd left her, my blood ran cold, colder than the water that was flowing over my feet, colder than the breeze that made my skin stand up in gooseflesh.

Because Layne wasn't looking at me.

Even though she was awake…

No. It was someone else.

Some*thing*.

I stared in horror at the scene before me. On the leather jacket where we'd spent the night, Layne was entangled with someone else. But this was far from the beautiful embrace the two of us had shared.

This was something sinister.

Layne was still nude, but it wasn't her tan skin that first drew my eye. It was the blood, blood that poured over her skin, pooling down onto her stomach from the two ragged holes in her neck. The blood flowed over her muscles, and for a long moment, time itself seemed to stand still as I watched the gruesome progression of the blood, as I stared in horror at my lover, bleeding from brand-new wounds.

My eyes were drawn to the blood first, but very quickly, my gaze latched onto what had *caused* those wounds. Because Layne was struggling with a woman, trying to kick her away.

The woman was slighter than Layne...but also much paler. I watched in horror as she snarled at Layne, as she lunged down at her. There were several details that I noticed, all in a flash. Like the fact that the woman was wearing a plain white button-down blouse and slacks. The kind of outfit you'd find on any woman in an office, but here and now, the contrast of her normal clothing with the surreal situation was startling.

Because the woman's incisors were long, curved and wickedly gleaming in the light of day.

This woman, this stranger, had bitten Layne savagely, torn into her flesh with such power that the blood pooling from Layne was like a river, wide and powerful as the blood flowed so fast that my heart rose into my throat.

All of this, all in the flash of an instant, because the vampire who had been staring down at Layne looked up at me again. She looked up at me, and even though there was a great deal of distance and beach between us, I could still see her, still see her clearly because of the rising sun, because of my adrenaline pulsing through me making everything that much more focused and clear.

The vampire looked at me with searing, blood-red eyes.

And she smiled at me.

God, I'll never forget it: the expression on her face, the fact that she was trying to kill my lover... All of that is still crystal clear in my memory, but nothing is preserved as clearly as the singular moment in which the vampire's eyes met mine.

I knew the vampire was going to kill Layne. And I knew that she was going to kill me. And there wasn't a single thing I could do to stop her.

Everything seemed to slow as the vampire stared at me, her eyes flashing with a deadly light. Time itself crawled as she pushed off from Layne, shoving the werewolf into the sand as she staggered to her feet. The vampire was already sprinting when she hit the ground, and the sand was flying up behind her.

She maintained an eerie smile, turning it into a too-wide, terrifying grin, as she raced toward me at an impossible speed. She was moving faster than a cheetah. Hell, she was moving faster than a car, and that was utterly impossible. But it was happening, all the same. She was moving across the beach with such startling power that there was nothing in the world that could stop her.

I had lost.

It was over.

When the vampire hit me, I didn't have time to brace for the impact, not that bracing could have made any difference. Because when she collided with me, I felt like I'd been falling through the air and had suddenly made contact with a brick building. My body was toppling backwards into the tide, and the cold water closed over my head.

But the chill of that water, the frigid ocean against my skin as it consumed my body was *nothing* in comparison to what the bite felt like.

There was no ceremony, no wait. It was sudden, and it was absolute, how the vampire bit my neck. She drew her arms around my shoulders as she fell beside me in the water, and she was embracing me, holding tightly to me, like we were locked in a lovers' embrace. But we weren't. It was a hideous mockery of love. She was holding me too tightly, painfully so, as her teeth found the beating pulse at my throat, and the chill of the ocean faded away, replaced by the violent heat of the puncture.

Her teeth, searing and white-hot, connected with my skin, entering me easily. A rush of adrenaline pulsed through my entire body like a bolt of lightning, but though my body was reacting to the vicious intrusion, there wasn't a single thing I could do to stop her. I *tried*: my body, instinctively programmed to fight and keep itself alive, tried to push her away, kicking; I jabbed her with my fingers, my hands, my elbows, churning up the water into a salty foam. I screamed. Salt water filled my mouth and burned itself all the way down to my lungs, and I was gasping violently, unable to get a breath as the water filled me. But that was secondary, everything was secondary, even my body's fight to survive was secondary...

Because my whole self was focused on those two incisors, piercing me.

I will never forget the pain. It would be impossible to forget.

Imagine the worst physical agony you've ever been in in your life. Now imagine heat added to that pain, like a burn that races over your skin, incinerating you, reducing you to ash. It was heat and pain that dove deep, deeper inside of me, and though that heat came first, fast, it was followed by a rush of cold that is difficult to describe.

The kind of cold you feel walking over a grave at night.

The kind of cold you feel when you stare at someone who once loved you but no longer does.

The kind of cold you feel when you...die.

And I knew, in that moment, that that was exactly what was happening to me now. I was dying, my physical body failing me as the vampire bit deep and drank even deeper, holding me down like a predator, going in for the kill.

The agony, the heat, the cold: it all began to drift away from me. I felt myself leaving my body. It was effortless, the way I slipped out of that physical vessel, as easy as removing a dress and leaving it crumpled on the floor. I remember light, light all around me, and the great relief I felt as the last remnants of the white-hot, searing pain and that chill, aching cold left me, all at once. The memory of that pain still moved through me, and it hurt me, even as a memory, but I knew that I was safe here. Safe outside of myself.

I stared down at the vampire, wrapped tightly around the woman, drinking her dry, lying in the shallows of the sea, the tides washing over them. I recognized myself, my physical body, far below me in the shallow water, and I knew I was dead, and that seemed so sad to me. Not depressing or bone-chilling or painful. Just...sad.

As I watched the scene, the waves lapping over the two bodies, everything began to slowly change, because my attention was drawn to a movement. A person moving on the beach. She was naked, and she was covered in blood, blood streaming out of so many wounds that it was shocking, even in the altered state I was inhabiting, to witness.

It was Layne. It was Layne, I realized, as I watched the naked woman crawling across the sand, her mouth caught in a snarl of deep pain and even deeper fury. She struggled to her feet, pushing up and off of the earth like it was the most excruciating action she'd ever taken, but she managed to do it, and then—wavering, blood dripping to the sand as she shuddered and shook—she threw back her head to the bright, cheerful, incongruent morning sky, and she opened her mouth.

And she howled.

The sound of that howl was bone chilling. Mournful, but there was also a fire to it, a deep, abiding fire that came through in that perfect, poignant note. It went on for only half a heartbeat, and then her body was curling forward at the waist, and a snarl erupted from her. A snarl of anger and of pain as the woman I saw in front of me transformed.

Layne became the wolf.

The gray wolf was enormous, almost as big as a horse, as her front paws touched down on land. She was beautiful as she moved across the sand into the water, her body sailing with a sleek, raw grace, her lupine head curving toward the vampire and the woman—me—still wrapped together in the waves. The wolf's eyes flashed with a dangerous, pulsing light, and then she lunged at the vampire.

The action was so quick, it was almost surgical in its precision: the wolf closed her jaws around the vampire's shoulder, biting down with such strength that the vampire flung back her head and screamed. There was a wet snapping, as of breaking bone, and the wolf tore the vampire off of the woman in the waves, and the wolf flung the vampire, her body arcing through the air.

Gently—ludicrous, really, considering the amount of power I'd just seen displayed in the mauling of the vampire's shoulder—the wolf nosed my body out of the water, her blood-flecked snout tenderly propelling the woman I once was up onto the shore. My body lay, face up, the waves tenderly pulsing against my feet, and for a long moment, the wolf stood there, her gray sides heaving as she stared down at the body. She huffed out, her nose twitching as she nuzzled my neck, where the wounds looked so ragged and raw, blood coursing from them down into the sand beneath me. The wolf nudged my chin softly, but I didn't move. For a long moment, she stared at me, her face tight, her nose quivering with pain as she watched me and how very, very still I remained. And then the wolf turned her sights on the vampire once more.

Because the vampire was, of course, not really deterred by that single bite in her shoulder, no matter how viciously it'd been delivered, and no matter how deep the bite had been. She'd fallen into the ocean some ways away from the woman and the wolf, and she was rising unsteadily to her feet once more now, her smile even wider. It was terrifying to behold, how wide the grin that stretched across her face really was, how long and distended her teeth had become, folding over her lower lip as if she were some sort of big cat, not a human-shaped creature at all. Her eyes were bright, blood-red.

The wolf snarled, her hackles raised, her lips drawn over her own long teeth, and she lunged at the vampire again, leaping over the woman's prone body to collide with the vampire in the water. With the wolf and vampire locked in a desperate tangle, I had to look away…and instead, I glanced down at the body of the woman lying on the beach as the little waves ran over her legs. Her eyes were closed, her chest utterly still, no sign of breath or rising or falling coming from it.

I should have been afraid. I mean, I was staring down at myself, at my physical body, and *it was not breathing*. But I didn't feel anything except this thin strand of sadness that seemed to be winding its way around me slowly, like a snake strangling its prey.

Everything was so simple in that moment. Because I knew that I didn't want to die. I didn't want to leave my father. I didn't want my father to grieve for me.

But when I looked at the wolf and the vampire, locked in their deathly battle, I felt something even stronger move through me.

I didn't want to leave Layne.

I loved her.

The wolf and the vampire squared off again after the vampire pushed the wolf out of the water, up and onto the sand. The vampire rose out of the water, too, her short, blonde hair soaked and darker now. She stared up at the wolf, the wolf who trembled as she rose to her four feet, blood visibly dripping from her sleek gray pelt, falling onto the sand—and the vampire smiled.

The vampire and the wolf both knew that someone would have to die today. But the vampire had just devoured all of my blood. I am assuming that this made her strong, stronger than Layne, who had already bled out that morning from the vampire's wounds. And maybe the vampire had drunk some of Layne's blood, too.

Layne was, right now, at a great disadvantage.

And that meant she was in danger.

I stared at the wolf as she rose unsteadily to her feet, and for the first time since leaving my body, I knew fear. I didn't want her to die.

I didn't want Layne to die, and I would do anything I could to help her.

I gasped as I felt searing-hot pain, followed by searing-cold pain, colder than anything I'd felt in my entire life. I started to cough…

And that's when I realized I had returned to my body.

Layne had brought me back. My love for her had brought me back.

And now I had to save her.

As I struggled up to a seated position, my head spinning, seawater running out of my nose and mouth, I realized that I wasn't going to be much help. The world spun, and I realized with a very cold sense of shock that if I *was* back in my body, it would probably be for a very short time. I felt as if I'd already stepped through death's door: I'd never been in more pain, and blood poured from the wounds in my neck, heat that coursed over my cold skin and made me shiver as I pushed up from the sand. I stared at the battle scene in front of me. The vampire and the wolf moved too quickly for me to follow with my eyes; how did I imagine that I could help in any way?

I felt the cold rush of hopelessness, but I also knew that I couldn't allow myself to be weighed down by it. Not today. I needed to get up, and I needed to try. And somehow, somewhere inside of me, I had to find the strength to do it.

I pushed up, onto my knees. Everything, *everything* inside of me, outside of me, screamed with profound pain. Still, I'd managed to rise to my knees.

I watched the wolf and the vampire, watched the wolf fall to her side as the vampire pushed her over, watched the vampire climb on top of her, watched the vampire rear her head back, her incisors extended, ready to tear into Layne and drink her dry.

And then I did the only thing I could think of to do.

I took a deep breath; I braced myself.

And I screamed.

The vampire stopped in her tracks, on top of Layne, about to bite her, and she turned to look at me, instead. Her eyes were surprised, probably as surprised as I was. After all, she'd thought I was dead. But I wasn't. I was here, on my knees, on the beach, and I screamed, hoping against hope that it would provoke her to get off of Layne and come toward me, instead.

And it did.

In one hideous heartbeat, the vampire came for me. She crossed the sand between us in the blink of an eye, her face bearing fury. Her eyes were wide, impossibly wide, and red. She shoved me down onto the sand with a single hand, using so much force that all of my bones shuddered from the impact. The pain that had been rippling through my body skyrocketed. She shoved me down, and I cried out, and then the vampire did exactly what she'd done to Layne. She straddled me, and she reared her head back, her incisors long like a snake's as she made ready to make her final strike.

I stared up at her, feeling myself falling away deep inside of me. I knew that I was about to rise out of my body again. I didn't know if my ruse had given Layne enough time to get away, to get help, to be safe, but I'd tried my best. I hoped it was enough.

God, I loved her. And I hoped, so much, that this was enough to save her.

I realized, as time again slowed, as I stared up at the vampire with her jaw gaping above me, that I didn't want my last moment alive to be spent looking at something so horrific.

I wanted my last moment alive to be spent looking at something beautiful.

To be looking at Layne, at the woman I loved with my whole heart, the woman I'd been drawn to from my first moment of meeting her, like there was a shining, bright line connecting her heart to mine. I still felt it, even as I lay there dying. I could *feel* the bright, silver thing connecting her heart to mine, and that's why I knew to look to my right. I knew that if I turned my head, she would be there.

And my last sight as I left this world would be of the woman I loved.

So I turned, ready to look at Layne and then close my eyes and fall away. But Layne was not there. Or, rather, she was, but she was moving too quickly to see clearly.

Layne was moving, I realized, toward us.

The wolf barreled across the sand, racing with her sleek gray body to devour the space between us. With one last thrust of strength, Layne's body collided into the vampire on top of me. She bit down on the vampire's neck with a growl so savage that the earth itself seemed to shake.

I fell away, deep inside of myself, and then, just as quickly as I was falling, I was rising, too. Rising right out of my body to stare down at the scene below me without any judgment at all.

The vampire lay on the beach, her neck bent at an awkward angle, her eyes still open, her mouth still smiling—but she was very, very still.

The woman that I'd once been lay in the shallows of

the sea, the little waves lapping over her thighs, her skirt moving like bits of flotsam in the water, her eyes closed, her mouth softly smiling—and she was very, very still, too.

And Layne lay between them both, no longer a wolf but a woman once more, her body marked by bites and scratches. I stared down at the werewolf who lay there bleeding, the beautiful woman I loved, that I still loved, even though I knew I was leaving this world, and it hurt so much to see her as she crawled over to my physical body, tears pouring down her face, her sides heaving with a sob that she was trying to hold in.

But when she reached my body, she did sob, a great, wracking sound that tore the air in two. I stared down at the two of us, at Layne as she drew me into her arms, as she rocked me side to side, as she lifted her head to the bright morning sky...and she howled. She wasn't a wolf. She was a still a woman, but the exquisite sound that came out of her mouth sounded exactly like a wolf's howl, bright, clear, and mournful. She howled again, tears pouring from her eyes as she held tightly to my dead body.

I started to rise higher. Higher and higher. I looked down at the scene on the beach, feeling that depth of sadness, until I couldn't see anything anymore, white rushing all around me as if I were standing in the middle of a waterfall. There was white, and there was rushing...

And then there was silence.

I was standing in a dark room. A room without a light. There was blackness all around me, but I wasn't afraid. I lifted my chin, and I gazed at the darkness, and then I lifted up my hands to try to find a light switch. Or, at least, I *tried* to lift up my hands. But I found that I couldn't.

"Elizabeth?"

I remembered that voice. I hadn't thought about that voice for such a long time, and if you'd asked me, I wouldn't have been able to tell you what she sounded like. But, even after all these years, I still recognized it.

"Mom?" I whispered.

The light came on.

I was standing in my old bedroom in my father's house. But this wasn't the bedroom that I had left when I went off for college. This was the bedroom I had when I was a little girl, with Rainbow Brite posters on the walls and my violin standing in the corner, piles of sheet music next to the little red chair where I practiced my heart out every day.

And there, on my bed with its My Little Pony comforter and Care Bear pillows, sat my mother.

She smiled gently at me and held out her hands. She was dressed in jeans and a flowy blue peasant blouse, wearing no makeup, and when she looked at me, her face lit up like a star. I smiled, too, because my mom had always had the type of smile that was contagious. I walked over to her. She took my hands, and she squeezed them tightly before pulling me down to sit on the bed beside her.

"Baby, this is really important," she told me, and she pinned me to the spot with her gaze. I'd forgotten that she had eyes just like mine, bright blue.

"What's important?" I asked her, and she was frowning a little, squeezing my hands so tightly that they actually hurt.

"Honey, you have to listen to me," she said, and she pronounced every word clearly, like she was announcing something over a loudspeaker. But there were just the two of us in the room, no one else. I stared at her uncertainly. "You have to go back," she told me then.

"Go back?" I asked, and I turned and looked at the door of my bedroom. "Go back where?" I asked her.

"You have to go back. It's not your time. You have to help your father, and you have to help Layne."

At the sound of the word *Layne*, I shuddered a little.

Why did I know that name? Why was it so familiar?

I couldn't remember, though it seemed, so much, that I *needed* to remember something important. Something very important.

"Who's Layne?" I asked my mother, my brow

furrowed.

"Sweetheart, she's the love of your life, and it's very important that you understand that you *can't* stay here," she told me, her eyes shining, but there was pain hiding in them, too. "Do you understand me?"

"But I *want* to stay here. I've missed you," I said. I didn't really understand, though, why I had missed her. It seemed like we'd never been parted. Like I'd just come home from school. We couldn't have been apart that long...right?

I was so confused as I looked at her face. I couldn't remember anything except for my mother and my father and the life I'd had with them before...

Before...something. Something terrible happened.

To her.

"Baby," said my mother, and she was crying now. "I wish that you could stay with me. I'm so proud of you and of everything you've done. You're amazing, you know that? But you can't stay with me. It would hurt too many people. And you have too many amazing things to do, sweet girl. Do you understand?"

"No," I told her, but I was starting to get distressed that my mother was upset. "Mom, what's going on? Where do I have to go? What are you talking about?"

"Honey," said my mom, and she cleared her throat now as she held my gaze. She gave my hands a squeeze for good measure, and then she told me quickly, the words coming out all at once: "Honey, you just... You just died, sweetheart."

I stared at her, and when I did, the lights in the room started to flicker.

"How is that possible?" I whispered, licking my lips, feeling anxiety start to crawl through me, a sizzling bit of electricity that really didn't feel good. "Dead?" I said, and the word ended on a little laugh, like, "You're joking, right?"

But she wasn't joking.

"It's okay," she said, and she put her hands on my

shoulders. "It happens. You did a brave thing, trying to save Layne."

"Layne," I repeated, and the lights in the room flickered again.

"Layne," said my mother. "That's right. Say it again, baby. It's important."

"Layne," I whispered, and the lights in the room went out.

"I love you, sweetheart," I heard my mother say, her voice breaking. "I'm with you. I promise you. I'm always with you."

And that's when I felt the pain.

The Protector

Chapter 21: Forever Changed

Pain roared through me. Pain that was ice, pain that filled my entire body until I couldn't remember a time that I hadn't been pain, all of me, pain alone.

But that was just the beginning.

The pain was followed immediately by heat. I felt that I had been swallowed by an inferno, that I had somehow been locked in a burning building and I would never be able to get out before the fire had consumed me. Because it was consuming me already. I felt the fire burn me, and then...then...

I was only ash.

But no. That wasn't quite right. From somewhere, far away, I heard someone call my name. And I knew, in that moment, that I wasn't just ash.

I was something else.

Elizabeth.

I took a breath. It was, I realized, from somewhere far distant, the first breath I'd taken in a long time, and that wasn't quite right, either. I should have been breathing all along.

If I was alive, I should be breathing.

I took another breath. And it hurt; it hurt so much to draw that breath into my lungs, but I managed it, and then I realized I was saying a word. I was repeating it over and over, whispering the syllable like a prayer.

"Layne," I murmured, and I took another breath. "Layne."

Like the heat that raced through me just a heartbeat ago, I now felt the immensity of cold spread through my entire body. The exact opposite of that heat filled me with cold so leaden I felt entombed within it, and as the cold stole through me, I wondered if I'd ever felt warm before, or ever would again. The cold inched along with precision, as if each individual cell was invaded by it; every part of my body was frozen. The cold ate me up, and when it was all done...

Everything became still.

I took another deep breath, and that's when I realized that I was held between two people. I knew that without opening my eyes, because I felt it. But...when I say I "felt" it, that's not the whole truth of the moment, because when I *felt* it, it wasn't with the knowledge of my skin, my limbs feeling two people surrounding me. Instead, I felt it with my whole self, with every fiber of my being, felt it with every atom that made me, built me into the person I was.

I knew that there were two people holding me tightly because I could feel their arms around me, their legs pressed against mine, their hips snugly fitting against my own. But I could also smell them, knew they were Layne and Mikagi Tasuki before I opened my eyes, because there was a difference in their scents. Layne smelled like the wild woods, like rich, good earth and rain and everything that was fierce and free. Mikagi smelled like honeysuckle flowers and rosin and violins and sheet music. She smelled like paper and practice rooms, wood polish and antiques, and underneath it all, the scent of something that isn't really alive and isn't really dead...but that simply is. Beneath Layne's scent there was something fierce and raw and beautiful, something that drew me like a flower follows the sun.

And I could hear them, could hear everything, like how Layne's pulse was racing just under her skin, and how Mikagi took long, even breaths. I could taste the salt in the air so brightly that I felt like I'd just taken a bite out of a block of salt, and when I opened my eyes, I could see the sky and its many clouds so clearly overhead, it felt as if I were looking through a telescope.

That's when I smelled blood, and when I inhaled, when I breathed the scent in deeply, I—somehow, some way—knew the blood to be my own.

Mikagi lay on my left side, her leg swung over my hips and legs, over Layne's, too, as the werewolf held me close, tenderly, gently, even though I knew the strength she was capable of. Layne had drawn me snug against her, my back to her front, and it was comforting to bask in that warmth. Comforting, because there was something amiss about the moment. Something very strange.

I inhaled deeply when I glanced to my left and I saw Mikagi—because her teeth were long. I glanced sidelong at her, at her pointed fangs, razor sharp and wickedly pointed and wet. Wet with blood. And there was blood on her lips, on her mouth, a single drop tracing its way down her chin. She raised a brow as she glanced at me, as she lifted up her left hand slowly and dragged the back of it across her mouth, wiping it, giving me a sly little smile as she did so.

"Hello," she said companionably. Her tone, lighthearted, carefree, was at odds with the rest of the moment, because when she lifted her left hand, I stared at it, and I breathed out in horror. There was a jagged wound cut across her wrist, a wound like one made by teeth. And blood flowed from it, dark blood that looked almost black in the warm morning sunshine.

I licked my lips nervously, and when I did so, I tasted blood. *Her* blood. Mikagi's blood. I tasted the sharp, tangy metal of it, the chill of it, and I knew, in that moment, that I had drunk it.

I stared up at the morning sky, slumping back against the sand, held in the embrace of these two women as I tried to make sense of what had happened to me.

And that's when I felt Layne's mouth at my neck, tenderly kissing me. I glanced at her, could see the tears rolling down her face. She was wearing a suit jacket—and nothing else, I realized—and she was weeping over me as she squeezed me tightly, as she held me close.

Something was...wrong.

Mikagi disentangled herself from me, and she sat up, or at least struggled to a seated position in the sand, drawing the back of her hand over her mouth again. Someone was beside her and helping her stand; Mikagi had to sag against her. Kane. The woman who helped Mikagi up was Kane. With her long white-blonde hair and her blazing blue eyes, she stared down at me with concern, then crouched beside me once she was sure that Mikagi could stand on her own.

"Elizabeth?" said Kane, her low voice a growl, her eyes narrowed. "Are you all right? How do you feel?"

I stared up, up, up at the bright blue sky. Far overhead, too far overhead for my human eyes to see clearly, a plane soared. As I stared up at that plane, I suddenly knew that it contained one hundred-and-twelve passengers, that the captain was arguing with his co-pilot about whether organic peanut butter tasted better than Jif, and I knew that there was a stewardess in the back crying because she'd just lost her cat to cancer. I stared up at that plane, mystified that I suddenly knew all of these things about it, could hear snatches of conversation from the passengers and crew, could make out small details, like the fact that there was a little girl in the last row of the plane who kept kicking the seat in front of her.

I took a deep breath, and I felt myself fall back to earth, feeling the firmness of the sand beneath me, Layne's arms wrapped around me.

When I looked up, looking out at the ocean, I knew the animals that existed in the wave that was cresting toward shore. I knew that there was a dolphin not far from where we sat who was excited about her breakfast...and a little farther out, there was a seagull diving into the water, trying to get a fish—but the fish evaded him, spectacularly happy as it sped into the deep.

Every detail of the world around me stood out with such clarity, with such brightness, as if everything I noticed were outlined with a thin layer of light. Not a specific color, just...*light*.

I sat up slowly, because every motion I made was *too much*. There was blood rushing through me, but as I licked my lips again, I realized how cold they were. Blood should warm you, should make your skin flushed.

But my body was strangely cold.

"Elizabeth?" Layne whispered beside me. She ran her fingers across my face, wincing a little when she did so. "You're so cold," she murmured, pinning me to the spot with her worried gaze, her heartbeat thrumming in her fingertips. "Are you all right?"

Two people had asked me this now, and I didn't know the answer to that question. I didn't know if I was all right, because I didn't know what I *was*. But as I looked up at Mikagi Tasuki, standing, slumped—now being supported by Tommie—and as I looked at Kane Sullivan as she stared at me, sympathy evident on her face, I realized what had happened.

I wiped my fingertips across my mouth and then looked down at my hand.

Black blood covered my fingers. Blood as black as the blood that oozed from the wound on Mikagi's wrist.

I licked my lips again, and I squinted at Kane.

"What am I?" I whispered, my voice shaking. I knew the answer to the question, knew it before I even asked it. Kane reached out to me and touched my shoulder with cold fingers, her brow furrowed, her sympathy making her mouth downturn into a gentle frown.

She took a deep breath, but she said nothing. Instead, she looked to Layne, who still sat beside me, and I turned, and I looked to her, too, holding her gaze with my own.

"You're a vampire, Elizabeth," Layne whispered, her eyes dull with deep sadness. "Mikagi turned you. You...you were dead. And it was the only thing we could do to save you. You're a vampire now."

I stared down at the black blood on my fingertips for a long moment, uncertain, feeling the surety of the words wash through me. I considered what she said. I felt the chill of my own skin, felt the heightened world around me.

And then slowly, carefully, after much thought, I lifted the fingers back up to my mouth.

And I licked them.

The taste of the blood was metallic, but it was also something...more. Something richer, darker, stranger. And when I tasted it, my eyes slowly rolled into the back of my head, my back arched of its own accord, and Kane reached out and snatched my wrist before I could lick my fingers again.

"When you're a vampire, you can't drink another vampire's blood," she warned me gently, when I opened my eyes and stared at her, not understanding. "You can't drink Mikagi's blood anymore, or it will hurt you."

But I was suddenly so thirsty; if I didn't drink something right *now*, I knew I would die again. And when Kane looked at my face, she seemed to read my thoughts. She took a deep breath, and then she was glancing at Layne again, the frown harder on her face now.

"Elizabeth is... She's very thirsty," Kane said in her low voice as she gazed at Layne. "She needs to drink, or she might be in danger of being too weak."

"There are no humans at the hotel now who know what we are," said Tommie with a small frown.

Layne shook her head. She shook it wearily, and then she was letting the suit jacket that had been placed around her shoulders pool to the sand. She was streaked with blood from the wounds in her neck, blood that had dried on her body in horrific hieroglyphics. "I know," she said, and the words sounded exhausted.

But then she inclined her head away from me, the long, beautiful curve of her neck exposed. And when she did, a new sensation entered me.

Hunger.

Her jaw clenched, and I saw the wounds on her neck clearly, saw the blood flow sluggishly from them. My senses lit up as if a switch had just been flicked on. All I could focus on was the the blood.

It was all I could see.

The bright blood flowed over the beautiful curve of her neck. As human beings, you are trained to believe that the sight of blood is wrong. After all, if you see blood, something has gone awry, and you need to protect yourself. It's one of the oldest instincts.

But for a vampire, blood looks...different.

It was as if, in that moment, Layne had red roses all along her neck, the petals sensuously brushing against her skin. Roses that were fragrant and velvet-soft, and as beautiful as art. That's how I saw the blood. And when I leaned forward, when I wrapped my arms around Layne and bent my head, when I inhaled, I realized I'd never smelled anything lovelier. Because the scent of Layne fused with the blood. There was a wild freshness about it, a fierce beauty that undid me. I wrapped my arms around Layne, and then I was drawing her to me, and I pressed my mouth to that flow of blood.

And I drank.

At the very first taste, every atom in my body seemed to come alive. I inhaled, licking my lips, running my tongue over my teeth as I tipped my head back, and I experienced that first taste of blood, my eyes rolling, the sensation of pleasure sweeping through me as brightly as any orgasm. Because that's what it felt like: an orgasm that swept through every part of my body. Pleasure poured through my cells, but what followed on its heels was a type of hunger that was all-consuming, absolute. And when I swallowed the blood in my mouth, I bent my head again, and I began to drink in earnest.

I drank and I drank, and as the sweet blood flowed over my tongue and down my throat, everything in the world became more focused, brighter, tinged with a clarity and light, until the world itself seemed like paradise. And still I drank. I drank when I heard my name from somewhere far away, my name spoken with increasing fervor and dread, and then shouted. I drank when there were hands at my shoulders, at my arms, at my middle, pulling me away from Layne.

And when we came apart, then and only then did I stop drinking from her.

I am ashamed to say it now, but I think that if Kane and Tommie hadn't stopped me, I might have drunk Layne dry. I didn't know it then, but I know it now: it's common for first-time vampires to drink their hosts to death. I'm so grateful that Kane and Tommie stopped me, and I can only imagine how hard I must have fought against them.

But when I came to from my pleasurable stupor, there was Layne on the ground, wrapped in the suit jacket again, and she was looking at me with a soft, wan smile. And she was so pale. Her skin is normally tan; I'd never seen her look so weak, so wan, and it honestly frightened me. I stared at her, and then I was on the ground on my hands and knees beside her, wrapping my arms around her.

"Are you all right?" I asked her, holding her tightly. I remembered everything in that moment, remembered how she'd saved my life, remembered how she'd fought with that vampire to make certain that I stayed alive. She had fought for me.

I remembered the pain she'd gone through to keep me safe, the wounds that had been inflicted upon her.

And I knew all of that, knew it deeply, as I held her close, and I loved her as I always loved her, that love growing in my chest until it pushed against my ribs, threatening to spill out of me.

But when I smelled her blood again, that fragrant, beautiful blood, something…well, *changed* inside of me. And, for half a heartbeat, I still knew that I was holding my lover in my arms, my lover who had almost given her life for me…but I also knew that I wanted something so desperately, was so infinitely hungry, that I pondered, for half a heartbeat, exactly what I would do to taste her blood again.

"Elizabeth," Kane growled, crouching beside me. Her voice, usually low, had a commanding tone to it suddenly; the very earth seemed to shift beneath our feet. I glanced her way, my eyes wide, as she got through to me, cutting through the hunger with her voice like a knife. "Fight it," Kane told me then—simply, succinctly. "You have the power to fight it, but you *must* want to. If you drink from Layne once more today, she is going to die. Your beloved is going to *die*." She held my gaze, her blue eyes sparking. "Do not do this to her. Fight the craving, and fight it *now*."

When she spoke those words, her voice low and commanding and a bit hypnotic, what she said began to cut through the need inside of me like a white-hot knife sawing through the cord of hunger. I blinked, taking a deep breath, and then I looked at Layne, really looked at her, glancing down at my lover wrapped tightly in my arms, my lover whose eyelashes fluttered against her cheeks, because she could barely keep her eyes open; she was so weak. And as I stared down at her, as I saw her breathing slow, as I saw the paleness of her lips, her cheeks, felt the blood beating so laboriously through her, I knew that she was in pain, and that, by drinking her blood from her, I was perpetuating that pain.

And, God, that knowledge hurt.

"I'm so sorry," I whispered to Layne, and I held her gaze now. She opened her eyes, and she stared into mine with such softness. Though I wanted to drink her blood again with all of my heart (wanted it so much; I was ravenous), I knew that I couldn't. Wouldn't. I knew that I was capable of being strong enough to resist.

I wanted her blood. I didn't *need* it.

I took another deep breath as Layne gazed at me, her beautiful hazel eyes filled with pain...and also love.

"It's all right," 'she growled to me, and she reached up and gripped my shoulders in a pained embrace. She held me so tightly, and I held her so tightly; I felt in that moment that we were never going to let each other go again. "It's all right," she repeated, and her words were even softer this time. "I'm so glad you're okay," she said then, and there was a sob in her voice, a sob she didn't fully let out. "I thought you were dead," she told me, searching my eyes.

From somewhere behind us, Tommie cleared her throat. She stood there on the beach, her men's dress shoes sinking into the sand as she raised a brow. "She really *was* dead, Layne," said Tommie, not unkindly. "And if she hadn't been turned, she would have stayed that way."

The pain in Layne's face was so poignant that it took my breath away. I wrapped her even tighter in my arms, drew her ever closer to me, before I took another deep breath.

And I remembered that, yes, I'd died. And I remember what had happened to me while I was dead.

I remembered my mother.

"Something happened while I was, um—while I was dead," I told them then. The vampires—and werewolf—watched me expectantly as I tried to put into words what had happened to me not so very long ago. It felt so surreal.

"It's..." I trailed off, looking at Layne in my arms. She had given me so much of herself from the very first moment we met, and now she'd given me her blood. "It's nothing," I told them then, glancing up. "It's nothing," I repeated a little more firmly when Layne gazed at me, one brow raised, her face concerned. "I'll...tell you later," I said to her, my voice low.

After all, there were bigger, more important things happening today.

And then, somehow, we rose and stood, side by side. Layne and I struggled until Kane stepped forward, hooking her hands under my shoulders and helping me to my feet, Tommie drawing Layne up. Once I was fully upright, wavering unsteadily, I gazed down at my once-wounded thigh with wonder.

Because my unsteadiness wasn't coming from the wound; it was from the fact that I still felt a little woozy, what with being dead and all not so long ago. The wound itself, the wound that had hampered my days, was now completely gone. There were still stitches in my skin, but the stitches stitched up, well, perfectly healed skin, which was kind of disconcerting to look at.

"You were reborn," said Tommie dryly, when she noticed me lifting up the hem of my skirt and staring down at my leg with as much surprise as if I'd just sprouted a new one. "That means that your old wounds have all healed."

"That's crazy…" I murmured, touching the skin on my leg in awe.

Kane took up the suit jacket from the ground—her suit jacket, I realized, since she was just in her dress shirt and tie now—and she draped the jacket around Layne's bare shoulders kindly before she turned to me with her brow up. "How do you feel?" she asked, her head to the side and her hands on her hips as she swept her eyes over me, assessing me for damage.

I stood there and flexed my fingers, curling my hands into fists at my sides and then curling them again. As I stared down at them, I could *feel* Layne's blood beginning to flow through me, filling every vein. I took a deep breath, glancing down at the sand, too, and again, I could make out the tiniest of grains, could make out microscopic bits of shell and rock; everything within my view had become intensely sharpened.

"I feel weird," I told Kane, glancing up at her as I bit my lip. "Is it always going to be like this—so sharp, so focused?" I flexed my fingers again and shivered a little. "It's a little overwhelming."

"You'll get used to it," said Kane, and she put an arm around my shoulders then, gazing at me with warm eyes. "I know it's disconcerting in the beginning, everything so bright and clear, but your body has to adjust to the fact that it's no longer human. The vampire parts of you are taking over, and it's going to take awhile for you become accustomed to everything."

"I mean…" I trailed off and looked up at the sun, already climbing its way toward its zenith in the heavens. I sighed. There was no time for me to ask the questions I wanted to. Because I needed to be in Boston by tonight. Mikagi had said it took about four hours to get there.

Which meant that we needed to leave soon.

"I don't know anything about being a vampire," I told Kane then, gazing at her with wide, frightened eyes. "Is there anything else I *need* to know? Anything super important?"

"In the beginning, you're going to need blood in order for your body to change itself over completely and not start to backslide toward death," Kane warned me, the warmth fading from her gaze. "But this is easy to achieve, especially if you have a donor who is giving you the blood willingly." She glanced sidelong at Layne, who nodded as she held the suit jacket a little tighter around her shoulders. But when she looked at me now, she looked paler. And she swallowed.

"It will be fine," Kane told the werewolf then, her voice softening. "You know that your body heals quickly. You will soon make all of the blood that has been depleted from you, and you will be able to feed her without any fear of hurting yourself."

Layne nodded again, watching me closely. "Is there anything else she needs to know?" Layne persisted. "Her father will tell her much, but the very important things—"

Kane looked as if she was going to say something, but Tommie stepped forward then.

"I hate to burst your bubble," she said pointedly, gazing up at the sun, too, "but it's not good for Elizabeth to be out here like this. There was cloud cover up until now, but that's fading away. She needs to get out of the sunshine."

"*Sunshine* hurts me?" I muttered, as Kane nodded, glancing sidelong at Tommie.

"We need to get going; I trust you can take care of the body?" Kane asked, a brow raised, and Tommie glanced at the dead vampire on the beach and nodded, grimacing.

"Yeah," she murmured, and then she moved away from us, toward the husk that had once been the vampire, rolling in and out on the little waves that hit the shore. Kane gestured for us to head back toward the sloped path that led up to the Sullivan Hotel and to leave the grisly scene.

"It doesn't *hurt* you to be out in the sun, Elizabeth, so much as it will burn your skin if you spend too much time in it," said Kane then, as we began to ascend the path. "But there are more pressing matters at hand. You need to get to Boston in time for your father's Council meeting, and we Sullivans are going with you. So I can answer your questions later, if you'd like." She watched me with her bright blue eyes, unblinking.

I gulped down air and nodded, following her up the steep path, Layne beside me. I didn't exercise often, so normally walking up such a steep incline would have left me a little breathless. But as I followed the vampire, as I wrapped my arm around Layne and helped usher her along, I realized that I wasn't winded at all as we hiked. My breathing remained perfectly normal. I didn't even break a sweat.

Well, at least there was *something* positive about being a vampire.

Kane must have seen my worried expression because she cleared her throat as she slid her hands into her suit pants pockets. "It's not as bad as all that," she said companionably, falling into step beside me. "The sunshine thing—it's a little inconvenient, especially when you have someplace to be during the day. But that's one of the very rare urban legends about vampires that's true. We don't sleep in coffins. We don't have Transylvanian accents—

unless we're from Transylvania. We don't endorse chocolaty breakfast cereals," she quipped with a laugh, casting me a sidelong grin. "Just make sure that you get blood every day for about two weeks, and then you can wean yourself off of it if you choose to do so." She glanced to Layne. "I know the first time was rough," she acknowledged, "but when a vampire isn't *desperate* for blood, blood donors find it quite...pleasurable," she said, and her smile turned a little suggestive as she raised a brow.

"I'll keep that in mind," said Layne dryly, and Kane chuckled a little, walking a little faster to climb the path ahead of us.

"Everything that comes after this—it's all going to happen so quickly," said Layne, and her voice sounded pained. When I looked at her in surprise, there were tears standing in her eyes.

"I've got this," I told her, even though there was no part of me that thought that was true. I felt so gangly, as if I were taking my very first steps in life, even though my first steps were about thirty years behind me. Everything felt so surreal, as if I were in an art gallery where they were showing a photographer's work, and all the photographer did was take close-up pictures of day-to-day life. As a new vampire, the world was too bright, too loud, and I had no way to shield myself from that. So I winced as I walked along, as I held onto Layne tightly, feeling my lover sag against me; she'd fought for me against the vampire. Fought for me and won.

"I've got this," I repeated, and Layne's gaze, obviously exhausted, weary, shifted a little. "You've taken care of me," I whispered to her, squeezing her shoulder. And though I was afraid, though I had no idea how tonight was going to go, I took a deep breath, and I told her, "Now let me take care of you. I'm *going* to fix this. I'm going to fix all of this. I'm going to keep my father safe, and Magdalena..." I cleared my throat. "Well, Magdalena isn't going to be a problem anymore."

When Layne looked at me, her eyes were full of love. She nodded slowly. But I knew she wasn't certain. "You're new to this vampire thing, Elizabeth," she whispered, and her voice was so soft, so warm, but there was an undercurrent of doubt to it. "I believe in you," she told me quickly, "but I've been your bodyguard from the very first day, and your father hasn't stopped paying me yet. I'm going to do my best to heal on the way down to Boston, but I've *got* to be there for you tonight. And I will be," she growled, clenching her jaw.

"You're too injured," I told her, and my voice was firm. "How long does it take a werewolf to heal?"

She breathed out, and she wouldn't meet my gaze. "Twenty-four hours to heal fully. But—"

I shook my head adamantly. "Then you have to heal for twenty-four hours. Period. No buts about it, Layne."

"I don't…" she murmured, her head to the side as she gazed at me, her eyes flashing with a more subdued version of her usual mischief, "…take orders from you."

"That's not what you said last night," I replied lightly, and when Kane glanced over her shoulder at us, we must have made such a ridiculous sight—the newly created vampire sagging against the bloody, half-naked werewolf as they both tried to hold each other up because they were laughing too hard to stand.

But, underneath it all, beneath the false bravado, ran an undercurrent of uncertainty.

I was trying my best to be brave.

But the thought of tonight terrified me.

Magdalena wanted my father dead. She wanted to take my father's place…

And now, essentially, I was the only person standing between her and that possibility.

The Protector

Chapter 22: The Calm Before the Storm

We rolled into the parking lot of my apartment building around six o'clock in the evening.

We were spectacularly late.

I was nervously shifting in my seat, curling and uncurling my fingers as I watched my beloved city pass by the passenger side window. Mikagi was driving—it was, after all, her rental car—and she had, unsurprisingly, not spoken a word to us during the entire trip here. Not after what had transpired on the beach last night between us. I'd tried to make conversation with her a couple of times on the way down from Maine, but each time, she either grunted or snorted but continued to remain silent. So we all sat without speaking.

Layne had sprawled in the backseat the entire way to Boston. Occasionally, she would groan or moan, and I'd glance worriedly behind me, and she'd always give me a wan smile, sweat beading on her brow as she grimaced. "I'm just healing," she'd explain to me quietly, sometimes in a growl as she'd wince, reaching up and touching one of her healing wounds. "It hurts to heal," she'd tell me quietly.

When we finally pulled up to my apartment building, I glanced in the passenger side mirror, expecting to see Tommie's red Mustang directly behind us. The Sullivans had set out for Boston soon after us, Kane driving a sleek black sports car and Tommie driving a sexy red Mustang, and they'd both been behind us all the way down from Maine thus far—but now they were nowhere to be found.

"The Sullivans are heading directly to the Council meeting," Mikagi told me flatly then, setting her car into park. "But I could not go there directly. I needed to drop you off at your own car." She glanced sidelong at me now. "Because I must get to the airport."

"Oh…you're not coming with us to the Council meeting?" I asked and—even to me—my voice came out high with worry. Mikagi chuckled, but when she looked at me again, there was kindness in her eyes, and the chill that had descended over the car on the way down was gone.

"No, I can't. I have a gig in London that I have to get to," she said, and I stared at her with wide eyes as I thought about the "normal" lives the both of us lived. I hadn't thought about the normalcy of our music careers since last night, when I'd played with her and Branna, because so much had happened since then. So much had changed.

Honestly, yesterday evening seemed like a lifetime ago. And, in some ways, it actually was.

"Of course," I told her then, and I unfolded my legs from the passenger side and stood up in the parking garage, stretching a little. It had been a long drive. Mikagi got out of the car, and then she was lifting the trunk door, taking out our suitcases and my violin case and placing them on the concrete beside me. I helped Layne out, and then all three of us stood there beneath the guttering fluorescent lights of my parking garage, still not saying anything. The awkwardness grew until I couldn't keep quiet anymore.

"Look," I blurted out, clearing my throat. "I'm…I'm really sorry about last night."

Mikagi raised a brow as she settled her weight into her heels. "I'm not," she said with a little shrug. "It was nice to get to know you, Elizabeth. You're a superb violinist. We would have, together, made a very good couple." Her mouth twisted into a sad smile. "But your heart belongs to another. And who am I to say what's wrong and what's right? You're happy?"

I nodded, threading Layne's fingers through mine as Layne gazed sidelong at me with a small, tight smile, holding her side.

"Yeah," I said, though the nervousness was flooding my entire body, and I had no idea how tonight was going to turn out. But I knew Mikagi was talking about Layne. Was I happy with Layne?

The answer to that was a very resounding *yes*.

"Well, here's the thing, Elizabeth," said Mikagi, rocking back on her black heels. "I know we'll see each other again. I will play with you again," she said with a wink. "And I wish you luck." The mirth suddenly disappeared from her face as she looked at me, really looked at me with her dark glittering eyes. "Don't do anything stupid tonight, and you might survive all of this," she said mildly.

"Stupid?" I asked, and my mouth was suddenly dry.

"Don't let her get killed," she said, turning to look at Layne, her eyes flashing.

Layne clenched her jaw and nodded once, twice, before sighing.

"I won't," she promised, her voice a firm growl of resolution.

I glanced at Layne, but she wasn't looking at me. A flicker of recognition passed between Layne and Mikagi before Mikagi took a step backward, then moved around to the driver's side door of her rental.

"Good luck," she repeated, and then she was in the car and revving it, pulling out of the lot before disappearing into the city streets.

For a long moment, neither Layne nor I said anything as the exhaust faded from the car, as the silence filled the parking area. I squeezed Layne's hand, I took a deep breath...and then I was watching her again.

It was time.

"Layne," I told her, taking a step back, "you have to wait for me in my apartment. There's no way that you can help me with this—all of this," I said uncertainly, circling my

331

hand in the air, "if you're still wounded." I indicated Layne's side.

And it was true—Layne had promised that she would try to do her best to heal on the way down from Maine. But, at the time, I still didn't understand how werewolves *worked*, and Layne's promise that it took around twenty-four hours had proven true...more or less. Some werewolves can heal faster than others, and there are times when a burst of adrenaline or—for lack of a better term—a werewolf's *wolfiness* takes hold, and power surges through them; then they can heal quite quickly. This is what happened to Layne the night that the bullet ripped through her leather jacket and through *her*. Because it did rip through her, I would learn later. But, at the time, she was capable of healing herself almost instantly because of her pure fury.

Here and now, that wasn't the case at all. The vampire had done too much damage to her, and it would be almost another full day before the injuries had healed themselves adequately.

Which meant that, right now, I had a werewolf on my hands who had been patched up as best as possible (Kane gently cleaning every wound and applying the bandages herself) but who was weakened tremendously.

She stood there on the concrete now, and she was wavering, though she was trying her best to stand with strength. Layne was bent forward a little, and her face bore the expression of someone who was in fierce concentration. There was a thin sheen of sweat on her forehead as she flicked her gaze to me now.

Layne was concentrating on standing. I knew she was trying to hide it from me, but that much was obvious. She wavered as she stood there, shifting her weight from foot to foot because it was so painful to be upright.

This was not a woman who could come with me to a Council meeting, to what might turn into a battle, pitting the members of the Council who were on my father's side against the members who were on Magdalena's. I had no idea if things were going to get ugly, but I had a pretty bad feeling that this wasn't going to be enjoyable—for anyone.

I picked up my violin case from the ground and my suitcase, too, and then I had an arm threaded around Layne's waist, and I was gently propelling her toward the building's elevator.

"You need your rest," I told her, but she was already shaking her head, and then she actually dug her feet in, making us both come to a standstill on the concrete.

"No," she growled. She cleared her throat. "No," she repeated, and she turned to me, wincing as she did so, because my fingers were pressing a little too hard and a little too close to one of the wounds on her side. I flinched, withdrawing my hand but leaving my fingertips gently grazing her hip. "I don't care if you think I need my rest or not, Ms. Elizabeth Grayson," Layne said, and she drew herself up to her full height. "We don't have time for this, and there is not a *world* in which you can go to the Council meeting by yourself—"

"I wouldn't be by myself," I shot back, a brow raised. "The Sullivans are probably already there, and they're with me. Layne, you can't—"

"No," she repeated, shaking her head, and her voice was coming out in a growl again. "This is *ridiculous*. How are we even arguing about this? You need me to come with you. You need my help."

"I need you to—" I began, but I didn't get that far.

Because Layne was kissing me.

It was a strong kiss, a kiss with power behind it...but there was also sadness in the way her mouth melted against mine, and as I wrapped my arms around her shoulders, pulling her a little closer to me, she winced as I, again, brushed my fingers too close to *a* wound. There was desperation, too, to this kiss.

Her mouth was soft against mine, soft and hot, and as she kissed me, wrapping her hands with strength around my waist, I realized that I'd never felt her warmth so acutely.

Was it just because I was a vampire now, naturally colder, and she was so much hotter than me? Either way, the sensation was delicious, her heat against me, and when I took a step back, when I was ready to be firm with her again, tell her that, no, absolutely not, she couldn't come with me—I found that I didn't have it in me.

Selfishly, I didn't *want* to go to the Council meeting alone. I was in over my head. But at the same time, I didn't want Layne to get hurt. I didn't want Layne to experience any more pain because of me.

When I took that step back, our mouths separated, and we were looking at each other now, the two of us. I reached up, and I brushed some of her beautiful black hair from her eyes; she hadn't had time to do it up in her usual rakish style. She gazed into my eyes with such an openness then, and it took my breath away.

"I can't let you go alone," she told me, and her voice was gruff, but that's because there was so much emotion in it.

I took a deep breath. "Can you drive me there?" I asked her, and as Layne started to nod, I put up my hand. "And then, when we get there, can you come back here to the apartment and get some rest?"

"You're joking, surely," she told me, and her right brow was arched. She shook her head, and when she spoke again, her voice was low, but every word was passionate as she stepped forward, as she gripped my hands with strong fingers. "I was hired to keep you safe," she reminded me, searching my face, "but beyond that, I *want* to keep you safe. I love you, Elizabeth."

As she stared into my eyes with her own bright gaze, I looked up at her, and I felt the weight and strength of those words move through me. I knew, in the moment, that she was telling me the truth. And that she meant it with her whole heart.

"I hear you," I murmured to her, drawing her face down to mine and pressing my forehead against hers as I breathed her in. "And I love you, too. But...but tonight's going to be... I mean..." I didn't know how to say it, so I didn't look for the right words. I just said, "I want you to be safe," passion making my words low, too, and just as fierce as hers. "I want you to stay *alive*."

Layne gazed into my eyes with her own bright, burning gaze. "And I want the same for you. So you need me to come with you," she said simply.

We stood there for a long moment, staring hard at one another. Here's the thing: I'm stubborn. God only knows how stubborn. It took so much tenacity, so much stubbornness to get to where I am in my music career: thousands of hours of practicing, of wanting it badly, more than I wanted anything else in the world.

But Layne was stubborn, too.

And it looked like I'd met my match.

I took another deep breath, and then I drew her close, laying my head on her shoulder. "Okay," I breathed, the word breaking at the end. "But if you get hurt again because of me—"

"Not *because* of you," Layne whispered, placing her chin on the top of my head and cradling me close, wrapping her arms around me so that I was held in the most comforting embrace in the world. "Because *I* want to do this. Because *I* want to keep you safe. I am making these decisions because I want to make them, Elizabeth. I love you."

"I love you, too," I told her.

But the words came out in a whisper.

There was a very real chance that she was going to die tonight. That my father was going to die tonight. That *I* might die tonight. How in the world was I okay with letting Layne come with me, with putting her at risk?

But I just couldn't fight it. Not anymore.

I glanced down at my wristwatch and grimaced.

"It's time," I told her.

And, hand in hand, we walked through the parking

lot toward my car and the inevitability of whatever this night had in store for us.

She squeezed my fingers reassuringly, but I could feel her blood pounding through her veins.

"I've already lost you once today," she told me, opening the passenger-side door of the car with a flourish before taking my suitcase and violin from me and setting them in the backseat. "I'm not going to lose you again."

I hoped she was right.

Chapter 23: The Battle of Boston

"The Council holds their meetings *here?*" I murmured, gazing up at the skyscraper.

Layne shrugged a little, digging her hands deeper into her leather jacket's pockets. "Your father thought it was ironic," she said, a trace of sarcasm in her tone.

We were staring up at my father's skyscraper. Dad had been bringing me here since I was a kid, and I'd never thought it was strange that a (self-proclaimed) king of fishing would have a skyscraper. My dad made a lot of money, had a lot of business to attend to, a lot of employees beneath him. His company had many departments, so it made sense to me that he required a skyscraper for the management aspect of things—but, of course, in my twenties, a friend commented that it was kind of odd that someone who sold fish for a living owned and operated his own skyscraper. So, I'd asked my dad about it, and he'd thought that the question was funny, but there had been a pained expression on his face.

Now, with everything I'd just learned and the person I'd just turned into, I wondered if the reason my father had a skyscraper had more to do with the fact that he was the vampire leader of the Nocturne Council of Boston than it had to do with his business.

"Many vampires work here," said Layne mildly, confirming my suspicions right out of the gate. "And there are many who are loyal to your father—don't get me wrong. But there are probably several people who work here who are loyal to Magdalena, as well. So, when we head into the building, the only people you can trust are your father and the Sullivans. And me. Got it?"

"Yeah," I muttered, straightening the hem of my skirt. I had no idea what sort of outfit one might wear to a potential "battle," so I'd gone with my gut instinct and the thing I always felt the most comfortable in: the outfit I wear for concert performances. My plain black skirt and white button-down blouse. The clothes had felt safe, familiar, when I'd put them on earlier today in Maine, ready to head to Boston.

And now I was in a familiar place. My dad's skyscraper was where I'd spent so much of my time practicing, growing up, because I'd come here after school, after my mother died, rather than go home right away. My dad had even given me a back corner office so that I could practice in peace. He had soundproofed the room so that his employees wouldn't complain about his kid practicing her violin.

Much of my childhood had been spent here. When I looked up at the skyscraper, I felt the nostalgic weight of love, of family, that I had always felt when I looked at it.

But overhead, heavy banks of gray clouds were masking the light of the setting sun, and darkness seemed to be arriving early. The lights on the skyscraper were already illuminated, and the Grayson logo was shining brightly, the two intertwined fish looping endlessly together above the streets of Boston.

I reached out across the space between us and brushed the back of my hand against Layne's leg. I cleared my throat nervously as she slid her hand out of her pocket, taking mine and threading our fingers together.

"Well," I said, and I took a deep breath. "Let's do this."

I was starting to walk up the steps toward the building when Layne pulled me back. I glanced at her, and I paused, waiting.

"No matter what happens in there," she whispered to me, her voice thick with emotion, "I want you to know that I love you. That I'll...I'll always be—"

"Don't," I whispered, and I stepped close, pressing my first finger against the fullness of her mouth. I breathed out, my heartbeat quickening as I felt the heat of her lips against my skin, as she held my gaze with her startlingly clear eyes. "Don't say anything like that," I whispered to her. "Because...because there's no need, okay? We're both going to get out of this."

"The odds are that we won't," she told me simply, earnestly, still holding my gaze. "And I want you to know the truth." I began to shake my head, but she kept going fervently: "That I do love you. That I have done everything in my power to keep you safe, and that I will continue to do everything in my power—until I take my very last breath—to keep you safe and well, Elizabeth. Because it is my duty to do so. And because I love you with my whole heart."

I watched her for a long moment, feeling my heart pound inside of me with uncertainty. With fear.

And with love—a roaring, raw love that I felt deeply.

"I love you," I told Layne fiercely, my heart rising inside of me. God, I was afraid. I was afraid that I was about to die, that *she* was about to die. The chances were, as she'd said, pretty good that we weren't going to make it out of this alive. I had no idea what to expect in there; I had no idea how many people were on my father's side and how many people were on Magdalena's.

But, no matter what happened, we'd had this. Us. And as I stood there, as I held Layne tightly, I tried to find the words to express that to her. That I was so glad that we'd come together, the two of us. That I was so glad we'd had last night.

And that last night had been the best night of my life.

It was true, I realized. It *had* been the best night.

I'd spent some of the happiest hours of my life with this enigmatic, powerful werewolf, falling head over heels in love with her. And I was so grateful for that.

"I love you," I repeated then, because I couldn't phrase everything I wanted to say, and we didn't have time for me to say everything I wanted to say. I think we both knew that.

"I love you, too," she said simply, arching a perfect brow as a look flickered across her face, and she smiled at me, grinning wickedly. "Now..." And Layne inclined her head toward the skyscraper. "Shall we?"

"Sure," I said, biting my lip, and hand in hand, we ascended the concrete steps outside of my father's skyscraper and entered through the wide glass doors, which shut smoothly behind us.

We were inside.

"Elizabeth!" said the doorman in shock, glancing at me with wide eyes. His name was Frederick, and he'd worked as my father's doorman in what Dad had always called his "downtown building" for over twenty years.

Was *he* a vampire? I stared at him for a long moment before I realized I was staring, and then I just smiled at him.

"Nice to see you, Fred," I told him with a nod. "I'm here to see...Dad." I actually had no idea where we were supposed to be headed, funnily enough. Where would a Council meeting be held?

"Your father's in the middle of a very important meeting," said Fred, with a small frown.

"Yeah, I'm supposed to be there with him," I said, and Fred's were as round as saucers. "Can you tell me where it's taking place?"

"The seventeenth floor," he said promptly, then called up an elevator for us as he gazed at Layne apprehensively. "Eh..." He cleared his throat, obviously nervous. "Are you sure you're supposed to be in a meeting with your father *today*, miss?"

As I stared at him, my eyes narrowing, I knew that he was aware that there was a Nocturne Council meeting going on right now.

"Yes," I told him, and as the elevator dinged open, Layne and I moved into the gilded box. All at once, my mind went blank. "What floor did you say it's it on?" I asked, swallowing as I held the doors open with my hand.

"Seventeen," said Fred, and his eyes lowered as the doors shut.

I pressed the golden button for floor seventeen.

When I glanced at Layne, she nodded, her nostrils flaring. "He's a vampire," she told me, confirming my suspicion. "Soon enough, you'll be able to detect one of your own kind," she told me soothingly, but that's not what I was upset about.

It would take time, I realized, to sort through all of my childhood memories, all of my memories of my growing-up years, wondering about my father's colleagues and sorting them into neat "vampire" and "not-vampire" categories. It was just so disconcerting. Was most of my childhood a lie?

I knew my father had kept all of this from me to protect me. I knew that my mother's death, now that I understood that it wasn't truly an accident, had been very hard on him. I couldn't blame Dad for all of the lengths he'd gone to in order to keep me safe, especially after his wife had been taken from him. I would have blamed myself for her death, too, were I in his position.

This revision of my life was just going to take some getting used to.

I stared down at my pale hands as the elevator ascended, hands that I'd known all of my life, hands that had worked tirelessly to master the violin, hands that had held lovers, hands that had learned the curves of Layne, a woman I'd fallen in love with so deeply. Hands that were now, I realized, different from the hands I'd had yesterday.

I was different.

It was only a single moment of contemplation, but it

341

unsettled me as the elevator rose higher and higher into the building I'd known since childhood, the building that—I now recognized—I'd never really known at all.

When the elevator *dinged* open on the seventeenth floor, I wasn't prepared for what was about to happen next. I wasn't prepared for anything. My life had moved at such a fast pace these past few days, and I hadn't had any time to catch up. But that's just...life, I guess. It moves faster than we can comprehend, and we just have to try our best, no matter the circumstances.

My heart was in my throat as the doors slid smoothly back, my own black blood pounding through my veins too quickly as we stepped into the corridor; the doors slid shut behind us.

We were in a hallway like any of the hallways in my father's building. A sumptuous oriental-style rug spread out ahead of us, centered on the tiled floor. But, little by little, I began to notice that there *was* something different about this floor.

I'd never been on the seventeenth floor—I hadn't visited many of the floors because I'd never had a need to do so—but I was struck by how dim the overhead fluorescent lights were here. The rug, too, had an unusual pattern, made with varying shades of red rather than the typical neutral palette. The colors, the swirls...they reminded me of blood.

I tilted my head. From somewhere far away, I heard voices. And then there was a roar, as of applause. I glanced over my shoulder at Layne, who had narrowed her eyes, her mouth pressed into a thin, hard line. Then, as if by an unspoken agreement, we started walking down the corridor side by side, following the sound of the voices.

The hallway wound around the outer perimeter of the building, and we walked along it, listening to the voices coming from our right—the internal core of the skyscraper. But there weren't any doors to get into where the voices were coming from. On our left were windows that looked out at the city of Boston, windows that were heavily tinted so that the remaining sunlight of the day could barely shine through; it was a little like looking seeing the world through sunglasses. And to the right of us, there was only a steel-gray wall with occasional paintings of modern art and cubist shapes. No doors.

We walked and walked for a comically long period of time, still with absolutely no doors to be found, and with the seemingly never-ending windows spanning to our left, until we turned a corner.

"This makes no sense," I told Layne, gazing up at her with frustration. "Where are the *doors*? Where are the voices coming from?"

Layne jerked her chin ahead of us, her eyes narrowing even further as she worked her jaw. "Up ahead," she murmured, and she almost imperceptibly changed a little beside me. There was a subtle shift to her shoulders, to the way she carried herself. It's almost as if she grew in size, though I knew that was impossible. It was her presence that grew to fill the corridor around us, not her physical body.

"How do you do that?" I asked her then, my voice quiet as I glanced sidelong at my lover and realized there were things about her I didn't understand. But I wanted to understand them. I wanted to know her, to her very core.

"Do what?" she asked, surprised, as she glanced at me.

"You became...bigger, somehow," I told her, waving my hand as she stared at me in surprise. "Kind of like your hackles are raised or something. Is it a wolf thing?" I asked.

She chuckled a little, though there was no actual humor in the sound. "Maybe. I'm just mentally preparing for what's about to happen..." Her voice trailed off. I reached across the space between us, and I took her hand in mine again, threading my fingers through hers, squeezing softly.

We turned the corner and kept walking, and that's when I first saw it. Coming up on our right was a set of doors.

They weren't like the rest of the doors in my father's building—you know the type—boring pre-fab wooden doors that are so common in offices. No, these were different.

For one, they were solid black. For another, they were floor-to-ceiling. And, on either side of the doors themselves stood two black pillars. Not the type of pillars *anyone* would expect to see in an office building. These were Roman in style, and as we came closer to them, I realized that they were made of solid marble.

I was beginning to think that we were beyond the office portion of my father's skyscraper and had entered the, well, *vampire* part of it. Which was very, very weird to consider, even though I was a vampire now, too.

Standing beside the pillar closest to us was Kane. She leaned against the wall, and her entire body projected nonchalance. Still, I had spent some time with her over the past couple of days, and I could sense that she was on edge. She was taking a long pull on a cigarette when she glanced at us; she pushed off from the wall, stubbing the cigarette out against the marble column.

"Good, you're here," she said, her voice a low growl as she stepped forward and put her hand at the small of my back, leaning her face close to mine as she murmured into my ear, "It's not going so well. We need to be prepared." She cast a glance at Layne and her jaw tightened. "All of us."

"What do you mean?" I asked, my heart in my throat, but Kane shook her head, nodding toward the doors.

"We've got to go in. Now," she told us, and then she was stepping forward. Her long fingers gripped the silver door handles, and she swung the doors open wide.

The room beyond was very dark—and packed with people. But beyond that, my eyes couldn't make anything out, not until we stepped inside and Kane shut the doors behind us. Even though the hallway had been dim, this room was fully black, or so it seemed at first.

Above the hushed noise of the crowd, there were loud voices—two of them—pitched in a heated argument. I recognized one of them as my father's.

I blinked rapidly, willing my eyes to adjust as Kane, her hand still pressed at the small of my back, gently propelled me forward. I began to make out the shapes of the people surrounding us, and my eyes focused while I scanned the crowd, my heart in my throat as I listened to my father.

"You must understand—" he was saying, but he was cut off by a derisive snort.

"We've been *understanding* for too long," the woman's voice snarled. "And we have no patience anymore. Not for you *or* your human-loving ways."

Yeah. I knew that voice, too.

I swallowed as a cold chill crept over my skin. The people around us began to part as Kane cut a path through the crowd. That's when I realized we were up on a balcony, because we'd reached the balcony railing. And there, down below us, was a scene that gave me pause.

I stared at my father, standing tall and proud at a lectern that had been elevated above the sea of people. Kane, Layne and I were situated on a balcony that ran all around the perimeter of the room, overlooking the open floor below us, almost as if we were in the stands of an amphitheater. This space was definitely not something that had been designed for a standard office building; it was so unexpected, so out of place. But I knew that I shouldn't really be surprised by anything, not at this point.

I watched my father, my heart hammering, but he didn't notice me. Not yet. Instead, he had his eyes locked on the woman opposite him, the woman standing behind the second lectern on another dais. She was beautiful, with her long blonde hair spilling over her shoulders in dazzling waves, her body filling out the curves of a tight-fitting black dress.

Magdalena.

As I stared down at her, my stomach turned, and I tasted bile in my throat. This was the woman who had gouged at the wound in my leg. This was the woman who had tortured Layne, almost killing her.

This was the woman who *had* killed my mother.

Magdalena had proven that she would stop at nothing to take over the Nocturne Council, and she would stop at nothing to overturn my father. She would murder anyone—everyone—who stood in her way.

My mouth was dry as I regarded her cruel face. The rest of the people gathered around us—the railing was packed shoulder to shoulder—watched the proceedings in eerie silence.

Kane stood at my back, but gradually Layne eased close enough to press against my side, peering over my shoulder.

And that's when Magdalena looked up in our direction.

She stared at us, and my father did, too. He looked relieved for half a heartbeat when he glanced my way, and then his face regained its former composure. But Magdalena? She didn't looked relieved at all. Her lips bared her teeth in what could only be called a grimace, and her incisors lengthened as she snarled at us.

But then her face…changed. Her snarl softened, smoothed, and then she was watching us with triumph, her eyes narrowed shrewdly. "How is it possible," she asked, and her voice was low, "that any of you would consider supporting a man whose daughter is sleeping with a wolf?"

That's when the silence broke, because Magdalena looked up at us again—pointedly—staring at me with a wicked, gleaming smile. And the other vampires in the room, standing ear to ear in order to watch my father and Magdalena square off, stared at me, too. A murmur spread…and it was low, but it was heated.

"Animal," I heard.

And "wolf," whispered in the most derogatory tone, as if the man saying it was spitting out the word to the floor.

My father caught my gaze, and though his face bore perfect serenity, something flickered across his eyes. Pain. Regret. Fear. I balled my hands into fists, and I stared down at Magdalena now, my blood pounding through me too quickly for me to remain silent, to just sit back and permit this bigotry.

"Funny that you'd have problems with a werewolf," I called out, and I was so proud that my voice was strong and clear, "when *you're* the only animal in the room, Magdalena."

The snarl returned to mar her pretty face, contorting it into something that should only be seen in horror movies. Her grotesquely long incisors descended over her lower lip.

"Go home, little girl," Magdalena laughed derisively. "A vampires' Council is no place for *humans* and their *pets*."

"Hmm." I lifted my chin. "As far as I can tell, Magdalena, there is not a single human here," I told her, glancing around at all of the vampires, watching me now in silence, some of them looking pretty damn amused, eager to find out what might happen next.

And what happened next *was* worth watching.

Because the look that came over Magdalena's face just then was legendary. It was quick—you'd have to be watching for it—but I certainly was. Her brow furrowed for half a heartbeat, as if she wasn't quite certain what I was saying. And then there was fury, bright, raw fury that fell over her like the mask of a monster.

"No," she whispered, but I shrugged, leaning on the railing as I stared down at her.

"Magdalena, you tried to have me killed. You tried to kill me *yourself*," I said, and my voice was ringing through the room. "You tried to kill me *multiple* times, actually...and *every single time*, you failed.

"Now it's too late. Like my father before me," I said, and there was purposeful pride in my tone, "*I* am a vampire now, *too.*"

And when I glanced at my dad, he was still gazing up at me, and his face was no longer cool and controlled. He was beaming at me, and there was so much love evident in his features that I was reminded me of the night of my very first violin recital. I was six years old, and I'd sounded horrendous with my little child-sized violin and my butchered version of Beethoven's fifth, but Dad was beaming at me from the audience as if I were the best concert violinist in the universe.

That was the look he had on his face now. Pride, mixed with the purest love.

And though things were tense, though there was fear rushing through my body, I smiled down at my father, and I gave him a little nod.

No matter what happened, going forward, we were in this together.

There was more murmuring among the assembled vampires now, and behind me, Layne leaned close to Kane, who murmured something into her ear.

Down below, one of the vampires stepped close to Magdalena's dais. He was an older gentleman, and he was wearing a sharp suit, his white mustache curled up at the ends, and his mouth drawn in a thin, downturned line. "Magdalena," he said, and there was a sharp tone to his voice, "is this true? Did you try to *kill* Grayson's daughter?"

Magdalena said nothing, only stared up at me as if were was something small and slimy that she would love to squish beneath her heel.

But I stood tall above her, and I clutched the railing so hard with my hands that my knuckles shone white in the dim light.

"Magdalena," said the older man sharply. "Answer me."

"All is fair in love and war," Magdalena replied somewhat airily, but she kept staring at me with brightly flashing eyes.

"I doubt," said the older gentleman dryly, "that you tried to kill her out of *love*."

"You're slipping, Magdalena," said my father then, drawing himself up to his full height and crossing his arms over his chest. He cocked his head and smiled a little ruefully at Magdalena, as if he pitied her. "This is not your day."

My father was using his most cajoling voice, the kind he brought out on the phone when he was talking with someone he was trying to convince of something. But Magdalena was not so easily convinced. She stared at my father, her nostrils flaring, the fury in her face making her expression chilling.

"The Council has been irrevocably divided, Alexander," she said, tapping the top of the lectern with one long fingernail. "There are those who side with you, yes. But I think there are more who side with me. We are *tired*," she spat out the word, "of hiding in the shadows. It is time for the vampires to rise as the better race. The more powerful race. Humans have feared us for millennia, and now they will know the reason why."

But my father was laughing. It was a bold move, and one I knew that he had calculated, reading the room to gauge whether this would infuriate Magdalena…or cause her to calm down.

It achieved a little bit of both.

The energy in the room was palpable, heavy. Tension crackled throughout the crowd. A soft, silent roar seemed to fill the space, and my heart was in my throat as I stared down at my father and Magdalena, standing behind each lectern as if they were poised at the prows of ships, trying to steer in different directions.

"I think that the Nocturne Council needs new leadership," said Magdalena, drawing herself up to her full height again, straightening her shoulders and staring daggers at my father. "And there are many who agree with me. For too long we have remained in the shadows."

"We are *not* in the shadows," said my father with another indulgent chuckle, though there was a stiffness to his words as he tried to keep his tone lighthearted. "We are giants among men. We own corporations and businesses. We have great wealth and power, all of us. We do not *suffer*," he scoffed, his head tilted to the side. "Do not imagine that we do."

"We shouldn't have to hide who we are!" Magdalena roared.

"We don't hide," said my father pointedly. "We walk among them. We are part of them. We have no need to subjugate them."

"It is always the same argument," said the older gentleman, standing on the floor between to the two platforms as he looked from Magdalena to my father and back again. "But Alexander has been a good leader for many years, and I do not see any reason to change the way of things."

"We deserve to be kings and *queens*," said Magdalena, her eyes flashing with a frightening fury. "We deserve *blood*, whenever we wish it."

There was a low murmuring among the assembled vampires now, and it wasn't necessarily a murmur of disagreement. There were a few vampires, definitely, who frowned as they gazed down from the railings. But there were also several who were—fervently—nodding their heads.

"This world should be *ours*," Magdalena hissed, and the murmuring quieted. "We are powerful, and we could take it—*all* of it—so easily from the human race. And then we would rule the planet. All of us. Together."

"You forget where you came from," said my father, and there was such strength to his words that few people probably noticed the slight tremor to his voice. I heard it because he's my father, and I knew his mannerisms well. I stared down at him, my heart beating too fast.

If my father was worried…this wasn't good.

Tension still electrified the gathered vampires, and when Dad glanced up at me, his eyes were dark.

"Things never change between us, Magdalena," said my father then, and he spread his hands in front of him. He looked at ease as he stood there, behind the lectern, but I could tell that he was anxious. There was a subtle rise in his shoulders. "We always come back to this place. We debate this issue again and again. I feel as if I have deja vu," he remarked wryly.

"We return to this place because the people want change," Magdalena hissed.

A hush of voices rose up again. The hairs stood up on the back of my neck, and I looked out toward the crowd of people, and I wondered how many there were here who were loyal to my father, loyal to the idea that humankind deserved to live as we—or, rather, they—had been living.

I was no longer human, but I knew the type of world that Magdalena wanted. She had a dictator's mentality. She wanted everyone to obey the oppressor, in fear for their lives, used and abused. I couldn't imagine the planet falling into such discord. It was an idea plucked from the pages of a horror novel.

The Nocturne Council, I'd been told, only presided over the northeast. There were other councils in the world, and they must have leaders who were similar to my father, because nothing truly terrible had happened to humanity yet—as far as I knew—brought about by the whims of vampires. If the balance shifted, even if it was only in this region of the United States, what havoc could be wrought?

Could the world itself *end* because of one small action here tonight?

I didn't know the answer to that question, but it was a terrifying thought. My heart in my throat, my blood beating quickly through me as I considered the apocalypse, brought about by vampires, I realized that I was leaning a little over the railing of the balcony as I stared down at my father—my father, who was watching me now with a furrowed brow.

But, no, he wasn't looking at me, I realized, as he opened his mouth, as he began to speak.

He was looking at Layne.

"I know how to settle this, Magdalena—once and for all," said my father, his words easy, but with an unsettling sharpness in his tone. When he flicked his gaze from Layne to me, there was deep pain in his expression.

My breath caught. What was he up to?

Magdalena stared at him, waiting for him to continue.

"Let us have a Match," said my father then, his eyes dark as he held Magdalena's gaze.

Everyone in the entire room began to whisper among themselves, and I stood there, perplexed, but no less worried.

What in the world was a Match?

"Layne, what..." I whispered, turning to her.

But Layne was gone.

Chapter 24: Match

I tried to whirl around to look at Kane, my eyes wide, but Kane remained in place, her hand at the small of my back, as if to keep me still. "Where's Layne?" I whispered to her, but Kane shook her head, her mouth set in a grim line.

"Layne is doing what she must do," Kane told me then. And there was an unmistakable note of regret in her low voice. "I'm sorry, Elizabeth," she murmured, searching my face, exhaling heavily.

"What? Oh, God, what's happening?" I asked her, but Kane inclined her head toward the balcony railing again, and, shaking, I peered over.

There, standing beside my father's dais, was Layne.

She stood tall, motionless, her chin lifted high, her hands behind her back and her legs spread apart, as if she were a soldier in the military. Her eyes trained on Magdalena. And I seemed to hear Layne growling, even from here. Her full lips were drawn back from her teeth, and she was snarling quietly at the blonde vampire.

"A Match," Magdalena repeated, almost as if amused. "And who would be your Champion?"

"I volunteer," said Layne immediately, and though her voice was low, every person in the room heard her, because they had fallen silent.

Magdalena tilted her head back, and she began to laugh.

"Do you see, everyone?" she said then, once she had

composed herself. "Do you *see* how he mocks us all, as vampires? Alexander proposes a Match to settle the differences among the Nocturne Council, and his Champion would be a *wolf?*"

"We have Matches all the time with shapeshifters," said my father dismissively, his eyes narrowing. "This instance is no different."

"This is *vampire* business," snarled Magdalena then. "Not *animal* business."

I stared down as the two of them argued, but I wasn't looking at my father or Magdalena.

I was staring at Layne.

Layne, who was staring straight ahead, her chin lifted, her eyes flashing dangerously. Layne, who had told me that she *must* come with me. I understood why now. My father and she had already arranged this, hadn't they? That she was to be his Champion…whatever that was. But as I listened to my father argue, I was fairly certain I knew what was about to happen.

There was about to be a duel of sorts between Layne and…someone else. Between Layne and, in all probability—considering how passionately and derisively Magdalena was arguing against "animals" in a Match—a vampire.

This couldn't be happening. A vampire had nearly killed Layne this morning, and she wasn't yet healed; she was still covered in a map of wounds, all over her body.

No.

She hadn't had enough *time.*

She knew this. She *knew* this, and yet she still came.

Layne was going to die. It wasn't certain, but I had a terrible feeling in the pit of my stomach as Magdalena and my father ceased arguing, as Magdalena descended from the dais and entered the thick throng of vampires to murmur quietly to them, selecting her own Champion.

I turned around. I tried to push my way through the press of bodies, but they were tightly packed together, angling their heads and trying to see over the balcony, down to the floor. Kane was right behind me, and she grimaced, shaking her head.

"I'm sorry, Elizabeth," she said. "You'll never make it down there before the fight starts."

"Layne's wounded," I told her as I gripped her arm. "Kane, she can't fight a *vampire*, not in her condition."

"Layne's remarkable," Kane soothed me, though there was worry in her expression as she flicked her eyes back toward the scene below us, her mouth drawn in a flat line again.

Layne *was* remarkable, but—oh, God, there were so many things that could go wrong...

My heart seemed to stop beating as I watched Magdalena climb back up to the dais, her eyes glittering wickedly. "My Champion has been chosen," she called out.

That's when Layne looked up. She stared across the distance, and her gaze locked with mine. In that moment, so much passed between us. She knew I was terrified of losing her; she knew that there was a great and terrible chance that she could die. But still, she stood strong on the floor far beneath me, and she regarded me with so much fierce, wild love that my heart, formerly stopped, began to beat again.

She didn't mouth the words *I love you*, but the sentiment was evident in her gaze as she carefully unzipped her leather jacket. She took the jacket off and placed it neatly on the edge of my father's dais. She stood there now in her jeans and her plain blue t-shirt, her hands fisted, her legs spread hip-width apart. She tipped her chin down, and she stood her ground.

She watched me.

And she waited.

I felt a presence come beside me, squeezing through the crowd, and when I glanced at the woman who had just bumped against my hip, tears sprang to my eyes.

It was Mikagi.

I embraced her tightly, and she hugged me just as

tightly back before peering over the railing, her nose wrinkled.

"I'm glad I got here before it began," she said, her accent clipped as she gazed at me with darkly glittering eyes. "I couldn't go to the airport, not in good conscience, with...all of this going on here."

"I'm glad you came," I told her, biting my lip, worry making my words high-pitched as I gripped the railing. "Mikagi, Layne's going to—"

"I know," she said, her head tilted. "Did the wolf tell you she intended to do this?"

"No," I groaned, glancing down. "I would never have let her if I'd have known."

"Ah. Then you know why she didn't tell you," Mikagi quipped, setting a violin case down by her feet. She crouched, opening up the case, and then she drew the violin and its bow out, grasping them in her sure hands.

"What are you doing?" I asked Mikagi as I peered distractedly down at the floor again. Magdalena was crooking her finger behind her, toward a shadowy figure, and my father was descending from his dais. Vampires pulled the daises back, and then the vampires down on the floor below formed a wide circle around the empty expanse of the floor.

"There's about to be a fight," said Mikagi brightly. "And a fight requires musical accompaniment, don't you think?"

I was too distracted to respond to her joke. I wanted to go down there, to stop Layne, to stop *all* of this madness—but I was too late.

The Match was starting.

Magdalena had motioned for a man to step forward. In the shadows, he had looked smaller than he actually was. The guy was pretty tall—not basketball-player tall, but he was still head-and-shoulders taller than Layne. He came forward and stood beside Magdalena with his arms crossed. He was wearing a long black leather jacket, and he had very muscular arms; the leather creaked when he shifted his shoulders.

The room had fallen as silent as a cemetery as Magdalena stood beside her chosen Champion—and Dad stood beside Layne.

"So, to be clear," said Magdalena, lifting her chin and pinning Dad to the spot with a wicked smile, "we're Matching our Champions based on who will control the Nocturne Council moving forward...yes?"

Dad did not answer for a long moment, an unreadable expression passing over his face. And then he said simply, "Yes."

The weight of responsibility that must be pressing down on Layne's shoulders right now... God, I can't imagine it. I stared at the scene below me, stricken, as Layne stood calm and steady, her breathing slow and even, her face relaxed, smooth. She didn't seem unsettled at all.

I knew, in that moment, why my father was doing this.

I could tell by the tenseness of his stance that he wasn't certain about Layne being able to fight—and win—in her current state. Still, he obviously felt that he didn't have a choice. Something about the mood of the room must have forced him to goad Magdalena into agreeing to a Match, rather than continue debating as they were—in order to prevent a potential riot from breaking out.

He had wanted to stop the possibility of widespread violence before it started, because he knew something that I didn't. He knew, somehow, that a battle was imminent.

I mean, even to me, the room felt like a short-fused bomb. The vampires were quiet, but the tension was taut, and it seemed to grow tighter, heavier, with each passing moment.

And then, suddenly, Mikagi began to play.

First, she plucked at her strings softly, to make sure that the violin was in tune. She didn't have much time to tune it, though, because everyone in the room shifted to look toward her, searching out the source of the music. She launched right into one of her original works, a fast-paced piece called "The Beast in Me." It was full of discordant, staccato notes, sounding like something broken, fractured...

Then Magdalena stepped forward, and all eyes left Mikagi, redirected toward the vampire on the floor.

"I'm ready. Are you?" she asked my father.

He nodded once, a small nod, and he took Layne's elbow. Then he murmured something into her ear, too low for anyone else to hear. She nodded almost imperceptibly, her stance straight and firm.

My father, with slow steps, moved away from Layne, again glancing up at the balcony, at me. His face was creased with agony, and my heart shuddered with fear in my chest.

Kane squeezed my arm in encouragement as Mikagi dove into the second, much faster verse of her song—and then Magdalena and my father stepped back from their two champions.

Mikagi's violin hung on one perfect high note for a long moment before descending into chaos; the music that flew from her strings was an agitation of notes. They made the hairs on the back of my neck stand on end.

And that's when the vampire man attacked Layne.

The two of them had been standing about five feet apart, and they were both being too casual, nonchalant. My entire body ached with tension; I felt it in my bones when he struck her, marrow deep.

He came for Layne with such lightning speed that it was difficult to follow his movement with my eyes. He was so much bigger than her, not just in height but in build. He was thicker than her, more muscular. Still, I knew that Layne was strong, that she could hold herself in any fight—and if the vampire attack on the beach hadn't happened this morning, I would have been confident, assured that she would win.

But she was injured, weakened, and, heart in my

throat, my confidence was shaken further as Layne sidestepped the vampire when he barreled toward her. Or, rather, she *tried* to sidestep him. And she nearly succeeded—but not before the vampire grabbed a scrap of her t-shirt sleeve in his hand, tearing it.

There was a flash of bright red on her arm, and I assumed he'd wounded her with—what? His fingernails? There was blood dripping down her bare, muscled arm. If the scratch hurt her—it must have hurt her—Layne paid it no mind. Instead, she drew herself up to her full height, and then she was bending forward...

And Layne became the wolf.

She was so beautiful.

I had only witnessed Layne's wolf form a couple of times, but I was always struck by how elegantly fierce, how awesomely lovely she was. The sleek silver pelt, the narrow lupine face—graceful and wild, all at once.

She stared at the vampire across from her, lips drawn over her teeth...and then it was dazzling, how fast she moved, covering the distance between them as if there were no distance at all.

After that, the wolf and vampire became a blur. It was impossible to follow them with my eyes, but I tried to, anyway, my blood pumping like quicksilver. Their limbs were caught together in a vicious tangle, both of them snarling. There was the movement of teeth through air, of snapping jaws, of claws extended...

And then: a whimper, like that of an animal being struck, and Layne bounced back, her paws hitting the earth lightly as she loped around the vampire, circling him.

But behind her, on the floor, dripped a steady stream of blood.

The vampire had gotten her—badly.

Because her fur was so thick, it was difficult to tell where the blood was coming from; I gripped the railing and tried to calm my breathing, but all I could do was gasp. I gulped down air as Mikagi played, her violin mournful now, the music complementing the pace of the fight as the opponents circled one another. The vampires surrounding the pair on the floor were deeply, eerily quiet.

Because of the silence, I could hear Layne's blood dripping onto the floor. *Drip, drip, drip*, and with each drip, my heart was breaking.

I found the wound now as Layne turned, placing paw over paw like a dancer; she kept her snout facing the vampire. The wound marred her shoulder, a big, jagged gash with blood flowing over her leg, down to her paw. The sight was macabre, her beautiful silver pelt vandalized by that garish red.

"Look," Kane whispered in my ear, and her voice was tense. I followed the line of her finger, pointing down below us, and I let out my breath in a hiss.

Magdalena was *laughing*.

Her mouth was hidden behind a hand, but as she looked at the blood that dripped over Layne's paw, she laughed. She was *laughing* at the wounded wolf. Her laughter was quiet, so quiet, but I could still hear notes of it all the way up here, a tinkling sound of delight—amusement over the fact that Layne was bleeding, blood that Magdalena's vampire Champion had caused to flow.

The scent of the blood itself was slow to reach me, but when it did, I was shaken, trembling. God, it smelled so good—so...delicious. I inhaled deeply, rising to my tiptoes to follow the scent, and that's when Kane's grip on my arm tightened, and she pressed her short nails painfully into my skin.

"Layne needs you," she murmured to me, not unkindly. "I know it's difficult to focus when you are new, but you must try, Elizabeth."

And I did. The blood was the most enticing scent I'd ever smelled, but I shoved down that want, shoved it into the deepest, darkest place inside of myself, and I locked the door. I was so ashamed for even thinking about tasting Layne's blood, but I couldn't help myself. As I glanced back at Kane, she gave me a soft, encouraging smile.

"It's all right. You should have seen me when I turned," she said, raising a brow. "Really, it's all right. Just… I don't know how this is going to go. And Layne needs your full attention right now."

I glanced back down at the two Champions circling one another, and I nodded. "Listen, Kane—can I get down there now? Please?" I asked her, the words faint as I whispered them in her ear. I didn't want to be overheard; Magdalena's people could be anyone, and anywhere.

In response, Kane glanced over her shoulder with a soft frown. "Yes. Come," she said, and then she was turning and letting go of my arm; I began to follow her.

"Good luck," said Mikagi, in the middle of playing a long, beautiful note. I nodded to her, offering a halfhearted smile, and then I trailed Kane around the balcony, toward a set of stairs that I hadn't noticed before.

We descended the steps and then had to push—hard—to get through the crowd surrounding the wolf and vampire. I couldn't see what was happening; there were two women ahead of me who stood so close together that I was having to peer around them on my tiptoes—but I heard, then, the smack of flesh on flesh, and my heart stopped as I heard another mournful whimper.

Now the vampire was taunting Layne, goading her to come attack him. I could hear him chuckling as we rounded those two women, as I pushed past them, and then I was standing on the outskirts of the circle where the wolf and vampire crouched.

Layne had been struck again. Now her other shoulder was coursing with blood, blood that rushed down, pooling on the floor beside her massive paw.

"Hey," said Tommie beside us, her mouth flat as she glanced at Kane and me. "This is bad," she murmured, leaning close to whisper into my ear. "Layne's not, well, *on*. She's too lost in her head. That guy's having fun, just toying with her."

And as I watched the fight continue, Tommie's words proved to be true. For a moment, I hoped that it was Layne's strategy to take a few blows, coax the vampire to lower his guard...

But she was in trouble.

It was obvious that Layne was trying to put up a strong front, but I knew her well enough by this point to recognize that that was all it was. She had very minute tells, but they were still there. There was a slight limp to her front right paw; she was trying to keep her breathing even, but it was coming faster and faster now, even though all she did was try to avoid the vampire's blows—and he wasn't exactly raining them down on her. Every few minutes, he'd make a feint at her, and then they'd simply start circling again.

But on the last feint, the vampire came too close, and his incisors were so very long: he grabbed Layne roughly by the shoulders, shoved her to the ground, and then he bit her neck.

His teeth had to go through her thick fur, but they managed the task just fine. Layne was on her feet before he could drink too much of her blood, but he'd taken *some*, all the same. His mouth was red as he smiled at her—a sick and twisted smile, a wide smile that made me shiver—the blood coating his lips. One thin drop of it trailed a wicked red line down his chin.

"Stop!" someone shouted. And as everyone in the room turned to look at me, I realized that I had finally voiced the word that I had been screaming in my head since the fight began.

"Stop," I said again, and then I was stepping forward.

Behind me, Kane's eyes were wide, and Tommie had her arms folded in front of her, watching me with a hint of amusement on her lips.

I had no idea what I was doing.

"There's no *stopping* a Match," said Magdalena, and she stepped into the circle. Above us, the violin music paused mid-note, and I glanced up toward the balcony, where Mikagi stood, violin and bow in one hand. She peered over the railing with a smile, watching me. As I looked up at her, she winked—and that small gesture of friendship gave me a little bit of courage.

"*I'll* take her place," I said then. The words were spoken so quickly; they tumbled right out of my mouth. My hands curled into fists at my sides.

"Elizabeth," began my father on the other side of the circle, but Magdalena lifted her hand.

"Accepted," she said at the exact same moment that my father was saying my name.

"That's not how this works," roared my father, and I stared at him in surprise—I'd never heard him so angry—but Magdalena rounded on him.

"*You* wanted the Match," she hissed in delight, "and now look at what you've done. Your daughter has entered the Match, and there's no getting out of it alive. Well, unless she wins."

Unless she wins. I swallowed, my heart thundering inside of me, and I pushed all of the fear out of my head as best as I could. I made my way over to Layne, who was still in her wolf form. She panted as she stood there, trying to keep all four of her paws on the floor.

As I watched her snout became shorter, her silver fur began to reverse, and then Layne was crouching on the ground, naked and dripping blood. She stood easily and unashamedly, but she hissed out her breath as she took a step toward me, a wound on her leg, a wound I hadn't noticed earlier, starting to gush out onto the ground.

"Don't do this," she told me, gripping my shoulders, but I stepped forward, I wrapped my arms around her neck, and I drew her to me for a kiss. Her mouth tasted like metal, like blood, and she was so hot against me, blood from the wound in her right shoulder dripping down onto my arm...but I ignored it. I shoved away my want for it, and I held her tightly, fiercely.

I had no idea what was about to happen, and as I stepped back from her, as Kane and Tommie both moved forward to wrap Layne's arms around their shoulders and help her limp back into the audience, I lifted my chin, and I told her my deepest truth: "I love you," I whispered.

"Don't let her do this," Layne begged Kane. "Kane, please, *don't let her do this.*"

"It's already done," said Kane, glancing at me with sad eyes. "Good luck, Elizabeth."

What have I done? I thought to myself, staring down at my hands. I'd just volunteered for a *fight?* I'd never fought anyone in my entire life. I played music. I had a normal, quiet life.

But nothing about this was normal or quiet; the crowd of vampires surrounding us stepped forward, as if they were interested to see what sort of Match this was going to become. My opponent just grinned at me, his fangs dripping with the blood of my lover.

The circle was growing smaller as the audience drew closer, everyone angling for a better view of the action. I stood there, stunned, reeling. I knew nothing about being a vampire, knew nothing about the new strength and speed that I possessed, knew nothing about how ruthless a vampire could really be. Because I'd never been ruthless. I'd never been cruel, at least not intentionally.

I was not a killer.

But the man across from me was.

And he took my hesitation, and he made the most of it.

The vampire lunged at me, and there was no way that I could have prepared myself for his attack. He was standing there, completely nonchalant one moment, and then the next, he was propelling himself toward me. I dove to the ground and fell out of the way, but it was a lucky move. The vampire spun around, and just as quickly, he was coming for me again.

I couldn't just keep falling to the floor, but I didn't

even know how to make my teeth grow and become pointed on command. But my body understood exactly what I needed, or perhaps the adrenaline pouring through me had something to do with it. Either way, when the vampire came for me again, I lifted my arms to block him, and my head came forward of its own accord: I was biting his arm with my long, very sharp teeth.

There had been a strange pulsating feeling in my mouth as the teeth grew, and then my body had moved on instinct to bite him. I remembered somehow, in the back of my head, that someone had told me not to drink vampire blood, so when I withdrew my fangs, getting up and bouncing away from him as fast as I could, I wiped my mouth on the back of my hand, and I spat the mouthful of black blood to the ground.

The vampire across from me growled in anger, and he was coming for me quickly, the veins in his neck and forehead throbbing as he launched himself in the air. Again, instinct was taking over, and I was moving to the right—but not before my hand darted out, and I raked my fingernails across the side of his face.

It wasn't *me* doing this. Was it? It felt so odd, as if something took over inside of me, something that was doing everything it could to keep me alive and intact. My fingernails weren't long—as a violinist, they have to be closely trimmed—but they were long enough to cause black blood to well from the scratches on his face.

When he turned toward me now, murder gleamed in his dark eyes.

He came at me relentlessly. I stumbled back from him, and I almost tripped over my own shoe because I wasn't paying attention to where I was going. I was keeping the man in my sights—this man, this man I didn't know, who was hellbent on killing me.

I was angry, and I tried to avoid his attacks, my body taking over and managing to draw blood one other time, with my fingernails, by clawing at his face again. His face was crisscrossed with dripping black gashes, and the fury in his eyes was almost sparking, as if fire burned deep inside of him and was in danger of burning him down.

But right after I scratched his face, I tripped backward as he swiped at me, and he managed to hit my belly with his hand. His nails tore through my shirt and into my skin.

I crumpled to the floor, and I immediately tried to get back up again, but he sideswiped my legs, and I came back down.

The man towered over me as I sat on the floor, holding my stomach. He offered me an inhuman smile—triumphant, gleeful. And his incisors grew as I watched them; he was about to descend on me...

But someone said, "Wait!"

And, surprising no one more than me, the person who had spoken was Magdalena.

She strode forward, her high heels clicking on the tiled floor, and she crouched beside me for a long moment, staring at me with bright eyes that didn't blink, didn't even flicker. It was unnerving as she stared down at me so intently, as if she were watching an insect through a magnifying glass.

"I'm taking over," said Magdalena then, standing and addressing the vampire man. Without a word, he shrugged, wiping the arm of his leather jacket over his face as the crowd parted and then closed around him.

Magdalena whirled to face me.

And when she did, I gasped. Her incisors had grown freakishly long, and her eyes were as red as blood. They *glowed*.

I was dimly aware of the sound of someone arguing, insisting that Magdalena shouldn't be the one to fight; they were offering to take my place... But all of this was muted, faraway. I felt my cold blood flow over my fingers, dripping dully onto the floor beneath me. The blood moved slowly, as if it had the consistency of molasses. I glanced down at it, unseeing, but then I flicked my gaze to Magdalena, who towered over me.

As I stared up at her, I knew that the only reason she'd volunteered to take over for her Champion was because she wanted to be the one to finish me off. She wanted to be the one who killed me.

I thought about my mother, my mother who had loved my father, who had died too soon because of her love. My mother, who had been murdered.

And as I sat there, as I stared up at Magdalena, I knew that I didn't want the same thing to happen to me. I didn't want to give Magdalena the satisfaction of taking me from this world, too. I wouldn't be another notch on her homicidal belt.

No.

I gazed past Magdalena, then, and I looked at Layne, who stood on the edge of the crowd, Kane's suit jacket wrapped around her shoulders, gripped in white-knuckled hands. She stared at me, stricken.

"Elizabeth!" she called; tears were falling down her cheeks. Kane held her back, but Layne struggled against her. "Elizabeth, look up!" she called, and her eyes were bright with pain—but with hope, too.

I narrowed my brows.

Hope?

Magdalena was tilting her head back, her incisors growing longer, sharper. She was poised to finish me, but I noticed this only peripherally, because I wasn't watching her. I was staring toward the balcony.

Mikagi stood on the narrow railing as if she were a tightrope walker.

She held her violin aloft, and she gazed down at me in encouragement, in *triumph*.

And then, with a tremendous shout, she threw the violin.

The instrument arced through the air. The sight was surreal... One of my recurring nightmares looked just like this: an incredibly expensive violin was plummeting about twenty feet toward the ground. There was no way that I could reach it in time, and I think Mikagi had accounted for that.

When the violin crashed down in the middle of the circle, everything seemed to stop, just for a moment. The whole world slowed in its spinning, and the voices in the space became so hushed that I could hear every point of the instrument's impact, which began at the base of the violin. For half of a heartbeat, I wondered if the violin was going to somehow, impossibly, survive its fall. But of course it wasn't, couldn't. It had fallen from such a great height, there was no way that it could fail to break.

But it didn't *break*, exactly.

It shattered.

I watched the violin splinter apart in slow motion, broken wood and strings pinging into the air, the bridge of the violin hitting the floor so hard that it became a small pile of bouncing wood bits. The neck of the violin alone stayed intact, skidding across the floor until it was close enough to my hand to touch.

I glanced up at Mikagi, who still stood easily on the railing; she stared down at me with her hands on her hips, an imperious—and meaningful—smile on her face.

There was something I was missing. Why did she throw down her violin, her priceless, custom-made *concert* violin, only to break it apart?

Unless…

I picked up the jagged neck of the instrument, the neck that had been lovingly and passionately played countless times. I stared down at the wood in my hands, and I recognized, with surprise, how pointed the broken edge was. It came to a point.

I was, I realized all at once, holding a wooden stake in my hand. While facing down a vampire.

Again, the world around me seemed sluggish, slow, as Magdalena screamed out into the stillness; she bent toward me, her mouth open, her incisors frightfully long. This was going to be the moment, the moment that she'd been waiting for.

This would be the moment in which she killed me.

But I was holding the neck of the broken violin. And as Magdalena descended toward me, I brought the neck around, and I held it up, the pointed edge aimed toward Magdalena.

And with that...time began to move normally again. The earth resumed its spinning as I gripped the violin's neck, its surface slippery now. Because the neck was now buried, up to the very first turning peg, in Magdalena's stomach.

She slumped down onto the ground, the neck of the violin still sticking out of her, and I stood there, completely shaken, blood dripping from my hand...

But I was alive.

The crowd erupted. Everywhere, there was cheering, echoing off of the ceiling and floor and filling the entire room. It was disconcerting, because all had been silent before, so silent that I could hear the drops of blood falling from my fingers onto the tiles, but now there was auditory chaos, rising in a crescendo all around me.

I stared down at Magdalena, and I wasn't sure if I was relieved or if I was unhappy that she stared up at me with hate-filled eyes, taking the neck of the violin—wet with her own black blood—and yanking the thing out of her stomach, placing her hand over the wound and pressing down hard upon it.

So I had just learned something about vampires: wooden stakes don't really kill us, but they can certainly slow us down.

Layne, my father, Kane, Tommie, and even Mikagi swarmed me, and they were surrounded by nearly every other vampire in attendance. Some people were talking about Magdalena being banished for what she'd done; others were talking about my father continuing his leadership of the Nocturne Council—but I heard all of this in bits and snatches, because I was having difficulty paying attention to the noise around me.

Instead, I was focused on Layne, only Layne. I threw my arms around her, drew her to me so tightly that there wasn't a whisper of space between our bodies; I curled my fingers around her hips, and I kissed her fiercely.

For a moment, Layne felt a little stiff against me, and when I backed away, when I looked up into her eyes, I frowned.

"What's the matter?" I asked her, worried.

Layne shook her head, her hair falling into her eyes as she glanced around us, concern creasing her features. "You shouldn't kiss me here, Elizabeth. Not in front of the vampires," she said, her voice low. "Think of what I am. Think of your position—"

"You know what?" I told her, and I held her hips a little tighter. "Screw it." And then I was kissing her again.

And the werewolf melted against me, putting her arms around me with so much passion that, for a moment, I forgot how to breathe.

There was a lot of celebration going on around us: Mikagi clapping me on the back, Kane and Tommie beaming with happiness, while my father appeared to be in deep talks with Magdalena about her impending banishment.

But I held onto Layne, and I kissed her with all my heart.

Nothing else in the world mattered.

Epilogue

"Elizabeth." Tracy stared at me with wide, awestruck eyes. "Mikagi Tasuki said that she's coming back to perform with us because of *you*. Do you understand how *cool* that is? *Do* you?"

I smiled across the tabletop at my friend and chuckled just a little as I wrapped my fingers around the steaming mug of coffee. It was Sunday morning. In a little over two hours, Tracy and I were going to play our traditional Sunday matinee with the symphony.

Life was, for all intents and purposes, returning to normal.

Well...the *new* normal.

"Yeah, I'm pretty sure Mikagi also mentioned that our orchestra is awesome, Tracy, and that had something to do with her decision," I teased her back, taking a sip of the aromatic drink before setting the mug back down on the tabletop and leaning back in the booth.

Tracy's phone *dinged* with another received text, and this time she blushed when she stared at the screen's face. "I really... I have to call him, okay?" she said, practically gushing as she dialed her boyfriend's number. "He's getting tickets at will-call, and there's some kind of snafu. I'll just be a minute," she promised me, before patting my shoulder and bouncing down the aisle to take the call outside.

Tracy was so happy with him.

And I was pretty happy with my new sweetheart, too.

Speak of the devil...or, wolf, as the case may be, Layne slid into the booth seat that Tracy had just occupied, glancing across the table at me with one brow raised and a rather wolfish grin slanting across her gorgeous mouth.

"You know you can sit with us, right?" I asked her, placing my chin in my hand as I gave her a pretty sultry smile.

Layne chuckled, leaning against the booth and placing her arm along the back of the seat as if she owned the place. She shook her head. "Bodyguards must watch from afar," she observed with a small chuckle, "or else how will I know if someone's out to steal your coffee?"

"Don't even joke about that," I warned her, curling both hands around my mug.

"Speaking of jokes," said Layne, fishing her phone out of her jeans pocket and setting it on the tabletop between us carefully, as if it might bite her, "your father is, I think, trying to befriend your new girlfriend."

"How so?"

"He keeps sending me...jokes."

I almost snorted coffee out of my nose. "Oh, my God, are they knock-knock jokes?"

"They're knock-knock jokes," Layne groaned, but I could tell that she was amused, because she was grinning when she met my gaze. "But this last one was different, because he probably ran *out* of knock-knock jokes."

"Hey, it means my dad *really* likes you if he's sending you jokes. Trust me. So, how bad was the last one?" I asked her.

Layne's face became perfectly serious as she stared across the table at me. "What's a vampire's favorite holiday?"

Without skipping a beat, I answered, "Fangsgiving."

"Ah. You've heard that one before."

"He breaks it out every Thanksgiving. Ever since I was a kid," I chuckled. Absentmindedly, I was turning my mother's ring on my finger as I smiled at Layne. My mother had always loved my father's corny jokes—or so Dad insisted. I liked to imagine her laughing at them, really laughing at them, her eyes full of love.

I had told Layne about my near-death experience, about my conversation with my mother, and she, like me, really wasn't sure what to make of it. But she'd held me close and kissed me over and over, whispering that she would never lose me again.

"Any word on Magdalena?" I asked Layne—for what was probably the eighteenth time that week.

She shook her head and reached across the table to take my hand in hers, squeezing it gently. "Banishment... It works," she promised me.. "Magdalena won't come back for a couple years, if—in fact—she ever comes back. She was pretty humiliated this time around. And," she said, holding up a finger when I started to protest, "there are even more people on your father's side now. But I don't think she'll cause us any more trouble."

"I'm not so sure about that. I don't know if she'll stay down forever," I muttered, swirling the rest of my coffee in the bottom of my mug.

"No matter what," said Layne, squeezing my other hand tightly, "we have each other. And no vampire is ever going to pull us apart ever again." Her tone was lighthearted, but there was a sincerity to her words, and when I gazed into her hazel eyes, the brightness of them filled me up, heart and soul.

"God, you're so hot," I grinned, squeezing her hand before I let it go, sliding out of the booth and picking up my violin case. But Layne took my case from me and carried it over her shoulder as we exited the coffee shop.

"And *you're* so cold. We make a good pair," Layne quipped, putting her arm around my shoulder and drawing me close.

We met up with Tracy outside and made our way toward the orchestra hall, moving quickly across the sunny sidewalk, because—it's true—vampires don't enjoy the sunshine.

    But, with my wolf by my side, and with love in my heart, a little sunshine didn't bother me all that much.

The End